"You went to an awful lot of trouble for me today. I guess I have to wonder why."

"I didn't want you dropping from exhaustion at the day-care center," Hudson said wryly, skirting the question.

Still, she kept her gaze on him. "So you'd do this for any of your employees?" She motioned to the meal and the house and he knew what she meant.

"No, I wouldn't. You're special, Bella."

Her pretty brows arched. "Usually when a man does something like this, he wants something in return."

He put down the wing he had been about to eat. "Maybe I do. That kiss didn't just happen out of the blue. There's been something simmering since we met. Don't you agree?"

She looked flustered. "I don't know what you mean. I—"

"Bella, tell me the truth. If you can honestly say you don't feel any sparks between us, I'll drop the whole thing, take you home, not approach you again with anything in my mind other than a boss-and-employee relationship."

"That's what we should have," she reminded him.

"Maybe. Are you going to answer my question?"

HOME ON THE RANCH:

MONTANA CHRISTMAS SECRETS

USA TODAY Bestselling Author

KAREN ROSE SMITH

PATRICIA JOHNS

Previously published as *The Maverick's Holiday Surprise* and *The Cowboy's Christmas Bride*

ISBN-13: 978-1-335-44567-4

Home on the Ranch: Montana Christmas Secrets

The Maverick's Holiday Surprise
First published in 2016. This edition published in 2019.

The Cowboy's Christmas Bride
First published in 2016. This edition published in 2019.

This edition published by arrangement with Harlequin Books S.A.

For questions and comments about the quality of this book, please contact us at CustomerService@Harlequin.com.

Printed in U.S.A.

CONTENTS

USA TODAY bestselling author **Karen Rose Smith** has written over ninety novels. Her passion is caring for her four rescued cats, and her hobbies are gardening, cooking and photography. An only child, Karen delved into books at an early age. Even though she escaped into story worlds, she had many cousins around her on weekends. Families are a strong theme in her novels. Find out more about Karen at karenrosesmith.com.

Books by Karen Rose Smith

Harlequin Special Edition

The Montana Mavericks: The Great Family Roundup

The Maverick's Snowbound Christmas

The Montana Mavericks: The Baby Bonanza

The Maverick's Holiday Surprise

Fortunes of Texas: All Fortune's Children

Fortune's Secret Husband

The Mommy Club

The Cowboy's Secret Baby
A Match Made by Baby
Wanted: A Real Family

Reunion Brides

Riley's Baby Boy
The CEO'S Unexpected Proposal
Once Upon a Groom
His Daughter...Their Child

Montana Mavericks: Rust Creek Cowboys

Marrying Dr. Maverick

The Baby Experts

Twins Under His Tree
The Texan's Happily-Ever-After
The Texas Billionaire's Baby

Visit the Author Profile page at
Harlequin.com for more titles.

THE MAVERICK'S HOLIDAY SURPRISE

KAREN ROSE SMITH

To my dad, who would have been 100 years old this year. With his 35 mm camera, he gave me my love of capturing memories with photography. I miss you, Daddy.

Chapter 1

Hudson Jones was used to getting his own way. But as he stood in the doorway of his office at the Just Us Kids Day Care Center, he had a feeling he wouldn't get his way this time. Bella Stockton had him stymied.

The day care manager was beautiful—tall and willowy with wispy short blond hair. He'd tried to flirt with her over the past month that he'd been here to see to the day-to-day running of the center. After all, a cowboy could get lonely underneath the big Montana sky. But unlike the other pretty women he'd flirted with over his thirty years, Bella didn't respond to him.

He studied her as she talked with a mother, one who'd apparently been involved in the parent-teacher conferences scheduled at Just Us Kids after normal business hours. Hudson recognized the expression on the parent's face. Over the last couple of months, he'd dealt with his share of upset parents. An outbreak of RSV—respiratory syncytial virus—had hit Just Us Kids, sending one of the children to the hospital, which had prompted her parents to file a lawsuit. The day care had been cleared, but the damage to its reputation had been done.

He moved a little closer to the main desk in the reception area where Bella sat.

Marla Tillotson was pointing her finger at Bella. "If I even see another child here with sniffles, I'm pulling Jimmy out and enrolling him in Country Kids." She turned on the heels of her red boots, gave Hudson a glare and headed for the door.

Although Hudson usually didn't commit too much time to any one place, he had taken this job more seriously than most. After all, it was an investment he didn't want to fail. He owned the property the day care sat on; his brother Walker owned the franchise. He'd let his brother talk him into staying for a while in Rust Creek Falls to oversee the staff and handle the PR that would put Just Us Kids back in the public's good graces. But, to be honest, mostly he stayed in town because he wanted to get to know Bella better.

As soon as he saw Bella's face, he didn't hesitate to step up to her desk. "It wasn't your fault," he said adamantly.

As day care manager, Bella ran a tight ship. She enforced policies about not signing in sick kids, incorporated stringent guidelines for disinfecting surfaces and educated the staff. But it seemed she couldn't put the whole awful experience of the lawsuit behind her.

Bella brushed her bangs aside and ducked her head for a moment. Then she raised burdened brown eyes to his. "I just can't help thinking that maybe I slipped up somehow. What if I wasn't vigilant enough before the outbreak? What—"

Hudson cut her off. "I'm going to say it again, and I'll say it a thousand times more if you need to hear it. You didn't do anything wrong," he assured her. "I read numerous blogs about day care and RSV when Walker asked me to take over here. RSV looks like a cold when it starts. Kids are contagious before they show symptoms. That's why it spreads like wildfire even with the best precautions. It's going to be *our* job—" he pointed to himself, and then he pointed to her "—to make sure an outbreak doesn't happen again."

Bella met his eyes intently. Suddenly the day care center seemed very quiet. Maybe it was just because he was so aware of her gaze on him. Was she aware of him? They could hear low voices in one of the classrooms beyond where tables were set up for the parent-teacher conferences. But other than that, the facility suddenly had a hushed atmosphere.

Hudson noted that Bella seemed to be gazing intently at him. That was okay because he was studying her pretty oval face. He missed seeing the dimples that appeared whenever she was with the kids. That's when she seemed the happiest. Her hair looked so soft and silky that he itched to run his fingers through it. But he knew he couldn't. This was the first time she'd even stopped and looked at him like this. Had she thought he was the enemy, that he'd pick apart everything she did? That wasn't his style.

He found himself leaning a little farther over the desk. He thought she was leaning a little closer to him, too.

All at once there was a *rap-rap-rap* on the door.

Sorry that they'd been interrupted, he nevertheless excused himself and went to the door. When he opened it, the brisk November air entered, along with Bart Dunner, a teenager who was a runner for the Ace in the Hole. Hudson had ordered a mess of ribs from the bar for anyone who was still around when dinnertime came. He paid Bart, gave him a tip and thanked him. On the way to the break room, he glanced over at Bella. *Nothing ventured, nothing gained*, he told himself.

"Have you eaten?" he asked her.

"No, I haven't. I've been making out schedules and ordering supplies for the new year."

He motioned to the bag. "Come join me."

At first he thought she was going to refuse, but then to his surprise she said, "I skipped lunch. Supper might be a good idea."

As they washed their hands at the sink, Bella kept a few inches between them, even when she had to reach around him for a paper towel. Was she skittish around all men…or just him? Maybe she was just shy, he told himself. Maybe she was a virgin. After all, she was only twenty-three.

At the table, they each took one of the Styrofoam containers with ribs, crispy fries and green beans. "These ribs smell delicious," she said, and he didn't think she was just making conversation. But it was hard to tell.

As they ate, he tried to get her to talk. "You know, we've been working together for over a month, but I don't know much about you, except that you live with your brother and help with his triplets. I also know lots of people in town signed up to create a baby chain to care for the kids." Jamie Stockton had lost his wife, leaving him with the newborns to care for and a ranch to run. "That says something about Rust Creek Falls, don't you think?" If he could just get Bella talking, maybe she'd realize he was interested in her.

"That's the way Rust Creek Falls works," she responded. "Neighbors helping neighbors. And what you know about me is probably enough."

"Come on," he coaxed. "Tell me a little more. Did you grow up here?"

"Yes, I did. I was born here."

"Have you and your brother always been close?" he prompted.

"We have. I love my nephews and niece dearly." She took a forkful of green beans, then asked, "What about you? I know Walker is your brother."

"I have four brothers. But we aren't that close. Maybe because we've always had our own interests, or maybe because—" He stopped.

Bella studied him curiously. "What were you going to say?"

Hudson hesitated and decided he had to give to get. "Maybe because my parents never fostered closeness."

She gave him an odd look at that. "Our parents died in a car accident when I was twelve and Jamie was fifteen. We always had to rely on each other."

No wonder she didn't talk about her childhood. Losing parents had to be traumatic. "I'll bet you did rely on each other. Who took you in?"

"Our maternal grandparents took us in—the Stockton grandparents had both died. But Agnes and Matthew Baldwin didn't really want that responsibility."

"How can you know that, Bella? What starts that way sometimes can turn into something else—a real family."

Looking troubled now, Bella shook her head. "When our grandmother died of a heart attack, I was fifteen. Jamie was eighteen. Our grandfather blamed us."

"You can't be serious." Hudson was outraged for her. How could her grandfather have even given that impression? But then he thought about his own parents and how cold his mother seemed.

"You don't know the situation," Bella said gently. "Jamie and I weren't the easiest kids to raise, and our grandfather was probably right."

Hudson was horrified that Bella actually believed that. She was one of the sweetest women he'd ever met. "You can't blame yourself for what fate hands out." But he could see she did.

Bella had torn apart her ribs at that point, and instead of trying to eat them with a fork as some women might, she nibbled the meat off the bone. Her fingers were sticky, and so were her lips. Hudson couldn't stop looking at her lips. She was in midchew when she realized he was staring. She stared back.

All eating stopped as they gazed at each other, and it was quite possible there was even a hum in the air. He wondered if she was just a little bit attracted to him.

But he never got to ask because one of the teachers popped her head into the break room.

"Got enough for me?" she asked.

That broke Hudson out of his trance. "Sure do, Sarah. Come on in and join us."

As the boss, he knew that was the right thing to do. But as a man, what he really wanted was to be alone with Bella. To find out more about her. To get to know her.

To kiss her.

* * *

Hudson let himself into the ranch house on the Lazy B, thinking that living in Rust Creek Falls for a while wasn't a chore. He tremendously liked where he was staying. He'd met Brooks Smith, the town's veterinarian, on one of his first trips to Rust Creek Falls. He knew the town vet could always recommend the best place to ride or rent out a horse. Brooks had done better than that. He'd suggested Hudson rent Clive Bickler's ranch.

Clive, an eccentric wealthy man who'd bought the property after the big flood several years ago, traveled a lot. Besides the main ranch house there was a smaller log home on the acreage where an older couple lived. They'd lost their ranch in the flood, and they lived on the Lazy B now and ran the place. Clive rented his home to high-end clients who appreciated his art collection and other niceties. Hudson, basically a trust fund cowboy, filled the bill. Living here was not only convenient but downright pleasant.

As he tapped in the code for the security alarm, he heard noise in the kitchen. That didn't bother him because he knew who was there—Greta Marsden. She wasn't only the wife of the foreman, but she also made sure Hudson had meals and treats to eat. Now she was loading a casserole into the refrigerator. The kitchen was all shiny stainless steel and high-end appliances. Not that Hudson cared because he didn't do much cooking.

Greta was in her fifties with silver hair that fluffed around her face. She had a wide smile and a kind disposition. She might have been a few pounds overweight, but she was fit in jeans and a plaid shirt. Her wool jacket hung over a nearby chair.

She glanced over her shoulder at him as she made room in the refrigerator for the casserole dish and smiled. "Do you need supper?"

"No, I had ribs. Not that they could stand up to anything you make."

She closed the refrigerator door, blushing a little. "You sure do know how to charm a woman, but save that for the ladies your age. I'm beyond it."

Hudson laughed. "You're not."

She waved his comment away. "When kids are grown, companionship and affection mean more than anything else. I'm relieved I don't need to look hot for anyone."

So that was what marriage developed into—companionship and affection. He wasn't sure his parents had that.

On the drive here, he'd thought about everything Bella had told him about her family. In fact he hadn't been able to get her story out of his head. He was still distracted by it now.

Greta bustled around the kitchen and pointed to a plastic container on the counter. "Oatmeal raisin cookies. These cold nights they'll go good with hot chocolate before you turn in."

"So you think I'm still a growing boy."

She laughed. "No, just a hardworking man with a big appetite."

Hudson wasn't sure about the hardworking part. He'd never really had to work too hard because his family was wealthy, so he was wealthy. He tended to take on jobs as he liked and then move on. His last project in

Cody, Wyoming, had been about helping a friend start up a ranch—buying horses, choosing computer programs to manage the place efficiently. Over the years he'd managed ranches, wrangled cows and trained horses. This gig with Just Us Kids Day Care Center was something entirely new to him.

Greta looked around the kitchen and shook her head. "Edmond needed me to do bookwork today, so I didn't clean up here," she explained. "I'll be back to do that in the morning."

Hudson wasn't concerned about collecting a few dust bunnies. "No problem."

As he remembered Bella saying *Our grandfather blamed us when Grandma died*, he considered Greta's comments about marriage.

"Do you mind if I ask you something personal?"

Greta shrugged. "I suppose not."

"How would you feel if you suddenly had teenage grandchildren to raise? What if it happened overnight? What would you do?"

Greta didn't even hesitate. "Edmond and I would try our best to love them to bits. The people who come in and out of our lives are gifts."

When Hudson thought about Bella, he realized how she usually seemed sad unless she was around the kids. Had that been because of the way she'd been raised?

Apparently her grandparents hadn't considered her and her brother as gifts. That had to color the way she looked at herself and the rest of her life.

Hudson nodded, suddenly a bit pleased with the evening. Though she hadn't revealed too much over their quick dinner, he had learned quite a bit about Ms. Bella Stockton.

* * *

When Hudson entered Just Us Kids the following morning, Bella was already there.

As he walked into the reception area, he tipped his Stetson and gave her a cheery good morning. Yet she simply murmured hello and hardly lifted her head. What was *that* about?

He wondered that same thing again when she wouldn't meet his gaze at a brief staff meeting before the children began arriving. He was sure something was wrong midmorning when Bella dropped time sheets on his desk without even looking at him.

She didn't act like a beautiful young woman of the millennia. It wasn't that she lacked self-confidence, because she didn't. With the staff, with the kids, with every aspect of organization, she was confident in her abilities. But not around him.

He had to get to the bottom of it.

Hudson had found he enjoyed being with the kids. It was odd, really. As an adult, he'd never been around children much. Several times a day he'd wander through the sections of children in different age groups. He knew many of the children by name, and they knew his name. He often stopped to help with an art project or just to converse with a curious four-year-old. They came up with the darnedest questions. He pretty much stayed away from the babies, watching over them from afar. The teachers didn't seem to mind him wandering through. They often gave him a thumbs-up, and he praised them for the way they handled the kids. It wasn't an easy job, and he knew it. He'd handled two-year-old horses, and *that* task had seemed easier.

Throughout the day he often glanced at Bella and

wondered why he was so interested in her. Her beauty, for sure, that pretty face, that pixie hairdo, that slender figure. There was something else, too, though—something that both unsettled and intrigued him.

He'd never been seriously involved with a woman. He'd never wanted to settle down because he'd seen the coldness in his parents' marriage. When he had dated, he'd seen that women wanted to tie him to one place. Moving from place to place gave his life the excitement romance couldn't. No woman had ever meant as much to him as not being tied down.

However, something about Bella Stockton made him want to get to know her a little better. He wanted to know why she'd gone all shy on him.

Late in the day, when only a few stragglers remained to be picked up, he had his chance.

He went to Bella's desk and asked, "Can I see you in my office?"

She looked up at him with startled eyes. But then she asked, "Do I need my tablet to take notes?"

He shook his head. "Not about this."

That brought a frown to her pretty face. But she followed him into his office, and this time he closed the door. He didn't claim to be a human resources expert. Yes, he could spin a good story. However, this moment called for some honesty.

"I suspect you're not happy that I'm here to oversee Just Us Kids. But I want to reassure you I know you do a good job. My being here is just necessary in the wake of everything that happened."

"I know that," she murmured.

"Do you?" He looked at her directly, making eye contact, not letting her look away.

"It's not just *you*," she said. "It's *me*. I don't want to make a mistake. I don't want anything to jeopardize Just Us Kids."

"I understand that. Up until yesterday, I thought we got along just fine. At least we could have a simple conversation."

She didn't say anything to that.

He went on. "And yesterday, I thought we were finally getting to know each other a little better. I'm glad you told me a bit about your childhood."

"I shouldn't have," she quickly said.

"Why not?"

"Because Jamie and I don't like to talk about it. We don't like to think about it. Those were hard times for both of us, and we don't want anyone to feel sorry for us."

"And you think I feel sorry for you?"

"Possibly."

Hudson shook his head. "I'm sorry you and your brother went through that. I'm sorry your grandparents didn't treat you as the gifts you must have been." He found Greta's conclusion absolutely fit the situation.

At his words, Bella looked surprised.

They were standing near his desk, she at one corner and he at the other. But now he took a few steps closer to her. He could smell the light flowery perfume she wore. He could see the tiny line across her nose because it wrinkled there whenever she laughed or smiled. She didn't wear much makeup, but what she did wear was perfect—just a bit of lipstick and a little mascara from what he could tell. Simply looking at her caused heat to build inside him. He tried to throw a dash of cold water on it with logic, but it was hard to douse the kind of attraction he hadn't felt for a very long time.

However, he kept his voice even when he said, "It's a good thing when people who work together share bits of their personal life. They have a better understanding of what the other person has gone through. Do you know what I mean?"

She considered that. "I guess the way I grew up taught me that children should all be treated with respect and kindness and love."

"I can see that."

"And why do you treat them as if you're one of them?" she asked as if she really wanted to know.

"Because I never grew up." He was half joking and half serious.

Bella finally broke a smile. She looked him up and down, from his wavy brown hair, to the razor stubble on his jaw, to the open collar of his snap-button shirt, to his wide leather belt, jeans and boots. Then she said, "That's easy to believe when I see you with the kids. But it's hard to believe when I look at you as the supervisor of this place. You wear the role very well."

"It *is* a role, Bella, believe me. I'm only here until we're sure Just Us Kids has its reputation back, then I'll be off again somewhere else. That's what I do. That's what I mean about never growing up."

She shook her head as if she didn't understand. "But what's your purpose?"

"My purpose?"

"Before this job, what made you want to get up every morning and face a new day?"

"A new adventure. I went looking for it, whether it was gathering wild mustangs in Wyoming or managing the books of a friend's ranch during start-up. I have skills, and I have purpose, but that purpose isn't always the same. I find a purpose in the places I travel."

"With no commitment or responsibilities?"

"No commitment and no personal responsibilities. It's an easy, uncomplicated way to live."

"My life is full of complications," she responded with a little shrug. "I guess I wouldn't know what to do without them. But my commitment to Jamie and the triplets, and eventually finding my own future, gives me purpose each morning. It's a continuing purpose. Do you know what I mean? It's going to take me into the years to come. Yours seems like it could fall apart easily and leave you adrift."

Oh, he'd been adrift. He'd been adrift in between jobs, and he'd been adrift when he'd just enjoyed the scenery. But Bella seemed to think adrift was a bad thing. He didn't.

They gazed at each other for what seemed like minutes, even though it was only seconds. He found himself wanting to slide his fingers through her hair. He found himself wanting to step even closer. There was a sparkle in her eyes when she looked at him that made him believe that maybe she was attracted to him, too. But he was sort of her boss, and she already thought he was judging everything she did. How stupid would it be to get involved with her? Yet *he* set the rules here, didn't he? If he and Bella ever did really connect…

He suddenly cleared his throat. "I'd better open the door before anyone gets second thoughts about what's going on in here. I wouldn't want there to be any gossip about your reputation."

A shadow passed over her face, a definite shadow.

Maybe he'd learned a little personal information about her, but not nearly enough. Just what was that shadow from?

But she wasn't going to confide in him any more than she already had. He could see that. She was already stepping away from his desk toward the door.

"Bella?"

She stopped.

"Are we okay?"

"We're fine," she said, raising up her chin a bit.

Fine. That was a wishy-washy word that didn't nearly begin to describe what he felt when he was in the same room with Bella Stockton. But he just nodded because he could see that's what she wanted him to do. He wasn't going to push anything…not yet.

Chapter 2

On Saturday afternoon, Bella was thankful for the baby chain that was helping her brother at Short Hills Ranch. This afternoon, Lindsay Dalton, one of the volunteers in Jamie's baby chain, had stopped by. She was taking over care of baby Jared while Jamie and Bella handled the others. By the stone fireplace in the family room, Bella was holding Henry and sitting in an old pine rocker she'd found at a flea market. His little eyes were almost shutting. Jamie had taken Katie upstairs to the nursery to try to calm her down. She was teething and couldn't be easily consoled today.

Lindsay sat on the sofa cooing softly to Jared. "If Henry starts crying again, he will, too," she whispered.

Lindsay was a pretty brunette and Bella could easily see why Walker, Hudson's brother, had fallen for her. Her own friendship with Lindsay had been strained by the lawsuit against Just Us Kids since Lindsay had been the lawyer suing Walker. But now Lindsay and Walker were engaged, and Walker was going to work mostly from Rust Creek Falls and travel when necessary. Lindsay and Bella were finding common ground again by helping Jamie.

"How goes everything at Just Us Kids?" Lindsay asked her, truly interested.

Bella continued to rock back and forth, watching Henry's fists curl. Holding a baby absolutely melted her heart, yet it made it hurt at the same time.

"Everything's going well," she told Lindsay. "At least it seems to be. We had a mother tell us that if she saw one baby with the sniffles, she'd pull her child and enroll him at Country Kids." Country Kids was their rival for clients.

"Sniffles and kids just go together," Lindsay said with a shake of her head. "Especially this time of year."

"One sniffle now and Hudson asks the parent to keep their child home. That's the way it has to be. I know that's a hardship on the parents, but we can't have another outbreak."

"I'm glad we can talk about this," Lindsay said. "I hated being on opposite sides of the fence."

Bella nodded. She'd missed Lindsay's friendship, too. "How are you and Walker?" she asked.

Lindsay's face broke into a wide smile. "We're wonderful. *He's* wonderful."

Then Lindsay asked, "How are you and Hudson getting along?"

"Fine," Bella responded airily. There must have been something in her voice, because Lindsay asked, "How fine?"

Bella felt her cheeks flush.

Lindsay said gently, "You know, don't you, that Hudson has a reputation for being a love-'em-and-leave-'em cowboy."

"His reputation doesn't matter," Bella said. "He's my boss. That's it."

Still she remembered the way they'd sat together eating those sticky ribs, the way they'd stood close and she'd felt heat from Hudson and her own heat in return.

"You don't resent him overseeing you anymore?"

"I'm still not sure how I feel about that," Bella admitted. "But I'm not as resentful as I was at the beginning. I understand that both Hudson and Walker have to safeguard the business. I just didn't want someone judging every move I make."

"Is Hudson doing that?"

"Actually, no, he isn't. His managerial style is hands-off, unless he has to step in."

She thought about how Hudson had stepped in after a parent had dressed her down. She also thought about Walker's brief visits to the day care center and his sometimes condescending attitude to Hudson because he was the older brother.

"I wish Walker would tell Hudson he's doing a good job. After all, Hudson handled the PR for the whole problem and managed to keep most of our staff and our clients. But I get the idea that Walker doesn't understand what a huge achievement that is."

Lindsay rubbed her finger along Jared's chin, studying his baby face as if maybe she was contemplating having a child of her own someday.

"I hear what you're saying," Lindsay assured Bella. "But you know, brothers will be brothers. I get the feeling that Walker and Hudson's relationship is complicated, so I think it's better if I stay out of it."

Bella admired Lindsay's honesty. "You're probably right. I wouldn't want anyone interfering in my relationship with Jamie."

After the babies fell asleep, Bella and Lindsay took them upstairs to their cribs in the nursery. Since Katie was still fussing, Jamie carried her to his bedroom so her restlessness and cries wouldn't wake the other two.

Downstairs once more, Bella and Lindsay cleaned up the living room and den. There were always baby things scattered everywhere, from bottles to diapers to receiving blankets to toys. After Lindsay left, Bella went to find Jamie, still in the recliner in his bedroom, rocking Katie. In a pink onesie with a teddy bear embroidered on the front, she looked like a little angel. He was looking down at her as if she *were* one.

"She's almost asleep," he told Bella. "But she's still restless. I want to make sure she's really into a deep nap before I put her down with the others."

"I can take her," Bella offered. "Why don't you go riding? You need a break." He'd been up half the night with Katie.

"I want to make sure this is merely teething and not something else. She doesn't feel hot, but I want to be certain she's not running a temperature."

Bella could hear the fatigue in Jamie's voice, and he looked exhausted. He hadn't shaved today, and beard stubble lined his chin. His blond hair fell over his brow as if he'd run his hand through it many times. But as he looked down at his daughter, his blue eyes were filled with love.

Jamie was often overwhelmed; she could see it on

his face and hear it in his voice. Yet he never gave up on the ranch, and he never stopped putting the babies first. He always gave them every ounce of love and caring in his heart, even if that meant he didn't have much of a life anymore.

She'd never regret quitting college and moving back in here with him. She loved helping him take care of the triplets. She loved being around the babies. But it was also painful. She so wanted to be a mother, but she knew she might never be able to have kids. Just how fair or right was that?

"What are you thinking about?" Jamie asked her. As a close sibling, he always could read her moods.

Her past played through her mind like a mocking newsreel. She could never forget about it, even though she tried. So she answered him truthfully.

"I'm thinking about how wild I was as a teenager."

"You were dealing with our parents' deaths."

"So were you, but you didn't jump off the deep end."

"Our grandparents didn't want us. I pretended I didn't care. I put my energy into sports. But you—" He shook his head. "You were younger. You needed Grandma's arms around you. You needed them to want you. They didn't. That's why we were separated from the others."

Bella sighed. Their sisters Dana and Liza had been younger, more adoptable, and had been sent to a group home for that purpose. Their brothers Luke, Daniel and Bailey had been over eighteen and had been turned out on their own.

"Don't you ever wonder where they all are?" Bella asked.

"Sure I do. But the fact remains that you and I haven't

left Rust Creek Falls. Our siblings could find us if they wanted to. They obviously don't want to. Case closed."

Bella understood Jamie's attitude. After all, they'd been rejected by their grandparents. They didn't need sibling rejection on top of that.

"Sometimes I don't understand how you help me like you do," Jamie said, looking troubled.

"I'm your sister."

"Yes, but..."

She knew what he was getting at. They rarely talked about it, but today seemed like a day for stepping back into the past.

"I think she's finally asleep," he said, rising from the recliner and carrying Katie into the nursery. There he settled her into the crib and looked down on her with so much love Bella wanted to cry.

Then he turned back to her. "When you got pregnant, I didn't know what to do to help you. After you lost your baby and possibly the chance ever to have another one, I didn't know what to do then either. I don't know how Grandma and Gramps kept everything that happened to you a secret, but they did. Grandma died so soon after you lost your baby, and Gramps blamed you. And me. But keeping the secret about your miscarriage wasn't good for any of us...especially you. You couldn't talk about what happened. You couldn't express your grief."

"Jamie," she warned weakly, not wanting to delve into any of those feelings.

"I feel like you're still grieving sometimes when you look at the triplets," he explained.

"You're wrong about that. I love being around Katie and Henry and Jared. They fill my life with happy times."

"I know sharing the triplets with you isn't the same as your having your own kids, but I want you to know I appreciate everything you do to help me and to take care of them. And even if you love being around them because they're your niece and nephews, don't you mind being around the babies and kids at the day care center? Isn't it just downright hard?"

"Actually, it's not," she assured him. "I think the day care center has been my saving grace. Your triplets and the kids there…they fill me with joy. I don't have time to be sad."

Jamie suddenly gave her a huge hug, and she leaned into him, grateful to have her brother. In that moment, she thought about having more, too—about having a man to love, a relationship, a life outside the day care center and Jamie's triplets. She thought about Hudson. She'd been attracted to him from the first moment she'd seen him. But she'd also realized what kind of man he was. He had a reputation, and she knew he wouldn't stay no matter what kind of electricity was flowing between them now. She shouldn't get involved…*couldn't* get involved. Besides, she had nothing to give somebody like Hudson. He had experienced the world.

And she was just a small-town girl who couldn't have kids.

Late Monday morning Hudson sat in his office much too aware of Bella at her desk in the reception area beyond. She really was an expert at handling the children. This morning he'd noticed the way she put her hand on a child's shoulder, or gave him a hug. Her smile when she was with the kids was absolutely radiant. Yes, it was safe to say there was a lot about the woman that intrigued him.

As if his thoughts had beckoned her, she stood and approached his office. He invited her inside.

"I set up a meeting for you with the holiday pageant director, Eileen Bennet, next Wednesday afternoon," she told him.

Every year the local elementary school put on a Christmas pageant, and this year they wanted the day care babies to get involved. "The pageant isn't that far off. I hope she doesn't have anything too complicated in mind."

"If she knows babies, she won't," Bella said with a smile. She filled him in on what she knew, then turned to go. She'd almost reached the door of his office when he asked, "What did you do before you managed the day care center?"

He'd heard the gossip that she'd quit college to help her brother, but he didn't know that for a fact.

"I was in college—my second year."

He must have looked puzzled because she added, "I worked after I graduated from high school to save money for college."

"What did you do?"

"Mostly I waitressed. Lots of long shifts so I could sock the tips away. Four years of that, and I applied for and received a grant from a women's foundation. I enrolled at Montana State University."

"What was your major?"

"Business administration. I eventually wanted to focus on public affairs and learn strategies for helping small towns survive. Maybe that's a pipe dream, but if someone doesn't inject life into a place like Rust Creek

Falls, it could become a ghost town. That was especially true after the flood."

"So your college courses gave you managerial skills that come into play here."

"I guess you could say that. I don't know when I'll be able to complete my degree. Working here will help me save the money to do it. But I plan to stick around Rust Creek Falls as long as Jamie needs me."

Bella's eyes sparkled with her dedication to her brother, as well as with the dreams that she still envisioned. More than anything, Hudson wanted to stand up and go over to her. He longed to brush her bangs across her forehead. Even more than that, he ached to tip her chin up, to bend his head, to put his lips on hers.

And that's why he stayed sitting. Yeah, he longed to kiss her, but they were in their workplace. Besides that, he wasn't looking for a long-term commitment, and Bella was the type of woman who deserved one.

This time when she moved to leave his office, he let her.

For the rest of the morning, Hudson felt unsettled. Finally he pushed away from his computer, stood and stretched. Truth be told, he wasn't used to sitting at a desk for most of the day. If he had to choose a job he liked best, it would be one training horses, cutting calves or walking through a field or pasture checking fence. He liked being a cowboy. Even now he rode whenever he could at the Lazy B, but it wasn't the same thing as being on a horse most of the day.

Leaving his office, he spotted Bella. Instead of at her desk, she was on a ladder at the bulletin board in the reception area. Instinctively, he crossed to her, fearful she was going to fall off.

As he stood a few feet from her, he could see that she was putting up photos of the babies who came to Just Us Kids. There had been an explosion of pregnancies after a wedding reception that most of the town had taken part in two summers ago. Rumor had it that old man Homer Gilmore had put something potent in the punch. The result: nine months later, nurseries had been full of babies. Many of those babies were enrolled at Just Us Kids.

He moved a little closer to study the photos, and Bella took notice of him.

"These pictures are good. Who took them?"

"I did," Bella said proudly.

She was still on the ladder, and he stood close to her, his shoulder at her waist. "You just didn't snap quick photos. These are well thought out, artistic even. Look at the eyes on this little guy. They absolutely sparkle." He pointed to another one. "And this expression is priceless. You have a real artist's eye and good timing. Kids move and change minute to minute, and you've caught some of their best expressions."

She glanced down at him, and their gazes met. "Thank you," she murmured.

Clearing his throat, he said offhandedly, "You'd probably enjoy looking at the paintings at my ranch house."

Bella seemed to almost lose her balance. She toddled, and he put his arm around her to support her. They stood frozen, staring at each other, her face above his but not so far away. Why had she lost her balance? Had she thought he wanted her to come back to his ranch house for other reasons?

Maybe he did.

"You have to careful," he mumbled.

She nodded slowly. "Yes, I do." Then she pushed away from him and made her way down the ladder.

Once she was on the ground, he asked, "Do you have other photos you've taken? Not of babies?"

"I do. I carry my camera with me almost everywhere I go."

"Get it," he said impulsively. "I'd like to see them."

"Now?"

"You're due for a lunch break and so am I, right?"

Bella didn't know what to think of Hudson's suggestion. Did he really want to see her photos? Why? And just what had he meant by that comment about going to his ranch? Did he really want her to see the paintings? Or did he have something else in mind?

Did *she*?

She felt her cheeks beginning to flush. She didn't know what was wrong with her. For years now she hadn't dated. She'd kept to herself. She'd been determined not to get into any more trouble, not to do something foolish or reckless. But in a way, her heart had been frozen during those years. She'd rebelled as a teenager, and that had gotten her into so much trouble. No, she hadn't loved the father of her baby. Yes, she'd been looking for love, and somehow she'd mistakenly thought that sex could give her love. But she knew better than that now. She knew better about a lot of things.

But having Hudson's arm around her when she'd almost fallen, catching the scent of his aftershave, looking into his blue eyes, foolish and reckless and impulsive had all seemed like good ideas.

No, no, no, she told herself firmly. *Hudson Jones is nothing but trouble for you.*

Knowing all that, she still said, "My camera's in my bag. I'll get it."

Going around her desk, she opened the bottom drawer. Inside her hobo bag she found her point-and-shoot camera. It wasn't anything special, but it worked for her.

Taking the small white camera to Hudson, she turned it on. Then she hit the button that brought up the display and the photo review. "My SD card is almost full," she admitted, handing him the camera so he could look for himself. She pointed to an arrow button. "Just press that to go backward or forward."

He was silent for a long time as he seemed to spend forever on each photo. When she glanced over his arm, she saw he was studying the sequence she'd taken on Short Hills Ranch. She'd shot the fall foliage with horses in the background. She'd captured Jamie astride a horse as well as a bay with a star on its forehead looking straight at the camera. There was a shot inside the stable, too, where a yellow light cast a horse in a golden glow.

As Hudson shuffled through one photo after another, she watched his expression. He had an expressive face, not stoic like her grandfather's. She saw his eyes widen with surprise when he glimpsed at a photo he especially liked. She spied his mouth turn up at the corners as he went through a sequence of the triplets more than once. There was Katie with cereal all over her face… Henry with his thumb in his mouth… Jared crawling toward a favorite toy. She'd also caught Jamie standing in a window at dusk, his profile in shadow.

Hudson suddenly lowered the camera. "Do you know how good these are?"

She analyzed every crease on his face, the openness in his eyes. Was he feeding her a line?

But his next words told her he wasn't. "I can see you don't know how good you are. Did you ever think about hiring out your services?"

"It's just a hobby."

"It's a hobby that could take you someplace. What if I tell you I know someone who might like to hire you to take photos?"

"Of what?" she asked suspiciously. After all, she'd learned to be suspicious of men and their motives.

"Do you know Brooks Smith?"

The name sounded familiar, and all at once she placed it. "He's a veterinarian. I've never met him. His dad usually comes out to Short Hills when we need a vet."

"Brooks and his dad have separate practices but cover for each other. His dad is cutting back his hours. Anyway, Brooks and his wife, Jazzy, run a horse rescue ranch out at the edge of town. The ranch is a passion with them, and they're going to have pamphlets printed about the facility. Jazzy mentioned she just hasn't had time to put it all together. Do you think you'd be interested in taking photos of the horses on the ranch?"

She was so busy now that she didn't know what to say. Between work and the triplets, she sometimes didn't have time to breathe. But the idea of taking photographs and making extra money was downright inviting.

"When would I have to do this?"

"Pretty soon, I guess. They mentioned handing out the pamphlets at their holiday open house."

"I don't have much spare time," she admitted.

"I know you don't, but this would probably only take a few hours."

"You don't know if Brooks and his wife would really want me."

"I can set up a meeting."

"Let me think about it. If Jamie has enough help, it would be a possibility."

Hudson motioned to the photos of the babies on the bulletin board. Then he pointed to her camera. "You have a gift, Bella. You see with your camera what most folks can't see with their eyes. You really should share that."

She thought about that, then asked, "Why? I mean, everyone sees what they want to see for the most part."

"But what if you can broaden someone's outlook? What if you could give them a positive spin instead of a negative one? What if you can make a difference?"

"We're talking about shooting a few photos." She couldn't keep the amusement from her voice because she thought maybe he was joking.

"No, not just a few shots. Each of your photos is a study of your subject that you've captured for eternity. That's not something to treat lightly."

She never expected something so deep to come out of Hudson. That just proved she didn't know him very well. And he certainly didn't know her.

"I'll check with Brooks and Jazzy," he said. "You think about it. I'm going to take a walk and get some lunch. Would you like some fresh air, too? You're welcome to join me."

She could hear the sound of children's laughter coming from one of the rooms. When she looked up at Hudson, she saw interest in his eyes. The children were safety. Hudson was danger.

As she had for the past few years, she chose safety. "I'd better stay here in case anybody needs me."

"You like to feel needed, don't you?"

"I do. It gives my life purpose."

He shrugged. "I've never had that kind of purpose. I'm not exactly sure what it feels like."

"Walker needed you here. Isn't that why you took over supervising Just Us Kids?"

"I never looked at it that way," he conceded. "I guess you're right." He motioned to the bulletin board. "It looks good. It will capture people's attention. Soon we'll have to decorate for the holidays."

"It's not even Thanksgiving yet."

"Not so far off," he reminded her as he moved toward the door. He opened it and looked back over his shoulder at her. "I won't be long. If anything comes up, you have my cell number."

She nodded. She did have his cell number. But she doubted she'd ever use it.

Chapter 3

As she approached Jamie's front porch, Bella couldn't stop thinking about Hudson and the way he'd studied her photos. He'd really seemed interested. She'd never thought of taking pictures for actual payment. That would be a breeze if it panned out because she loved photos and she loved horses, so she knew they'd be good. She hoped Hudson would really follow through with his offer.

As she opened the door to the ranch house, Bella heard commotion in the kitchen. Taking off her coat, she hung it in the closet and headed for the voices and the squeals.

She smiled when she saw the scene in front of her. Fallon O'Reilly was helping Jamie with the triplets by trying to feed Katie while he fed Henry and Jared. Bella felt warmth spread around her heart at the generosity of Fallon and others who were giving of their time so easily. However, the way Fallon looked at Jamie, Bella suspected there was more there than a friend helping a friend.

Fallon was a year older than Bella and came from the kind of family that Jamie and she wished they'd had. She was a product of parents who had been married for decades and who loved their kids dearly. In turn, Fallon was great with kids. She should be; she worked at Country Kids Day Care.

When Fallon spotted her, she smiled. "As you can see, applesauce is on the menu. Katie is wearing it exceptionally well, don't you think?"

The baby had obviously waved her hands around with applesauce-covered fingers. There was even some on the little pink ribbon in her fine hair. She smiled when she thought how Jamie always dressed her in pink and tried to keep the ribbon in her hair so everybody would know she was a girl. He was such a good dad.

On the other side of the table, Henry and Jared had smeared it all over their mouths, on the high chair trays and even on Jared's nose.

"This looks like fun," Bella said with a laugh. "Can I join in?"

Jamie motioned to a chair on the other side of Henry. "Pull it up and have a go at this."

As Bella settled in, she said to Fallon, "How's everything at Country Kids?"

She brushed back her curly red hair. "Busy as usual. I had a four-year-old today who hit another child, so I had to call his parents to come pick him up. He was having a tantrum."

"How did the parents react?"

"Not well. But I explained that he couldn't disrupt

the whole class just because he couldn't get his way. The mom admitted she and her husband are having some problems at home and that's why he's acting out. Her husband lost his job in Kalispell, and he's taken two part-time positions to try to make up for it. But they're having financial difficulties and arguing. All of that affects kids."

Bella exchanged a look with Jamie. Everything regarding home life affected kids. That's why she and Jamie were trying to give the triplets all the love and attention they could muster. With others joining in, the triplets should have a good start on life, even though they'd been born prematurely and had had to catch up. Even though they'd lost their mom.

"Fallon, I don't know if we say it often enough, but we're so grateful for your help," Bella said.

"I love helping." She turned her blue eyes on Jamie and then the triplets. "When these little ones follow me with their eyes, as they grab hold of my finger, or they eat their food instead of wear it, I feel like I've accomplished something important."

"I know what you mean," Bella agreed. "That's why I love working at the day care center, too. Babies are so easy to love." She thought about her background and Jamie's and added, "Unlike teenagers, who are angry and ungrateful sometimes."

"Our grandparents did their best," Jamie murmured.

Bella supposed that was true. People could do only what they knew how to do. But it seemed love should be easier to give than to withhold, and she'd always felt their grandparents had withheld their affection. She always surmised that they'd taken in her and Jamie out of guilt. Years before, they'd disowned their only daughter,

Bella's mother Lauren, when she'd gotten pregnant out of wedlock, and Bella suspected they regretted that decision. When Bella had gotten pregnant, it had brought back for her grandparents all those unwanted memories and stress—stress that no doubt contributed to her grandma's death. At the end of the day, she had blamed herself for all of it. She'd ended up believing that she was a burden who should have never landed on her grandparents' doorstep.

Jamie's thoughts must have been following the same course because he said with regret, "I wish things were different with Gramps, but that's too much water under the bridge, isn't it?"

"I wish things were different around the holidays especially," Bella agreed.

Gramps still lived in the same house in town, and they never heard from him or saw him. She wished he could be part of their lives, but he'd disowned her after she'd gotten pregnant, even though she'd had a miscarriage. That hadn't made any difference to him. He'd been cold and mostly unspeaking until she moved out when she was eighteen. There was so much resentment there—resentment for his wife dying, resentment for the financial burden they'd caused, resentment that Bella had acted out when she was looking for love. No, there was no going back there. She just had to look forward.

"Family is complicated," Fallon agreed.

"Yours doesn't seem to be," Bella offered. "You're close to your brothers and sisters, and your parents would do anything for all of you."

"That's true, and my parents are great role models for the marriage I'd like to have someday." Again her gaze fell on Jamie, but he was oblivious.

Bella knew her brother had always thought of Fallon as a kid sister. Would that change now that she was helping him with the triplets? Could that change when he was still grieving over Paula? Thank goodness for the babies and the others who were helping. Although Jamie didn't want to be beholden to anyone, the baby chain's presence in his life kept him from brooding, from being too solitary.

And then there were the babies. As she watched her brother wipe applesauce from Henry's little mouth, she knew the triplets had saved Jamie from grief that could have swallowed him up.

"As soon as we're done feeding them, we'll start supper," she said to Fallon. "Would you like to stay? I just plan to make tacos."

"I can chop tomatoes, lettuce and whatever else you want to put on them," she offered after she accepted the invitation. "That is if we get these rapscallions settled so we can have supper."

"We can take turns watching them and cooking, even if we have to eat in shifts. We'll manage it," Jamie insisted.

Her brother's gaze met hers. Yes, they were managing. But life was about more than managing, wasn't it?

She thought again about Hudson. All too easily she could picture his face and his mesmerizing blue eyes.

Bella stopped in the break room the following morning for a bottle of water to take to her desk. She was surprised to see Hudson there, opening a carton he'd set on a side table. Every time she looked at him, a little tremor started inside her and she wished she could will it away. It wasn't like she ogled calendars with pictures of buff firemen or handsomely suited *GQ* models for a little female thrill. But whenever she looked at Hudson, she felt a quiver of excitement.

She wasn't sure if it was caused by his long, jeans-clad legs—those jeans fit him oh so well—or the Western-cut shirt with its open collar where a few chest hairs peeked out. He was long-waisted and lean, and she could imagine exactly how he'd look seated on a horse. His brown leather boots made him seem even taller. Even without his tan Stetson, there was a rugged-Montana-guy feel to him that had to do with the lines of his face, the jut of his jaw, his dark brows. His thick hair waved a bit as it crossed his brow, and she found her fingers itched to ruffle it.

Crazy.

He smiled at her now as he flipped open the carton and took out…a blue teddy bear. Then he dipped his hand inside again and produced a green one and then a brown one.

She couldn't help but smile, too. "What are those?"

"Christmas presents for the young'uns. The day before Christmas they can each take one home."

"Did you do this?"

"Do you mean did I pick them out and order them? Yes, I did. It seemed like a great idea. There are three more boxes of them out in my truck. I'll stow them in the storeroom until Christmas Eve."

She approached him, telling herself she just had to pass by him to get to the refrigerator. When she did walk past him, she caught scent of his aftershave, something woodsy that made her think of pine forests.

She took a closer look at the bears. "They look child safe with their embroidered eyes and noses."

"That's what the online description said," he assured her. "I know how careful the teachers and parents are about those things. I learned that the first week I was here."

"You had a crash course in child rearing from the teachers."

"I did, along with the most tactful way to speak with parents. But it's darn tiring being politically correct all the time. It's much easier just to say what you think."

"You usually say what you think?"

"I try to. Less misunderstanding that way. I've had a few sharp lessons in life, teaching me to get to the bottom of people's motives really quick. Straight speaking does that."

She nodded, opened the small refrigerator and pulled a bottle of water from the shelf.

Now he moved a few steps closer to her. She wrapped her hand around the cold bottle of water, suddenly feeling hot. He unsettled her so, and she didn't know what to do about it.

"You were busy all morning, and I didn't want to interrupt you. I spoke with Jazzy Smith, and she'd like to see your photos."

Bella had considered the project but had doubts about becoming involved in it. "I don't know, Hudson. I don't even have a professional camera, and I don't know when I'd have the time."

Hudson gave her a long studying look. She had a feeling he was debating whether to say something. But then he said it. "You're around babies and kids all day at the center, and you're around your brother and the triplets the rest of the time. Don't you think you deserve something of your own?"

She didn't know why his comments felt like criticism of her life. She'd had a whole ton of criticism from her grandmother and her grandfather. She didn't need any more from outside sources, making her second-guess what she was doing. Even her friends had been judgmental when she'd quit college to help Jamie. So before she thought better of it, she decided to say what *she* thought.

"You've no right to tell me how to live my life."

He didn't look shocked or even surprised, but rather he just gave her that same steady stare. "No, I don't have any right to tell you how to live your life. But maybe, just maybe, it wouldn't hurt for you to talk about it with someone." After closing the flap, he hefted the box of teddy bears into his arms and left the break room, heading for the storage closet.

See? she thought, mentally chastising herself. *Say what you think and it causes tension.* Yet on the other hand, her retort wasn't quite fair, not when he'd just seemed to be looking out for her. She sighed and went after him.

He was shuffling things around in the closet, apparently making room for the teddy bears.

Teddy bears. How many men would have thought of that? Let alone gone ahead and taken care of it.

He didn't look her way as she entered the closet, so she went right over to him and stood in his path.

"Hudson, I'm sorry. I shouldn't have responded like that. I guess you just hit a sore spot. That was my rebellious teenage side making an appearance."

He didn't seem angry. In fact, the look in his eyes made her breath hitch a little when he remarked, "I can't see you as a rebellious teenager." His lips twitched up a little in amusement.

If only she hadn't been, her life might be so much different now.

"You have no idea," she told him. As soon as she said that, she was afraid he'd ask questions. To forestall those, she said simply, "I'd like to meet Jazzy Smith. Did she have a particular time in mind?"

"Matter of fact, she said this evening would be good. If you're free."

Bella thought about it. "I'll have to call Jamie and make sure he has help for dinner."

"No problem. Just let me know. I can pick you up at your brother's. No reason for us to take two vehicles."

She considered riding in Hudson's truck, maybe finding a common interest that didn't include diapers and rattles.

"I'll call him now," she assured him and took her phone from her pocket, heading back to her desk. She could think better and breathe easier when she wasn't in Hudson's presence.

When Hudson picked up Bella a few hours later, Jamie was upstairs giving Henry a bath while Fallon finished feeding Katie and Jared downstairs. She called upstairs to her brother that she was leaving.

Bella explained to Hudson, "Giving a baby a bath can be tricky. Henry has his full attention."

"I'll meet him another time," Hudson assured her.

But Bella wasn't all that sure she wanted Jamie and Hudson to meet. Jamie was too intuitive, and her brother would sense her attraction to the man and zero in on it. She didn't want that happening. It was difficult enough to deal with her reaction to Hudson, let alone Jamie's reaction, too.

Hudson easily made conversation with Fallon. "I suppose you're getting ready for the holidays at Country Kids, too."

"We are. Artwork turkeys everywhere."

Hudson laughed.

"Fallon's such a good help with the triplets because she knows exactly what to do most of the time," Bella explained.

"Experience definitely helps when you cope with kids," Fallon agreed.

"I'm surprised you stop in here after work," Hudson noted. "Kids can be draining. I admire the way Bella works and then comes home and helps with the triplets."

"It's easy for me just to stop in on my way home," Fallon said. "And, like Bella, I love kids."

Katie banged her spoon on her high chair tray while Jared pushed round cereal pieces into his mouth.

"Are you sure you're okay for me to leave?" Bella asked.

"I'm fine. After Jamie's done with Henry, I'll take Katie up and give her a bath."

After goodbyes, Hudson walked Bella outside to his truck. He went around to the passenger side and opened the door for her. "Need a leg up?"

Oh, no, he wasn't putting his hands around her waist and giving her a boost into the high truck. She could just imagine those long fingers and those big hands and the warmth she'd feel through her jacket...

Quickly she assured him, "I'm used to boosting myself up onto a horse. No problem with a truck."

Fortunately she was telling the truth. Clutching her

purse and the photo album she was going to show Jazzy and Brooks, she hopped onto the running board and slid inside. Hudson closed the door for her, and she wondered if he was this chivalrous with every woman. Rumor had it he wasn't seeing anyone in town, but he could have a long-distance relationship with someone.

Once he was inside the truck and they were on their way, she felt she had to make conversation. Dusk had already fallen, and the inside of the cab seemed a little too intimate.

"Is the rescue ranch far?"

"Just about a mile from here."

"You said you're staying on a ranch."

"The Lazy B."

"That's a big spread," she said. "Any horses?"

"Oh, yes, some fine ones. Clive, the owner of the spread, has a good eye. He has two quarter horses, an Arabian, a Tennessee walker, a horse who pulls the buckboard and a Thoroughbred that was supposed to be racing but wasn't real successful at it. She's a beauty, though."

"Do you have a favorite?"

"I do. The Arabian, I have to admit it. I'm used to quarter horses for cutting cattle and rodeo training. But that Arabian has eyes that can see into your soul. She seems to intuitively know what I want to do next, with a flick of the rein, with a slight pressure of a boot. Amazing, really."

"What's her name?"

"It's Breeze. Clive found her at the rescue ranch. Someone had abandoned her. After Jazzy worked her magic and got her back into shape, the mare actually trusts humans again. Clive named her Breeze because she runs like the wind. She knows her name now. At least, I think she does. She comes when I call her."

After a moment, he asked, "What's your horse's name?"

"How do you know I have a horse?"

"You said you liked to ride. So my guess is, Jamie has one just for you."

"Her name's Butterscotch. I ride her in the mornings when I can."

"I can almost picture her. Flying blond mane?"

"You got it."

Horses were an easy conversational gambit for them. Horse lovers were like any animal lovers. Talking about the beautiful creatures created a bond.

After a bit of silence, Bella decided to be a little bolder. "So what life did *you* leave when you dropped in here to take care of Just Us Kids?"

He glanced over at her, maybe to gauge how much she wanted to know. She could see his profile by the light of the dashboard glow. She imagined he could see her face only in shadow.

"I was helping a friend in Wyoming who'd bought a ranch. He needed help with the start-up."

"I imagine traveling place to place, you meet a lot of people."

"I do."

"Do you make friends easily?" From what she'd seen, he did. But she wanted to know what he'd say.

"I find something to like in most people. That allows for friendship, especially if I go back to a place more than once. It's really hard to keep up a friendship once you leave. I know the tech age is supposed to make it easier, but friendship still requires commitment."

He was right about that.

"Have you ever been committed to a woman?" she asked. She supposed that was one of the better ways to phrase it.

"No. Never anything serious," he answered with a shrug. "How about you?"

That was the problem with asking questions. The questionee thought he should return the favor. "Not lately," she said nonchalantly.

"Did you leave someone behind at college?"

"No. I really had my mind on my studies, so I didn't date."

He seemed to mull that over, and she wondered if he'd ask more about her past.

To her relief, he flipped on his turn signal and they veered down a lane to the ranch. "Brooks could move his practice out here, but he prefers to keep it in town."

Since darkness had fallen, Bella couldn't see much except for the floodlights on top of the barn that glowed over their surroundings. There were at least three barns and a house that looked like a typical ranch house but was much newer. It appeared big for two people, but maybe Brooks and Jazzy were planning on having a large family. Bella felt that stab of pain again that was never going to go away. It was one regret that haunted her.

Apparently divining her thoughts, Hudson explained, "Brooks and Jazzy plan to fill this house with kids. But they also have a first-floor suite set up for Brooks's dad when he's ready to move in with them one day."

"Then they must have a wonderful sense of family," Bella said, thinking about her absent brothers and sisters and whether she and Jamie would ever see them again.

When Jazzy opened her door to them, Bella admired her natural beauty right away. She was slim in skinny jeans and a tunic sweater. But her smile was wide as she welcomed them. She didn't hesitate to give Hudson a hug.

"It's good to see you again." She held out her hand to Bella. "It's nice to meet you."

"And you, too."

Bella handed the photo album to Jazzy. "I thought you might want to look at these. I don't have a professional portfolio, but I keep an album of the best ones."

"I can't wait to see them," Jazzy said. "Come into the living room. I fixed a few snacks. Brooks is out in the barn. He'll be in shortly."

Bella quickly glanced at the cheese tray, the biscuits that looked warm from the oven, jam and butter for those, and a fruit platter, too.

"You didn't have to go to all this trouble."

"It's no trouble. Brooks and I often don't eat till much later. I have something simmering in the slow cooker. I grab a snack with him when he gets home, and then we go out to the barns for a couple of hours. Rescue horses need a lot of kindness, soft talk and gentle touches. That takes time."

"Do you have help?" Bella asked.

"Some part-time help. There are also a group of kids from the high school who mount up service hours for working here. They learn from the horses, and the horses learn from them." She motioned to the food again. "Help yourself. I can't wait to take a look at these." She positioned the album on her lap and began turning pages. After a few pages, Jazzy glanced at Hudson. "You were right. She has a good eye—for scenery, for animals and for kids. That's a winning combination."

Just then Brooks emerged from the kitchen. "I came in the back way," he said, "so I could wash up. Hey there, Hudson."

Hudson introduced him to Bella.

"Look at these," Jazzy said.

"Before I even look, I can hear it in your voice. You like them," her husband guessed.

She just smiled at him and handed him the album. Bella lifted her camera, pressed a button and showed Jazzy photos she hadn't yet had printed. They were the same ones Hudson had seen of the triplets and of Jamie's ranch.

"Those are unedited," Bella told her. "I play with them a bit when I have time—cropping, adding a little light, studying them with black-and-white effects."

"I can see that with these," Brooks said, motioning to the album. "I think we should hire you."

Jazzy nodded and named a sum Bella could easily accept.

"I'd like a day with perfect weather," Bella said, and they all laughed. "Well, near perfect," she amended. "Do you mind if we do a last-minute shoot? I'll keep checking the weather day to day and, when I can get free, I'll text you to see if it suits you. Is that okay?"

"That's fine."

Now that business was taken care of, they snacked and talked, and Bella felt she really liked the couple. It was easy to see that they were deeply in love, as well as passionate about their work.

After she and Hudson left and they were in the truck, she said as much to him.

"You'd never believe they married for convenience's sake, would you?" Hudson asked.

"You're kidding."

"No. It had to do with Brooks's dad and him letting his son into the business. Then his father had health problems, and Brooks felt marriage was the only way to convince his dad to slow down."

"But they have more than a marriage of convenience."

"Oh, yes, they do. Jazzy and Brooks will be the first ones to tell you that they thought they were marrying for convenience, but they were really marrying for love."

Bella and Hudson didn't talk after that, and she wondered if they were both thinking about what he'd said. She couldn't remember much about her own parents' marriage, but she believed they'd been in love. She remembered them holding hands. She remembered them kissing when they thought their children weren't looking. But she'd never know that kind of love. Men wanted children, and she couldn't have them.

Back at the ranch, she'd thought she'd just hop out of Hudson's truck and that would be it. But no, he was being chivalrous again. He came around to her side and opened the door for her. He even took her hand to help her out. That was the first they'd touched all evening. His fingers seemed to burn hers. And when she was on the ground, she looked up at him, confused by all of it. They walked side by side to the front door, then just stood there gazing at each other.

"It *was* nice," he finally said, "sitting there with Jazzy and Brooks, talking like we're friends."

"Yes. Most of my friends are single women."

"They really liked your photos. This could be just

the first of many assignments. Word gets around, you know."

"It would be fun to take photos to pay bills. I can also save some money for college."

"No splurging?"

She could hardly think straight looking into Hudson's eyes. "No splurging," she said softly.

He took a step closer to her, and Bella knew she should back away. But she didn't.

Hudson reached out and touched her cheek. Her face was cold from the winter night air, and his hand was large and warm. She could feel calluses on his fingers, and that was exciting. Everything about Hudson was exciting. When his hand went to the nape of her neck and he slid his fingers into her hair, she should have protested. She didn't. And when he bent his head, she knew exactly what he was going to do.

Chapter 4

If he'd thought this kiss was going to be something easy or quiet, Hudson had been dead wrong. Bella had a sweetness about her that revved up his male instincts and all his male needs. The hunger that welled inside him wasn't going to be satisfied with just a quick tasting.

Some essence of her made him want to get closer and know her in an intimate way. He wrapped his arm around her, maybe to steady them both.

He'd kissed a lot of women, and he'd wanted to demonstrate finesse with this kiss. But finesse floated out the window when his tongue breached Bella's lips. He swept her mouth with an intensity that disconcerted him. No, one brief kiss wasn't going to be enough. He felt intoxicated by their passion and confident in her response. She was tasting him, too, giving back passion as well as receiving it.

But then suddenly she wasn't. It was as if a switch had been flicked off. He felt her stiffen, and he knew exactly what was going to come between them. Rational thought. It had invaded her head before it had found its way to his.

Suddenly she was breaking away, her arms stiff at her sides. She was shaking her head, and he knew whatever she said wasn't going to be good.

Still, he was old enough and experienced enough and respectful of females enough, not to take what a woman didn't want to give. He tried to shut down the heavy beating of his pulse. With a deep breath, he willed his body to calm down, letting her escape his arms. He kept his hands by his sides even though he wanted to still touch her, even though he wanted to wrap her in another embrace.

"What's wrong?" he asked, surprised his voice had come out as even as it had. After all, that kiss had practically knocked his boots off.

"I can't do this," she said, shaking her head again. "I need my job. I can't get involved with you."

As if a bolt of lightning had made him see more clearly, Hudson suddenly realized that everything about Bella's life was so much more precarious than his. Although his parents had been distant emotionally, he'd had four brothers. Someone was always there. And besides his family, his father's wealth had been a life raft. His own trust fund had given him opportunities and saved him from embarrassing situations. When something didn't work out, he moved on to the next endeavor because he didn't have to count on a paycheck. Bella didn't have that luxury. She worried about her brother and her niece and nephews and about Jamie's financial situation. She worried about her own. She was trying to save enough money to finish college, and Hudson knew how expensive that was these days.

The porch lamp softly glowed across her face. He saw her expression that said she already might have done something that would put her job in jeopardy. That was because she didn't know him. She didn't know what kind of man he was, and that he'd never punish a woman for backing away from him.

"Bella, it's all right. I understand."

"You're not mad because I wouldn't—" She stopped, seemingly embarrassed to go on.

"Nothing's going to interfere with your job, whether we kiss or whether we don't."

"It's too dangerous for me to even think about getting involved with you," she responded. "I can't risk one of the few jobs in Rust Creek Falls that pays decently. It isn't just you. It's Walker, too. He owns Just Us Kids. If anything happened between you and me, he could blame me."

This time Hudson took hold of her shoulders. He couldn't help touching her. "Stop, Bella. I do understand. No repercussions. I read the signals wrong."

At that she blinked, and then she sighed. "I can't let you think that. You didn't read the signals wrong. But I remembered my responsibilities. I remembered who I am and who you are. We come from different worlds, Hudson."

"It was just a kiss, Bella."

After she studied him for a few seconds, she nodded. "Okay, it was just a kiss. I have to go inside. I'm sure Jamie heard the truck, and he'll wonder why I'm still out here."

Hudson dropped his hands away from her because he knew she was going to run. He couldn't blame her, for all the reasons she'd mentioned. Yet when she turned the knob on the door, when she glanced at him over her shoulder, he got the feeling she didn't want to go inside at all.

She said good-night, and so did he. But as he went to his truck, he remembered everything about their kiss, and he wondered if she was doing the same.

Hudson understood Bella's avoidance of him—he really did. That didn't mean he was less attracted to her. Nor did that change the electricity that zapped between them whenever they had to deal with each other. First, when he stole glances at her and saw the dark circles under her eyes, he wondered if the tension between them was causing it. But as the week passed, he didn't think that was it at all. Bella worked all day, and he'd heard her tell one of the teachers that two of the triplets had kept her and Jamie up for the past few nights teething. He might not understand what that was all about, but he did understand sleep deprivation. She wasn't smiling at everyone the way she usually did. The next day at lunchtime, he walked into the break room and found her arms crossed on the table with her head down on them. She was asleep.

She didn't stir as he approached her and stood at the table looking down at her. Her eyes were closed, the lashes fanning her cheeks. Her hair wisped along her face, looking as silky and soft as always. He couldn't let her try to function like this.

Placing his hand on her shoulder, he said gently, "Bella?"

Her eyes fluttered open immediately. She turned her head, spotted him and sat up straight. "Sorry," she murmured. "I was just—"

"You were catching forty winks."

"It's my lunch break," she said, almost defensively, as if he'd caught her doing something terribly wrong.

"I understand that, and if we had a cot in here where you could take a nap like the kids do, you'd be fine. But you're not getting enough sleep, are you?"

"Katie and Henry have new teeth coming in. They're miserable. At first Jamie and I took turns, but it's hard to handle two at once. So we've both been up rocking and walking them."

"You have to get some sleep. Take the afternoon off, go home and go to bed."

"I can't do that."

He suddenly realized she meant *can't* in a couple of different ways. "You mean because you're needed here?"

"Yes, I am."

"I can take over for the afternoon. It's Friday. Things have slowed down for the week."

But Bella wasn't convinced, and then he realized what the other problem might be. "You won't be able to rest if you go back to Jamie's, will you? I should have realized that. Let me take you to my house so you can get a few hours of sleep without disruption."

Bella's eyes went wide, and he knew exactly what she was thinking. "I'll let you in, turn off the alarm and then I'll come back here. You can sleep on the sofa or a bed or wherever you want. The place will be yours for a few hours."

"Hudson, it's your home. I can't just barge in and take over."

"Sure you can. Tell me, how much time have you had absolutely alone since you moved in with Jamie?"

The question obviously didn't need much thinking about. She answered immediately. "I'm alone in my drives to and from work, and if I manage to go for a ride to exercise the horses."

"And how often do you do that?"

"I haven't for a couple of weeks," she admitted.

"Exactly. You have noise and kids around you almost twenty-four hours a day. Give yourself a break, Bella. Just take a few hours for yourself. Come on, get your coat. I'll let Sarah know I'll be gone for about twenty minutes."

"I can just drive myself," Bella said.

"In your condition, you might fall asleep at the wheel. This is no big deal. Grab your coat and let's go."

As if she didn't have the energy to resist, she nodded, went to the closet and pulled out her coat.

Bella opened her eyes when Hudson switched off the ignition of his truck. They were in the driveway of the ranch-style house. She must have dozed a little on the way here even though it hadn't been that long a drive. She was really that exhausted. It was the only reason she'd taken Hudson's offer seriously.

Was he really going to just drop her here and leave? That's exactly what she wanted, right?

"We're here," he said cheerily. "And a good thing, too. I don't think that seat belt could have held you upright any longer."

"You're exaggerating."

"Not by much. Let's get you inside."

The stone-and-timber home was one story and sprawling, and it sat before her like a quiet haven. Hudson came around and opened her door. He offered his hand, and she took it to step down from the high running board. The cold air felt damp, as if snow was on its way. 'Twas the season.

As she walked beside Hudson, she felt…small. His height and broad shoulders made him tower above her. He was a substantial man, especially in his boots and suede coat with its Sherpa lining and trim. At the door, he dug into his pocket and pulled out a key. There was an overhang above the door, and as she stepped up beside Hudson, she felt as if the two of them were the only people in the world. She figured it was sleep deprivation muddling her thoughts.

He turned the key in the lock, opened another dead bolt, then pushed open the door. As soon as they stepped inside, he was pressing buttons on the security system on a panel on the wall.

The floor of the foyer was some kind of black stone. With just one look, she could tell this house was built with quality materials.

To the right, Bella caught sight of a dining room with a hand-carved oak table and chairs, and a beautiful hutch that showcased stoneware plates. Looking ahead into the center of the house, she saw an open-concept family room and kitchen.

Hudson motioned through the family room. "There are two bedrooms over that way."

Then he motioned to the left. "I've set up an office over there, and there's a master suite behind that. Where would you like to settle?"

The lone couch in the family room was upholstered in blue and rust in a chevron design and looked cushy with its back pillows for support and comfort. She didn't pay much attention to the accompanying leather recliner and wing chair with side tables and lamps. That sofa was exactly what she needed.

"That'll be fine." As soon as she reached the sofa, she took off her coat and laid it over the back. She sank down onto the couch, and it was like sitting on a cloud.

Hudson laid the key on the immense rough-hewn coffee table. "I'm going to leave you that key. I have a spare. Do you want me to set the alarm or not?"

"I don't want to set something off by mistake."

Hudson pointed to the hangings on the walls. "Clive owns some expensive art. That's why there's a security system."

"Not to mention this beautiful furniture and that huge flat-screen TV," she said, motioning to it.

Hudson chuckled. "Yeah, not to mention that." He took out a card and a pen and jotted down the alarm code. He slid it under the key ring. "I'll set the alarm. There's the code in case you need to turn it off."

"I'm not going to move," she assured him, settling back against the cushions.

A Pendleton blanket was folded over one of the side chairs. Hudson picked it up and brought it to her, spreading it out on the lower end of the couch. "Just in case you get a chill. This will warm you up."

Just looking at Hudson Jones warmed her up, but she wasn't exhausted enough to say that. She did have a few faculties about her.

"I'll come back here after the last kid's gone from the day care center and drive you back there to get your car. You have my cell number, just in case you need me for some reason."

When her gaze caught Hudson's, their kiss became a vivid memory once more. She had the feeling he was remembering it, too.

His eyes darkened. He took a step closer but then said, "The refrigerator's stocked if you get hungry. Greta takes care of that for me."

"Greta?"

"Her husband, Edmond, is the foreman on the ranch. They live in the log cabin just around the bend from the house."

After a last look at her, he turned and headed toward the door. She had the feeling if he stayed longer he could sit on that sofa beside her, and then who knew what could happen?

"See you in a few hours," he said.

She heard the beep of the alarm as he set it and the click of the door when it closed. She heard his truck revving up in the driveway and backing out. Taking one of the throw pillows from a corner of the sofa, she positioned it, curled up with her head on it and pulled up the blanket.

She saw Hudson's face in her mind's eye, right before she succumbed to her fatigue.

When Hudson returned to the Lazy B that evening, he let himself in and switched off the alarm. He'd stopped at Wings to Go, hungry himself and sure Bella was, too. Greta had left salads in the refrigerator, and they'd go great with the wings. He knew Bella would want to get home, but sleep and food and quiet had seemed to be a necessity for her today.

When he switched on the small side light in the family room, she didn't stir. He watched her from a few feet away. She was curled on her side facing the sofa, the blanket pulled up to her shoulders. He wanted nothing more than to go over to that sofa and finger her hair, touch her cheek, kiss her. Even sleeping, she awakened his appetite for more than barbecued wings.

Still, he let her sleep while he went to the kitchen and set the table for dinner. By the time he put out the salads and the wings, he heard the rustle of movement from the sofa.

"Hey, sleepyhead," he said with a smile. "Are you hungry?"

Pushing off the blanket, she sat up and tried to wipe the sleep from her eyes. "I didn't hear you come in."

"You got a good nap."

She yawned. "I did. I feel like I got more sleep than I have all week." She checked her watch. "Oh my gosh. I've got to get home. Jamie will wonder what happened to me."

"Text him. You can take another fifteen or twenty minutes to eat supper. You've got to take care of yourself, Bella. You won't be much help to him if you get run-down or sick."

She looked torn, but then she nodded. "I know you're right." She'd left her purse on the coffee table, and now she took her phone from it and quickly texted. Afterward she said, "Something smells great."

"I picked up wings. The rest of the meal was in the fridge. I'm a lucky guy."

He saw her look around as if she hadn't really done it before. He spent a lot of time in the family room. A flannel jacket lay over the top of one chair. His laptop sat on the coffee table beside an unfinished cup of coffee. Another pair of boots sat near the gas fireplace.

Standing, she started toward him. "It looks as if you've settled in."

"For now," he said, meaning it. After all, he didn't know how long his wandering spirit would keep him here. He motioned to one of the ladder-back chairs at the table. "Have a seat."

She washed up at the sink and then sat across from him, studying him rather than the food.

"What?" he asked.

"You went to an awful lot of trouble for me today. I guess I have to wonder why."

"I didn't want you dropping from exhaustion at the day care center," he said wryly, skirting the question.

Still, she kept her gaze on him. "So you'd do this for any of your employees?" She motioned to the meal and the house, and he knew what she meant.

"No, I wouldn't. You're special, Bella."

Her pretty brows arched. "Usually when a man does something like this, he wants something in return."

He put down the wing he was about to eat. "Maybe I do. That kiss just didn't happen out of the blue. There's been something simmering since we met. Don't you agree?"

She looked flustered. "I don't know what you mean. I—"

"Bella, tell me the truth. If you can honestly say you don't feel any sparks between us, I'll drop the whole thing, take you home, not approach you again with anything in my mind other than a boss-and-employee relationship."

"That's what we should have," she reminded him.

"Maybe. Are you going to answer my question?"

Stalling for time, she spooned potato salad onto her plate. Then she looked up at him with guileless brown eyes. "Yes, I feel the sparks, but I've been doing my best to ignore them."

He pushed the broccoli salad dish toward her. "That's only going to work for so long."

She sighed and took a sip of her sparkling water. Then she said, "Can we table this discussion for now?"

"Am I making you uncomfortable?"

"No. It's just I have my mind on getting home because I know Jamie's going to need my help."

"And you're afraid if we get embroiled in this type of discussion, you won't get home soon enough."

She picked up a wing. "Yes."

He nodded. "Okay, let's eat."

They were quiet as they ate but still aware of each other. Their gazes met often. Their fingers brushed when they reached for another wing at the same time. He noticed the pulse at the hollow of Bella's neck. He caught her studying the scar under his eye.

"I fell out of a tree house when I was a kid," he said, "and got scraped up pretty good."

She blushed a little. "Stitches?" she asked.

"Yep, twelve of them. How about you? Were you adventurous when you were a kid?"

She was silent for a few moments, then she said, "Not in the tree-climbing kind of way." She hesitated. "But after Jamie and I went to live with our grandparents, I was difficult—acting out, truancy, that kind of thing."

She looked as if there was a lot more to that story, but he didn't press. He just responded, "You don't look like the type. Now you seem to want to go by the book and obey every rule."

"Maybe because I stepped over the line one too many times." With that conclusion, she stood and carried her plate to the sink. Then she asked, "Can you point me to the powder room?"

He waved down the hall. "It's right across from the office."

She nodded and went that way.

He cleaned up in the kitchen, still wondering about her "acting out" escapades. When he heard her in the hall off the foyer, he met her there and pointed to the office. "Did you peek in there?"

"No."

"Not the nosy type?" he asked with a grin.

"Not usually," she answered agreeably.

"I'd like to show you the paintings in there. Come on. It will only take a minute."

He led her into the office, and when she joined him, she gave a little gasp of pleasure. "Oh my. Are they originals?"

"They are. Clive considers Barclay the best Western painter in America."

He gave his attention to the landscape of a Montana ranch near Billings, then another near Missoula—mountains with a stream running through.

"I noticed the wall hangings in the family room right away when I walked in. They're beautiful, too. Mr. Bickler has wonderful taste and deep pockets."

"Deep pockets can't buy taste," Hudson assured her. "But, yes, Clive has both. I'm fortunate this place was available when I was looking around to find somewhere to live. I thought you might appreciate these."

"I do."

He pointed to a vase sitting on a wide windowsill. "Most of his pottery is signed, too."

She came closer to the window to examine the vase. The darkness outside and the quietness of the house wrapped them in a type of intimacy. He was very aware of the master suite right down the hall.

When Bella looked up at him, he wanted to kiss her so badly that he could remember her taste. But he didn't want to scare her away. He was afraid another kiss right now might just do that. Timing, he knew, was everything.

His voice was husky when he said, "I'll take you back to the day care center, then I'm going to follow you home to make sure you get there safely." He put his forefinger to her lips. "And don't say I don't have to do that. I know I don't. I want to."

Her lips under his finger were warm, pliable, sexy, and he knew exactly how sweet. When he removed his finger, she was still looking at him. He suspected there was a depth to Bella that not many people probed. She kept up a wall of reserve, and that held them at bay. But he was going to break through that reserve.

One day.

A short time later, Hudson and Bella stood next to his truck at Jamie's ranch. Bella didn't know how to thank Hudson for what he'd done for her this afternoon. He confused her. She hadn't expected the kindness that seemed an innate part of his nature. She felt she had to return that kindness and maybe even take a figurative step toward him, toward admitting those sparks they both knew they felt.

"Can you come in for a few minutes?" she asked. "I'd like you to meet my brother." If Jamie saw the attraction between her and Hudson, he could help her sort it out.

There was a bright moon in the sky, and even though his face was shadowed, she caught the surprise on it. "I'd like that," he said.

And just like that, Hudson took her hand and they walked toward the door. He let go as she opened it. Inside the house, the TV was blaring. Paige Dalton Traub was on the sofa playing with Katie. Jamie was on the floor with Henry and Jared building a structure with colored blocks. He looked up when Bella came in.

"I'm glad you got some dinner," he said. "It was hit-and-miss here."

She'd texted him about the wings and eating with Hudson. She and Jamie had no secrets from each other.

Jared crawled quickly toward Bella. Bella dropped her purse, shrugged out of her coat and laid it over a chair. Then she scooped up the baby, hugging him close.

"Hi there, big boy. I hope you're not giving your dad too much trouble."

"He and Katie aren't as fussy today," Jamie said, getting to his feet and hauling Henry into his arms. "I'm hoping the teething crisis is over."

Bella introduced the two men.

They shook hands, and Bella noticed they seemed to be sizing each other up. They were about the same height and supremely fit from their outdoor work, though Hudson was a bit huskier. Then Jamie introduced Paige—Sutter Traub's wife, elementary school teacher and mom—to Hudson.

Paige said, "If you'll excuse me, I'll get this little girl started on her bath."

Jared suddenly leaned toward Hudson, holding his arms out. Not sure how Hudson would react, Bella said, "You don't have to—"

But Hudson didn't hesitate. He lifted the little boy from Bella and held him high in the air. "Hi there, big guy. I hear you've been stealing sleep from your dad and your aunt. I hope those teeth have settled down."

"Until the next one pops up," Jamie said wryly.

Hudson transferred Jared to the crook of his arm, and the little boy seemed satisfied to stay there for the moment. "I can't imagine caring for three of them," he said to Jamie with a shake of his head. "This is like having your own day care."

"I hope Bella's told you we have nothing against Just Us Kids. But since the triplets were preemies, I don't want to take the chance of putting them in day care yet. You understand, don't you?"

"Of course I do. And they're in good hands from what I hear."

"Our helpers are the best," Jamie said. "And so is Bella," he tacked on.

It was easy to see the bond between brother and sister and the way they communicated with their eyes, with a gesture, with no words at all. Jamie deposited Henry in his play saucer and then held out his arms for Jared.

Placing him in another saucer, he said, "Come on, fella, you're going to be next for a bath."

"I'd better be going," Hudson said. "It was good to meet you."

"Likewise," Jamie agreed with a nod. And then he maneuvered the two saucers into the kitchen.

Bella walked Hudson to the door. "It's always chaos here."

"Just like the day care center," Hudson said with a smile.

They were standing very close, and neither of them seemed to want to move away. Bella wasn't sure how to say goodbye to Hudson. She wasn't sure where they were headed. They were in between a working relationship and a personal one, and she wasn't even sure she should step into the personal one. But when she looked into Hudson's eyes, she wanted to.

"Thank you for this afternoon," she said sincerely. "I needed the sleep and the quiet, and those great wings."

Hudson chuckled. "Here I thought you were going to say you needed supper with me."

"All of it was really kind of you."

Hudson reached out and touched her cheek. "It was more than kindness, Bella. Sometime we'll continue the discussion we started over dinner."

Then he was stepping away from her, opening the door and leaving. She stood in the doorway, watching him until he drove away.

She found herself disappointed he hadn't kissed her.

Confusion? Thy name was Bella.

Chapter 5

On Saturday morning Hudson rose before sunrise. After downing a protein shake along with one of Greta's cinnamon rolls, he went for a ride on Breeze, contemplating his day. He considered what Bella had said about purpose and realized except for handling the day care's PR problems, he didn't have one. He thought about last evening, meeting Jamie and watching him handle the triplets, as well as his ranch. The guy needed more than a baby chain. Since he'd noticed fencing on Jamie's ranch that needed to be repaired, Hudson decided what he was going to do with his day before bad weather moved in. Throughout his adult life, he'd never had to consult anyone when he wanted to go somewhere or do something. So he didn't now.

He drove his truck to the lumberyard, bought the supplies he needed and headed out to the Stockton ranch, down a rutted road on the side field. The ground was frozen, so he couldn't repost fence. But he could replace slats and make repairs that would keep cattle in and horses safe.

Before 9 a.m. he was working on the fence line, the physical labor feeling good. He'd missed it. After an hour, he sat inside his truck, warmed up with another cinnamon roll, then went back at it. It was noon when he spotted Jamie rushing out the back of the house and across the field. Hudson didn't at all expect the reaction he got when Jamie was within earshot of him.

The rancher asked, "What are you doing out here?"

"I thought you needed help with the fence line. You don't want your cattle or horses getting out, do you?"

Hudson could see the angry expression on Jamie Stockton's face now that he was closer. "Of course I don't want them getting out. But I don't want *you* doing my work."

"I was trying to help out, just like the baby chain helps you with the triplets."

Jamie's words puffed white in the almost frigid air. "That's different. I have to accept help so Katie, Henry and Jared stay healthy and happy and content. But as far as the ranch goes, I can handle it on my own. Did Bella tell you I needed help out here?"

"No," Hudson said honestly and quickly. "I saw it when we drove by. Your fence slats are falling off. Your posts are leaning. I would have helped with those, but I can't with the ground frozen. If the snow rots them and takes them down, you might have to put up something temporary."

"That's *my* worry, not yours."

To top things off, Hudson caught sight of Bella running toward them. He could see she hadn't even taken time to zip her parka. She jogged toward them and came to an abrupt stop. When she did, he saw how troubled she looked. He hadn't meant to make things harder for her or for her brother.

He addressed Jamie again. "I understand if you want me to stop. But I already bought the supplies. What if I unload them in your barn?"

"I don't need charity," Jamie insisted stubbornly. "You can take your planks and nails and leave."

Bella went to her brother and put her hand on his arm. "Jamie."

"I mean it, Jones," Jamie said tersely. "You took over the day care center under Bella's nose when she'd done nothing wrong. Maybe you had to because you were invested in it. But you have no investment here. Just let me and mine take care of ourselves."

Hudson knew about pride. Walker had been the big brother who bailed Hudson out of scrapes and then tried to tell him what to do. Hudson had always balked and his pride got in the way of a good relationship with Walker.

Jamie had lost his wife. He had to juggle more than a man should have to. At the end of the day, his pride was a valuable asset.

So Hudson didn't argue with him. He just tipped his Stetson to Bella, nodded to Jamie and said, "I understand. I'm out of here."

He gathered up the few supplies he had lying about and stowed them in the back of the truck. When he stole a glance at Bella, he saw she was caught in the middle. He wouldn't want to be in her position. She had to support her brother, and if that meant watching him turn down help, then that's what she had to do.

Hudson climbed in his truck, and as he drove away, he peered into the rearview mirror. Bella looked appalled that he was leaving like this. But he'd had no choice. He'd miscalculated badly. What was that old saying? *No good deed goes unpunished.*

He'd found that out today. Wandering, rambling, not being connected to anyone seemed to be the easier road to take. Yet he realized now it might be a road that no longer satisfied him, a road that had kept him from forming real connections and friendships.

The Monday morning influx of babies and children under the age of five was the ultimate mayhem. But somehow Bella managed it and kept everybody, from parents to kids to teachers, smiling when she did it.

Hudson hadn't had a chance to talk to her, and he wasn't sure she'd want to talk to him. Now when he looked back on what he'd done, he saw how it could be misconstrued. His actions could be considered high-handed, arrogant, maybe even condescending. She might want to stay far away from him. So he was surprised when, after the last child was logged in for the morning, Bella came to his office and rapped on the open door.

He stood and came around his desk, not wanting a barrier between them. It seemed as if they had enough of those, though he wasn't even sure what some of them were.

"I wanted to talk to you," she said, looking as if she had something serious on her mind.

"I wanted to talk to *you*," he returned.

They were about two feet apart, and Bella looked lovely today in a pale blue sweater and navy slacks. She'd worn boots, too, no doubt in anticipation of the snow that was predicted for later. It seemed Bella was the type who liked to be prepared.

They both said "I'm sorry" at the same time. He stopped and waved at her to go first. "Go ahead," he said. "But you have nothing to be sorry for."

"I'm sorry for Jamie's behavior," she apologized.

"His behavior was my fault," Hudson assured her.

Shaking her head vigorously, she responded, "No, it wasn't. One thing I've learned is that we have to own our actions. Jamie simply overreacted. It was a wonderful thing you tried to do."

Hudson stuffed his hands in his pockets so he didn't think as much about reaching out and touching her. "*Wonderful* didn't turn out so well."

"It's nothing against you, Hudson. Jamie's already accepting so much help with the triplets, he's touchy about it. He feels as if his life is running him instead of him running his life. Do you know what I mean?"

Thinking about what she'd said, he nodded. "Yes, I do. I can see the responsibilities he has sitting on his shoulders. They're wearing him down. I think they're wearing you down a bit, too."

"I'm fine," she assured him. "But I am worried about Jamie. I had a break on Friday, thanks to you. I really needed that afternoon nap. *And* that dinner. But Jamie won't take a break."

"Maybe he feels if he does, everything will fall apart. I should have discussed fixing that fence with him before I did it. I never meant to cause such a ruckus."

"You did fix the worst part, and whether he realizes it or not, he's going to be grateful when he thinks about it." She took a step closer to Hudson, and he felt his heart beating faster.

Before he realized what she was going to do, she stood on tiptoe and kissed him on the cheek. That kiss was as light as the touch of a butterfly's wings, but he felt it in every fiber of his being.

When she stepped away, she said simply, "Thank you," and then she was gone from his office.

Hudson brushed his fingers over the place on his cheek where her lips had touched his skin.

He did that often over the next hour, aware that he'd been touched by that gesture as he hadn't by anything in a long time.

Throughout the morning, he found himself staring out the window more than at his computer. Around noon he watched the first snowflakes begin to fall. They didn't start lightly but multiplied quickly, coating the grass and the pavement in no time.

The phone began ringing, and he knew why. Parents would want to pick up their kids early. To his surprise, every single one of them did. Usually there were stragglers but not today. And that gave Hudson an idea.

After the teachers had left, Bella was reaching for her parka in the break room when he found her there and asked, "How would you like to go riding in the snow?"

She zipped up her parka. "Are you serious?"

"I am. If you're game, I'll follow you to your brother's, where I can apologize to him for my high-handedness, then we can go for a short ride and chase the snowflakes. What do you think?"

"At your place?"

"Yeah, at my place. There's a horse who will be perfect for you, a little chestnut named Boots. She's got four white ones."

Bella laughed. "Okay, I'm game. Let's go."

A short time later, they pulled up at Jamie's ranch. He parked behind Bella and walked up to the door with her. She opened it, went inside and called "Jamie? Somebody's with me who'd like to talk to you."

Jamie came from the kitchen, his finger over his lips. "Not too loud. All three of them are napping. I think it's a first. Country Kids let out early, and Fallon's upstairs sorting the triplets' clothes. Some of them are already too small."

As Jamie spotted Hudson, he went silent. But Hudson didn't hesitate to walk right up to the man.

"I'm sorry," he said. "I never meant to overstep. You want to run your ranch and your life your way. I get that. I should have talked to you before I brought in supplies and did anything."

Jamie was silent as he studied Hudson, maybe trying to figure out if he was being sincere. Then he extended his hand. "No hard feelings. You did a good job and saved me a lot of work. But I want the bill for those supplies and the time you put in."

"How about if we split it down the middle? I'll give you the bill for the supplies, but my time was free."

Bella's brother considered Hudson's words, then he nodded. "All right. But I owe you one. If you need a favor for something, you come to me."

"Deal," Hudson said with a grin. "For right now, though, I'd like to take your sister riding in the snow at my place. Is that all right with you?"

Cocking his head, Jamie seemed to weigh what Bella might want.

She said, "I'd like to go if you don't need me. Is Fallon going to stick around?"

"She is. She said she can stay the night if need be."

"I'm just going to change into warmer clothes. I'll be quick—five minutes."

As Bella hurried up the steps, Jamie murmured, "Riding in the snow. We did that when we were kids."

"Before your grandparents took you in?" Hudson asked, still curious about Bella's upbringing.

"Oh, yeah, before they took us in. After that, we didn't have a whole lot of fun."

"Bella told me they didn't want you. I can't believe that."

"Oh, believe it, because it was true. I'm surprised she talked to you about it. She never talks about our childhood. Did she tell you anything else?"

"Just that she believed her grandfather blamed the two of you for your grandmother's death."

"True, too, and he might have been right."

The way Jamie was looking at him, Hudson wondered if he expected him to go on, to say more that Bella might have told him. But there wasn't anything else. Now Hudson was even more curious.

He forgot about Bella's past, though, when she came rushing down the stairs in jeans, riding boots and a pretty pink-and-white turtleneck sweater. He had a sudden urge to cuddle her in his arms. To be honest, he actually wanted to do more than that. But the cuddling sure would be nice, too.

She grabbed her parka and made sure she had her gloves and hat.

"Let's go," he said. "I'll call Edmond on the way, and he can get the horses saddled up."

As Bella rode beside Hudson in his truck, she wasn't sure what had made her agree to this crazy proposal. Maybe it was Hudson's enjoyment of the idea. Maybe it was his enthusiasm. Maybe she just needed a little fun in her life.

Hudson didn't pull into the driveway at the house but rather drove farther down the lane and pulled over at a big red barn. She spotted a log cabin not far away.

"Is that where the foreman lives?"

"Yes. It's a homey place. Greta's into crafts as well as cooking. I think you'd like it. Maybe we can stop there afterward."

At the door to the barn, snowflakes swirled lazily around them as Bella said, "I feel guilty for leaving Jamie back there with the triplets."

"They're his kids, Bella, not yours."

For a moment, she was almost angry at the remark, and Hudson must have seen that. "I'm sorry. I shouldn't have been so blunt. But it's true. At some point he's going to have to be able to handle his own life. He said Fallon was there, so you don't have to worry about him, at least not for the next few hours."

"You can look at the situation pragmatically. I can't."

He took a step closer to her and held her by the shoulders. "Someone has to. Maybe I can help you find a balance."

"And what can I do for you?"

The way Hudson was looking at her, she knew exactly what she could do for him, and it involved a kiss. She kept perfectly still, but he didn't bend his head. He didn't squeeze her tighter.

Rather he said, "Not everything's a negotiation, Bella. I meant it with Jamie when I said I don't want anything in return, and I mean it with you, too. I just enjoy being with you. Maybe that will work to both our advantages."

"How's that?"

"You think I need purpose in my life. Maybe I'll get a better sense of that by being around you."

"Sometimes, Hudson, I can't tell if you're making fun of me or if you're serious."

"I will never make fun of you, Bella. You're a beautiful, intelligent woman who deserves to be listened to. Why would I want to make fun of that?"

A snowflake landed on her nose, but she didn't care, didn't move. Suddenly it had become more important that Hudson understand her and where she'd been, at least part of it. So she explained.

"My parents were great, at least what I can remember. I have some pictures of them in an album. Thank goodness, our grandparents let us keep those. In those photos, Mom and Dad were laughing and playing ball with us, and even jumping under the hose on a hot summer day. We felt listened to…important…loved. But after my parents were gone, my grandparents talked only to each other. They made decisions with each other. They never consulted us. They sent—"

She stopped. She wasn't going to tell him about the brothers and sisters they never saw. She didn't want him to feel sorry for her. She just wanted him to know the way it had been and why she reacted sometimes now the way she did. "My grandparents just didn't listen, and after Grandma died, my grandfather shut off. It was as if he wasn't even there. He put food on the table. He barked orders at us. But he was never kind the way a parent should be kind. He was never there to listen to what happened at school or after school. He was cold and hard, and I couldn't wait to leave."

Now Hudson did put his arms around her. The brim of his Stetson kept snow from falling on her face. He admitted, "I know about cold parents. My mother's that way. But she calls it reserved. It comes down to the same thing."

"I think Gramps was born that way. Then when he was in a situation he didn't want to be in, burdened with us, he withdrew more into himself. Why do you think your mom was cold?"

"I'm not sure. My guess is she wasn't happy in the marriage. When you're not happy, when the other person doesn't try to make you happy, what's left but resentment and maybe even contempt? That's always what I felt vibrating between them."

"But you had your brothers."

"Yes, I did. We established our own rules, kept each other safe, fought, yelled, but told each other our secrets."

"Like brothers should. Is that why you helped Walker when he needed you?"

"That's one of the reasons."

He brushed snowflakes from her hair, and the stroke of his hands almost made her purr. "Let's get you inside before you become a snow woman."

She laughed, and he opened the barn door for her.

"Edmond, how goes it?" Hudson called when he saw his foreman in one of the stalls.

"Just getting Boots ready. Your Breeze is champing at the bit. She can't wait to get out there."

"They might not be so happy once that snow's falling all around them. But we won't keep them out long."

"Greta wants to know if you'd like to come to supper when you get back. She has a huge pot of chili on the stove, and she says it's just what you'll need after a ride in the snow."

Hudson looked at Bella. "Do you think Jamie can do without you?"

She considered everything Hudson had said about having her own life, about Jamie needing a life of his own, too. Yet she knew right now their lives had converged. Still, Fallon was helping him, and she said she'd even stay the night. Bella had the feeling that Fallon wanted to spend as much time as she could with Jamie. Maybe it was a good thing if she stayed away for a little while.

"Let me give him a call and make sure before we saddle up."

The call took only a few minutes, and she was ready to mount Boots. Hudson stood next to the pretty horse holding its reins. "What did he say?"

"He said I should have supper here with you. Everything is under control back there."

"Good. I lowered the stirrup a bit so you could mount easier. Once you're up, I'll fix it for you."

He could have just given her a leg up, but she was glad he'd done it this way instead. Hudson's touch made her skittish, and maybe he knew that. What she'd heard about Hudson, about him being a love-'em-and-leave-'em cowboy, just didn't mesh with who he really was. She'd found him to be a gentleman, and she liked that. She liked it a lot.

She'd been right about the way Hudson sat on a horse. His back was straight and his shoulders square. Yet his body had enough flexibility that he seemed one with the horse. He looked as if he'd been made for riding. And he looked incredibly handsome, especially against the snow that frosted the landscape.

She followed Hudson since he knew the terrain better than she did. Besides that, she trusted him to lead. Odd that she thought of that now. She hadn't trusted him when he'd first come to Just Us Kids, but she'd learned better. Her experience with men—other than her brother—had been anything but positive. Trusting seemed as far away as dreaming or loving someone who would love you back forever.

The atmosphere out here was positively church-like. The tall pines, the hushed silence, the pure whiteness of fresh snow. Bella felt herself relaxing into the moment, simply enjoying being alive.

Hudson suddenly changed direction and gestured for her to follow him due south. They rode along a copse of pine and aspen and rounded a corner. She felt a gasp come from her soul when she saw a pond before her with white softness edging its borders. The water reflected the gray sky, but there were places where it picked up sparkle from somewhere.

Hudson waited for her to ride up beside him, then he asked, "Are you game to dismount for a while? Those trees will protect us from the snow." He motioned to a canopy that looked like a little haven.

"Sure," she said, giving him a smile. "It's beautiful out here."

He gave a nod and then dismounted first so he could give her a hand. She would have just jumped off her horse, but Hudson was right there, his hands on her waist, helping her to the ground. He lifted her down, and she felt like air in his arms. There was strength there and a sure grip that assured her she wouldn't fall.

He took hold of their horse's leads. They walked about twenty feet into the copse of trees, and she saw immediately why he'd wanted to bring her here. It was a more in-depth view of the lake, the snow on the reeds, the white birch on the far shore, the pine canopy that kept snow from falling on them.

"Sometimes we don't realize how much noise surrounds us all day until we're in a quiet place like this."

"Do you come here often?" she asked, almost in a whisper because that seemed fitting here.

"I do. I have that luxury because I don't have to take care of triplets when I go home."

Facing him, she asked, "Are you trying to make a point?"

He gazed down at her with sincerity in his eyes. "Nope. Just attempting to show you the other side of having a purpose."

She felt mesmerized by him…so drawn to him. "I think you have a purpose when you come out here."

"What would that be?"

"To connect with something outside yourself, something bigger than yourself. My guess is you find here what many people find in meditation or in church."

"Wide-open space has always meant freedom to me. I don't like fences or boundaries that predict where I have to stay."

That statement prompted her to probe deeper. "Do you think you were *born* to be a risk taker or an adventurer? Or did you learn it?"

"I only take calculated risks. And as far as being

born an adventurer, I'd say I learned it, in order to escape my siblings and my parents."

"I wish I had gone that route," she admitted with a sigh, and then was appalled she'd said it. What she didn't want to do was get into her background. What she didn't want to do was explain what had happened when she was a teenager rebelling against her grandparents who didn't love her, against fate that had taken her parents from her, along with her other siblings, too.

Apparently Hudson's thoughts ran in another direction from her teenage years because he turned to face her, adjusted the chin strap on her hat and said, "You can still be an adventurer. It's never too late to start."

The darkening of his eyes, the heat she suddenly felt between them, the vibrations that were all about male and female awareness made her ask jokingly, "You mean I should catch a plane to Paris?"

"No," he said honestly. "I was thinking that you should kiss me again."

When Hudson wrapped his arms around her, she didn't hesitate to let him pull her close. He dragged his thumb down her cheek and kissed the trail his finger had taken. His sensual touch sent tremors through her, and in spite of herself, she envisioned them naked in his bed. She should have stopped the thought right there. If she had, when his lips sealed to hers, maybe then she wouldn't have felt like melting into his body. The cold seemed to swell around them, but they were warm, getting hot, even hotter. His lips seemed to burn hers, and when his tongue breached her lips, forged into her mouth, took the kiss deeper and wetter, she wrapped her arms around his neck and held on for dear life.

Hudson stopped the kiss suddenly…didn't end it… just stopped it.

She knew he wanted another one because he kissed along her lower lip, then the corner of her mouth. After a deep breath, he said, "You make me feel too much."

"You make me shake," she admitted.

His soft chuckle said he liked that idea, and he came back for another kiss, and then another until time didn't matter. The swish of pine boughs didn't matter. Snow mounting around their boots didn't matter. Only Hudson's desire, his hands at the nape of her neck and his body heat mattered.

He broke away again, then he looked down at her, breathing hard. He assured her, "If we were someplace else, someplace warmer and more comfortable, we'd be doing more than kissing."

But we shouldn't be, a voice inside her yelled. *Why not?* echoed back. She ignored both and said to Hudson, "I'm not sure we *know* what we're doing."

"That's the fun of it—the adventure of it," he reminded her. "Let's just see where this goes, Bella." Just in case her response wasn't what he wanted to hear, he brushed her lips with his again and wrapped his arm around her. "I think that chili at Greta and Edmond's is good and done. Let's go get a bowl and warm up."

She didn't need chili to warm up. She'd been plenty warm when Hudson had been kissing her. She had a feeling she'd be plenty warm every time she thought about it, too. Could she be an adventurer and take it further?

Thank goodness, she didn't have to answer that question now.

Chapter 6

As soon as Bella walked into Greta and Edmond's house, she felt as if she were surrounded by warmth, and not just warmth coming from the woodstove. Whereas Clive Bickler's house was decorated with expensive paintings, fine-quality wall hangings and artist-signed pottery, Greta and Edmond's little house was simple and cozy. It was a log home, and Greta had kept the country look about it.

Everything was spick-and-span, shiny and authentic. The wide-plank flooring was worn. The living room's magnificently colored, large Southwestern rug needed repair in one corner and wore a straggling fringe in the other. The appliances weren't state-of-the-art, but Bella could tell they were used and used well. The colors migrating through the cabin—whether the fabric was striped, flowered or solid—were burgundy, green and yellow.

"I love your house," Bella told Greta. "It's charming."

Greta motioned to the curtains and the valances. "I made those myself. I still have an old treadle machine that works just fine. We managed to save it from the flood."

Edmond motioned to the table where a crock full of chili sat in the center. "Take a seat and we can talk while we eat."

"Our ranch was almost wiped out," Greta told Bella. "We saved what livestock we could first, then a few other things like my sewing machine, photo albums, framed pictures, a set of dishes my grandma handed down. But that was it. Everything else was wiped out when the house filled with water up to the second floor."

Edmond sat next to his wife and covered her hand with his. It was obvious that thinking about the flood was still an emotional experience for the couple.

Bella stole a glance at Hudson. He was watching Greta and Edmond, obviously trying to understand.

Greta's husband went on to explain, "We were living in the boardinghouse, not knowing what we were going to do next. No job, not much in the way of possessions. We basically had each other. We could have gone to live with our kids, but we didn't want to do that. They have their own lives. I was using my phone every day to search for jobs and not coming up with anything because lots of folks in town were in the same boat."

"But then fate stepped in, I guess," Greta said. "The owner of the Lazy B wanted to leave Rust Creek Falls, didn't think it would ever come to life again, and Clive Bickler saw the good deal that it was. Edmond and I had helped organize one of the old barns that wasn't underwater where we could give out supplies to people who needed it—bottled water, blankets, some clothes. Clive heard about that somehow, and the fact that Edmond knew horses and cows. So he asked us if we'd manage his place, room and board free. It was a deal we couldn't refuse. We just hope he never sells the place."

During the next hour, Greta and Edmond were full of lively stories about times on their own ranch when they'd had it, as well as this one. Eventually, Edmond and Hudson got to talking about horses while Bella and Greta spoke of good meals to make on the go. Bella was thoroughly enjoying herself and could see why Hudson liked spending time with these people. As a couple they were cute together, bumping each other's shoulders, touching each other often, and Bella could tell from the sparkle in their eyes that they were still deeply in love.

They were eating dessert, a delicious gingerbread with whipped cream, when Greta and Edmond exchanged a look. Edmond nodded, and Greta addressed Hudson.

"We have some really great news."

Hudson gave a chuckle. "What would that be? You can't make me any more food than you already do. It won't fit in the refrigerator or on the counter."

Greta waved his comment away. "This has to do with our children."

Edmond added, "One specifically. Our daughter Gracie is pregnant. She and Cole are overjoyed, and so are we."

Greta cut in, "Edmond can't wait to teach a little one how to ride a horse."

Hudson said to Bella, "Their daughter lives in Kalispell, so they'll be able to see their grandchild often."

"A little girl," Greta said with glee. "Can you imagine? Bows and pigtails and shiny shoes."

Edmond shook his head. "Not if she's a tomboy like Gracie was."

Bella saw Greta's and Edmond's radiant faces, and Hudson's happiness for them. She felt happy for them, too. "A baby is something glorious to look forward to," she said, and she meant it.

But inside she felt as if the evening had suddenly wilted because reality had struck again. These good people had reminded her what family was all about—meeting someone you loved, getting married, having kids. A sudden sadness washed over her, especially when she thought about her kiss with Hudson and what it could mean...what it *did* mean. They were so attracted to each other, and if she let that kiss go further, the next time—

There shouldn't be a next time. If they started a relationship, it couldn't go anywhere. No man wanted her because she couldn't have kids. She could not carry a baby to term. When would she finally let that reality take hold?

Maybe she could find love later in life, she told herself. When she was fifty? When having kids didn't matter to a man? Was that ever the case? She knew what Hudson was like with kids. She'd seen it over and over again. He enjoyed them. He could get down on their level. He could even *be* one at times. He would want children.

Somehow she managed to be part of Edmond and Greta's conversation, talking about kids, toys and even the day care center. She managed to smile and share in their excitement. But deep down, she hurt. That hurt would never go away.

* * *

Hudson was confused as he drove Bella home. They'd had a marvelous afternoon. Their ride had been romantic and fun—the snow falling around them, riding together, the grove in the trees that had sheltered them while they'd kissed. He knew he hadn't been mistaken about Bella being as involved in it as he was.

Dinner with Edmond and Greta had seemed to be enjoyable, too. But then suddenly, he could tell there'd been a change in Bella. She'd grown quieter, though not a lot quieter. He'd only noticed her gaze hadn't met his as often. There had been a tension there when he'd spoken to her, even about something as mundane as a child's toy. And he wanted to get to the bottom of it.

He felt as if he'd done something terribly wrong. Maybe once that wouldn't have bothered him so much, but this was Bella, and it did bother him.

When he arrived at the Stockton ranch and parked in the drive, he hadn't even turned off the ignition when Bella said, "You don't have to walk me to the door. I'll be fine."

That almost made him angry. He switched off the motor and said, "That sidewalk looks slippery. I'll walk you to the door." He knew his firmness brooked no argument.

Bella seemed to accept his decision, but she didn't look happy about it. She didn't wait for him to come around to her door. She opened it herself and hopped down.

When he rounded the truck, she was already on her way to the door. His legs were a lot longer than hers, and he caught up easily. He clasped her elbow and made sure she wasn't going to slip on the walk. At the porch she turned to him, and it seemed that she steeled herself to meet his gaze.

She smiled and said, "Thank you for today. I had a lovely time."

She'd said the words, but there was some kind of underlying message in them that he didn't like and he didn't accept. It was as if this was the last time they were going to have a lovely time.

"Bella, what's wrong?"

"Nothing's wrong," she said with a little too much vehemence.

"I don't believe that. Everything was fine, and then suddenly it wasn't. I want to know what's going on in that head of yours."

She gave him an almost defiant look that said maybe he didn't have the right to know what was going on in her head. She was correct about that, so he tried a different tack.

"If I did something wrong, I'd like to know what it was."

Now the defiance was gone, and she looked genuinely concerned. "Hudson, you didn't do anything wrong. I enjoyed the ride, I really did. And Greta and Edmond are a wonderful couple. I can see why you like spending time with them."

"But?" he prompted.

She shook her head. "No *buts*. It's just that our situation hasn't changed. You're my boss. I think we should keep our relationship colleague to colleague."

Settling his thumb under her chin, he tipped her face up and studied her. That might have been one of her concerns, but it wasn't the only one. Still he couldn't force her to confide in him. All he could do was try to gently persuade her with actions rather than words.

"We're more than colleagues, Bella. Deep down you know that."

Reluctantly he took his thumb away from her soft skin. Reluctantly he took a step back. "But I respect what you're saying. I respect you."

He turned to go. "I'll see you at Just Us Kids." Then suddenly he stopped and looked over his shoulder at her. "If you ever want to change our colleague status, just say so. I'm flexible." He left her standing on the porch contemplating his words.

As he climbed into his truck, he saw her step inside. He just hoped that someday soon she would confide in him what was bothering her.

Because if she didn't, they would just remain colleagues…until he left Rust Creek Falls.

On Tuesday afternoon, Bella stopped in Hudson's office. They hadn't had contact all day, and he was glad to see her now. She motioned to the classrooms.

"All the children are gone early for a change. We had a light day with the snow keeping some of the kids home. So I'm going to scoot. I called Jazzy, and I'm going out to the ranch to shoot photos. I have about an hour and half of daylight. With the snow and the sun on the horizon, I should be able to get some good shots."

"After I close up, do you want company?" he asked.

"I might be finished by the time you get there," she said. Then she paused and gave him a small smile. "You can help convince Jazzy that if she doesn't like the photos, she doesn't have to take any. So sure, come on out."

Because of Bella's attitude toward a relationship, he

didn't want to push. But he wasn't beyond coaxing a little. Just being around her would help convince them both exactly what they should or shouldn't do. Besides, he still wanted to find out what had happened at dinner last night, and why she'd turned suddenly…*sad.* That was the only word he could find to describe her mood.

After Bella left, he finished up some work, chatted with the teachers, then when they left, he made sure the facility was locked up tight. As he drove to Brooks and Jazzy's ranch, he felt energized at the idea of seeing Bella again. Had other women ever done that to him? Sure, he'd looked forward to dates, to finding satisfaction in the most physical way. But the idea of seeing Bella again just…lightened him. That was the only way he could put it, and he felt almost happy.

He didn't think about happiness often. He just lived his life. It was one of those things that if you searched for it you couldn't find it. But he'd figured out happiness had nothing to do with what he owned. It had something to do with where he went. Maybe that's why he traveled. This lightness he felt around Bella, however, was something different altogether.

At the ranch he parked beside Bella's car. Climbing out, he adjusted his Stetson and headed for a purple-coated figure standing at the corral fence.

Jazzy was staring into the pasture where Bella was shuffling through the snow, crouching down to get a shot, then standing to take a long view of another horse. He and Jazzy watched her as their breaths puffed white every time they breathed out. Bella wouldn't want to be out here too long in this cold, but she was dressed for it with practical boots and a parka, a scarf and knit cap.

He couldn't see her expression from this distance, but her stance said she was intent on what she was doing.

"She's good with the horses," Jazzy said.

As he watched her approach one of the animals and hold out her hand, maybe with a treat, the horse nuzzled her palm. She stroked his neck and put her face close to his.

"As good as she is with kids," Hudson noted. He could feel Jazzy's gaze on him as he watched Bella.

"You like her," Jazzy said, as if it were a foregone conclusion.

"You mean it shows?"

"If someone's looking," Jazzy answered. "It's in the way you look at her. The thing is, I've heard rumors that you don't stick around very long. Are you planning to settle in Rust Creek Falls?"

"No." The word popped out of his mouth before he thought better of it. "I'm going to be moving on soon. Walker can easily find someone else to oversee the day care center."

"That might not be as easy as you think. Rust Creek Falls isn't teeming with cowboys like you with managerial experience. I hear you've done a magnificent job of getting the business back on track since the lawsuit."

"I hope that's the case. It's hard to wipe out the impression of something gone wrong. But we're steadily signing up new clients, and the old ones are staying. That's what's important."

"Do you find what you're doing fulfilling?"

He thought about it. Then he said with a shrug, "Kids or horses. That's a tough decision to make. I sure do miss being outdoors, though, working with horses most of the day."

"So you like Clive's ranch?"

"Oh, I do."

"Do you really want to move on?"

"It's my nature," he said quickly, as if he had to convince himself of that, too.

Instead of focusing on Bella, Jazzy turned to him and looked him deep in the eye. "Maybe it's only your nature until something or someone convinces you to stay."

Jazzy's words were still echoing in his mind a half hour later as Bella waved to them that she was finished and came over to the fence, her camera swinging around her neck on its strap. She climbed the crossbars and swung her leg over the top.

Jazzy said, "I'll start inside and make us hot chocolate. Maybe we can thaw out our fingers and toes."

Hudson held out his hands to Bella. She hesitated only a moment, and then she took them and let him help her down. They glanced at each other now and then on the walk to the house but didn't speak. Hudson wanted to ask her how she thought the shoot went, but he knew she wouldn't answer, not until she got a look at those photos on more than her camera screen. And he had an idea.

"Did you bring along the cord to hook your camera up to the TV?"

"Brooks and Jazzy have a smart TV?"

"Oh, I'm sure they do. We'll check when we get inside. That way you can see what the pictures look like."

"I brought my laptop," Bella said.

"Wouldn't you rather see them spread across fifty-two inches?"

She laughed. "It's a guy thing, isn't it? Having a huge TV."

Hudson stopped and studied her. “Is that a sexist remark?”

“No, it’s the truth,” she said.

“You don’t want to watch a chick flick on fifty-two inches?”

“When I watch a chick flick, it’s for the content. I don’t care how big the screen is.”

He just shook his head. “Venus and Mars.”

“You think men and women are from two different planets?”

“I think they have two entirely different perspectives on the world.”

“You might be right.”

They were no sooner inside than Jazzy brought hot chocolate and sandwiches into the living room and set the tray on the coffee table.

Brooks grinned. “Perfect.”

He wasn’t looking at the food, though. He was staring at his wife. Her cheeks were rosy, her hair mussed. She was wearing slim jeans, boots and a heavy sweater.

“You were out there a long while,” he said. “I’ll switch on the gas fireplace. Extra heat won’t hurt.”

After Hudson and Bella had taken off their coats, scarves and hats, they came to sit down, too. Bella rubbed her hands in front of the fire. “That feels nice. I like the idea of not having to carry in the wood.”

“It has an automatic pilot, too,” Jazzy said, “so if the electricity goes out, we still have its heat. I imagine Clive has something like this,” she said to Hudson.

“Yes, he does. It’s come in handy the past few nights. No reason to put the heat up in the whole house when I’m just in one room.”

Bella gave him a glance that said she was surprised

he was economical about it. He had the feeling she underestimated him on a lot of things—his reputation, maybe his brother's sentiments about him, that he was a drifter and didn't settle down long in one place. Yet Walker was probably right.

Not wanting to think about that, he asked Brooks, "Can we hook Bella's camera up to your TV? Then we can all view the pictures on there."

"Without me previewing them first?" Bella asked, sounding nervous about it.

"Up to you," he said.

She chewed on her lower lip for a minute and then said, "I think I got a couple of pretty good shots. Let's do it."

After Brooks and Hudson accomplished the hookup, they all viewed the photos, one by one.

Hudson heard Jazzy's intake of breath at a photo of a light-colored bay against the sun setting on the horizon and glinting off the snow. He hoped that meant she liked it. There were so many others to like, too. Jazzy took a few steps back so she could get a better perspective and silently watched as one photo after another appeared on the big screen. She oohed over the one of the chestnut near the pine grove when the light was still full. She aahed over a blue sky as a backdrop against pristine snow and a gray equine beauty. Bella hadn't captured only the horses, but the ranch, too. He'd seen her run from one end of the corral to the other, snapping an action shot of three horses together, but then also taking her time, sitting on a fence, snapping barns and trees and Montana's big sky.

After they viewed the photos twice, Brooks said,

"Bella, these are fabulous, absolutely fabulous. I don't know how we're going to decide which ones to use."

"You don't have to decide now. I'd like to edit them a bit and do some cropping. I can send you the files."

"I have a photo printer at Clive's place," Hudson said. "Why don't we go back there and print them out. Then you can look at the printed photo as well as the digital file and decide which ones you want on the pamphlet. That might give you a better idea."

Brooks and Jazzy exchanged a look. "That sounds good to us," he said. "Now, let's have another round of hot chocolate."

Bella called Jamie to make sure everything was all right there. He said he had it under control and Fallon was keeping him company. Bella told him about the photo shoot and how Jazzy and Brooks seemed to like her photos. He was excited for her, and she saw that both of them needed something in their lives other than babies and diapers and laundry. She was glad Fallon was there with him.

An hour later they finally left for the Lazy B.

As they stepped inside, she asked, "Why do you have a photo printer?"

"I like gizmos and tech stuff, not just saddles and boots," he told her. "And I've been here long enough to have a collection. I have a camera, too. I sightsee now and then. I've gone out to the falls near Falls Mountain and taken a few shots, but mostly I use it for the day care center. My phone camera is fine, but I get better light with a point-and-shoot. If I see something that can be improved on at Just Us Kids, I take a picture so that I have a reminder of it. It's my way of working."

She followed him into the great room and took off her parka. "I'll pay you for the cost of printing the photos."

"Nonsense. I got you this commission, so to speak. It's my contribution."

As she walked with him to the study, she said, "You're a generous man, Hudson. Have you found people take advantage of that?"

"The ones who need the generosity don't. If somebody does, I chalk it up to experience learned. Giving usually isn't wasted. You give, too. You're generous with your time and your spirit, Bella. I'm sure your brother would attest to that."

When Hudson gave her compliments, Bella wasn't sure what to say. So she said nothing. As they sat next to each other at the desktop computer, their arms brushed. She didn't pull away. Being with Hudson was both unsettling and exciting. The exciting part coaxed her to let it continue. She knew she was headed for deep water and it was quite possible that she'd drown. But the attraction to Hudson was heady, like nothing she'd ever felt before. And she liked dwelling in it for just a little while.

The computer monitor was large enough to do the photos justice. When Hudson downloaded them, all the recent photos on the camera went into the program. He took a long time studying several of them that were taken at area barns and ranches.

"You're really good, Bella, even better than you know. I can frame any one of these for a wall grouping and it would stand out as artistic and meaningful."

"You're too kind," she said.

He turned toward her and pushed a strand of her hair behind her ear. "No, I'm not kind, not about this, not about you. I don't have kindness on my mind when I look at you."

"Hudson," she said on a slightly warning note.

He dropped his hand from her hair, leaned back and sighed. "You don't have to say anything else. I know how you feel about…everything. I can't say you're wrong…unless you want to enjoy the moment. Unless living for today means as much as living for tomorrow."

"Have you used that line before?" she asked, staring directly into his eyes. She knew Hudson was experienced. She knew he'd been around the block, so to speak. She knew he knew what he was doing.

For a moment she thought he was going to get angry, but then he rolled his chair away from hers. "It's not a line. It's just the way I think. It's the way I live. I'm not sure what you think my history is with women, Bella, but I don't need lines."

"No ego there," she murmured.

His serious face turned light, and he chuckled. "I never said I was a humble man. Come on, let's get these printed out. Then I'm going to follow you home to make sure you get there safely."

"No, Hudson. There's no need for that. I don't need a protector."

There must have been something in her voice that convinced him of that, but he was still a negotiator.

"All right. I won't follow you home if you promise to call me when you get there."

"I'll text you," she bargained.

He rolled his eyes but responded, "Deal."

Yet somehow, even though Bella had felt like she'd gotten her way, she knew that Hudson Jones would have the last word.

Chapter 7

Bella found herself humming a Christmas carol the following morning as she sat at her computer at the day care center. The holiday was still weeks away, but timing didn't dampen her mood. Nor did the statistics she was examining and organizing for a year-end report.

The photo shoot yesterday had gone extremely well. She loved the work she'd done. She'd been up late editing the photos, emailing files to Jazzy. Already this morning they'd gone back and forth in emails, and Jazzy had chosen seven of the photos she liked the best to use for her pamphlet. She was going to use others on her website. She'd told Bella when she had it updated, she'd let her know.

When Hudson had asked Bella if she minded if he dropped by to watch the shoot, she'd worried that he'd be a distraction. But he hadn't been. She'd liked having him there, sharing in the experience. His ideas were often good ones—like viewing the photos on the big-screen TV. The admiration in his eyes when he'd looked at her had almost made her tear up. She hadn't felt that kind of admiration in a very long time…if ever.

What if Hudson knew about her past? What if he knew she'd mistaken a hungry look in a teenage boy's eyes as love? What if he knew she'd gotten pregnant?

What if he knew she couldn't have children?

The statistics on her computer monitor seemed to blur for a moment. Hudson didn't need to know any of that, did he? After all, he'd said himself that he'd be leaving Rust Creek Falls. But a little voice inside her heart asked, *And what if you do get involved with him?*

The idea had been growing in momentum. It had even taken over many of her dreams. Every time she thought about the two of them together, really together, she had to struggle to push the thoughts and images away. But at night, her subconscious went wild. She woke up wanting his arms around her, needing his arms around her. But then like dreams do, they faded into reality. Her common sense prevailed, and she warned herself to keep her distance, or at least not let anything progress beyond a kiss.

However, Hudson's kisses were unforgettable.

As if she'd conjured him up by thinking about her dreams, he appeared at her desk. "I've been thinking," he said.

She gave him a smile, not knowing what was coming. "I thought I saw smoke coming from your office," she said with a straight face.

He gave her a mock scowl. "That smoke you saw was my coffeepot biting the dust. It's time I buy a single-serve brewer for in there. Any flavor you like best? I'd be willing to share."

The twinkle in his eyes told her he'd like to share more than coffee. She shook her head. "Break room coffee is fine with me."

"Until I give you Death by Chocolate to taste," he teased. "Just you wait."

She couldn't look away from his eyes, and she didn't want to. It would be so easy to get lost in Hudson and the sparks they generated…in a fire that could consume her. She took a deep breath and slowly let it out.

"So what have you been thinking about?" she asked, getting the conversation back on track.

"I've been thinking about using your photography skills as a moneymaker for the day care center."

She tilted her head, interested.

He could obviously see that because he went on. "How would you like to take photos of moms and their babies? It would be quite a keepsake for them, plus a good promotional tool for the day care center. We can put together a child care book where we lay out the photos with parent tips. I'm sure the mothers would have plenty of those. You've seen those community cookbooks? This would be something like that. Your photos would give it that aaah factor."

"It sounds ambitious, but I'd love to participate in it."

Hudson looked thoughtful. "We could do the photos after hours, or we could commandeer the corner of one of the classrooms. Moms can stop in whenever they like, and you could make it a priority to take the photos."

"Mothers love to be photographed with their kids. I think it would be easy to convince them."

"I'd like to have it all put together by Valentine's Day," he suggested.

"That's quick."

"I know. The owner of one of the ranches I worked at self-published a history of the ranch. I helped him with it. There's a formatter I can contact. I would trust your eye on the basic layout. If we shoot the photos between Thanksgiving and New Year's, it's possible."

"I should send out an email to the parents to explain the project and encourage them to get on board. I can write something up right now and have it to you after lunch for approval."

Hudson was again pensive for a few moments. She studied his expression, the character lines on his face, the way his hair waved across his brow. Standing at her desk, he towered over her and seemed larger than life. His chest was broad, his forearms muscular beneath the rolled-up sleeves of his snap-button shirt. There was strength in those forearms, and she became distracted by the curling brown hair that covered them. Just looking at him, any part of him, sent her pulse racing.

She didn't know how long he'd been talking when his words finally broke through her thoughts. "I don't want you to go to extra work if this isn't going to fly. I'll give Walker a call or text him. After I run it by him, I'll let you know if it's a go."

"It's a wonderful idea, Hudson. It really is. You *deserve* a new coffeepot."

At that he laughed, gave her a little wave and went back to his office. Her heart was still pitter-pattering when she turned back to her computer.

Hudson was eating leftovers from a casserole Greta had prepared when Walker breezed into the day care center and his office later that day.

"That smells good," Walker said, motioning to

the chicken-and-broccoli casserole that Hudson had warmed up in the microwave in the break room. "I don't imagine you made it."

"Greta made it. She doesn't let me starve."

"You settled into a good deal there. Not only horses but home cooking."

"In a way, it feels like home, more than our home ever did."

Walker gave him a surprised look. "In what way?"

"I like going there after a day here at work, or after a ride. I look forward to it."

Walker glanced around the office and the rest of the day care center. Hudson knew his brother had gone into the business because he wanted kids to have a safe, caring place to stay while their parents worked. Their own childhood with nannies who were overseeing them only because of a great salary was probably one of the reasons.

The lawsuit Walker had been involved in had also given him a new perspective. He was setting up a foundation, The Just Us Kids Pediatric Pulmonary Center, for children who need specialized medical care.

Walker returned his attention to Hudson. "So you wanted to talk to me about a scheme to make money?"

"It's not a scheme, it's a project." Hudson kept the defensiveness out of his voice. He was prepared with Bella's photos. He spread them across the desk, faced Walker and explained exactly what he had in mind.

"It would help if we could get some kind of child care expert to give quotes, too," Hudson suggested.

Walker seemed to think about all of it. "I'm surprised you came up with this."

Walker's comment irked Hudson. Yes, Walker was

the CEO type, the business-oriented brother, but Hudson knew he had good ideas, too, just in a different vein.

After Walker took another look at the photos, and at the schedule Hudson had devised along with the cost estimate, his brother nodded. Then he stared at Hudson as if he were seeing him in a different way.

"I have one question," Walker said. "Will you be staying until the project is finished?"

Hudson considered his brother's question. He also considered Bella and spending more time with her. "Sure, I can stay until it's finished."

That seemed to settle everything in Walker's mind. "Go ahead," he said. "Get it started. It will be good for the day care center. It's something the other franchises could pick up and do. We could even sell it on the biggest ebook seller there is. Child care tips can be relevant to moms across the country. Quite a moneymaker you've thought up here." He extended his hand to Hudson. "Good job."

Hudson shook his brother's hand, feeling a connection with him he hadn't felt in a long time.

After Walker left, Hudson told Bella the good news. "He feels it will be a good moneymaking project and that the idea will catch on with the other franchises. He thinks we might even be able to sell it through a nationwide channel."

Bella's face was all smiles. She threw her arms around Hudson's neck and gave him a huge hug.

The impulsive gesture made him catch his breath, which only made it worse for him as he took in the scent of her perfume or shampoo or whatever smelled like flowers and Bella. He couldn't help but tighten his arms around her, and for just a few moments, she tightened her arms around him. He could feel she was breathing fast, and so was he. He wanted to bury his nose in her hair, kiss her temple and more. But she leaned away, moved her hands to his chest and looked up at him. He had to give her time. He had to give her the opportunity to come to the realization on her own that they'd be good together. One thing he was sure of—he couldn't push Bella, or she'd run. He didn't know why. He wished he did.

As if she were suddenly embarrassed, she pulled out of his arms. "I'm so happy about this. I know it's not the same as professional credits, but if I wanted to do more of this photography work, I'd have a strong recommendation."

"You might want to change what you study at college when you go back," he offered.

She looked pensive. "You might be right. On the other hand, maybe I could have a major in business administration and take photography classes, too. The best of both worlds."

Wasn't that what everybody wanted, the best of the worlds they chose? He felt as if he had one foot in an old world and one foot in a new one. He knew the old world brought him satisfaction, and he was comfortable in it. A new world? That was always a risk. But was it a risk he wanted to take?

Bella gave him a look that said she didn't know if she should say what she was thinking, but then she seemed to make up her mind. "I couldn't help but notice you and Walker shaking hands as if you meant it."

"That's a novelty?" he joked.

"You have to get along for business's sake, I suppose. But you've never seemed...close."

"He really doesn't know what I've done on past jobs when I've worked at ranches. I guess he thinks I only wrangle calves."

"You don't talk about it?"

"Don't you know cowboys are men of few words?" Again he was teasing, but she seemed to take him seriously.

"Few words, maybe. But if they're the right words, they count."

"You and Jamie are different from me and my brothers. Maybe as kids we commiserated and told each other secrets but not as adults."

"That's a shame. But miles do make a difference. When I was at college, Jamie and I didn't talk as much or often."

"Distance can be a wedge," he agreed.

She said brightly, "But you and Walker are here now. Maybe you'll have a new start."

"Maybe," he agreed, wondering if that could be true. After all, the holidays were coming up. Weren't they the time for a new start, or a deepening of what was already there?

Bella glanced at the clock on the wall. "I told Sarah I'd help her with an art project with her class. Her aide is out this morning."

Hudson nodded. "And I have that meeting with the pageant director, Eileen Bennet, over at the school this afternoon."

"Let me know how it goes," she said as she stepped out into the hall, giving him one of those smiles that seemed to make his heart turn sideways. He stared at her until she stepped into Sarah's classroom.

Then he looked back down at the photographs he'd

printed out that were still spread across his desk. Walker had really studied them and admitted they were as great as Hudson thought they were. If Bella needed credentials to get more photography work, maybe he could help her out. He took out his cell phone and checked his contacts list. Yep, there it was. Miles Stanwick. He was the owner of a few galleries, including one in Kalispell. His headquarters, however, were in Billings. That was the great thing about cell phones. No matter where Miles was, Hudson could reach him. After two rings, Miles answered.

"Hi there, Hudson. Are you in Billings?"

"No, I'm in Rust Creek Falls. I've been taking care of business for Walker here."

"Your dad has always been one of my best clients. What can I do for you?"

"You scout out new talent, don't you?"

"I do, but I have a lot of fresh painters right now. What do you have?"

"How about photographers?"

Miles seemed to think about it. "With point-and-shoot digitals, everybody's a photographer these days. But I'm always on the lookout for something special."

"I think these photos are special, but I don't have a gallery owner's eye. Would you consider taking a look at them?"

"I'm getting into my busy season. But sure, I can spend fifteen minutes looking over photos. Do you have my email address?"

"I do. I can send you the digital files, but I also printed them out. I think you'll see they really come to life in the glossies. I can overnight them." After Miles gave him the Billings address, he asked, "If you feel the photos have merit, do you think you'll be able to place a few?"

"If they have merit, I can always make a place for them." He paused a second, then asked, "If you're working on business for Walker, then you're not traveling much, I take it?"

"Not right now."

"Well, if you're still in Rust Creek Falls when I come over to Kalispell for the holidays, I'll give you a call. Maybe we can have dinner."

"Sounds good. And thanks, Miles. I really appreciate this."

After he ended the call, Hudson gathered up the photos. He'd email Miles the digital photos, then he'd package up the glossies and mail them on his way to the school for his meeting.

He really did think the photos were something special. He hoped Miles did, too.

He decided to keep the whole gallery query a surprise. After all, he didn't want Bella to be disappointed if nothing came of it. For now she would be happy photographing moms and babies.

An hour later, before he left for his meeting with the pageant director, he went looking for Bella. He wanted to make sure she didn't need anything before he left. He found her in Sarah Palmer's classroom, where she was still helping with the art project, and what a project it was.

The four-year-olds were having a stupendous time with the art supplies. They were gluing and coloring without knowing they were practicing hand-eye coordination and fine motor skills. Sarah concentrated on that with every art project as well as burgeoning young talent. There were turkey heads and feathers cut out of construction paper, and feet, too, made of some fuzzy cord. Bella and Sarah were helping the children paste them all down on a plate that served as the turkey's body. The kids talked and laughed as they wielded crayons as if they were true artists, drawing faces on the plates.

Tommy, one of Hudson's favorites, pushed back his chair and came running over to him. "Mr. Hudson, Mr. Hudson, look at what I'm doing."

His turkey had black eyes and a mouth, and Tommy was coloring his body purple.

Hudson crouched down to Tommy's eye level. "So you've seen purple turkeys?"

Tommy looked at his turkey and the pictures of turkeys that Sarah had attached to the bulletin board.

"I didn't *see* a purple turkey," Tommy admitted. "But there could *be* purple turkeys."

At that Hudson laughed out loud. Anything was a possibility in a child's mind.

Hearing his laughter, Bella looked up. Their gazes met and Hudson could swear he felt the room shake. But no feathers scattered, mock or otherwise, so he knew it was his imagination. Purple turkeys could give a man delusions.

The curly-headed blonde four-year-old next to Bella tapped on her arm. Hudson remembered her name was May.

"Miss Bella, I made a mistake. My line went crooked."

Hudson walked over to where Bella was seated, and he could tell the little girl's picture was supposed to resemble a house. A purple turkey. A house in a turkey's tummy. What was the difference? he supposed.

Bella rested her arm around May's shoulders. "A crooked line doesn't have to be a mistake. Let's look at what you're trying to do." She gave the plate a quarter turn. "What if we made your crooked line part of the fence that goes around the house? Sometimes they're straight and sometimes they're crooked. Your line will fit right in."

"But it can't be red. Red is for the bricks on the house," May insisted.

Bella picked up a brown crayon. "Here, give this a try on top of the red. It will make it look just like wood."

May did as Bella suggested and then looked up at her. "It does."

"You'll have a fine fence there," Hudson encouraged her. "I see you have a house with a second floor. Does it have windows on the second floor?"

No windows were showing now.

May put her finger to her lips, and then her eyes sparkled. "My house has windows. I can put in windows."

Bella said to May, "You work on that for a little while. I'll be right back." She pushed her chair away from the table and stood.

Even so, Hudson was still a head taller. For some reason, Bella made him feel ten feet tall. He wasn't sure why. Maybe it was just this "thing" between them. He felt their breathing almost synchronized as they stared at each other. He wasn't sure why that happened when he thought about kissing her, but it did.

How could he think about kissing her when they were in the middle of a room with four-year-olds?

He waved at the table and the projects spread out everywhere. "Do you think you'll ever get this cleaned up?"

"Maybe with the custodian's help," she joked. "But it's amazing how little ones like to help when you ask them. They'll pick up their scraps."

"Their feathers, you mean?" Hudson said with a straight face.

"So you got sucked into a world of purple turkeys and green feathers?"

He laughed. "It's hard to resist. Maybe that's why I like being around the kids so much. It makes the real world go away."

"Or they take you back to when you were four."

"I don't even *remember* when I was four."

"I bet if you and your brothers got together you would. No clubhouse, jungle gym, forts made out of a blanket on the sofa?"

"Are you kidding? A blanket on the sofa? Our mother would have called the maid."

Bella blinked. "I forgot."

"Forgot what?"

"You grew up very differently than I did."

What Bella meant was, he'd grown up with money. Yes, his family had been wealthy. There had been maids and housekeepers and nannies.

"Maybe I did," he said. On the other hand, though, maybe their worlds hadn't been so different after all. "But that fort you speak of…my brothers and I escaped to the woodpile now and then and rearranged it. It was a grand fort. What my mother didn't know didn't hurt her."

Bella studied him. And maybe in the atmosphere with four-year-olds around, and Sarah not too far away, she felt brave to delve into his life a bit because she asked, "How else did you escape?"

"Riding did it the most, or just wandering the pasture with the horses. How about you? How did *you* escape?"

"Books. Books took me anywhere I wanted to go, with anyone I wanted to be with. They still do. When I get the chance to settle down with one."

One of the kids dumped a canister of crayons onto the table. The scattering noise took Bella's attention for a moment. Then she asked, "Are you leaving now?"

"I am. I just wanted to remind you to call me if you need anything."

"Will do. And if I may, I'd like to remind you of something. With the pageant being held the Sunday after Thanksgiving, we don't have a lot of time to get costumes together. I'm definitely not a seamstress, and I don't know if any of the teachers are. So if we have to do any type of costumes, we need to keep it simple."

Hudson nodded. "I'll talk to Eileen about that. You should definitely sit in on the next meeting. Or maybe you should be going instead of me."

"I can go to the next one if you'd like me to. We'll have to get permission slips from parents, work up the PR for the kids being in the pageant and get that out in emails and on the website so the parents know exactly what we're doing, too."

"All good points."

Tommy waved his turkey at Hudson. Hudson went over to the four-year-old and pointed to the turkey's neck. It was still white. "Are you going to color that?"

"Maybe I'll make his neck red."

"You'll have a colorful turkey," Hudson proclaimed with a straight face.

"Maybe Miss Sarah will hang mine up high so everybody can see it."

Bella came to stand beside Hudson. "She's going to hang everyone's turkeys so when your parents come to pick you up, they'll see what a good job you did."

"And we can take them home for Thanksgiving?"

"Yes, you can."

Thanksgiving. Hudson still had no idea what he was doing for the holiday next week. He supposed Bella was planning to spend it with Jamie. Maybe in their next conversation he'd ask her. He'd spent many holidays alone, and he'd told himself he liked it that way. Memories of long-ago holidays were faded and ghostly. He almost had a hard time imagining what a real holiday would be like surrounded by family and friends he actually cared about, and who cared about him.

He should be more grateful about what he'd had growing up. After all, look at everything Bella had lost.

"Is something the matter?" she asked him.

He was going to say no, but decided to tell the truth. "I was just thinking about holidays and families and expectations that aren't usually fulfilled. Look at these kids' faces when they study their turkeys. They're totally in the present. Maybe somehow that's what we have to do to appreciate Thanksgiving and Christmas."

"When you learn how to do that, you let me know," she responded, then added, "Maybe this year the triplets will teach me their secret."

"I'm always open to hearing secrets," he said.

Bella looked startled for a moment, and then she

backed away from him. “I’ll see you later,” she told him. “I have to get back to pasting on those feathers.”

The word *secret* seemed to have spooked Bella. He supposed no one got to adulthood without a few of them.

Just what was Bella Stockton’s secret?

Chapter 8

Bella sat at her desk that afternoon, composing letters to send to parents explaining about the photos she wanted to take and the child care tips they might want to contribute. Usually moms were eager to share everything they knew about kids. She'd certainly gotten experience helping Jamie with the triplets.

Despite the work, she found herself missing Hudson. The place just wasn't the same when he wasn't there. Yes, she'd resented him when he'd first moved in, so to speak, to check up on her. But now they worked in tandem. Not only that, she missed his physical presence, the sparkle in his eyes, the energy he projected. Cowboy or businessman, he was one difficult man to ignore.

When the phone rang, she picked it up. "Just Us Kids Day Care Center, Bella Stockton speaking. How can I help you?"

“Is Hudson Jones there?” a gruff male voice asked her.

“He’s not available at the moment. Can I help you?”

There was a pause. “No, I need to speak to Jones. If I leave a message, will you make sure he gets it?”

“Of course I will. Or I could put you through to his voice mail.”

“I don’t trust that stuff. I’d rather you hand deliver it.”

She smiled and wondered how old this man was. She pulled a pink message pad and a pen from her desk. “As soon as he comes in, I’ll hand it to him.”

“Tell him this is Guy Boswick from Pine Bluff Ranch. He can reach me at…” And he rattled off a number. “I have a problem for him to handle.”

“Can I tell him what this is in regards to?”

“No. I need to talk to him. Don’t worry. He’ll know who I am when you give him my name.”

That was a cryptic message if she’d ever heard one.

“All right, Mr. Boswick. I will do that.”

“If I don’t hear from him today, I’ll call back tomorrow,” he assured her.

“That’s fine. I understand.”

She hardly had the words out when Mr. Boswick said “Goodbye” and hung up.

A half hour later, Hudson blew through the door along with the wind and a few snowflakes. He had a smile on his face.

Bella couldn’t help but smile back. Hudson Jones was infectious. She just hadn’t figured out if that was a good thing or a bad thing.

As he took off his jacket and hung it in his office, she followed him inside, the message in her hand. “You look as if you had a good meeting.”

"I did. We figured out how to keep things easy for the babies."

"I'm not sure anything is easy with babies," she warned him.

He chuckled. "Probably not. But how's this for an idea? Reindeer antler headbands for the babies, and we put them all in carriages. That way, volunteers at the school can decorate the carriages and we don't have to worry about costumes."

"I think that's brilliant," she agreed. "Did you come up with that or did Eileen?"

"A little bit of both. Eileen knows kids and what will work and what won't. I'm sure some parents must have carriages. If they don't, I'll buy a few and we'll use those."

"Is that in the budget?"

He arched his brows. "If I have to make a purchase outside the budget, we just won't tell anyone, right?"

"I don't know. Walker could mark me down for being a coconspirator."

"Not if we pull off the pageant with a big kick."

When their gazes met, Bella experienced that shaken-up feeling all over again.

Hudson hung his Stetson on the hat rack. With his flannel shirt open at the collar, dress jeans and brown boots, he was as tempting a man as she'd ever seen. But that's all he was at this point—a temptation.

She broke eye contact first, remembered the message in her hand and held it out to him. "You had an odd phone call, a Mr. Guy Boswick. He wanted me to hand deliver this to you."

Hudson took the message and studied it. "He has a problem?"

"He wouldn't tell me what it was. He just said you knew him and you should call him back. He warned me that if you don't call him back today, he'll call again tomorrow."

"And keep calling until he gets me. That's Guy, all right."

"So you *do* know him."

"Yes, I do. I worked on his dude ranch a couple of years back. He became a father figure to me for a while. He's a tough old cowboy, but he has a good heart. I can't imagine what he wants now, though. I'd better give him a call." He looked back up at her, and she thought she could be wrong, but it seemed his eyes twinkled when he thanked her.

"Anytime," she said, meaning it.

As she went back to her desk, she realized she hadn't closed Hudson's door, nor had he. Apparently he didn't expect the conversation to be private. She liked Hudson's transparency. He said what he felt, and he meant what he said.

Bella couldn't help but overhear the beginning niceties of the conversation. After all, her desk wasn't that far away from Hudson's open door. She wasn't trying to listen, not at first. But then she heard, "You want me to accept a position in Big Timber with you at Pine Bluff? Why would I want to do that?"

He was being offered a job? Now Bella was all ears.

"I understand you have a problem you want me to solve," Hudson said. "But public perception can't be swayed easily. I have a commitment right now. Any PR firm can help you."

Bella supposed Guy Boswick was raging a powerful argument to sway Hudson to Big Timber, away from

Rust Creek Falls. Maybe an emotional argument if he'd been a father figure. After all, Hudson didn't really *need* a job. He was wealthy.

"All right, I'll agree to that." Hudson listened, then asked, "How soon do you need an answer?"

Boswick must have told him and said a few more things because Hudson ended with, "It was good talking with you again, too, Guy. Take care," and he set down the cordless phone.

Hudson looked Bella's way, and she couldn't pretend she hadn't heard. Rising from her desk, she went into his office. "Maybe I'm sorry I gave you that message. I couldn't help but overhear. Did he offer you a job?"

"Yes, he did. But I don't know all the details yet. Someone from the ranch is going to be contacting me. Then I'll know more."

"When would it start?" she asked hesitantly.

"Bella, there's really nothing to talk about. Everything's supposition at this point."

"But when we talked about putting together the child care book, I was under the impression you were going to stay until Valentine's Day, right?"

"I don't want to talk about this now, Bella. I have a lot to think about and information to get. I *will* tell you I'll be out for a couple of hours tomorrow. Actually, maybe I'll just take the whole day. I need to clear my head, go riding, maybe work some colts. That will probably be the best thing for everyone. If you need me, you can reach me on my cell."

Bella decided not to mope. She'd known what kind of man Hudson was when he'd arrived. He'd told her point-blank he was a traveling man and not one to remain in one place. So she certainly hadn't been weaving dreams about him staying, had she? Valentine's Day or sooner, he was going to be leaving again, and she'd better get used to the idea.

She raised her chin when she replied, "I won't need you, Hudson. I managed Just Us Kids just fine before you got here. I can certainly handle it tomorrow."

As she turned to leave his office, he called her back. "Bella?"

She stopped but kept her shoulders squared and her back rigid, her head held high.

"Life is about choices, and they happen every day. This is just another one of those choices."

"Commitments happen every day, too," she returned, then went to her desk and ignored Hudson for the rest of the day.

The atmosphere between Bella and Hudson remained excruciatingly strained after his phone call to Guy Boswick. This was one time when she had no idea what he was thinking. Could he seriously be considering taking a job in Big Timber? Riding the range again? Training horses? He was a man of many talents, that was for sure.

As she worked at her desk all day on Thursday, she couldn't stop herself from wondering where he was and what he was doing. Couldn't stop herself from missing him. It was odd when you got used to a person's presence. When the individual was gone, a piece of your heart was, too. No, not her heart, she told herself. She couldn't care that much about Hudson. Could she?

She thought about the days and weeks and months after she and Jamie had been split up from their other siblings. Each minute at first, and then each hour, and finally each day, she'd wondered where they were and what they were doing. She and Jamie had been too young and hadn't had the means to keep track of them. Their grandparents had made it clear their sisters and brothers were no longer their concern. Were Liza, Dana, Bailey, Daniel and Luke bitter and resentful? Was that why they never called or returned…because Rust Creek Falls had nothing but bad memories of the split-up after their parents' deaths? And sadness. All good reasons not to return, she supposed.

The day rolled along even though Bella didn't put much gusto into it. At least not until she visited the classrooms to talk and play with the kids. But when she returned to her desk, she fell into the same thoughts, missing Hudson and wondering if he was actually considering the job offer. Knowing she could only make herself crazy, she forced herself to stop. Her life certainly didn't revolve around his, and his would never revolve around hers. At least not with any permanence.

Could an affair assuage some of what she felt for Hudson? Or was it already too late for that? He could even be gone before Christmas.

In an effort to get her mind off him, she returned to her year-end report. She didn't pick her head up until one of the moms, the one who had threatened to take her son to another day care center if she saw evidence of a sniffle, entered Just Us Kids to pick up Jimmy. Marla Tillotson never seemed to be happy. Bella had glimpsed a smile on her face once in a while when she was with her son, but not often. Bella had also noticed that Marla stirred up gossip with the other moms. She managed a new laundromat that had opened up recently, so she was in contact with many town residents. When she heard news, she spread it around.

As Marla approached the desk, Bella pulled out the clipboard with the sign-out sheets. She handed it to her with a smile and asked politely, "Is it getting any colder out there?"

"Cold enough to trade leather boots for fur-lined ones," Marla said. Her gaze went to Hudson's office. "So Mr. Jones took the whole day off?" she asked. "I noticed he wasn't here this morning either."

Bella wouldn't gossip, but she would be honest. "Mr. Jones took a personal day today."

Marla gave her a wicked smile. "I'll say it was personal."

Bella couldn't keep her eyebrows from arching up. "Excuse me?" she asked, knowing she shouldn't pursue it, yet interested in most anything about Hudson.

"I stopped in at the Ace in the Hole for takeout for lunch. He was there with a very beautiful redhead. They seemed to know each other well, at least from the way he was patting her hand. They didn't seem in any hurry to eat and were enjoying glasses of wine."

Bella felt as if she'd been stabbed. Hudson had taken off today for a date? A long lunch with afternoon delight afterward?

Should she be surprised?

With Hudson's charming nature, he'd been in Rust Creek Falls long enough to make friendships, to meet lots of women. She turned back to Marla. "Mr. Jones's business is his alone," she said, her voice devoid of inflection. "Go ahead back to Jimmy's classroom. I'm sure he'll be ready to leave."

Marla gave Bella an odd look, then a little shrug. She went down the hall to her son's classroom.

Bella was not going to give another thought to Hudson Jones.

Not one more thought.

When Hudson came to work the next morning, he looked somber as he gave Bella a nod then went to his office. He didn't say good-morning. He didn't ask how the day had gone yesterday. In essence, he was quieter than she'd ever seen him, and he stayed that way.

Was it because of the kisses they'd shared that she now felt piqued that he was ignoring her? Was it because of their argument? The possibility he'd be leaving?

As the day progressed, and he stayed in his office on his computer, she imagined exactly what he'd been doing yesterday. Maybe he was so quiet because he'd had a marvelous afternoon and evening in bed with the redhead. Maybe the redhead had turned his head. Maybe…

Maybe too many things. She was tired of her mind running in circles or supposition playing havoc with her thoughts. Maybe they should just get everything out on the table and then worry about digesting it.

The afternoon seemed tediously slow as she thought about what she could say, what she could ask. Eventually she signed out the last parent and child, and she watched all the teachers leave.

That left her and Hudson. Now was the time.

He was still at his computer, studying the screen as if it held the answers to the universe, when she marched into his office.

He swiveled away from the monitor and gave his attention to her. "Are you leaving?"

"In a minute. First I have something to ask you."

"Go ahead."

"Why did you ignore me all day? Because I'd like to know whether you're keeping your commitment to Just Us Kids or not."

"I didn't ignore you today."

"I don't know what you'd call it. You hardly said two words."

"I have a lot on my mind. My mood had nothing to do with you."

For some reason that conclusion annoyed her more than anything else. It seemed she was becoming of no importance to him. Or was it that he had become too important to her?

Because she wasn't used to caring for a man, because she had too many thoughts spinning around in her head, she blurted out, "Oh, I understand it had nothing to do with me. That's probably because you must have had a spectacular time yesterday with the redhead."

After his brows arched and he leaned back in his desk chair, she realized Hudson looked totally surprised at her outburst. Meeting her gaze directly, he said, "Lunch with that redhead was all about business. Period."

Bella felt a red flush begin at her neck and start to creep up into her cheeks. She felt like an absolute fool, and she couldn't stand here and face Hudson another second. In one continuous motion she left his office, grabbed her coat that she'd laid over her desk chair, as well as her purse from the bottom drawer, and made for the door.

By that time, Hudson was standing in the doorway to his office. "Bella—"

But she couldn't look at him right now. She couldn't talk to him reasonably, not after she'd acted like a foolish teenager, the foolish teenager she'd once been. She rushed out of the day care center and into her car, then pulled away in a burst of speed.

Hudson had two reactions to Bella's sudden departure. The first—he was worried about her. But the second… Was that jealousy he'd detected? If she was jealous, did that mean she cared about him a bit?

He could go after her, but he expected she needed time to calm down, time to realize they were going to have to talk about this eventually. As he walked through the rooms, closing up the place, he realized he'd been wrong when he'd said his mood today had had nothing to do with her. It had actually had a lot to do with her. Yes, their argument. But more than that, everything else that was on his mind, too.

The woman Guy had sent to meet with him was basically his ranch manager; she took care of the books, scheduling, vet appointments, and kept all running smoothly. She had been a looker, that was true. And in the past, Hudson had wanted to look.

This time he didn't.

He hadn't cared at all what she looked like. But he'd listened to what she'd said, and that had caused him more turmoil. He tried to decide whether he should stay or leave Rust Creek Falls. Point one, did Just Us Kids still need him? The day care center was back on track now, the client base saved, rumors put to rest, the scare of another epidemic almost resolved. Was there a need for him to stay?

He'd told Walker he'd stay until the book project was completed. No, it hadn't been a hard-and-fast promise, but he did always keep his word. Besides, he'd found he actually liked living in Rust Creek Falls, especially at Clive's ranch. But there was one more reason compelling him to stay. And her name was Bella.

Bella drove home, her face still flushed from her encounter with Hudson and her own stupidity. She usually filtered what came out of her mouth. What had happened?

At the ranch house, she jumped out of her car and practically ran inside. This ranch had become a safe haven. But as she stepped over the threshold, she realized it might be safe, but it was noisy, too.

The babies were squalling for their dinner, and Jamie just shook his head. "Paige couldn't come tonight, so I said I could handle them on my own."

She could see that he was trying to, but more than anything, she could see how exhausted her brother was. Slipping out of her coat, she hurried to help him feed the triplets. With two of them catching spills, wiping sticky hands and playing airplane games, they soon had the babies fed. Bathing, however, took a little longer.

By the time they'd settled all three in their cribs and returned downstairs, Jamie looked at Bella with a weak smile. "You didn't get anything to eat."

"I'm not hungry," she said honestly, still remembering what had happened with Hudson. How was she going to live that down?

Her brother's shoulders slumped a bit as he picked up

dirty dishes from the table and took them to the sink. She could tell he was practically dead on his feet, and she knew he needed more than a good night's sleep. He needed a break.

She pulled out a kitchen chair and pointed to it. "Sit."

"I have to clean up the kitchen," he reminded her.

"No, you don't. I'll do it. I want to talk to you."

"That sounds ominous," he said as he sat in the chair, obviously too fatigued to argue with her.

"You have to take a break from everything or you're going to collapse." When he started to protest, she held up her hand. "I'm going to ask for Monday off. I want you to call a motel in Kalispell and leave tomorrow morning for a few days. I want you to get some rest while I take charge of the babies and the schedule and the ranch chores."

"You can't do it on your own."

"You're going to have to trust me, Jamie. The baby chain will help with the triplets, and if I need help with the chores I can call our neighbor's son." When he began to protest again, she cut him off. "You're not going to be any good to the triplets or the ranch if you fall over from exhaustion or get sick. You probably haven't had a solid night's sleep since they were born."

"Since they came home," he admitted. "I think I hear them, and I wake up to check, or I worry that I'm not going to hear them."

"Or one of them cries," Bella added. "Believe me, I understand. That's why you have to do this. You have to depend on me as I've always depended on you."

"What about you?" he asked.

"I've actually *had* breaks—like that afternoon I

went riding." Like the afternoon she'd slept on Hudson's couch. "I even get a break at work," she added.

"Around all those kids?"

"I don't have direct responsibility for them—the teachers do. I can take my lunch break without worrying or take a walk."

Or stop in Hudson's office to talk to him, she thought. But that wasn't going to happen again.

Jamie got quiet. He actually seemed to be considering her offer. Finally he looked at her and said, "I'll only do this if the neighbor boy can come over and help you with the chores."

"Call him and the motel. Any motel you want."

"Just something with a bed would be good," he admitted.

"I'll call Hudson and ask him about Monday." She hoped she'd just get his voice mail.

But that, of course, didn't happen. He answered his cell on the second ring. But before he could say anything, she launched into an explanation.

After a moment's hesitation, Hudson assured her, "No problem. Take the day off. I can cover for you."

"Great," she said, ready to hang up.

"Bella, about this afternoon..."

"I really have to go, Hudson. I think I hear one of the triplets. I'll see you Tuesday."

And before he could say more, she ended the call.

Was it the cowardly way out? Possibly, but she was also buying time. Maybe in a couple of days he'd forget about her outburst. Simply put, it might not have been that important to him. If it wasn't, she was off the hook.

If it was...she'd deal with Hudson on Tuesday.

Chapter 9

Hudson knew the longer a misunderstanding went unattended, the more mucked up life could get. That's why he decided to visit Bella on Sunday. He knew a phone call wouldn't do it. If she was taking care of the triplets with Jamie gone, she'd be too busy to focus on a call. Besides, this explanation required face-to-face time. He had a feeling she didn't believe him about his lunch with the redhead being purely business.

Considering the fact she thought he was the love-'em-and-leave-'em type, it was very possible. Love them and leave them. Yep, that's what he'd done in the past. It was easier than getting involved and getting hurt. He'd always made that clear at the outset with whomever he dated. But Bella?

She seemed to turn his world and his perceptions of it upside down.

When he arrived at Jamie's house and stood on the porch outside the door, he still wasn't sure what he was going to say. He did realize, however, that there wasn't another vehicle in the driveway. That was odd since the baby chain always helped on weekends as well as during the week. Hudson was aware of the sound of squalling babies from inside. Two of them, if he could make out the sounds. He rang the doorbell and heard Bella's voice.

"Oh my gosh, Paige, I'm so glad you could make it after all."

Then she opened the door and saw Hudson.

The baby in Bella's arms was squirming and squiggling and obviously wanted to be let down. He was squalling as loud as his little lungs would allow.

"Which one is this?" Hudson yelled above the din.

Though obviously surprised at his presence, Bella answered reflexively, "Henry."

More crying came from inside the living room. Looking past Bella, Hudson could see a baby dressed all in pink, so he supposed it was Katie, wailing with the best of them. She was seated in a play saucer, but that definitely wasn't occupying her.

He reached out and said, "Give me Henry. You go take care of Katie."

Bella didn't seem sure she wanted to give up the little boy, so Hudson took matters into his own hands. He reached for Henry with a big smile. "Come on, fella. You and I have to talk."

The baby reached his arms out to Hudson, and Hudson took him, raising the baby's face to his own. "You'll get ahead in life better if you don't scream so much. Come on, let's figure out what's wrong."

Hudson walked Henry into the living room and saw

the third triplet, Jared, sitting in a playpen playing with blocks. The only cooperative one in the bunch.

Henry had obviously been surprised by Hudson lifting him and talking to him. His cries subsided into hiccups until Hudson settled him into the crook of his arm. Then Henry started all over again.

Puzzled, Hudson jiggled him a bit. "What? Wet diaper? Hungry? Bored? You'll have to tell me."

Henry stopped crying as if he was considering it, and Hudson stuck his finger into the boy's diaper. "He's wet," he called to Bella. "Where are the diapers?"

Bella motioned to a changing table on the other side of the room, and Hudson went that way. He'd learned a thing or two working at the day care center. There, one had to be a man of all trades, so to speak. He not only learned how to change diapers, but also how to give belly rubs and tickle toes. Anything to get a baby to do what you wanted him to do.

Grabbing hold of a rubber ducky on the changing table, he laid Henry down and handed it to him. "You play with this while we take care of business."

By this time Bella had taken Katie out of the play saucer. The little girl had stopped crying as soon as Bella lifted her into her arms.

Now that Henry was concentrating on the rubber ducky, and Katie was quiet, Bella asked Hudson, "What are you doing here?"

"We need to talk." He unsnapped Henry's jeans and took off the wet diaper. "But more important, why don't you have any help today?"

"Fallon caught a flu bug she didn't want to give to the babies. Paige and the others couldn't cover because of church functions or holiday gatherings. Paige said she'd get here as soon as she could."

Hudson fumbled a bit with the dry diaper. He wasn't as adept at it as Bella or the teachers and aides at the day care center. The sticky tab caught on his thumb, bent over and stuck to itself. But somehow he managed to diaper Henry, even if it was a little lopsided.

"I was going to give them a snack," Bella said. "Maybe we can talk if we can get them all eating a cookie at the same time."

"Sounds good," Hudson agreed, snapping Henry's jeans and pulling down his little shirt. When he hefted Henry into his arms, the little boy gave him what Hudson thought was a smile. Hudson felt as if he'd accomplished something big.

After he carried Henry into the kitchen and settled him into a high chair, Bella did the same with Katie. Then she hurried back into the living room to gather up Jared. Soon the triplets were gnawing on cookies.

Bella turned to him. "Would you like something to drink? Soda, milk, juice?"

"Milk would be fine. I'm still a growing boy."

Bella shook her head and gave him a small smile as she went to the refrigerator, poured two glasses of milk and set them on the table.

Hudson was thinking about the best way to start when she plunged in first. "I'm sorry I reacted as I did on Friday. I had no right."

Hudson decided to ignore her remark about her rights. Instead, he said, "Tell me why you reacted as you did."

"Because of what Marla Tillotson said."

After she finished explaining, Hudson pressed, "And

why did that bother you so much? That I might have been having lunch with a redhead."

Bella suddenly gave all her attention to Katie, wiping a few crumbs from her cheek. "Hudson..."

"All right, I'll let that go for now. But let me explain the whole situation to you. Guy sent his ranch manager—who just happens to be a pretty redhead—to convince me he needs me in Big Timber. Apparently he thought she could do a better job at it than he could."

"Because you like pretty redheads?" Bella asked seriously.

Hudson knew a little honesty might go a long way with Bella. "In the past, I've been known to have my head turned by a pretty woman. Guy witnessed that."

"Why does he think you're the right person for this job? Exactly what is it?" Bella asked, moving away from the topic.

"Last season, one of the ranch's patrons had an accident. Guy took an economic hit over it. He had clients cancel their reservations. They're trying to get past it. They've seen how I turned around the reputation of Just Us Kids, and they want me to do that for them."

"Are you going to take the job?"

Hudson couldn't tell from Bella's voice or her expression whether she cared personally or professionally.

He said honestly, "I don't know. Just Us Kids really doesn't need me any longer. Guy is a friend. But any PR firm could help him."

Before she could respond, Bella's phone emitted a lively ringtone. Hesitating only a second, she took it from her shirt pocket and studied the screen. "It's Jamie. I need to take this. Excuse me."

He gave her a wink. “I’ll watch this tribe while you talk.”

She answered the call. “Hi, Jamie… Everything’s fine… I told you, you don’t need to check every few hours.”

Even though Jamie was taking a break, Hudson realized he still had the triplets and Bella on his mind. Of course he’d be checking in often.

“We’re good. Order room service. Eat a lot. Sleep, and watch mindless TV. That’s an order.”

Her brother said something that made her laugh. “Yes, that is a change, isn’t it? Really, we’re good. And I don’t want to hear from you again until you come home tomorrow night. Fine. I’ll text you after they’re all settled in for the night. And I’ll give them extra kisses from you. See you tomorrow.”

Ending the call, she pocketed the phone once more.

“I admire your loyalty to your brother,” he said sincerely.

Bella went to the refrigerator and pulled out a casserole dish. She showed it to Hudson. “Cherry cobbler. Our volunteers bring casseroles and desserts when they come. Would you like some?”

“Sure,” Hudson agreed. “That will go great with milk.”

Efficiently Bella microwaved two dishes of cobbler and brought them to the table. She sat across from him, the babies between them.

Despite everything, Hudson felt a connection to Bella, a connection that was growing stronger. Just now, when she’d offered him this snack, it was as if she’d made a decision of sorts, and he wondered what was coming.

She stirred her cobbler a bit, forgot about her spoon and looked him straight in the eyes. "Jamie and I have been a team for years."

"Anyone can see that," Hudson commented, lost in her face, the point of her chin, the tilt of her cheek bones, the brown of her eyes.

"We became a team for a reason."

"Your parents died. That brought you closer together," Hudson said. She'd already told him that.

"That wasn't the only reason we became a team. We have five other siblings—Luke, Daniel, Dana, Bailey and Liza."

Hudson was stunned. He didn't know what to say. But then he remarked, "No one in town mentioned it."

"Anyone who knows us respects what we've been through. They know we've had a lot of heartache, and some of that is due to not having any contact with our other siblings."

"Why not?"

"After our parents' accident, we were split apart. Dana and Liza were sent away and adopted because they were younger. Our grandparents considered me and Jamie too young to be involved, and they didn't tell us much about it. Luke, Daniel and Bailey were over eighteen and considered adults. Our grandparents said they couldn't handle more mouths to feed, so the three boys left town. They were just as traumatized by our parents' deaths even though they were older. On top of that, I think they were bitter and resentful that my grandparents essentially kicked them out on their own."

"Have you tried contacting them?"

"I've tried. Not directly, of course, because I don't

know where any of them are. But I've used search engines. I haven't had any luck."

"And none of them have ever contacted you?"

Hudson could see the anguish on Bella's face as she shook her head. "It hurts," she said. "Jamie has never left Rust Creek Falls, and I've been here except for college. It would be easy to find us. But apparently they don't want to. That's why Jamie and I have been as close as we are."

Finally Hudson thought he understood the depth of Bella's loneliness. As much as he and his brothers squabbled, they stayed connected. Reaching out, he covered her hand with his. "I'm sorry for all you've lost."

"I don't need anyone's pity," she said quietly. "That's why Jamie and I don't talk about it."

"Thank you for confiding in me. That means you trust me."

Bella looked as if she might say more, but then she pushed her chair back and stood. "Maybe we can settle this crew down for a nap. Getting them all quiet and sleeping at the same time could be an impossible feat, but we can try. That is, if you can stay. If you can't, I understand."

Hudson wasn't going anywhere, not until he was sure Bella could handle what she'd taken on.

Although they worked together at the day care center, Bella was surprised to find they also seemed to work well around the babies in the kitchen. She couldn't help sneaking peeks at Hudson as he wiped Henry's mouth or as he plucked a piece of cookie from Katie's hair. He was big and tall, but he was gentle and caring. He was almost as good around the babies as Jamie was.

When he'd thanked her for trusting him, she'd almost told him about her pregnancy and the baby she'd miscarried. She almost told him that she loved taking care of Jamie's babies because she might never have any of her own. Watching Hudson with Katie and Jared and Henry, she could easily see he'd want kids of his own someday.

She thought again about the job offer he'd received. Another good reason not to confide in him. There was no point. Whether she trusted him or not, whether he was attracted to her or not, he was most likely going to be leaving again. Rust Creek Falls was just a stopover in his nomadic lifestyle.

To her surprise, Henry was the baby who quieted first. After they laid him in his crib, he stuck his thumb in his mouth, and his eyes soon closed. It took longer for Katie and Jared. She and Hudson walked them and rocked them until finally they both dozed off. After settling them in their cribs, Bella gave Hudson a smile as they left the room and went downstairs.

In the living room, she made sure the monitor was turned on. "They could wake up in five minutes," she told Hudson.

"Or they could give you a break for at least a half hour or maybe longer."

"Do you always see the world in positive terms?" she asked.

"I try to. But then most of my life has been pretty positive. My family might not be all I want it to be, but I have one. I've never had to think about money. I can pretty much go where I want to go and do what I want. I'm grateful for all that. Every day at the day care center I see single moms struggling and dads working two jobs. I look at folks who were hit by the flood here and what they've lost. I can't help but be grateful for what I have."

"I like your outlook," Bella said.

He stepped closer to her. "Is that all you like?"

She tried to keep the moment light. "I could make a list," she teased.

"And I could make a list of everything I like about you. It would be a long one."

He was right there now, close to her. He loomed over her, but she didn't feel intimidated. In fact, everything about Hudson being near her excited her. Feelings surged through her that almost made her reach for him. When she thought about that redhead, she hated the idea of Hudson kissing another woman, holding another woman, making love to another woman. Bella wanted to *be* that woman.

He must have seen the hunger in her eyes because he took her into his arms and kissed her. His lips were unerringly masculine, supremely masterful, absolutely intoxicating. His arms held her a little tighter, and she pressed closer. His scent, man and aftershave, was intoxicating. He was so ultimately sexy. As they kissed, her hand came up to his cheek, and her fingers trailed over beard stubble. When he groaned, she felt as if she'd accomplished a monumental feat.

As if he wanted to accomplish that same feat, he laced his fingers in her hair. He swept his tongue through her mouth until she had no breath left for anything but Hudson. They kept tasting each other as if they could never get enough and gave in to desire that they'd denied for weeks. He backed her up, and she knew what was behind them—the sofa. She didn't protest or even think about refusing. Her head might know better, but her heart wanted Hudson…wanted him in a primal way.

They'd almost reached their destination…

Then the doorbell rang.

It took a few moments for Bella to realize someone was at the door. She tore away from Hudson, her head spinning, her mouth throbbing from his kiss, her senses filled with him.

"I have to get that," she murmured. "It could be… anyone."

No, she definitely couldn't think straight. That was for sure.

Hudson's eyes held a glazed look, too, and she wondered if he'd been as into that kiss as she had been. Was that even possible? Had she lost her mind? She'd just listed all the reasons she shouldn't confide in him and couldn't get involved with him.

Then what had she done?

She'd kissed him.

To her dismay, that hadn't been an ordinary kiss. That had been a lead-to-something-else kiss.

The doorbell rang again, and she practically ran to the foyer and pulled open the door. She was so glad to see Paige's face.

But Paige took one look at Bella and asked, "Is something wrong?"

"Oh, no. No," Bella assured her, pulling her inside. "I thought you couldn't get here this soon."

"Our meeting ended earlier than I thought it would. How are you coping?"

"Oh, I'm coping just fine. In fact, Hudson's here.

He helped me put the triplets to bed. Believe it or not, they're actually all napping."

Paige was giving her an are-you-sure-I'm-not-interrupting-something look.

But Bella kept shaking her head. "Come on in. I can use your help. Jamie called, and I convinced him I had everything under control." She prattled on, filling the air with chitchat, which was so unlike her.

Paige knew that, and Hudson did, too. But she had to do something to cover up that kiss, to process it, to absorb the way she felt when Hudson kissed her.

By the time she and Paige were inside the living room, Hudson had seemed to compose himself, too. He'd taken his Stetson off the table where he'd laid it when he'd come in and plopped it onto his head.

To Bella he said, "It looks as if you have reinforcements, so I'll be on my way. Nice to see you, Paige."

"Good to see you, too, Hudson."

There was an awkward silence until Bella offered, "I'll walk you out. Paige, I'll be right back. The monitor's on."

It would have been easier and less awkward if Bella had just let Hudson leave. But she'd just have to face him when she returned to work if she didn't deal with their kiss now.

He stepped out onto the porch and then turned to look at her. They were eye level. "It seemed right," he simply said, and she knew what he meant. Everything about that kiss had seemed right.

"Maybe, but I'm glad Paige interrupted. We both need time to think."

He shook his head. "Maybe we should stop thinking and just feel."

"Hudson, there's still a lot you don't know about me."

"So tell me."

If she did that, she'd be plunging into the unknown. If she did that, she'd be asking for rejection. Impulsively, she leaned forward and gave Hudson a light kiss on the lips.

"I'll see you at work on Tuesday morning," she said.

He looked as if he wanted to take her into his arms again, but she backed up, and he seemed to understand. He nodded. "See you Tuesday morning."

When Bella closed the door, she couldn't help but imagine exactly what would have happened if Paige hadn't arrived.

Hudson was out of sorts. When he arrived back at the Lazy B, he went straight to the barn. After a stop at the tack room, he saddled up Breeze, mounted and took a path through the fields where the snow had melted. He needed a horse under him, the wind in his face, the cold against his skin.

As he rode, he realized he just hadn't been able to go into the empty ranch house. The reason? He wanted Bella there with him. He wasn't sure yet what all that entailed, but he knew he wanted to make a few of his dreams come true—the ones that included Bella in his bed. If they hadn't been interrupted this afternoon, they would have had sex on that couch. The thing was, if Paige hadn't interrupted them, one of the babies might have. That would have been even more awkward.

When he made love to Bella, he wanted no interruptions and no one interfering. He wanted their attention to be focused on just the two of them. He also wanted Bella to be sure…to want him as much as he wanted her. To his surprise, that wasn't just about lust. It wasn't just about the fun they could have in the sheets, the satisfaction of two bodies coming together. No, these feelings went deeper. He felt protective toward Bella. He didn't want her to be confused or unsure. Most of all, he didn't want to hurt her. If they shared a bed, they'd both have to do it freely. Consequences and the future be damned.

The problem was, he'd never felt protective like this about a woman before. He'd never cared about her dreams, her insecurities, her past. He cared about all of that with Bella. She'd lost her parents, her brothers and sisters. He could understand why she wouldn't want to willingly lose any more.

He didn't want to lose anything either…especially not his freedom. He felt vulnerable and didn't like that at all. He didn't like the idea that a woman could cause upset or joy or create a hunger he just had to satisfy.

Bella confused him. That was a first, and he'd like it to be a last.

He had no idea what he was going to do about any of it.

Chapter 10

Hudson could fry himself a burger. He could even flip an omelet. What he couldn't usually do was bake. But he'd missed Bella at Just Us Kids, as did everyone else, and he wanted to bake something to welcome her back on Tuesday. She did so much for the teachers, the parents and especially the children, making them feel comforted and loved. In essence, she was the poster girl for Just Us Kids. More than that, she was the heart.

At first he hadn't known what to do that would be special yet not over-the-top. He'd nixed flowers right away. Spending tons of money on every rare flower there was and filling her desk with them was too showy and too impersonal. Besides, he wanted to show her another side of him—one that could be caring in ways that counted rather than only spending money.

After consulting a clerk at the grocery store, he found

a box of what she said were never-fail cupcakes. He had to do cupcakes, of course, so they could pass them out and share them with the kids. She showed him the muffin pans to buy and colorful little cups. After one look at him, and hearing his woe that he'd never made icing in his life, let alone a cake, she showed him canned icing. That would have to do.

Before he took all his supplies to the checkout, she asked, "Why don't you just buy cupcakes or a cake from the bakery? We'd decorate it really nice and even put her name on it."

But Hudson just shook his head. "That's not the same thing at all. I don't want to buy the cupcakes. I want to make them for her."

The woman gave him a wink and a nod as if she understood, and Hudson left with his purchases, full of hope.

Actually the baking went fairly well, except for a few spills when he poured the batter. The icing, however, was something different. When he realized he'd bought only white and pink, he decided to swirl it and get a little fancy with it. White with a pink swirl, pink with a white swirl. At the end of his project, he had to admit he would never be a cake decorator. But the cupcakes looked presentable, and that's what mattered.

He left early for the day care center, in plenty of time to hang the pink-and-white crepe paper the store clerk had told him would be a good decoration. He wanted everything ready before anyone else arrived.

And he was ready. As the teachers filed in, he was glad Bella wasn't among them. He wanted as many teachers and kids here as possible before she came through that door.

All of the teachers were there and some of the children, too, when she came in, saw the decorations and the big sign that said Welcome Back, Bella. Her mouth dropped open.

Her gaze went to Sarah, but Sarah just shrugged. "Not our doing." She pointed to Hudson.

One of the other teachers, Joyce Croswell, pointed to the cupcakes. "And just look at those. He made them, too." Her gaze went from Bella to Hudson, as if everyone should realize something more was going on than boss and day care center manager.

Bella looked absolutely paralyzed for a moment, but then she recovered and smiled. "I don't know what to say." She went over to Hudson, threw her arms around him and gave him a huge hug. "No one's ever done anything like this for me before. And I was only gone one day."

"Bella Stockton," he said seriously, loud enough for everyone to hear, "you make this place go round. We all felt the length of the day you were gone because you weren't here to experience it with us. We missed your smile and your energy and your caring, and we just wanted to let you know."

Bella looked close to tears now, and he hadn't wanted that. "Come on," he said. "Taste one of the cupcakes, then everyone else can have one, too. I made enough to go around." He took one of the paper plates they used for snacks with the kids and placed one of the pink cupcakes on it. Then he handed it to her. She studied the cupcake with its little white swirl on the top.

They were standing quite close together now, and she murmured again, "I can't believe you went to all this trouble."

"No trouble, Bella, not for you. Not to show you that I think about you and I care about you." He didn't think anyone else had heard what he'd just said, but he could see in Bella's eyes that she had.

"Aw, Hudson."

The door flew open, and two moms and their babies came in. Their special moment was gone.

"I'd better wait to eat this until I can really enjoy it," Bella told him.

"Lunchtime?" he asked.

"Sure, if no crisis erupts. But at least I can taste the icing." Taking her finger, she swiped at the white point on top of the cupcake. He watched her as she slowly placed it on her lip. Her tongue came out, licking the confection, and she closed her eyes and smiled. "It's sweet, Hudson, just like icing should be."

"It came from a can," he said, now wishing he had tried to make it himself.

"It's the thought that counts. It's pretty and it tastes good, and it's perfect on the cupcakes. I'll have a lot more than that little taste at lunchtime. I promise."

Rattled by the sheer sensuality of watching her lick that icing with her tongue, he almost broke into a sweat. Composing himself, he took trays of cupcakes to each classroom and passed them out to the children who were old enough to have them. The others he took to the break room, protecting them with a plastic covering. Then he waited for lunchtime.

Bella had seen that look in Hudson's eyes—the one that excited her. She was never so happy it was finally lunchtime. When she went to the break room, he was already there. Apparently Greta had made him some kind of casserole he could warm up in the microwave. He had the flowered dish in front of him, and he was forking pasta with ground beef into his mouth.

He stopped when she brought her bagged lunch and a paper plate to the table. "If you'd like something hot, I'll share. There's plenty here."

"I'm fine with this." She nodded at her turkey sandwich. But as she ate it, the smell of the casserole made her mouth water. He must have seen her eyeing it because he took her paper plate and forked some of the casserole onto it. Then he gave her another fork that had been sitting beside his dish.

"Did you expect company?" she asked.

"Sure did. I want to make sure you enjoy your cupcake." And before the electricity zipping between them got a little too hot, he asked, "How's Jamie?"

"He looks better, and he seems rested. I think the time away did him good."

"And you survived," he said with respect in his voice.

"I did...with help. Including yours."

His visit to the ranch house brought to mind that kiss. That kiss she'd never forget.

After that, they made small talk about the day care center while they ate. When they'd both finished, Hudson rose, chose two cupcakes from the tray and brought one over to Bella.

"Coffee with that?" he asked.

"Sure." She'd never had a man serve her cupcakes and coffee before. This was truly a first.

He took milk from the refrigerator and poured just the amount she liked into her mug, then set it on the table. He poured a black coffee for himself.

Trying to be ladylike, she took the paper from the

cupcake and then used her fork to take one bite, and then another. "These are really good. Maybe you can give Greta a run for her money in the baking department."

He ate his cupcake in three bites, then responded, "I doubt that. This was just a lucky first try. Or maybe I just had good motivation."

Her fork stopped halfway to her mouth. They gazed at each other, and Bella's heart beat so fast she could hardly swallow.

He leaned forward and with his forefinger touched the top of her lip. "You have some icing there," he said. His touch held fire, and she couldn't help wishing it was his lips that were meeting hers.

"I'd kiss you again," he said, as if reading her thoughts, "but that wouldn't be proper at the workplace."

With Hudson looking at her with those bedroom eyes of his, proper didn't seem to have a place in her world. Should she be fighting this attraction? What if she just gave in to it and enjoyed it? Enjoyed herself with a man? Maybe for the first time ever.

"I should get back to my desk," she murmured, to put that very temptation out of her mind.

But before she could rise to her feet, Hudson covered her hand with his. "Look, I don't know what you've heard about me or my reputation, but I don't just go around kissing random women."

She didn't know what to say to that, so she waited for Hudson to go on.

He cleared his throat, as if putting his feelings into words was hard for him. "You're such a pretty woman. I'm sure lots of men want to kiss you."

Considering her history and her situation, nothing

could be further from the truth. Most of the men in town now considered her standoffish. That was ironic considering her wild teenage years when she was anything but. She couldn't help but laugh wryly at his comment.

But when she did, Hudson leaned away, took his hand from hers and seemed to be insulted. She knew he was when he asked, "Do you consider my kissing you amusing, or our kisses just a joke?"

Anything but. He actually looked a bit vulnerable, and she wondered if she'd hurt him. Could he really care about her?

"I'm just botching this and making a fool of myself," he said, standing.

But before he could stride out of the room, she hopped to her feet and caught his arm. "I didn't mean to laugh, but you don't know—"

"I know how much I'm attracted to you. Are you attracted to me?"

She gave a small nod, and suddenly she was in his arms and he was kissing her again. It was a short kiss, though a deep, wet one.

He set her away from him. "I know you're worried about your job. Considering what happened with my brother and Lindsay, I understand your concern. Believe me. But there are no repercussions with what's going on with us here. You can walk away, and your job will still be safe. I've wanted you for weeks, but I understand that you're young, and I'll back off if that's what you want."

She was deeply touched by everything he'd said because she could see he meant it all. She could also see something else. Because she was young, he could possibly believe she was a virgin, that she was inexperienced. She had to be honest with him and set him straight.

"Hudson, this isn't my first rodeo."

He looked a bit surprised at her comment, so she went on. "You've been on my mind for weeks, too. I have so many decisions to make in my life. Helping Jamie is one of them, and I don't know how long he'll need me. And you're right about my needing this job here. I do. But I also want to go back to school soon. Everything is in flux, so I was trying not to add something else to complicate my life."

"You think I'd complicate your life?" Hudson asked with a crooked smile.

"I don't think it. I'm sure of it. But the more I get to know you, the more I want the complication…the more I want *you*."

His eyes darkened with that unsettling hunger again. He seemed to take in a deep breath, as if he was reminding himself not to hurry anything. "After work, do you want to come back to my place?"

If she answered him affirmatively, she knew exactly what she was agreeing to. Her hand on his arm, she looked up at him with the wanting in her eyes.

She said simply, "Yes."

Hours later as Bella parked in back of Hudson's vehicle and they walked together to the ranch house door, he realized how surprised he'd been at her remark that this wasn't her first rodeo. He'd really thought she might be a virgin, not only because of her age, but because of her demeanor. But apparently he'd been wrong. Had she been hurt terribly by someone and that's why she held back?

After they entered the foyer, they were a bit awkward with each other. He wasn't going to just jump her bones, or rip her clothes off, or carry her to his bed, even though he wanted to do all three. More than anything, he wanted to do this right. Though he wasn't sure why that was so important.

He motioned to the great room. "Would you like something to drink?" he asked. "It might break the ice so we don't feel so rattled."

She smiled at that. "Something to drink would be nice."

"Hot chocolate, coffee, tea?" He wasn't going to suggest wine because he didn't want their senses dulled. He wanted to be aware of absolutely every moment tonight.

"Hot chocolate would be great." Looking nervous, she glanced around the room. Her eyes lit on the photo albums under the coffee table. "I saw these when I was here the last time. Do they belong to Mr. Bickler?"

"No, they don't. They're mine. Believe it or not, I take them wherever I go. Sometimes in a bunkhouse I might not have much else than my boots and my jeans and my sheepskin, and my Stetson. But keeping these with me when I travel helps me stay grounded. I remember I have a family, and I had a home where I grew up. It's just a way of remembering my roots."

"Do you mind if I page through them?"

He thought about that. "No, I don't mind. You'll have a good laugh at some of the pictures in there. They're candid shots, nothing like the photos you take."

"Candid shots are sometimes the best ones." She unzipped her parka, shrugged out of it and laid it over one of the chairs. Hudson felt himself relax. This evening was going to be everything he wanted it to be.

Hudson had learned hot chocolate was almost as important as hot coffee on a cold winter night. He'd become somewhat of a connoisseur and used a mix he special-ordered. Minutes later he carried in two mugs topped by a mound of whipped cream and sat on the sofa beside Bella, putting the mugs onto coasters.

She looked at the hot drink and smiled. "How did you know I liked whipped cream?"

"Just a good guess, I imagine."

She had a photograph album open on her lap. There were photos of him and his brothers as kids. His parents were in a few of them, but it was mostly just them.

"You and your brothers are *all* handsome," she murmured. She pointed to one of the pictures. "Who is who?"

He pointed to each in succession. "That's Autry, Gideon, Jensen and, of course, Walker."

Then she pointed to another picture. "Your mom and dad?"

"Yes."

Hudson's mother looked guarded in that particular photo. His father looked as imposing as ever with a shock of white hair and cold blue eyes. Yet Hudson knew he definitely bore a resemblance to them.

"You look like him—the same jaw, the same high forehead," she noted, mirroring his thoughts.

"I might look like him, but I hope we're different in lots of ways. He and Walker are more alike, all about business and money, maybe even power. Maybe that's why I took a left turn when they took a right."

"Do you respect them?"

"I respect Walker for what he's accomplished. And now he seems a bit different with Lindsay, as if he knows what matters. But my dad, maybe he's just been with the wrong woman all his life and they don't make each other happy. Or maybe they just don't want to work at it."

"I think about my parents often," Bella admitted. "If they had lived, I wonder if the Stocktons would be a close family. Would they have kept us all connected?" She looked up at Hudson. "The way it sounds, you and Walker might be different, but you *are* connected. That's why you're here helping him."

"That's why *you're* helping Jamie."

She nodded her agreement as she sipped the hot chocolate. He saw the whipped cream that gathered on her upper lip and suppressed the urge to lick it off. *Don't rush this. Let her get comfortable. You'll know when she wants you just as much as you want her.*

At least he hoped he would.

Bella placed her mug down as she swiped at her lips. "I have some good memories from before my parents died."

"Tell me," he encouraged her.

"There was this lake where Mom and Dad took us to go swimming. It had a grassy, stony shore, and the older kids would help the younger kids wade in. We had the best times there in the summers, swimming and picnicking. Jamie and I don't talk about those days much because it hurts to think about them. I guess because we miss our siblings. Yet I know remembering would be good for us, too."

Hudson pointed to a photo in the album. "I remember Walker and me being rivals at a lot of things. Roping a calf was one of them. Neither of us was very good at it at first, but our rivalry made us better."

Bella pointed to another photo of him inside a grand room. The Christmas tree he stood before had to be at least ten feet tall. "That's a beautiful tree."

"Mother always had a decorator come in and do the trees, along with other Christmas decorations. That's far different from a tree I'd like to bring in here for the holiday."

"What do you have in mind?"

"I want to go cut it myself and put it right over there." He pointed to a spot by the window. "When I told Greta I wanted to do that, she said she has a box of hand-crocheted white ornaments that she'd made one year for their tree. She has others that she uses now and she said I could have the crocheted ones if I'd like. I *would* like to use them, with lots of tiny lights."

"I'm sure the kids at Just Us Kids would make you ornaments if you asked them."

"I'm sure they would."

Suddenly it seemed that both of them had run out of conversation. Hudson couldn't take his eyes from Bella's, and it seemed Bella couldn't take hers from his. He slowly circled her with his arm and moved closer. He could smell her floral perfume, like flowers in the middle of winter. Everything about Bella was sweet and pure. Sweeter and purer than he deserved.

"You can still change your mind," he whispered. And he meant it. He wanted nothing about tonight to be uncertain.

"I don't want to change my mind," she said with a small smile that made him ache even more with desire for her.

When he bent his head to her, when his lips captured hers, he felt possessive. He knew his mouth was claiming, and that's the way he wanted it. He wanted Bella to be his. He'd never been so in the moment with a woman before. He was excruciatingly aware of the softness of her skin as he stroked her cheek, the taste of chocolate on her tongue, the small moan that escaped her as they kissed. He gathered her into his arms and wondered how in the heck he was ever going to make it to the bedroom.

"I should have turned on the fireplace," he said when he broke for air.

"Or we could just keep warm under the covers," she suggested softly.

That did it. He rose to his feet and gathered her up into his arms. When he carried her to the bedroom, he felt like a caveman. Somehow Bella made him feel as if he could accomplish anything.

In his bedroom, he settled her on his bed. He found he didn't want to let her go even for a second. So he sat beside her, kissed her again and decided their clothes had to go.

"Light or dark?" he asked her before he started, curious as to what she'd say. The room was in shadows now, and they could hardly see each other's faces even with the hall light glowing.

"Let's turn on the light," she said. "I want to see your face."

Her response pleased him. Loving her in the light meant she felt free about what they were going to do. She felt right about being with him. There was no reason for darkness or shadows or hiding what they were feeling.

After he switched on the bedside lamp and fumbled with a condom packet from the drawer, he reached for her. Not long after, their clothes were on the floor and he'd turned back the covers and rolled on the condom. They were naked on the steel-gray sheets, and he soaked in the beauty of Bella's body.

"Are you cold?" he asked.

"No. Every time you touch me I feel like I'm on fire."

"Same here."

He palmed her breast, wanting her to be ready for him in every way. She moaned, and he kissed her again, this time covering her body with his. He ran his hand up her thigh and then teased her until she wrapped her legs around him.

"I can't wait," he said.

"I'm ready," she whispered.

And just like that, he was inside Bella and he felt as if he'd come home.

She held on to him tightly, but when he kissed her again, he was aware of tears on her cheeks.

"Bella?"

"It's wonderful. *You're* wonderful."

Her words drove him to prolong each stroke, to kiss her more passionately, to touch her everywhere he could. He held off his own pleasure until he felt her body tense, until he heard her cry his name, until she clung to him as if she'd never let him go.

Then he gave in and knew pleasure as he'd never known it before. With Bella in his arms, he felt as if he'd conquered the world.

Chapter 11

Bella awoke slowly, realizing where she was and whom she was with. Hudson's arms surrounded her as she lay on her side with him spooned against her. She held no illusions about what had happened last night. She had no expectations. Disappointed before, she didn't want to hope. Yet she couldn't help but remember each kiss, each touch, each word they'd exchanged.

She ran her hand lightly over the hair on his forearm, knowing in her soul that Hudson's strength was more than skin-deep. She admired the man. No, she more than admired him. She'd tumbled over a cliff and fallen in love with him.

Love. How long had it been since she'd known love from anyone other than her brother?

However, she suspected Hudson's feelings didn't run as deep. She'd learned the hard way that men's sexual desire often dictated their actions. Certainly Hudson was no exception. Wanting her and loving her were two entirely different things.

She thought Hudson was still asleep, but a light nip on her shoulder told her that he wasn't.

Could she face him and the fact that one night might have been enough for him? After last night, how would they react to each other at Just Us Kids? She'd followed her heart and now felt foolish.

She started to inch toward the edge of the king-size bed. Better to leave than to face the awkward conversation that told her it was over before it had begun.

But she didn't get very far. Hudson's arm tugged her back to him. He moved over a bit so she could turn to her back, and now she had no choice but to face him.

"Where do you think you're going?" he asked.

"I have to get dressed and go back to the ranch."

"It's not even sunrise," Hudson reminded her.

"When babies are hungry, they don't care if the sun's up or not. I told Jamie I'd be home this morning to help him."

Hudson studied her, then removed his arm from around her. "Do you want to go?"

Just what was Hudson asking her? To be vulnerable and lay her feelings out on the bed? She didn't know if she could do that. "I thought you'd want me to leave."

He stroked a wisp of hair behind her ear. "I don't want you to leave. If it was up to me, we'd stay here all day. I know we can't. We need to talk about how we're going to handle our relationship in public."

She felt heart-tugging joy that he wanted a relationship. Was it possible she could dream again and have that dream come true?

"We should probably keep this—" she motioned to the bed and everything that had gone on there "—a secret."

"I thought you might say that, but I disagree. We have to think about our situation realistically. I would agree, no public displays of affection at work, even though at times I don't know how I'm going to resist kissing you."

She felt a blush start to creep into her cheeks.

He leaned forward, possessively captured her lips and said good-morning in a way that had her tingling all over.

When he broke the kiss and backed away, he asked, "See what I mean? You smile that certain way and I just want to pull you into my arms. I won't do that at work, but I don't want to be secret about us being together either. If someone sees you here, so be it. We're consenting adults. What we do on our off time is no one's business but ours."

"I don't know how much off time we'll have," she said honestly. "Yes, Jamie has help, and Fallon stayed late last night because he asked her to, but I can't do that often. I can't leave him in the lurch."

"Then I guess we'll just have to steal as much time as we can in between, including lunch hours. My truck is roomy, and the heat we generate should counteract the cold weather, don't you think?"

The idea of a quickie with Hudson was as exciting as spending all day here with him. His crooked grin told her he wasn't just daring her to have sex with him in the truck. He was serious about it.

"And just where would we park your truck?"

"Oh, believe me, I'd find us a secluded spot. And the

falls aren't so far out of town that we couldn't make it there and back in an hour. If we put our minds to being together, we *can* be."

He slid a hand under her and nudged her in his direction.

"You did say we were two consenting adults," she drawled coyly. "And we could practice for that truck rendezvous."

With a low growl, he grabbed a condom packet from the nightstand. After she helped him roll it on, he pulled her on top of him, then ran his hands down her bare back. She could feel him against her, fully aroused and ready whenever she was. Maybe that's why he wanted her on top, so she could set the pace. This morning her pace would be as fast as his. She slid back and forth against him until he groaned.

"Keep that up and this will be the shortest rendezvous on record."

"Practice makes perfect," she teased and rubbed against him again.

"Bella, really, if you don't stop—"

"I'm not going to stop," she warned him. "I'm as ready as you are."

One look into her eyes and he was assured of that fact.

She rose up on her knees and then guided him inside her. She watched pleasure overtake him. Her orgasm came quickly, surprising her.

"We're not done yet," he said as he continued to stroke her. As she kept riding him, she found her body tightening all over again, the tension mounting till she thought she'd go wild. He pulled her down on him, and together they climaxed in a thunderous orgasm.

"Was that quick enough for you?" she asked after she'd collapsed on him.

"*Quick* enough but not *nearly* enough," he responded, and she smiled against his chest.

Hudson felt shaken up, off balance, unsettled and definitely out of his depth. Making love with Bella had blown his mind, and he couldn't seem to sort his thoughts or his feelings. He felt rattled to his core, though he thought he'd hidden it well. He'd tried to be practical about the whole thing. But now at work, catching glimpses of Bella now and then, he just wanted to pull her into his arms and take her to bed again.

Would they be able to work together? He wasn't sure. He had to think about their relationship at work, but he wasn't considering much more than that. The job in Big Timber? Bella's commitment to her brother? His own wanderlust? The questions seemed too big to fit into the mix right then.

Though it was the day before Thanksgiving and many of the kids were home with their families, it was almost noon by the time Bella left her desk. She came into his office, and he braced himself for the feelings that came rushing back when he saw her.

"Are you busy?" she asked.

"No more than usual. What can I do for you?" He hadn't meant the question to have a sexual undertone, but it seemed to.

She blushed a little. "We could talk about that later," she said and gave him a big smile.

He laughed, and that broke the tension—tension that had been caused by mind-blowing sex and possibly the consequences of it. But he didn't want to cut off whatever was happening between them, and apparently she didn't either.

"Jamie has help tonight, so I'm free…free for a few hours. I thought we could spend some time together."

When he didn't answer right away, she hurried to say, "It's okay if you don't want to. I just thought I'd ask." She turned to leave his office.

But he was out of his chair before she could reach the door and blocked her way. "You didn't even give me a chance to think about it."

"I didn't want to put you on the spot. It's okay if you have other things to do."

He was aware of where they were, in his office with glass windows, and teachers and kids not far away. So it wasn't as if he could hold her and reassure her.

"How would you like to put up a Christmas tree with me?" he asked.

"Really?"

He nodded. "Since we're closing early today, we'll have enough light to find one to cut down. Then I'll set it up. I have Greta's crocheted ornaments. We could buy a few more on the way to the Lazy B."

"Sounds good."

"If I didn't have glass windows where everybody can see in, I'd kiss you."

"Later," she said with a wink.

Again, he felt as if his world had rocked on its axis.

Later that afternoon, Hudson could see Bella was excited about the prospect of putting up a Christmas tree at his house. He wondered if she hadn't had many Christmas trees since her parents had died. Would her grandparents have even thought of getting a tree for two kids who needed a little Christmas?

After a stop for ornaments, they'd gone to the Lazy B, then to the stables. Now they were bundled up, riding on a buckboard to a stand of trees he'd seen while on his horse one day last week. "I'm glad we got to the general store early while they still had a collection of balls and garlands. I like your idea of blue and silver mixed with Greta's white ornaments."

"I've always wanted to decorate a Christmas tree with blue and silver," she said.

"Can you tell me why?"

"I remember one like that when my parents were still alive. Mom said it reminded her of heaven and the stars. I've always remembered that."

"Did you have Christmas trees after your parents died?" After all, if they were going to be in some kind of relationship, they should be able to ask the tougher questions.

She was quiet for a little while, but then she told him, "A Christmas tree was too much trouble for my grandparents. I snuck a little one into my room one year, after Grandma died, but Gramps said it would just make a mess and I should get rid of it."

"Did you?"

"No, I didn't," she said defensively. "I put it in my closet. Jamie and I couldn't get each other much. I used my spending money to buy yarn, and I knitted him a scarf. He gave me a card of barrettes for my hair, and we put our presents under the tree in the closet. That probably sounds silly to you."

He transferred the horses' reins to one hand and wrapped his arm around her. "It doesn't sound silly at all. The two of you were trying to make the day special."

After they rode a little bit farther, he asked, "Do you think Jamie will put up a tree this year?"

"I don't know. The triplets are still too young to understand what it would mean, even though they might like looking at all the lights. I'm afraid it would remind Jamie of his Christmases with Paula, so I don't even want to suggest it. If he decides to do it, then I'll certainly help him with it any way I can."

Hudson drew up in front of a stand of pines. He said, "We have to walk a little ways in."

"I wore my boots."

He laughed. He liked the way Bella seemed to take things in stride. He liked the way she was ready for a new adventure even if it was just cutting down a Christmas tree.

"Look around and see if you can find one you like. They might have bare spots from being too close to the other trees, but we can always fill that in with garland or ornaments."

While Hudson took a saw from the back of the buckboard, Bella forged ahead, circling the pines, one after another. He had to smile as she looked at each with a critical eye.

"Imagining those blue and silver balls on them?"

"You bet, and a silver star on the top. We were lucky they had one of those."

Yes, they had been. That silver star could make some of Bella's dreams come true. At least her Christmas tree dreams.

She called from around a pine, "If Jamie doesn't put up a tree, maybe I can bring the triplets over to see yours."

That thought startled him for a moment. The babies

in his house. Well, not *his* house, technically. What kind of havoc could they wreak? But once he thought about it, he decided he wouldn't care. Having the babies and their laughter in his house would fill it in a way that it hadn't been filled before.

Bella called from the end of a row. "I think I found one. It will be perfect."

From Hudson's experience, rarely was anything perfect. But he had to admit, Bella had found a pretty nice tree. It was about eight feet tall with no gaping holes. Now all he had to do was cut it down.

As he told Bella to stand back and he scrambled under the tree with the saw, she asked, "Have you ever done this before?"

"Believe it or not, I once worked on a Christmas tree farm."

"Why am I not surprised?"

He looked up at her. She wasn't wearing a hat, and her hair was being mussed by the wind. Her eyes were bright. Her cheeks were pink from the cold air. She'd never looked more beautiful.

"I bet I have a few more surprises up my sleeve. Or maybe not exactly up my sleeve," he said with a wink.

"You're incorrigible."

"You're not the first to tell me that. I think that was my dad's favorite word for me."

"Did you purposely try to live up to that opinion?"

"Sure. It set me apart from the others."

While she was still shaking her head, he took the saw to the base of the pine. It took elbow grease and a bit of work, but a short time later, he called to Bella to step way back, and the tree fell.

"Do you need help carrying it?" she asked.

"No. You run ahead to the buckboard and get out of the snow or you're going to be an icicle."

"No more than you are," she shot back.

"All right, if you want to help, make sure the tarp's laid out across the buckboard. That way when we want to take it in the house, we can just wrap it in the tarp."

Bella made sure the tarp was spread from one side of the wagon to the other. It seemed to cause Hudson no stress at all to pick up the tree by its trunk and load it.

Once he had, she looked at it and said, "It's going to be a beautiful tree."

Beautiful. Just like her. As he looked at her, he felt a wet flake on his nose and realized snow was falling now.

"It's just like in the movies," she said with a laugh of sheer joy. "Cutting down the Christmas tree, putting it in the buckboard and having snow fall." She lifted her hands up to the heavens as if to catch a few flakes.

There were no glass windows around them now, and no one to see them for miles. He captured Bella in his arms and swung her around. "I've never cut down a tree quite like this before."

"What do you mean?"

"Oh, I've cut down trees, but not with someone I cared about. That changes everything."

Still, if he had to list what, he probably couldn't right then. He just knew that this seemed to be the start of something.

He was still holding her when he put her on the ground. "We could have a quickie out here," he whispered into her neck.

"And literally freeze our buns off?"

"Of all times for you to be practical," he grumbled.

"Of all times for us to think about whether we'd want the exciting experience of polar lovemaking, or if we'd rather go back to your place, switch on the fire and think about doing it there."

"Both are tempting," Hudson admitted with a joking air. "Snow, pines, the buckboard and a tarp. Or a glass of wine, a blazing fire, fewer clothes to fumble with."

"I think you're convincing me. But just to make sure, let's experiment a little."

With that he took her cheeks in his hands. They were as cold as his hands were warm. The sensation of touching her like this was a once-in-a-lifetime experience. They didn't kiss at first, but rather rubbed noses. They laughed and teased, snuck cheek kisses and neck kisses before they finally came together in a lip-lock kiss.

Bella had removed the top of her gloves. Although her palms were covered with fabric, her fingers weren't. She could dive her fingers into his hair that way. And when she did, he realized they were taking freedoms with each other, and that was good.

The snow began falling harder as they experimented, him burying his nose at the base of her throat and giving her a kiss there, her reaching her hands inside his coat so she was plenty warm. He could have stood with her all night like that, rocking back and forth, kissing, snuggling.

But the snow was becoming a fuzzy curtain of white now. He whispered close to her ear, "We have to get back."

She nodded as if she knew it were so, but she gave a sigh. What they had done had been fun. They'd just have to do it again sometime.

They both had snowflakes on their hair and their eyelashes by the time they returned to the house. Edmond was at the barn to help Hudson dismantle the buckboard and take care of the horse. Hudson suggested Bella go into the house instead of staying out in the cold. He'd bring the tree inside and set it up, and then they could start decorating.

Bella said, "I'll make hot chocolate to warm us up."

Hudson gave her a look that said they didn't need hot chocolate for that. Edmond no doubt caught the look because as soon as Bella left the barn, he gave Hudson a thumbs-up.

"Something's different between the two of you," he said. "Are you a couple now?"

Hudson shrugged. "We'll see."

Were they a couple now? That was a question to ponder while he set up the tree.

Less than an hour later, Bella watched Hudson string the lights on the tree. They'd chosen tiny white twinkle lights. She thought about their excursion to cut down the pine, and she had to smile. She was so glad Jamie hadn't needed her tonight. She was so glad she could do this with Hudson. She suddenly realized that she wouldn't want to be doing it with anyone else.

The problem was, she didn't know what Hudson expected next. For that matter, she didn't know what *she* expected next. Was this just an affair or a fling? Or could it be more? If it could be more, what would happen if she told Hudson she couldn't have children? Or that at least the likelihood of it happening was very slim?

He was great with kids, even babies, but as he turned to her now and said, "Ready for the ornaments," she pushed questions and doubts out of her mind. It had been years since she'd lived in the moment, and that's what she wanted to do now. Tomorrow, her world could crash down around her. For just today, she wanted to be happy.

Hudson took a break to sip his hot chocolate. "Yours is getting cold."

She went over to the coffee table and picked up her cup. She clinked her mug against his, then she turned toward the tree. "We're doing a fine job. Do we put the star on first or save it till last?"

"Let's save it till last. Are you getting hungry?" he asked. "I put that casserole Greta made into the oven."

"That sounds good," Bella agreed. "I'll start unpacking these ornaments." As she took blue ones from the box and attached little hooks to each one, she heard Hudson moving around in the kitchen. Then she heard the buzz of his cell phone and the rumble of his voice as he spoke with someone. But she couldn't hear the conversation.

Five minutes later he returned to the living room. His expression was thoughtful. "That was Walker on the phone. We were discussing Thanksgiving tomorrow. I know you'll probably want to spend it with Jamie and the triplets. Do you have plans?"

"It snuck up on us so quickly we didn't even buy a turkey. I told Jamie I'd stop at the store on the way home tonight to buy fixings for a dinner."

"I might have a solution for that. Walker and Lindsay want you and Jamie and the triplets to come to dinner at the Dalton ranch."

"All of us?"

"All of you. Lindsay has a huge clan who think the more the merrier. Do you think Jamie will go for it?"

"He might. It would be good for all of us to get out."

"Do you want to give him a call, then I can call Walker back?"

"Sure. I can check in and make sure everything's okay, too."

At first Jamie wasn't sure he wanted to join the Daltons, but then Bella said, "Don't you think it would be good to spend the holiday away and make a new memory?"

After a moment of silence, Jamie responded, "I suppose it would. All right. Tell Hudson to tell his brother he'll have five more at his table."

When Bella did, Hudson laughed. "Apparently it's going to be a big table." He approached Bella and motioned to the ornaments on the coffee table. "We'd better get to tree decorating. What time did you tell Jamie you'd be home?"

"I told him around nine."

Hudson stepped even closer. "When we have limited time together, we have to decide what's most important—decorating the tree, eating or..."

The *or* turned into a kiss that took Bella to a place where happiness was possible, where dreams could come true and where Hudson filled her world.

Hudson was passion and sensuality and all man. Hunger swelled inside her, a hunger like she'd never known. Conscious thought didn't seem possible as Hudson's tongue plundered her mouth, as she chased it back into his, as they kissed each other like they might never do it again. She slid her hands into his thick hair, then needing the touch of skin on skin, she massaged the nape of his neck. When Hudson slid his hand under her sweater, she wanted to give him freer access. She backed away slightly, and he broke the kiss.

"We have too many clothes on," he mumbled, finding the edge of her sweater and bringing it up over her head. After he tossed it onto the sofa, he just looked at her for a few moments.

She was glad she'd worn the bra edged with lace. He unhooked it, then he began unbuttoning his shirt. Not long after, they were on the floor in front of the fire, both naked.

"Decorating the tree seemed important when we were cutting it down, but now this is more important." He whispered his hot breath against her skin as he trailed his lips down to her nipple and suckled it.

Bella thought she was ready to make love with Hudson again. But he apparently had no intention of rushing it. He laid her back on the rug and swept her body with featherlight kisses and butterfly touches, sensual, heady and thrilling. Everywhere they touched, his hands ignited a heat that threatened to sear her skin. As his hands slid down her stomach to her thigh, exquisite sensations bombarded her. This much need, this much want and this much hunger couldn't be right, could it?

She didn't have an answer to that question because she'd never experienced anything like this before. She felt like one of the logs on the fireplace grate that glowed with an inner heat that couldn't be contained.

Although Bella could feel Hudson's hunger in his kisses and his touches, she could also feel tenderness. That's what undid her most of all. Leaning over her on the rug, Hudson kissed her once more while his hand slipped between her thighs. He wanted to see how ready she was. She passed her hand down his back to his backside and heard the growl that came from deep in his throat.

"Do you know what you do to me?" he asked her.

"Probably the same thing you do to me."

"Don't move," he said, sitting up, reaching for his jeans. She knew what he was doing. He was getting a condom from his pocket. She should tell him now. She should reveal that she could become pregnant yet would probably never be able to carry a baby to term. But she didn't say anything. She didn't want to spoil this day by ending it with a conversation that could separate them completely.

A minute later he was poised over her again, looking down into her shadowed eyes, and she wished she could take a picture of him right there and then. Then he entered her, and she held on to him tightly, wishing the moment could last forever. Wishing reality wouldn't poke its head back into her life. Wishing she'd been more responsible as a teenager so that she didn't have a secret to keep now.

She knew she couldn't keep the secret much longer because she wanted honesty between her and Hudson as much as she wanted anything else.

Chapter 12

Jamie's huge SUV maneuvered easily over a light coating of snow on the way to the Dalton ranch—the Circle D. It was located about a half hour out of town.

Bella glanced over her shoulder at the triplets, who were in their car seats behind her. "They seem content for the moment."

"Let's wait and see what happens when we get into a crowd. I'm not sure this was a good idea."

"They have to get out sometime, Jamie. Besides, did you really want to spend the holiday alone?" Sometimes she suspected it was more than protectiveness that kept Jamie from being out and about with his children. Was it grief or was there something else?

"I wouldn't have been alone," he said wryly.

"You know what I mean. Spending the day with the Daltons should be fun."

"We'll see," he responded, obviously not sure of that fact. He glanced at her quickly, then moved his eyes back to the road. "I think this was more about you spending the holiday with Hudson."

He had her there. Still, she said, "It's not like we'll have time alone."

"I'm sure you can steal a few minutes. You're getting more involved with him, aren't you?"

If "more involved" meant sleeping with him, yes, she was. But she wasn't willing to go into that with her brother.

When she was silent, Jamie said, "I worry about you."

"You don't have to."

"You gave up your life to help me. Of course I have to. You *are* going to go back to school, aren't you?"

"Eventually."

"Sooner, rather than later."

"Jamie, I don't know what's going to happen next."

"You mean with Hudson?"

She sighed. "With Hudson. With my job. With the triplets, even. I want to make sure you and the babies are stable before I consider doing anything else."

"We have our routine. We're doing well. If you go back to school, I'll look around for somebody else to help. Even if I have to pay them."

"You can't afford to do that. The ranch expenses are up, not to mention everything you need for the triplets."

"You're not trapped, Bella. I don't want you to think you are. I would figure something out."

She was sure he would. Still, she felt that he needed her.

"Did you tell Hudson yet about your miscarriage and your…problem?"

"No."

"How serious does it have to get before you do?"

"Everything with Hudson has happened so fast. I have to feel the time is right."

"The longer you wait, the harder it's going to be to tell him."

"I know," she said. But today wasn't going to be the day, not in the middle of a family Thanksgiving celebration. She was sure of that.

Shortly after their conversation ended, Jamie took the turnoff to the Circle D. At the fork in the road, Jamie said, "One of the Dalton brothers lives over there in that white house with the green shutters."

Each Dalton sibling was allotted land within the ranch borders. Although Ben Dalton and his wife, Mary, owned the ranch, Ben was a lawyer and didn't devote much time to it. His son Anderson was in charge and managed it for him. As Jamie drove a ways, Bella wondered what it would be like to belong to a large family and have everyone live close by. That would be nice.

After driving farther, Bella caught a glimpse of the stables. When they reached the main ranch house, she stayed in the car with Katie and Henry, while Jamie took Jared inside. She expected to see Jamie come back out, but instead Hudson did.

He approached the car door and said, "Your brother trusted me to help get the babies inside."

That was saying a lot, she supposed, because Jamie didn't trust just anyone with the triplets. They detached both car carriers from the backseat and carried them into the house.

Already there was a group of adults gathered around

Jared, oohing and aahing. When Hudson and Bella brought the other two over, everyone made room. Lindsay and Walker welcomed them, and then the entire Dalton clan descended on them. The parents, Ben and Mary, as well as Anderson and his wife, Marina, with their blended family of eleven-year-old Jake and baby Sydney. There was brother Travis, a bachelor; Lani Dalton with her fiancé, Russ Campbell; and Caleb Dalton and his wife, Mallory, and their ten-year-old daughter, Lily. And, finally, Paige and her husband, Sutter, who cast watchful eyes over their two-year-old son, Carter.

In the center of the crowd, Lindsay smiled. "And this is just the tip of the Dalton iceberg. Uncle Charles is having Thanksgiving with his five kids. My other uncles, Phillip, Neal and Steven, have big families, too, but they live in another part of Montana."

Lindsay's mom, Mary, was particularly welcoming. She picked up Katie from her car carrier and said, "Aren't you pretty? With two brothers to treat you like a princess."

"Or pull her hair," her husband, Ben, said, and everyone laughed.

"We have high chairs so the triplets won't miss any of the celebration." She looked at Bella. "Do you want to come with me to see what else they might need?"

Hudson offered, "I can set up those high chairs."

"Thank you," Mary said. "Come on with me."

"I'll take Katie," Lindsay offered. She whispered to Bella, "It will do Walker good to be around babies."

For the second time in the last few weeks, Bella wondered if Lindsay might be wanting a child soon. Would Walker take to kids as his brother had?

Kids. It always came down to kids.

"What's wrong?" Hudson asked her as they followed Mary to the kitchen.

"Nothing," Bella said lightly. "I'm just hoping we can keep the triplets occupied during dinner so everyone can enjoy it."

"We can always take one out at a time and walk him or her. The Daltons are used to kids. I'm sure everyone will be sitting around the table long enough that a little excursion in and out with a baby won't spoil dinner at all."

In the kitchen, Mary pulled dishes from the cupboard, and Bella chose the ones she thought would be best for the triplets. "I have baby spoons in the diaper bag," she said. "Jamie will warm up their food right before we eat, if that's okay. He likes to maintain a stable diet for them."

"Maybe with a spoonful of mashed potatoes or two?" Mary asked with a twinkle in her eye.

"Maybe," Bella agreed.

A peal of laughter came from the living room, followed by lots of chatter.

"This is a real Thanksgiving," Hudson said.

"Your family doesn't get together for the holidays?" Mary asked him.

"My brothers are scattered all over now, and Mom and Dad are traveling. So, no, we don't. It's rare that even Walker and I are together."

"This *must* be a treat then. One of those holidays to remember. I'm glad you all could join us."

Hudson picked up one of the collapsed high chairs that were leaning against a wall. "Any place special you want me to set this up?"

"No. Just fit them in wherever you can. I'm sure whoever is next to a baby will see to their needs. This is a child-friendly family."

Hudson carried a high chair into the dining room.

Mary turned to Bella. "What about you, child? I suppose you and your brother spend most of your holidays together."

"Yes, we do."

"I imagine this one is particularly hard for him. I hope being among friends will help. I've heard about the baby chain that takes care of the triplets."

"I don't know what we'd do without them. Not only in the care of the babies, but they've helped Jamie not draw into himself even more. They're kind and considerate, and he almost thinks of them as family now."

"One of the things I like most about this community is that we help others. I'm sorry that Lindsay and the day care center were at odds for a while. You know, don't you, that she was just doing her job?"

"Oh, I know that. I'm just glad everything turned out as well as it did."

"I hear that's your Hudson's doing."

"Oh, he's not *my* Hudson."

Mary laughed. "You can say that, but I see something else."

When Hudson returned to the kitchen for a second high chair, Bella knew her cheeks were flushed. When he left again, Mary said to her, "After dinner, when everyone's settling in to watch TV or chat, you and Hudson ought to take a walk down to the stables. There's a new horse there you both might enjoy. Her name is Trixie…a fine quarter horse."

As Hudson returned to the kitchen, he heard the last part of that.

"Wouldn't you like to see our new horse?" she asked him.

"I'm always interested in a good horse. I'm sure Bella is, too. She doesn't just ride them, she photographs them. She did some work for the Smith Rescue Ranch."

"Really?" Mary asked.

"Jazzy and Brooks liked some of my shots, and they're using them on their pamphlets and on their website," Bella explained. "The redesigned website should be up by Monday. You should take a look if you get a chance."

"I'm not much into computers, but my husband and all my kids have them. So sure, I'll take a look. Now, come on. We have potatoes to mash, beans to dress and a turkey to carve."

When they were all finally seated around the table for the Thanksgiving meal, it was loud and fun. Many conversations traversed the room, and Bella couldn't keep track of them all. The triplets seemed mesmerized by all the people, let alone the food being passed around. So they were entertained while they ate.

She and Hudson had been seated next to each other. Every once in a while, Hudson would reach over and place his hand on her thigh. That simple contact sent a charge through her body, and she hoped it didn't show on her face. Now and then, however, she saw Lindsay looking at her speculatively. And one time Mary Dalton gave her a wink.

The talk among the men turned to ranching for a while. The women shared recipes, as well as caught up with their careers. Bella felt as if she were somewhere in between. Managing the day care center was not going to be her career. She took care of the triplets with Jamie and could easily discuss that. But she had her foot in two different worlds. Throw in her feelings for Hudson, and it was difficult to come up with a life plan, especially when she didn't know if he'd be staying or going…especially when she didn't know if he could accept not having children of his own.

She joined conversations, but her thoughts were jumbled. The only thing she did know was that she loved being with Hudson. She loved making love with him. She loved *him.*

By dessert time, the triplets were getting restless. Bella, Jamie and Paige took them from the high chairs and set them on their laps, distracting them with rattles and little toys.

Paige said, "The pageant on Sunday is going to be a hoot. Imagine all those babies, kids, costumes and Christmas."

"I'm going to have a look at the carriages tomorrow," Hudson said. "They're at the school and all decorated. I want to make sure there's nothing the babies shouldn't get hold of. I also need to get a few basic instructions to take to my staff. We aren't having a dress rehearsal with the rest of the group." He shrugged. "It's not as if our little ones have a script."

Everybody laughed.

"I'm sure they'll cause a lot of ad-lib moments," Ben said. "You can't have babies around and expect everything to go as planned."

"How about more whipped cream on that pumpkin pie?" Mary asked.

Mary and Ben had blocked off one area of the living room so the babies could crawl around and play with their toys in relative safety. Jamie sat on the floor with them, and Paige did, too. Jamie said to Bella, "If you want to go for a walk or anything, go ahead. We're fine for a while."

Paige waved at her. "We've got this."

Bella looked up at Hudson, who immediately got to his feet.

"I'll go get our coats," he said. "We'll take a look at that new horse."

As they made their way from the house to the barn, Hudson took Bella's arm. "Do you think you can get away for a few hours Saturday evening? I'd like to take you into Kalispell for a surprise."

"I'll have to talk to Jamie and see if he has other help."

"That's fine. I'd just like to take you on a real date. We can get dressed up, go to dinner, and then I'll show you my surprise."

Bella had no idea what Hudson was going to surprise her with, but whatever it was, the idea excited her.

The stables on the Circle D were a classic rectangular shape. Hudson opened the door for Bella and flipped on a switch just inside. The overhead light revealed a long center aisle with stalls on each side and a door at the other end, too. As they walked down the aisle, they saw plaques with the horses' names. They passed one for a giant black horse named Zorro.

"I think they have the heater on in here," Hudson said. "It's not as cold as outside."

Hudson was right, and Bella unzipped her parka as he unbuttoned his. They walked farther in, finally stopping in front of Trixie's stall. She was a cute little chestnut. The horse turned from her trough and gave them an interested look.

Bella held out her hand. "Come here, pretty girl. Let me pet you."

The horse apparently liked the sound of a friendly voice, because she turned and came to Bella, hanging her head over the slats so Bella could touch her nose. "No matter how many times I touch a horse's nose, I'm always amazed at the softness."

"I know what you mean," Hudson said. But there was a huskiness to his voice that made her think he was talking about her rather than the horse.

"You and Mary seemed to hit it off," he said.

"Yes, we did. She's nice."

He laid a hand on Bella's shoulder. "I feel for you that you lost your mother."

"Thank you. Lindsay's lucky. This whole family is lucky that they're still together and have each other."

"I think they realize that. Anderson does a great job managing the place. He wants to do it not just for himself, but for his family."

Bella had noticed more than the family atmosphere today. She'd noticed the couples in love—Lindsay and Walker, Anderson and Marina, Paige and Sutter, Caleb and Mallory. Had she been aware of them because of her own feelings for Hudson? If happily-ever-after was possible for *them*, maybe it was possible for *her*.

Suddenly she was very aware of Hudson beside her. He sidled closer and put his arm around her.

"Every time I'm close to you, I want to kiss you," he murmured in her ear.

She turned into his arms. "I feel like that, too."

Slowly he lowered his mouth to hers. This wasn't one

of those quick let's-do-it-before-we-can't kisses. It was one of those I-want-to-take-my-time-with-you kisses. He began it softly but with the firm pressure of his lips. Seconds later, his tongue teased the seam of her mouth.

Her heart was beating so fast she couldn't breathe. But she didn't have to breathe. Not when Hudson was giving her his air, his taste, his desire. Her hand slipped into the collar of his jacket, felt his sweater and then the skin of his neck. Hudson's body was becoming more familiar now. She could feel the tension in it because of the need coursing through him, just like the need coursing through her.

His hand caressed the side of her face, then moved down her sweater to her breasts.

She nipped at his mouth, and he took that for assent of what he was doing. She was assenting all right. She couldn't seem to get enough of him. The stable seemed to spin around her, and she clung to Hudson as if he were the only thing in her world that was stable. He took her tongue deeper into his mouth, and she melted against him. His palm on her breast was replaced with his fingers as he kneaded her and searched for her nipple under the sweater. When he found it, she knew it was hard, and she could imagine him doing things to it with his tongue.

He groaned, dropped his hands to the waistband of the sweater and dived underneath. Skimming her stomach, they came to rest on her bra. Masterfully he flipped open the front catch, and then he was holding her, caressing her breasts, making her want him with a need so strong she could only hope it would soon be satisfied.

He said roughly, "I want you." He brought her hips

tight against his so she could feel how hard he was and just how much he wanted her.

All of a sudden, Trixie neighed. The sound penetrated Bella's passionate haze. Then she heard bootfalls and the clearing of a throat.

"I was going to turn around and leave, but you might as well know that I know."

It was Walker's voice.

Hudson backed away slowly, but made sure Bella's coat was closed over her sweater. He wrapped his arm around her and faced his brother. "Don't you say a word," he warned Walker. "Not after what you and Lindsay did."

Bella knew her eyes were wide, and she felt stricken. No matter what Hudson had said, Walker owned the Just Us Kids franchise. Would her job be in jeopardy?

As if Hudson understood what she was thinking, he said to Walker, "This won't affect my working relationship with Bella."

Walker focused on Bella. "Your job is safe. You don't have to worry about that. No one could have handled everything as well as you have, especially with Hudson coming in to oversee you." He motioned to his brother and then to her. "In fact, this attraction between you might have helped that along, encouraged both of you to work for the good of the center."

"Then why does it matter that you *know*? You could have turned around and left and saved us a lot of embarrassment."

"I could have. But I still need to know if you're staying until Valentine's Day, or if you're going to leave before that for the job in Big Timber."

"And you have to ask me *now*?"

"Maybe it's a good thing I am, because Bella has to know, too, doesn't she? Or is she just another diversion until you're on your way?"

Bella's heart sank because Walker knew Hudson's history. And he knew Hudson's nature, too. If she was just a diversion, was she going to let their affair continue?

"I have to give Big Timber my answer on Monday," Hudson said. "I'll give you my answer then, too."

"So you haven't made up your mind?" Walker asked as if he expected nothing less.

"I'm still considering the pros and cons."

Again Walker looked from one of them to the other. And then he nodded and walked away.

They both heard the barn door close. They'd been so engrossed in their kiss, they hadn't heard it open.

Quickly Bella reached under her sweater and fastened her bra. She moved away from Hudson, thinking about everything Walker had said. Then she looked up at the tall cowboy and asked, "So you really don't know yet if you're staying or going?" Though she knew that if he stayed until Valentine's Day, that didn't mean he was going to stay longer.

He took her by the shoulders. "Bella, there's a lot to think about. Believe me, I'll tell you before I tell anyone else what I decide."

She supposed that was something, but it certainly wasn't enough.

"Are we still on for our date Saturday night?" he asked.

She thought of saying no and ending it then, so she could start nursing her heart back to health. But her heart wouldn't let her say it.

"Yes, we're still on for our date." Whether he stayed or whether he left, she loved Hudson Jones. For this weekend, that was going to be all that mattered.

Hudson glanced over at Bella on Saturday evening as she stared out the front windshield, eagerly anticipating where they were going. So far, everything had gone smashingly well. She'd joined him at the dress rehearsal for the pageant, so she'd be able to give teachers direction, too. Although there was tension between them because his decision about Big Timber was still in the offing, they'd seemed to put that aside during the dress rehearsal as well as at dinner tonight.

He'd taken her to the fanciest restaurant in Kalispell. She'd dressed festively in a beautiful long-sleeved red dress. Although the dress seemed modestly cut, its folds accented all her curves in just the right places. When he'd picked her up, she'd looked at him as if he were some kind of *GQ* model, which was crazy since he was wearing a Western-cut suit and bolo tie, a Stetson and boots. She'd given him a smile that had practically twirled his bolo.

Dinner was incredible, but the night wasn't over. He still had one more destination. To make conversation while he drove, he asked, "Do you think we're really ready for the pageant tomorrow? All those babies and kids at one place at one time—"

"We're as ready as we're ever going to be. Sometimes the more you regiment children, the more chaos you provoke. For the most part, all we have to do is make sure the babies are in their carriages and hope that the carriage decorations don't fall off. The one that looked like Santa's sleigh was pretty elaborate."

"The older kids really worked hard on them." Hudson was finding that he liked kids more and more… from babies to high-schoolers. And when he thought of kids, he thought of Bella. He didn't examine that thought too closely because he knew exactly where it might lead—Bella as a mom, him as a dad, a family like the Daltons had someday.

He glanced at Bella again and decided to concentrate on the here and now—on his attraction to her and on her surprise.

There were several cars parked in front of the building already. He pulled up to the curb in front of a bakery storefront.

Bella looked puzzled as he went around his truck and helped her out. She was wearing high-heeled boots, and he didn't want her to slip or fall.

"The bakery's closed," she said in a puzzled voice.

"We're not going to the bakery. I'd have you shut your eyes, but there are some icy spots."

"Why would you want me to shut my eyes?"

"You aren't used to surprises, are you?"

"Not good ones."

Hooking his arm into hers, he guided her along the sidewalk until they came to the Artfully Yours gallery. She looked up, saw the name and blinked. "You want to buy a painting?"

"You never know," he said with a smile.

They went up the steps, and he opened the door to lead her inside. At first, there didn't seem to be a huge selection. The gallery owner was selective on what he hung where, on what sculptures he positioned on pedestals.

The gallery manager came to greet Hudson, and they

shook hands. Hudson had spoken with Jim Barringer on the phone several times. Jim gave Hudson a nod, and he led Bella to a side exhibit set in an alcove.

"Aren't you going to let me look at the paintings?" she started to ask, but then her eyes settled on the photographs hanging in the alcove. "Oh my gosh! They're mine. My photos. They're matted and framed."

"As well they should be. This isn't your own show… yet. But it is a showing. Notice the little red dots on two of them? That means they're sold."

Bella's mouth dropped open as she noticed the two sold prints—the landscape she'd shot at sunrise at the Stockton ranch and the close-up of one of the horses. The frames were perfect, rough-hewn like barn wood.

Bella turned to Hudson. "Did you do this?"

Hudson wondered again if he'd been too high-handed by doing it without her permission.

But then she threw her arms around his neck. "I can't believe you did this."

He squeezed her hard. "I didn't do the framing. I left most of that up to Jim, though he did ask my opinion. I just happened to know the gallery owner and asked him to take a look at your photographs. He thought they were well worth showing. You could have more than one career, if you want it, Bella."

Unmindful of where they were and who was around, Bella gave him a smacking kiss on the lips. When she broke away, she said, "Thank you."

"I'd do it again for another kiss like that," he teased.

She looked around the gallery. "I can't believe my photographs are hung here with all these talented artists."

"You're talented, too. You have to know that."

"Maybe I'm starting to."

For the next hour, they went from painting to painting...from sculpture to sculpture...from photograph to photograph until Bella had her fill.

On the drive back to Rust Creek Falls, Hudson thought that Bella might want to call Jamie and tell him her news. But she didn't. She just kept glancing at him, putting her hand on his thigh, looking at him as if he was Christmas all wrapped up in a cowboy package.

"Do you want to stop at my place?" he asked as they neared town.

"More than anything," she answered with such fervor that it took Hudson's self-control to the limit not to press down hard on the accelerator.

When they reached his house, he hurried out of the truck, going around to her side. When he opened her door, he saw longing in her eyes, too. He lifted her down from the truck and held on to her as they walked to the door. He fumbled with the keys as he tried to get the door open. All he could think about was holding her in his arms...naked. Time alone with her was precious, and honestly, he didn't know how much more they'd have.

After he punched in the code for the alarm, he took her into his arms, kissing her the way he'd wanted to kiss her all night. The ride home had seemed endless. He shrugged off his jacket, letting it fall to the floor. She was still unzipping her parka when he helped push it from her shoulders and let that fall, too. Her breath and his heightened and so did every look between them, every brush of their fingers, every touch of their skin. Bella's ability to return his hunger still amazed him. She undid his tie while he found the zipper at the back of her dress and ran it down its track. She unbuttoned his shirt while he pushed her dress down off her shoulders. It weighed on her arms as she was trying to undress him.

He laughed and said, “I can probably do it faster.”

By the time he finished undressing himself and her, their clothes lay in a pile in the foyer. They couldn’t seem to wait to reach the living room to touch each other. When her hands slid up his chest, he was a goner. He kissed her hard, and she returned his fervor, clutching his shoulders, pressing against him until he thought he’d die from the wanting. Lacing his fingers into her hair, he angled her head for another kiss.

When he broke away this time, she murmured, “I’m ready. We don’t have to wait.”

“Yes, we do,” he said. “I have to grab a condom. Don’t move.”

She didn’t.

“Turn around,” he said, and she followed his gentle order, bracing her hands on the wall.

He wanted to give Bella every experience, every pleasure, every peaked orgasm. He just had to hold on a little longer. Stepping close behind her, he ran his hands over her breasts, teased her nipples, then slid his hands down her sides to her hips.

She understood what he wanted to do, and in the next second, he was thrusting inside her, pulling back, then doing it again until she moaned with as much pleasure as he felt. The wall braced them both as he felt her release come first, and then his followed. He rested his chin on her shoulder, and then he just held her.

When he could breathe again almost normally, he said, “Now we can try that in bed and take it a little slower.”

She turned into his arms, wrapped hers around his neck and placed a kiss on his lips so tender that he thought he'd fall apart at the seams.

Scooping her up into his arms, he carried her to the bedroom, wanting to make each moment they had together last as long as it could.

Chapter 13

On Sunday afternoon, Hudson felt a bit like a horse in the midst of a cattle stampede. It looked and felt as if everyone in Rust Creek Falls had come to the holiday pageant! That was understandable, he guessed, since the pageant was an important event and there wasn't much else in the way of entertainment in the small town.

Chairs had been set up in rows in the elementary school gymnasium with an aisle down the center. Teachers and volunteers milled about backstage along with a few parents, under the watchful eye of Eileen Bennet.

Classes from the elementary school had already performed. Scenery for the production had been swiveled around for two different segments. The first was an old-time scene where kids in costumes from the 1900s paraded onto the stage. The audience had been invited to sing traditional Christmas carols. The second segment depicted the 1960s with women and girls dressed in maxi-coats, fur rimming their hoods, and men in peacoats. More carols accompanied by the piano had brought a rousing response from the audience.

Now the audience awaited the third and last segment, a modern-day rendition of the holidays. In this segment, children would parade across the stage in Christmas finery. Bella had decked herself out in her red dress. Hudson had complied with the theme by wearing a green sweater and black jeans. Other teachers had dressed in holiday colors, and they would push the decorated carriages onto the stage. They would be followed by a wagon with kids and, of course, Santa Claus, who was actually one of the big, burly, white-bearded dads.

From the sidelines, Hudson heard one of the teachers call, "Quentin spit up! Paper towels, quick."

Another teacher shouted, "Mary's carriage is supposed to be in line before Monica's. Switch them. The parents know the order and will be upset if we don't have it right."

Bella, who was two carriages behind Hudson's, caught his eye. She gave him a thumbs-up and smiled. That smile. He remembered the sleepy expression on her face and the sparkle in her eyes after they'd made love last night.

Suddenly the baby in Bella's carriage lifted up his arms to her. She didn't hesitate to lift him out even though they were almost ready to go on. A baby's needs would certainly take priority over the pageant. She cuddled him and cooed to him, straightened his reindeer antlers and set him back in the carriage, handing him a rattle.

Hudson suddenly felt the need to go to her. Snagging the attention of Sarah Palmer, he asked, "Can you watch this young gentleman for a moment? I need to talk to Bella."

"Sure," Sarah agreed. "We have about five minutes until we push our carriages out onto the stage."

Going to Bella's side, Hudson asked, "How do you think things are going?"

"Great, so far. The audience is really involved. Now, if not too many babies cry once the carriages are on the stage, we'll have succeeded."

He chuckled, then looked over the scene before him with all the carriages lined up and children and teachers milling about. He motioned to the carriages. "I remember all the rumors about how these babies were conceived because of the wedding punch at Jennifer McCallum and Ben Traub's wedding. Supposedly, Homer Gilmore spiked it with a magic potion and there were lots of romantic hookups because of it. When I first came to town, I heard that some couples came here who were hoping to have a baby because they thought the magic might rub off on them."

Bella's face suddenly took on an odd expression. The sadness was back in her eyes, and he didn't understand any of it. But he did understand one very important thing, as if a lightning bolt had hit him. He never wanted her to be sad. He wanted to protect her...forever. He realized that he loved Bella Stockton, and he was going to do something about it.

Someone near the curtain gave a signal, and he gave Bella's arm a squeeze. "I have to get back to my carriage. See you after?"

She nodded and said, "Sure."

A few of the babies did cry as the carriages rolled out

in front of Santa and the children on the stage sang "Jingle Bells" with the audience. Hudson, however, wasn't living in the moment right now. All he could do was stare at Bella and wish the pageant was over. He had something to say to her, and he couldn't wait to say it.

He should have seen his love for her before now, but maybe he'd been blinded by the chemistry between them, by the passion that seemed to supersede everything else when he was around her. Bella Stockton was everything he'd ever wanted in a woman without even realizing it. She was smart and challenging and sweet. Most of all, she knew how to care and she knew how to love. That was evident in her loyalty to her brother, her love for the triplets, her care of every child at Just Us Kids.

Hudson realized now that home wasn't so much a place. It could be a person. He wanted to make Bella his home and hoped she felt the same about him. He realized now he could make a life in Rust Creek Falls with her, and he had an idea about that. He was going to get on his cell phone and make sure that dream could come true as soon as he talked to Bella. Maybe he'd always been a rich man, but he hadn't felt rich before. With Bella by his side, he knew he could be a better man than he'd ever been. They'd raise a family together, and they'd hand down values that could last through the years. She'd never said how many kids she might want, but he didn't care about that. Two, four or five. They'd talk about it. They'd kiss about it. They'd make love about it.

Hudson spotted Walker and Lindsay in the audience. Not far away, he spied Jamie with the triplets in their stroller. Fallon was with him. Hudson gave him a big smile and a thumbs-up, and Jamie grinned back. The green headband on Katie's little blond hair tilted sideways. Jamie straightened it with such a loving expression on his face that Hudson knew he couldn't wait to be a dad. Would Bella want to have kids right away, or wait awhile? There was so much to talk about, so much to look forward to, so many dreams to fulfill.

With all the people and babies and kids involved in the pageant, it was almost an hour later until the scenery had been stowed in the wings, until parents had been reunited with their children, until the audience who had come to mingle as well as to watch the show drifted out of the auditorium.

Bella, who had helped stow the babies' reindeer headbands in a plastic bin, snapped on the lid and stacked it with boxes that held other costumes. Hudson was about to burst with what he wanted to say to Bella.

As they walked to the exit, he cloaked his excitement and asked her, "Do you have to get back to the ranch right away?"

She zipped up her parka and hoisted her hobo bag over her shoulder. "I do," she said. "Fallon helped Jamie at the pageant, but she can't stay. I told Jamie I'd be there to help feed and bathe the babies."

Hudson felt a pang of disappointment, but he knew this was Bella's life. They'd have to talk about that along with everything else. But right now, he had to take a few minutes to tell her how he felt. He couldn't hold it in any longer.

"I know we don't have much time…" He took her hands in his. "But I want you to know how much last night meant to me."

"It meant a lot to me, too," she responded. "I can't

thank you enough for recommending me to Artfully Yours. But beyond that, Hudson, I've never spent time with a man like you."

"And I've never spent time with a woman like you. And because of that, I have to tell you something, Bella." He drew in a shaky breath and then went for it. "I love you. I want to marry you and make a life with you that includes lots of babies." He gave her a broad smile. "Will you marry me?"

Hudson expected an enthusiastic "yes." He expected Bella to throw her arms around his neck and say that she loved him, too. He expected they'd both be hearing wedding bells instead of silver bells. But none of those things happened. Instead, Bella burst into tears, turned away from him and pushed out the exit door.

It took him a moment to realize what had happened. The door had swung shut, and he pushed out after her.

"Bella, wait," he yelled.

But she was headed to her car.

He took off at a run after her, but when he caught up to her at the driver's side door, she was shaking her head. "I can't give you want you want. Not ever."

Hudson was so shell-shocked he couldn't move, think or talk. In the next few moments, she started the engine, backed up and drove away.

Just what had caused *that* reaction? More important, what was he going to do about it?

Hudson spent the rest of the evening trying to decide the best thing to do. He could make Bella face him, but he wasn't sure that would do any good. She had to *want* to talk to him. He didn't want to force her.

That evening when his cell phone beeped, he grabbed

it up, hoping beyond hope it was Bella. But Jamie Stockton's number showed up.

"Jamie, is Bella all right?" he asked before the rancher could get a word out.

"She asked me to call you. She's taking a sick day tomorrow."

"A sick day? To avoid me?"

He heard Jamie's sigh. Hudson knew Bella might be right there and her brother couldn't talk freely. With insight, he realized talking to her brother might be better than talking to Bella right now.

He asked, "Can you get an hour away at lunch tomorrow?"

Jamie responded cautiously, "I might be able to. Why?"

"Can you meet me at the Ace in the Hole? I need to talk to you about Bella. I only want the best for her. I love her, Jamie."

"All right," Jamie said.

"Around one okay?" Hudson asked.

"If it's not, I'll let you know."

Jamie ended the call without saying more, and Hudson knew Bella was probably listening and Jamie didn't want her to know about their meeting. She might feel her brother was betraying her.

Hudson didn't want to cause a rift between them, but he had to find out what was going on.

The next morning dragged on so slowly Hudson could count each second. He left for the Ace in the Hole fifteen minutes early, found a table there, ordered coffee and drummed his fingers until Jamie Stockton walked in the door.

Jamie saw him and headed toward the table. After

he unzipped his jacket, he looked at Hudson's coffee. "I thought you might be drinking something stronger."

"I need a clear head for this conversation," Hudson said. "I need a clear head for this whole situation."

Jamie signaled a waitress and pointed to Hudson's coffee and at his own place. She nodded. Seconds later, he had a mug of black coffee in front of him, too.

"What's on your mind?" he asked Hudson.

"We need to talk, man-to-man, brother to the man who loves your sister."

"I don't know if a talk will do any good," Jamie said.

Hudson felt there was a closed door in front of him, but he wasn't going to let it stay closed. He was going to open it. Heck, he was going to push through it. "Look. I know Bella has a lot of baggage. I want to know the best way to help her deal with it."

Jamie eyed him and asked, "What do you want?"

"I want a future with her. I want a life with her—a family and kids."

A shadow passed over Jamie's face, the same shadow that Hudson had seen on Bella's. Then Jamie seemed to make up his mind. "Yes, Bella has a lot of baggage. She felt abandoned like I did when our parents died. She felt rejected when our grandparents didn't want our siblings and didn't want us either, though they took us in. But her hurts aren't as simple as all that."

"Simple? There's nothing simple about being abandoned. What else is there?"

"I'm only telling you this because I think it's best for Bella. She rebelled against our grandparents' rejection. She became a little…wild. She looked for love in the wrong places. She got pregnant, and she had a miscarriage. Because of that miscarriage, she probably will never be able to have children."

If Hudson had been shocked by Bella's response yesterday, he was even more shocked by what Jamie had told him. He felt numb. She might never be able to have children? It was so much to take in, and he didn't know how he felt about all of it.

He thought about how intimate he and Bella had been, and he couldn't help but mutter, "Why didn't she trust me enough to tell me?"

"I think you can answer that yourself. For a lot of years, I don't think she's trusted anybody but me."

"I feel so sorry for her."

"But?" Jamie asked with a probing look.

"My heart hurts at the idea of not having kids with her."

"That's why I told you this. If you can't deal with the idea of no kids, then you should walk away now. Don't hurt Bella further by rejection later." He nodded to Hudson's coffee cup. "Do you want something stronger than that now?"

Hudson glanced at the bar and all the bottles behind it. "No, I still need a clear head to think this through. Thanks for your honesty."

Jamie picked up his mug, took a couple of swallows of coffee and set it back down. As Bella's brother rose to his feet and then left, Hudson was hardly aware of it. He was too lost in his thoughts.

The sun was barely up the next morning when Bella stood at Hudson's door and rang the bell. She was shaking. She didn't know if this was the right thing or the wrong thing to do. She didn't know if Hudson would even let her inside after the way she'd left him.

When he didn't answer the door, Bella wondered if he'd gone riding or already left for the day. She could check the garage to see if his truck was there.

Just as she was about to do that, the door opened and Hudson stood there, his expression totally unreadable. She could tell one thing, though. He looked tired, as if she'd gotten him out of bed. His hair was sleep-mussed, there was a heavy stubble on his jaw and his feet were bare under a pair of sweatpants.

"I'm sorry if I woke you," she said.

"No harm," he returned evenly.

She wasn't sure about that. "May I come in?"

He ran his hand through his mussed hair and pulled down his T-shirt. "I haven't even had a cup of coffee yet. Are you sure you want to talk to me now?"

There was an edge of something in his voice, and she supposed she deserved that. She hadn't wanted to talk to him Sunday or yesterday. Coffee or not, she'd take her chances today.

"Yes, I need to talk to you."

His eyebrows arched at the words. He backed up in the foyer so she could enter.

After she did, she closed the door behind her, wishing he'd react more, say something, do something. Like kiss her?

That was wishful thinking.

She had done nothing but think and cry and worry since she'd left him Sunday. She'd helped Jamie with the triplets but told him she didn't want to talk about any of it. She couldn't, not until she figured out what she was going to do. Jamie had pretty much left her alone because he'd known this was her problem to solve and her life to lead. All she could think about all day yesterday and last night was how her heart hurt because she loved Hudson so much. She loved him enough to walk away if that's what he wanted. But she had to be honest with him, and she had to tell him everything first. That was only fair after what they'd shared.

Hudson led her into the living room and sat in the armchair. Maybe he expected her to sit on the sofa, but she didn't want to be that far away. She needed to make eye contact with him, and she needed to be close. So she sat on the large ottoman in front of him.

He looked surprised and maybe a bit uncomfortable.

How could she mess this up any more than she already had? But she wasn't going to scurry away now. "I'd like to tell you…everything."

"Everything?"

"You know most of it, but…" She couldn't lose her courage now. She plunged right into her story. "I felt so lost after my parents died."

She thought she saw a glimmer of compassion in his eyes, but she couldn't be sure. But she hadn't come here for pity, so she hurried on. "Jamie and I missed our five other brothers and sisters. It was like one minute we had a family and the next we didn't. Grandma and Gramps didn't want us, and…" She lifted her hands as if she didn't have to explain any more about that. "I told you I was wild, and you didn't believe me, but I was. I'm not the woman you thought I was, Hudson. When I was a teenager, I wasn't smart or mature. I was fifteen, and I ended up dating and sleeping with an older boy."

"How old?" Hudson asked, and she couldn't tell if there was judgment there or not.

"He was almost eighteen. I got pregnant. I thought he loved me. I thought we'd have a family. But I was so stupid. He didn't want any responsibilities. When I told him I was pregnant, he said it wasn't his."

"You could have proved otherwise."

"I could have. My guess is Gramps would have made me prove it to get child support. But we never had to do that." She heard the quaver in her voice and swallowed hard. When she spoke again, she'd regained her composure. The only way she'd get through this was to blurt it out. "There were complications with the pregnancy. I lost the baby, and the doctor said I might never be able to have another one. I have a weak cervix. I can possibly *get* pregnant, but I'd never carry the baby to term."

Before Hudson could say anything, she pushed on. "My grandparents kept the whole thing secret. I wasn't showing when the miscarriage happened, and I certainly hadn't told anybody but the boy, and he wasn't saying anything to anybody. After Grandma died, Gramps said I caused her heart attack with the stress of my pregnancy and what happened afterward. That's what killed her."

"He was wrong," Hudson said with more expression than she'd heard yet.

"I don't know if he was or not. The only saving grace was that my parents weren't alive to see it."

"If your parents had been alive, the whole situation probably wouldn't have happened," Hudson reminded her.

"I know you probably think less of me now. I know you probably want your own children more than you want me. It wasn't fair that I didn't tell you about all this before we made love."

Suddenly Hudson moved forward in his chair and took her hands into his. "I already know about all of this."

She felt as if the breath had been knocked out of her. Recovering, she asked, "How could you?"

"I had a talk with Jamie yesterday. I don't think he wanted to tell me. He wanted you to confide in me. But he also didn't want you hurt any more than you already were."

"Maybe I should go," she said softly and tried to pull away from him.

But he held on to her and wouldn't let her move. She was as mesmerized by the look in his eyes as she was by the hold of his hands.

"I thought a lot about us in the past two days, Bella, and I know exactly what I want."

She held her breath as panic seesawed in her stomach.

"I love you. I don't want to live without you. I would be fine with adopting kids if that's what you want to do. If you want biological children, there are ways to make that happen. There are advantages to being rich, you know. I can have access to the best doctors in the world, or we can hire a surrogate."

Tears burned her eyes, and she felt a few roll down her cheek.

He went on. "Did I mention that I love you and I can't live without you?"

She was full out crying by then and so in shock she couldn't move or speak until he asked, "Will you marry me, Bella Stockton? Make a family with me? Grow old with me?"

Now the look in his eyes sunk in. It was the look of love. It warmed her, surrounded her and made her free.

"Yes," she said jubilantly. "Yes, I'll marry you!"

Hudson gathered her into his arms and held her on his lap. Then he kissed her with so much promise that she knew she'd remember this day forever.

Epilogue

Hudson and Bella, filled with the Christmas spirit, were decorating Just Us Kids for the holiday. They'd erected an artificial tree in the lobby and were adding ornaments, one by one, their fingers brushing often, their gazes connecting.

They were still working out their plans to get married. Hudson was hoping Jamie would accept some financial help to hire someone to take Bella's place with the triplets. He'd talked to Jamie about it, and Jamie said he'd consider it. Bella's brother was just happy that she was finding happiness.

Hudson had a couple of surprises for her and decided now was as good a time as any to produce one as they put the finishing touches on the tree. Bella had wrapped empty boxes to place underneath it in bright shiny paper and pretty ribbon. It had been only three days since she'd accepted his marriage proposal—three days of giddy happiness, work and, last night, a long night of lovemaking.

Taking a box from his pocket that was wrapped in silver with a gold bow, he handed it to her. "The bow's a little smashed," he said, "But I didn't want you to see it before now. Open it."

"It's early for a Christmas present," she teased.

"We're going to have one long Christmas," he assured her.

She took the bow from the box and set it aside. Then she unwrapped the silver paper and did the same with that. Taking the lid from the black box, she found a velvet-covered one inside.

She looked up at him.

He saw her fingers tremble as she opened the ring box. Inside, on white velvet lay a platinum ring with a large center diamond and tiny diamonds circling it. It reminded Hudson of a snowflake.

He explained, "I hope you like it. I saw this ring at the jewelers, and it reminded me of that day we went riding and the snow started falling. I wanted something unique for you. What do you think?" He took it from the box and slipped it onto her finger.

Bella's face was glowing as she said, "I think it's perfect."

"I hope you'll think something else is perfect," he suggested.

"Uh-oh, another surprise."

"I hope it's a good one. I'm buying Clive Bickler's ranch. We'll have a real home and a place to ride and lots of room to raise a family."

Bella had hung a ball of mistletoe in the doorway of Hudson's office. Taking his hand, she led him to it now. On tiptoe, she wrapped her arms around his neck and gave him a kiss Hudson knew he'd long remember.

His fervor was exploding into downright fiery passion when he heard a noise. Still holding Bella, he broke the kiss slowly, then turned toward the lobby. There were two moms there with strollers with babies. They were grinning from ear to ear.

But Hudson didn't care. He was ready to shout from the mountaintops that he loved Bella Stockton and she was going to be his wife. Bella must have felt the same way because she drew his head down to hers again and kissed him once more.

They were going to have the merriest Christmas of both of their lifetimes.

* * * * *

Patricia Johns writes from Alberta, Canada. She has her Hon BA in English literature and currently writes for Harlequin's Love Inspired and Heartwarming lines. You can find her at patriciajohnsromance.com.

Books by Patricia Johns

Harlequin Heartwarming

Home to Eagle's Rest

Her Lawman Protector
Falling for the Cowboy Dad

A Baxter's Redemption
The Runaway Bride
A Boy's Christmas Wish

Love Inspired

Montana Twins

Her Cowboy's Twin Blessings
Her Twins' Cowboy Dad

Comfort Creek Lawmen

Deputy Daddy
The Lawman's Runaway Bride
The Deputy's Unexpected Family

His Unexpected Family
The Rancher's City Girl
A Firefighter's Promise
The Lawman's Surprise Family

Visit the Author Profile page at Harlequin.com for more titles.

THE COWBOY'S CHRISTMAS BRIDE

PATRICIA JOHNS

To my husband, the real-life guy who inspires my heroes: strong, stubborn and a heart that beats for me. Who could ask for more?

Chapter 1

Andy Granger sat across from Dakota Mason—the one woman in Hope, Montana, who had never fallen for his charms. Yet here they were, and Dakota looked less than impressed to see him. A pile of ledgers teetered next to a mug of lukewarm coffee and outside a chill wind whistled, whipping crispy leaves across his line of sight through the side window. It was getting late in the winter for there to have not been snow yet, but it looked like it wouldn't hold off much longer.

Andy leaned his elbows on the table and pushed the coffee mug aside. "Didn't expect to see me here, did you?" he asked, a half smile toying at his lips.

Dakota pulled her fingers through her thick, chestnut hair, tugging it away from her face, cheeks still reddened from the cold outside. She'd always been beautiful; the years only seemed to improve her.

"I was expecting Chet," she said. "He said he needed some extra help on the cattle drive. I'd rather deal with him, if you don't mind."

Yeah, everyone was expecting Chet. Andy was here for a couple of weeks at the most. He'd agreed to do the cattle drive this year for his brother and then he was heading back to his life in the city. This ranch—this town even—wasn't home anymore, and he'd been reminded of that little fact repeatedly since arriving.

"Afraid I can't oblige," he replied. "Chet and Mackenzie are in the city. There were some complications with her pregnancy. That can happen with twins, apparently. Anyway, I'm here to take care of things until they return."

That was why Chet had held off on their cattle run to bring the herd from the far pastures in the foothills back to the safety of nearby fields for the winter months. The warm fall and late winter had felt providential with Mack's problematic pregnancy, but the cattle had to come back soon, and now Andy would be the one to do it. As long as he was back out of town before Christmas, he'd call it a success.

"Mack's okay, though?" Dakota asked, her expression softening a little.

"Yeah, she'll be fine." He leaned back in his chair. "So, how've you been?"

"You haven't heard?" Dakota tugged her leather jacket a little closer around herself. She looked uncomfortable, not that Andy blamed her. Everyone seemed ill-at-ease around him since his return, and he'd rolled with it, but he didn't like seeing that discomfort in Dakota's eyes. She'd always been one of the few to see straight through his act—which had generally taken the form of telling him he was an idiot—and this time he wished she could still see what no one else seemed to…that he wasn't all bad.

"I've been out of the loop lately," he confessed.

"That's an understatement," she retorted. "But thanks to you selling off that land to developers, our ranch is now bone dry."

"What?" Andy frowned. "What are you talking about?"

"The streams that ran through your pasture watered ours," she said. "The developers blocked the main ones to make some sort of reservoir. We're down to a trickle."

"Sorry, I didn't know." Those words didn't encompass half of what he felt. That sale had been a mistake, and while he'd been able to buy a car dealership in the city, which had turned into a rather lucrative investment, he'd never been able to shake the certainty he'd made a monumental error when he sold his half of the inheritance and the family pasture.

"But glad to know you made some money off it." Her tone dripped sarcasm.

"It was my land to sell, Dakota."

It wasn't like he'd stolen something from his brother. What was he supposed to do—dutifully step back and forget about his inheritance altogether because his brother was using it?

"Yeah, but to Lordship Land Developers?" she snapped. He'd seen the sign beside the road, too—a bit of a jolt when he'd first driven back into town.

Dakota wasn't so far away from his position. Sure, her parents were still alive, but every ranch faced the same problem. When the owner had more than one child, and the bulk of his financial worth was wrapped up in that land, how did you divide it in a will and still keep the business intact? Who got the ranch and who got cut out?

"What if your brother inherited your dad's ranch?" he pressed. "Let's say your dad leaves the whole thing to Brody. What if you were left with some scrub grass and some memories, and that was it? What if you were pushed out and had to find a way to deal? Are you telling me you wouldn't have done the same thing? It's not much of an inheritance when no one expects you to lay a finger on it."

"Then you sell to your brother," she said with a shake of her head. "But you didn't. You turned this grudge between you and Chet into something that put a black mark on this whole community. Who says anybody is okay with having some resort built here? We're a ranch community, not a vacation spot."

"Take it up with the mayor." He was tired of defending himself. Everyone had the same complaint—he'd sold to an outsider. That was the kind of misstep the town of Hope couldn't forgive.

"Trust me, we tried," she retorted. "Especially when our land dried up and we had to try and graze an entire herd on dust."

Andy's stomach sank. Was it that bad? It wasn't like he could've anticipated that, but people around here didn't seem to care about what was fair to blame on him and what wasn't. Things had gone wrong, and he was the target for an entire community's animosity.

"Look, I'm sorry. I had no way of knowing that would happen."

She didn't look terribly mollified, and he didn't really expect her to be. The truth was he could have sold to his brother, but he'd erred on the side of money. The developers had offered more than he could turn down—enough to buy the dealership in the city free and clear.

And, yes, he'd harbored a few grudges against his perfect brother, Chet. This cattle drive was a favor to his brother, nothing more, and the last thing he needed was a distraction. He'd messed up and he didn't need a four-day-long reminder of that in the form of Dakota Mason, but Chet had asked her to lend a hand before Mackenzie's pregnancy troubles, and Andy was just filling Chet's shoes until he got back. This was all very temporary.

"Changed your mind about helping out?" Andy asked. "My brother isn't going to be back for a while, so you'd have to deal with me, whether you like it or not."

"Thanks to you, we need the extra money," she retorted. "So, no, I'm in."

Working with a woman who couldn't stand him was a bad idea. He knew that plain enough, but he couldn't shake the feeling he owed her. Just like the rest of this blasted town. He had a debt hanging over his head that he'd never be able to repay. Andy glanced at his watch. Two drovers had quit on Chet, and they needed two replacements to get the job done. After Dakota, there was only one other applicant to the job posting he'd placed. He wasn't exactly in a position to turn down help.

"Have you done a cattle drive before?"

She shot him a sidelong look. "Are you seriously asking me that?"

It wasn't a completely inappropriate question. Andy hadn't gone on more than two cattle drives in his life. His brother had always been the one who cared about ranching operations—and was the consummate favorite—so their father had taken him along most years. Andy needed drovers who knew what they were doing, because while he was the face of the family for this drive, he didn't have the experience, and he knew it. Getting the job done was going to rely on the expertise of his team. Which brought up an important question.

"All the other drovers are men," he said. "Can you handle that?"

"If I can handle cattle, I can handle men." She narrowed her eyes. "Can *you* handle a woman on your team?"

Andy shot her a grin. He'd never been one to shy away from women. He'd managed to garner a bit of a reputation for himself over the years. In fact, he'd even dated his brother's wife back when they were in high school—and when he'd been dumb enough to cheat on her with another girl. Not his proudest moment. But while Hope might remember him as the flirt no one could nail down, the last few years had changed him in ways he'd mostly kept to himself. Seeing Chet and Mack fall in love, get married and now start a family made him realize what he wanted—the real thing.

"I have no problem working with a woman," he replied. "But if we're going to be working together for the next four days, maybe we could drop the personal vendetta. Like a truce."

She met his gaze without even a hint of a smile. "I can be professional."

Professional. Yeah, he'd had his fill of professional at the dealership. And if he had to spend the better part of a week with a group of people, he'd rather not feel their icy disapproval the entire time.

"I was actually aiming for friendly," he said and

caught a flicker of humor in her direct gaze. "I'm not your favorite person, I get that. I hadn't realized how bad it was—" He swallowed, weighing his words. "You aren't the only one with a grudge around here. Do you know what it's like to order breakfast at the truck stop and have everyone there, including your waitress, glare at you? I think my eggs tasted funny, to boot. Goodness knows what they did to them. So I get it. I'm the bad guy. I'm the jerk who sold you all out, but I do have a job to do, and this isn't for me, it's for Chet."

Some of the tension in her shoulders loosened at the mention of his brother. That's the way it always was around here. People liked Chet. They respected him. They sided with him, too.

Her direct, cool expression didn't flicker. "I'll meet you halfway at civil."

"I'll take what I can get. If you want this job, we have to be able to work together. You know what it's like out there, and if we can't count on each other, we're wasting everyone's time."

"*I'm* not going to be your problem," she said, and he knew what she was talking about—the rest of the team.

"Leave the other guys to me." He wasn't exactly confident in his ability to lead this team of drovers, but if he could bridge the gap with Dakota, it would be a step in the right direction.

"So, what are the plans?" she asked.

"It's four days in total. I haven't done this particular ride before. It's to the far side of what used to be the Vaughn ranch. We're driving back four hundred head, so it's no small job."

Dakota nodded. "When do we start?"

"Monday morning."

"Okay, I'll be here bright and early." She rose to her feet and turned toward the door. Her jeans fit her nicely and he found himself having to pull his eyes away from admiring her shape.

"Dakota—"

"Yeah?" She turned back, brown eyes drilling into him, and he felt the urge to squirm.

This was the hard part—this was where he had to reveal that he needed help—and his stomach tightened. He didn't like admitting weakness, but needed an outside opinion, and she was the most qualified person in the room.

"You sold Chet some horses last spring," he said.

"What of it?" She raked a hand through her hair.

"I need to choose my horse for this drive, and I thought you might have some advice." More than advice. Dakota was something of a horse whisperer, able to calm even the most spirited animal, and while he knew she didn't much like him at the moment, he did trust her instincts. There was a horse he'd warmed up to over the last couple of days—Romeo. Chet thought Romeo wasn't ready for a cattle drive, but there was just something about that horse that Andy couldn't dismiss. Maybe he and Romeo were alike—not exactly ready but still perfectly capable. He wanted Dakota's take on it. Maybe she'd see something Chet hadn't.

When Dakota didn't answer right away, he added, "I know I'm not in the best position to ask you any personal favors, but it's been a long time since I worked a ranch, and Chet is counting on me to take care of things. Once I'm done this job, I'll go away and never bother you again. That's a promise."

She sighed. "Do you have time now? I'd need to see

the horses again to see where they're at. They all needed work when they left my stables."

Andy shot her a grin and rose. "You bet. I have an hour until my interview with another potential drover."

"Who?" She frowned.

"Harley Webb. Heard of him?"

She shook her head. "No. He from around here?"

"Doesn't seem to be," he said. "I'll find out later, if he shows."

She gave him a curt nod and pulled open the door. There was something about this woman, her slim figure accentuated by morning sunlight, that made his mind stray into territory it didn't belong in. Just before that hazy summer, when Andy had dated Mackenzie, Dakota had started dating Andy's best friend, Dwight. She'd almost married him, so he'd seen quite a bit of Dakota back then. You'd think that would have made her more inclined to be friendly with him. But even back then she'd seen straight through his attempts to look tough and suave, and she hadn't liked what she'd seen. Now the woman had every reason to resent him; he had to keep that thought front and center.

Meanwhile he had a job to do. He'd do this cattle drive and, when Chet got back, he'd stay true to his word and get out of Hope for good. He'd celebrate Christmas in Billings and put all of this behind him. He'd seen enough over the last few days to be convinced that Hope would never be home sweet home again.

The fact that someone at the truck stop had meddled with Andy's morning eggs was mildly satisfying. He had it coming after what he'd done to this community, and he didn't deserve to swagger back into town and be welcomed with open arms. He'd formerly been a town favorite—up until he'd sold them all out. He'd been so cocksure of himself, and the girls had swooned for that auburn-hair-and-green-eyes combination—the Grangers were a good-looking family. It didn't help that Andy was a flirt, either, but Dakota had never been the kind of girl to be taken in by that kind of guy. She'd seen straight through him from the start.

Dakota respected substance over flattery, so after Andy broke about a dozen hearts around town after Mack's, and then up and sold his land to the developer, her sympathy—and everyone else's for that matter—was spent. Andy Granger was a flirt and an idiot. As for the scrambled eggs—whatever they'd done to them, he'd had it coming.

Andy walked half a step ahead of her across the ranch yard. A tractor hooked up to a trailer was parked along the western fence, a few bales of hay and some tools on the trailer bed. Several goats were in the field beyond it, and they bleated in greeting as they passed. A chicken coop sat at the far end of the yard by the big, red barn and a rooster perched on a fence post nearby fluffed his feathers against the chill. A few hens scratched in the dirt outside the coop, but it looked like most had gone inside for some cozy comfort.

Andy angled his steps around the coop and Dakota noted how broad and strong he was still. City life hadn't softened him physically. It had been almost five years since she'd last clapped eyes on him, and she'd forgotten how attractive he was up close… Not that it mattered.

A breeze picked up, swirling some leaves across their path, and she hitched her shoulders against the probing wind.

Word had spread about Andy, even when he was away. He'd spent a decade in the city, where he'd gotten engaged and then got cold feet, from what she'd heard through the grapevine. Then he'd sold the Granger pasture and left town again. It would have taken some courage to show his face after all that, but here he was, and he was doing this for his brother, which was the only reason she was being helpful at all—well, that and the money.

Dakota had known Andy quite well back in the day. He'd even asked her out once, leaning against the hood of his pickup and casting her a boyish grin. Truthfully, she'd been tempted to say yes—what girl hadn't? But she'd just started dating Dwight and she wasn't the two-timing kind of person. And what kind of a guy moved in on his best friend's girlfriend? She'd turned him down flat, which was just as well because a few weeks later Mackenzie Granger came to town and soon they were a smoldering item. That just went to show that the boyish grin wasn't to be trusted.

Ironically enough, Andy turned out to be less of a threat to her peace of mind than Dwight had been. The minute Dwight turned twenty-one, he did two things: propose and start drinking. She accepted his proposal, but the wedding never happened. With the booze, Dwight got violent, and she couldn't stay in a relationship like that. Still, canceling her wedding had been the hardest thing she'd ever done. And Andy had been Dwight's best friend—it said something about the kind of man Andy was, in her estimation. Birds of a feather and all that.

"So your eggs tasted funny, did they?" she asked, casting him a wry smile.

Andy shook his head. "You know, in a place this small you get to know everybody, but you also get to tick everybody off in one fell swoop, too."

"So why come back?" she countered. "I've heard that you're set up pretty well in Billings, and while I get helping out your brother, Elliot could have led this drive easily enough."

In fact, she'd heard that Andy was rich, if she had to be entirely honest. Apparently he was making money hand over fist in the city, which was one more reason for people around here to resent him. It was easier to feel sorry for a guy who ended up down on his luck after pulling a stunt like that, but to have him actually prosper…

"I am set up pretty well." His tone became more guarded and he looked away for a moment. "Let's just say that some sentimental nonsense got the better of me."

"Is that code for a woman?" she asked dryly. With Andy it usually came down to a woman.

"No." He barked out a laugh. "Is that what you think of me, that I'm some kind of womanizer?"

Dakota shrugged. She couldn't see any reason to lie. He had to know his own reputation. "Yes."

He eyed her for a moment as if not sure how to take her frankness, then he shrugged.

"Well, this particular sentimental nonsense has nothing to do with a woman. This is about my dad, rest his soul, and my brother. I guess I missed…them. This. Fitting in. Like I said, nonsense. There is no turning back that clock."

She didn't miss the fact that he hadn't exactly denied being a womanizer, but she did feel a little pang of pity at the mention of his father. Mr. Granger had died about four years earlier in a tractor accident. The whole town had showed up for the funeral. Even the truck stop closed down for a couple of hours so that everyone could attend; that's how loved Andy's father had been. She inwardly grimaced.

"I didn't send the horses out to pasture today," Andy went on, saving her from finding an appropriate reply.

He led the way around the side of the newly painted barn toward the corral. As they stepped into its shadow, the December day felt distinctly colder. This winter would make up for lost time; there was no doubt about it.

Andy glanced over his shoulder and his green eyes met hers. "Thanks for this, by the way."

Her pulse sped up at the directness of that look and the very fact that he was working his blasted Granger charm on her was irritating.

"This isn't for you, Granger. It's for Chet."

She wasn't falling for any of Andy's charms, but she could certainly understand why some women did. He was tall, muscular, with rugged good looks and scruff on his face that suggested he'd missed a couple of days of shaving. But Andy also represented something that hit her a little closer to home—the kind of guy who could walk away without too much trouble. Her brother had fallen for the female version of Andy Granger in the form of Nina Harpe, and she wasn't about to repeat Brody's mistakes. She had a lot of reasons to be wary of Andy Granger.

The corral was attached to the back of the barn, bathed in midmorning sunlight. At this time of year the sunlight was watery, but the air was surprisingly warm—about four or five degrees above freezing. Beyond the corral was a dirt road that lead toward different enclosed pastures, rolling hills of rich, golden cinnamon grass glowing in late autumn splendor. And beyond the fields were the mountains, rising in jagged peaks, hemming them in like majestic guards.

Several horses perked up at the sight of them, ears twitching in interest. Andy reached into a white bucket that sat in the shade and pulled out a fistful of carrots. He rolled them over in his hands, rubbing off the last of the dirt, and headed for the fence. Two of the horses came right over when Andy walked up—a dun stallion named Romeo and a piebald mare. Chet's horse, a chestnut gelding named Barney, stood resolutely on the far side of the coral, ignoring them.

"Have you ridden any of them yet?" Dakota asked, stopping at Andy's side. He held a carrot out to the mare.

"I've ridden Romeo, here," he said, reaching out to pet the stallion's nose. Romeo leaned closer, nosing for a carrot, and Andy obliged.

"How about Barney?" she asked, nodding toward the gelding that was inching closer around the side of the corral, wanting his own share of the treats.

"He bit me," Andy retorted.

Dakota choked back a laugh. "Not sweet old Barney."

"Sweet?" Andy shook his head. "That horse hates me. Every chance he gets, he gives me a nip. I just about lost the top of my ear last time."

"Okay, well, not Barney, then," she replied with a shake of her head. In fact, if Andy wasn't going to ride Barney, she was inclined to take him herself. He was an experienced horse for this ride, a sweetheart deep down…if you weren't Andy, apparently.

"So what do you think?" he asked.

She paused for a moment, considering.

"Romeo, here, is young and strong. He's a runner. He'll go and go, so he'll definitely have the energy for a cattle drive. But he doesn't have the experience."

"I like him, though," Andy said. Romeo crunched another carrot, his jaw grinding in slow, satisfied circles. "He wasn't Chet's first choice, either."

"Which horse did Chet recommend?" she asked.

"Patty," he said, nodding to the piebald mare. "But what do you think?"

Dakota looked over the horses. "I'd have said Barney, but if he really hates you that much—"

"And he does," Andy replied in a low laugh.

"Patty is a good horse. She'd do well." She paused, watching the way Romeo stretched toward Andy for another carrot. "But you seem to have a good bond with Romeo. I don't know. I'd say it's between Patty and Romeo. Patty would be my first choice. I think Romeo's a risk."

Andy nodded. "Thanks. I appreciate it." He gave the last carrot to Patty and showed Romeo his empty hands. "Sorry, buddy. All out."

Andy pushed himself off the fence and Dakota followed him as he headed back the way they'd come. Sunlight warmed her shoulders and the top of her head. She glanced around the yard as they walked, inhaling the comforting scent of hay and autumn chill.

"So?" she prodded.

"When have I ever been one to take good advice?" he asked with a grin. "I'm taking Romeo. If I'm going to ride for four days, I'd rather have it be with a horse that wants to move."

Somehow this didn't surprise her in the least, and not in a pleasant way. Andy Granger had always made his own rules. "Fair enough."

"What?" He cast her a quizzical look.

"Did you really want my advice, or just a vote for what you already wanted to do?"

"Hey." His tone grew deeper and his eyes met hers. "I might not be the rancher of the family, but I'm not exactly a lost kitten, either. I can ride."

Dakota dropped her gaze, her cheeks warming. Andy had an effective stare.

"I grew up here, too, you know," he added. His stride was long and she had to pick up her pace to keep up with him.

He may have grown up in Hope, but she knew he'd never taken ranching very seriously.

"You clowned around," she retorted. "I remember that horse show where you arrived late and—"

"I had my fun," he interrupted. "And why not? No one else took me seriously."

"They might have," she shot back, "if you'd shown that you cared about this land at all."

"And if I were punctual." He gave her a look of mock seriousness. "So very punctual."

He was making fun of her now and she shook her head. Andy had been late for that horse show, and she'd told him off for it when he finally did arrive. It was that joking attitude of his that rubbed her the wrong way—it always had. Always joking, never saying anything of any substance. In her own humble opinion, Andy's father had made the right call in who got the ranch.

"You were late, and I came in first at that show," she said. She'd enjoyed beating him.

"I was late and I still came in third," he quipped. "Imagine what I could've done if I'd arrived on time."

"Yes," she retorted. "Imagine."

The thing was Andy hadn't lacked in skill or talent, just focus. At least that was the way she saw it. And he hadn't focused because he hadn't cared about ranching life. But Dakota did—she cared more than a guy like Andy could ever imagine, and while he was horsing around and flirting with girls, she'd been working hard. It wasn't just a junior horse show, it was a matter of pride.

"I was joking." He came to a stop in front of the house and shoved his hands into his pockets. He didn't sober entirely, that smile still teasing at the corners of his mouth. "You'll get used to it."

From where they stood she could see the barn on one side and the drive leading toward the main road on the other. It wound through bushes of amber and nut brown, a few cattails growing in the ditch where water collected. The cluck of the chickens mingled with the faraway call of a lone V of geese that soared overhead. She could see the beauty here—the life, the rotation of the seasons, the work to be done and the harvest to be enjoyed. She could see things she was quite sure Andy didn't. The land wasn't a joke, it was a responsibility.

"I'm already used to it," she retorted. "You're acting like I don't know you. If you want to know why people are so ticked with you, this is it. This is all a joke for you, just a way to pass the time. But for the rest of us, this is our life, something we care enough about to dedicate every waking hour. When you sold that land, you made a dent in this community and it's affected us all—my family especially. You might be joking around, but the rest of us are dead serious, and we're left paying for it."

"And I doubt there's any way you'll forgive me, is there?" He'd sobered finally, the joking look evaporating from his face, leaving those chiseled Granger good looks to drill straight into her.

"Probably not." Dakota sucked in a breath and nodded in the direction of the corral. "I still recommend Patty, for the record. Not that I expect it to matter to you."

"Noted. And I should add that just because I joke around doesn't mean I'm not dead serious about some things, this cattle drive included."

"Good." She swallowed, uncertain of what else to say. There was nothing left, really. She'd stated her position and he'd stated his. They weren't friends. They weren't anything, really, except two people forced to work together for a few days. What he thought of this land didn't much matter. It didn't belong to him.

"So I'll see you Monday morning," he said. "I want to start riding at sunup."

"I'll see you then," she said and turned toward her truck.

"Dakota—" She turned back and he shrugged. "Thanks for meeting me halfway."

Halfway at civil. It wasn't much, but it seemed to mean something to him. Melancholy swam in those green eyes and then he gave her a nod of farewell and turned back toward the house. For all of his joking around, he was carrying a heavier load than she'd given him credit for. While she'd always hoped he'd live to regret what he'd done to this town by selling out, she'd never considered what it would mean to see that regret reflected in his face. Karma was best reported secondhand, not witnessed…something she'd already learned with Dwight.

A few years ago, right around Christmastime, she remembered putting up the family tree in the living room with her brother. She'd been dating Dwight at the time, and no one knew about his violent outburst yet, but apparently, his boozing had put up some warning flags. Brody had given her some sound advice. "Don't get caught up with a guy who will ruin your future," he'd told her seriously. "You already know what you want. Dwight doesn't—and even if he did, he'd have to stop drinking if he wanted to achieve anything. So you'd better put together the life you want. No guy is going to give it to you, least of all Dwight. You need to dump his sorry butt before it's too late."

That advice still applied—both about steering clear of Dwight and any other guy who didn't share her priorities. The wrong man could demolish everything she'd worked for.

Chapter 2

Dakota put her truck into reverse and pulled a three-point turn before heading out the drive that lead to the main road. She steered around a pothole, the dried fingertips of bushes scratching across the side of her vehicle. Mission accomplished: she'd secured the job. When Chet had called several days ago asking her to lend a hand on their late cattle drive for a decent sum, she'd been relieved. They needed the extra money rather badly, especially with Christmas coming up. Sometimes blessings came in the form of hard work.

Andy had been a surprise, though.

She turned onto the main road and heaved a sigh. She'd been more nervous than she'd thought when she realized she'd be dealing with Andy and not his more likeable brother. But a job was a job, and with her mother's medical bills for her emergency hysterectomy last year and the down payment they needed to put down for the new hydration system, she'd take a paycheck any way she could get it, and this drover position was paying relatively well. Chet was like that. He knew better than to offer the Masons charity, but he'd offer a job for fair pay. That was the sort of kindness Dakota could accept.

The road divided the land—one side an endless, rippling carpet of golden wheat, the other what used to be the Granger's pasture, a mixture of maize yellow with olive green and sienna—the different grasses maturing together into a rich expanse, the beauty of which was marred by muddy roads. The growl of large machinery surfed the breeze, tractors creeping along the ground in the distance, and every time she looked at them, a new wave of anger swept over her. Lordship Land Developers had friends in powerful places to get the zoning for this eyesore, and all the petitions she'd filed had made no difference at all. Apparently money spoke louder than righteous indignation. And Dakota had plenty of righteous indignation.

This county—this road—was as much a part of her as her own blood, and seeing it torn apart hurt on a gut level. Andy had seemed properly surprised at the impact his choice had had on their ranch, but it didn't change where the blame lay. He'd had one foot out of town for as long as she'd known him. Again, a lot like Nina Harpe—the woman engaged to her brother, Brody... whom her brother still believed he'd marry. Except, Nina had up and married Brody's best friend while he was stationed overseas with the army. Nina was more than beautiful—she was voluptuous and sexy, a Marilyn Monroe singing Happy Birthday to the president. Apparently, one of her virtues wasn't patience.

Dakota wasn't given to petty grudges. She believed in second chances and people's ability to grow, unless that person had singlehandedly impoverished her family's land or broken her brother's heart. Her benevolence had a limit. To be fair, Brody's heart wasn't broken yet…but that clock was ticking.

And yet, in one small corner of her own heart, she found herself pitying Andy. He deserved what he got—there was no ambivalence there—yet the softer side of her still hated to see someone suffer. Even Andy Granger.

A few miles farther led to her own drive and she slowed to make the turn. As her tires crunched over the gravel, her phone chirped on the seat beside her. It was an incoming email. She glanced down and saw that it was from Brody. It was always a treat to hear from him, except lately, when he was asking more persistently about Nina. There was more to that story and she couldn't be the one to tell him.

Dakota and Brody always had been close as kids. She'd been fiercely protective of her quiet big brother, and he'd never really treated her like a little kid. Before he'd left, they'd discussed the future of the ranch in depth together, and it felt weird to have him so far away. But this was what Brody had always dreamed of, joining the army and protecting his country.

A brown, floppy-eared mutt raced after the truck as she pulled to a stop next to the single-level ranch house. Shelby bounced excitedly, planting several muddy footprints into Dakota's jeans when she opened the door.

"Hi, girl," she said, scratching the dog behind the ears.

"That you, Dakota?" Her mother's voice came from

the house and then she appeared at the screen door. Her sweater was rolled up to the elbows, her front covered in a floral print apron and her hands—held up like a surgeon's—were covered in flour.

"Hi, Mom."

"Where were you?"

"I was just lining things up with the Grangers for their cattle drive." Dakota gave Shelby another rub and then headed toward the house. She kicked her boots against the step on her way in.

She glanced down at her phone and skimmed her brother's email as she came in past the screen door.

"What are you reading?" her mother asked, glancing over her shoulder. She was working on some cinnamon buns, rolling out the fluffy dough with a heavy, wooden rolling pin.

"Email from Brody."

"How's he doing?"

They all missed Brody. He'd been gone a full year now, and anyone who heard from him was honor-bound to share with the rest of the family. He was serving the country, and Dakota was so proud of him it almost hurt sometimes, but that only made their secret here at home all the heavier.

"He's asking about Nina again," Dakota said as she came into the kitchen, and she and her mother exchanged a look.

"What did you say?" her mother asked, reaching for the butter plate.

"I haven't answered him." Dakota sighed. "I really don't like lying to him, Mom. He's going to hate us for this."

Brody was the big, burly kind of guy who kept his

thoughts to himself, but that didn't mean he didn't feel things deeply. Dakota had often thought the girl who ended up with her brother would be lucky, indeed, which was why his choice of Nina Harpe had been such a disappointment. But he'd asked Nina to marry him and she'd accepted. What could they do?

"I don't want him distracted over that little idiot when he's dodging bullets," she retorted. *That little idiot* was what her mother had called Nina since she'd sheepishly announced she was marrying Brian Dickerson eight months after Brody had been deployed. She'd followed through with that—a tiny wedding she'd agreed to keep secret—and then promptly moved to the city with her new husband. To add insult to injury, Brian had been Brody's best friend since elementary school. They both were going to have some explaining to do when Brody got back home. As was Dakota when she'd have to tell her brother why she'd kept the secret, and she wasn't looking forward to coming clean. Brody was going to be crushed.

Brody was better off without Nina, though. She was flighty and more preoccupied with material objects and celebrity gossip than she was anything worthwhile. She had perfectly coiffed red hair, swaying hips and breasts like melons. She left a cloud of perfume in her wake, and a string of gaping men.

Nina was a self-involved flirt, much like Andy Granger, but having Nina take up with Brian behind her brother's back was worse. Brody's taste might be a little lacking, but he deserved better than that while he fought for his country. Apparently, Nina hadn't been able to wait long before she got sidetracked by the next available guy. They'd all agreed to keep the secret until he got back. Then Nina could rip his heart out at her leisure, when he was safely home again.

"Don't worry, I have plenty to distract Brody with," Dakota said with a wry smile. "Did you know that Chet and Mackenzie are at the city hospital right now?"

"I just heard that from Audrey," her mother said with a frown. "Apparently the babies are low in amniotic fluid and she needs to be under medical supervision. Who's taking care of the ranch while they're gone?"

"Andy."

"What?" Her mother looked back. "Seriously? So the prodigal son has come back, has he?"

"As a favor to Chet, he claims," she replied, her mind flashing to the meeting at the Granger ranch. "So he'll be the one leading the cattle drive. I don't think Andy knows enough to lead one on his own, but apparently he's going to try."

Her mother fell silent and they exchanged a tired look. Andy Granger was old news. They'd talked about him on a regular basis, and he'd grown bigger and badder with each mention.

Dakota remembered coming back late one night after the construction had started and the water had dried up, and could recall overhearing her parents talking in the kitchen, their voices filtering through the open window. Her father had sounded so gutted, so deeply sad, that his deep voice trembled.

"Millie, we might lose this place..." There had been a pause so long Dakota's leg had almost cramped as she'd tried to stay still. "That Granger kid... He did this. I don't think I'll ever forgive him."

Dakota had never forgotten those words or the quivering sadness in his voice. Because of Andy, her father stood to lose the land that fueled his heart, and she was determined to do whatever it took to keep them ranching.

Hence looking for side work and extra income. She'd taken anything she could get for the last several years, but it had never quite added up to enough.

"The cattle drive starts Monday," Dakota said. "So, like I said, I'll have plenty to update Brody about without having to say much of anything about Nina."

"Are you sure you want to do this?" her mother asked. "You agreed to work with Chet, not Andy."

"There aren't that many jobs posted right now, Mom." Dakota picked up an apple from the fruit bowl and polished it on her shirt. "And the Grangers are paying pretty well. Don't worry. I can deal with Andy Granger for a few days." Dakota shot her mother a grin. "I'm pretty sure he's more afraid of me than I am of him."

Her bravado was only partially sincere, though. She wasn't looking forward in the least to doing a cattle drive with Andy, but the last thing her mother needed was to shoulder more guilt about the family finances. It wasn't her fault that she'd gotten sick or that the insurance company had fallen through when they'd needed them most. What mattered was that she'd gotten the hysterectomy she'd so desperately needed and was back to full strength.

"As for Nina..." her mother added. "We only have to keep the secret until your brother gets home in February. Just a few months longer. I'd rather have him find out when he has family support."

It was an old conversation—one they'd had a hundred times before—and Dakota stared down at the polished apple in her hands.

"What about Dad?" she asked cautiously. "I know how he feels about Andy and all—"

"He'll be fine. A paycheck is a paycheck." She smiled wanly. "As long as you think you can handle it."

Dakota took a bite of the crisp apple and chewed thoughtfully. Times like these she missed her brother the most. Brody would have some wisecrack to make them laugh and he'd manage to cut Andy down to size in no time.

"I'm going to go fill the feeders before it gets too late," Dakota said. They'd done their own cattle drive last month and the whole herd was back in the nearby fields. The cows wouldn't wait, and she still had to sort out how they'd manage the work while she was gone for a few days. There was one thing she wanted more than anything else, and that was to ranch this very land she was raised on, if only she could get her father to let go of his hopes for Brody taking it over. She glanced down at her brother's email.

Is Nina okay? She seems distant, but I guess I'm a bit distant, too. I want to do the right thing and marry her when I get back. I know you don't like frilly stuff, but any chance you'd pitch in and help to put together a wedding?

This family was in tatters; their finances were shaky. Right about now, doing a cattle drive with the man who'd dried up their land didn't seem half bad compared to facing the rest of their problems.

She needed a paycheck. She'd start with that.

* * *

Harley Webb arrived on time with a cigarette behind his ear and a worn New Testament tucked into the front pocket of his fleece-lined jean jacket. He looked young—too young for this job. He'd barely grown a mustache and the rest of his face looked smooth as a boy's. A cowboy hat sat firmly on his head and his hands looked too big for his wiry physique, like an overgrown puppy. So this was the bottom of the barrel, apparently.

"Harley, I take it?" Andy asked, shaking the kid's calloused hand—at least he'd done some hard work in his life.

"That's right," Harley replied. "Good to meet you."

While Dakota had the unpleasant surprise of seeing Andy instead of Chet, Andy had been the one to call Harley for an interview, and it was mildly relieving not to have to explain his presence to someone. That being said, he didn't know this kid from Adam, and he was used to having some sort of personal association with the men who worked the ranch—either they'd worked on a neighboring ranch in the past or were related to someone from the county. Harley, however, seemed to have dropped down from above—a gangly, questionable gift.

"So where are you from?" Andy asked, leading the way into the house.

"Idaho," he replied.

"And what brings you here?" Andy stood back while Harley came inside. He gestured to a kitchen chair and both men sat. Harley took off his hat, his thin, brown hair flattened against his forehead.

"I came out here to visit some family," Harley said.

He fiddled with the edge of his hat. “Decided to stay a bit longer, and I need to make some money.”

Andy nodded. It sounded plausible. “How old are you?”

“Twenty-two.” Harley laughed self-consciously. “Trust me, I get carded a lot.”

“You have some ID?” Andy asked, and Harley shrugged, leaned the side and pried a wallet out of his back pocket. His Idaho driver’s license confirmed his age.

Andy handed it back. “All right. So let’s talk experience, then.”

“I was raised on a ranch,” Harley said. “I’ve done it all. I can rope, herd, brand—you name it. I’ve done cattle drives before.”

He sounded confident enough—and today was Saturday. There wasn’t much time to find another drover if he didn’t take Harley.

“You know anyone around here who can vouch for you?” Andy asked. “You said you’re visiting family. Who are they?”

“My sister—her name is Holly Webb. She lives in town here.”

That didn’t help. He’d never heard of her. “Anyone else?”

“Sorry.” Harley shook his head. “But I’ll work hard. You can count on that. I’m honest and I’ll earn my keep.”

Andy paused, considering. Hiring someone at the car dealership was different, since he had a human resources official to check into work histories and the like. He had no way of checking out Harley’s story on such short notice. This one was left up to his gut. The way he saw it right now, they could ride with Harley or without him. Even if he wasn't much of a drover, he'd be an extra body for night watches. That was something. On the bright side, he might be as good as he claimed. Besides, he'd showed up on time and, despite Andy's teasing of Dakota earlier, he did value punctuality in his employees; it showed the kid wanted the job.

"Okay, well, this is what we offer." Andy wrote a number on a slip of paper and slid it across the table. "That's not negotiable."

"Looks fair, sir," Harley replied with a nod.

"If you want the job, you're hired," Andy said. "We start out Monday at sunup. Be here an hour early and we'll get you fitted with a horse. I'll need a copy of your ID..."

The next few minutes were filled with legalities and forms. There was something about Harley that Andy liked. Maybe it was that Harley was oblivious to Andy's past and only seemed to relate to him as a boss and source of a potential paycheck. Call it vanity, but it felt good to be called "sir" again instead of the other, less flattering descriptions he'd overheard. Ordinarily he'd be more cautious about an unknown ranch hand, but lately he was a little more sympathetic toward people wanting a fresh start. They weren't so easy to achieve and he envied those who managed it.

Plus, with Christmas coming up, he was more sentimental than usual. Christmas was hard—it had been ever since his mother had passed away right around the holiday when he was thirteen. Christmases were never the same without her. It wasn't anything concrete like her cookies or the way she always found the perfect gift for the people she loved...it was her. Without Mom, it was like the sun dimmed and the moon went out. Those were some of the memories he hoped to escape when he left Hope after this cattle drive. Christmas needed to be in Billings this year—in his modern apartment with his new life. He couldn't face another Christmas in Hope.

After Harley left, Andy took the paperwork into the office. He pulled out a fresh file folder and grabbed a ballpoint to write out the newest employee's name. Andy wasn't quite the lackadaisical jokester that Dakota took him for, but her assumptions weren't her fault. He'd worked for that reputation out of a deep sense of hurt and betrayal. He wasn't a guy who liked to advertise his vulnerability because, ironically enough, even though he'd put his teenage energy into proving he didn't care, the thing he'd wanted most from the people in his community was their respect. Maybe even a "sir" now and again.

But that was long gone.

When he was a kid, his brother and his dad would go out to check on the cattle. Andy used to go with them, but he felt the inequality in how they were treated. Chet was his dad's favorite, the one he talked to when he was explaining how something worked. Andy was just along for the ride—or that was how it felt. He was treated like a little kid, even though he was only two years younger than Chet, and when he told jokes, his dad would say, "Enough," and the growl in his voice said it all. Mom wasn't like that, though. When Andy told her a joke, she'd throw back her head and laugh.

She also made an amazing blueberry pie.

He'd never be like his stoic father, but he wanted a woman like his mom—full of love and laughter, who stood by her man through thick and thin. If there was one thing about Mom, she was loyal. Even when the laughter stopped and her eyes turned sad, she was still loyal.

He tucked the photocopies of Harley's ID and his signed contract into the file folder. He dropped it in the back of the employee section of the file cabinet the way Chet had organized it.

Andy turned off the light on his way out of the office. For some reason an image of Dakota kept rising in his mind when he thought about what he wanted in life, and it was like his subconscious was taunting him. Dakota was the one woman who never would fall for his charms. She never had. In fact, she was the woman with the biggest grudge against him.

And yet there was something about the way her eyes snapped fire when she'd stood there in the driveway, cheeks pink from the chilly wind and a thumb hooked in her belt loop… *If you want to know why people are so ticked with you, this is it.*

Apparently he was a sucker for punishment. He'd come back to help out Chet in his time of need, and that was where it was supposed to stop. He'd known full well it would be hard. He'd known he'd have to deal with some painful memories. He'd even known he'd be resented. He just hadn't counted on feeling this attracted to the one woman who resented him most.

Andy pushed the thought aside and grabbed his hat off the table where he'd tossed it. There were chores to be done, animals to check on… He had enough to worry about for the next week or so. Keeping his mind on his job was the best solution he could think of.

Chapter 3

Monday morning, the sun was just peeping over the horizon as Andy cinched the girth on his saddle tighter. Early rays of sunlight, pink as a grapefruit, flooded the fields, sparkling on the frost that clung to every blade of grass. Dawn made the ranch cozier somehow. It was the rose-splashed sky and the long, dusty shadows—a moment in time that hadn't changed over the years. He could remember this exact moment of the day when he was a kid holding a bucket of chicken feed, staring at the sky.

"Get 'er done, Andy," his father would say on his way past, Chet in his wake. Get 'er done. Staring at the dawn wasn't efficient use of his time, but it was something his mom could understand.

"Just look at that sky..." She'd stare at the sky for long moments. Mom got it.

The rooster let out a hoarse crow and Romeo stamped a hoof as Andy ran a hand down the horse's dun flank. His team consisted of four regular ranch hands who rode along for cattle drives every year, and the two newbies—Harley Webb and Dakota Mason.

Dakota was getting Barney ready to ride a few yards off. She slid a feedbag over his head and patted his neck affectionately. Andy found it ironic she'd chosen Chet's horse, the beast that kept nipping at Andy every time he came close. He looked gentle as a lamb with Dakota, though.

The sunrise made her milky skin flush pink in the growing light, her dark hair pulled into a ponytail, revealing the length of her neck. Her coat was brown leather, tough and formfitting, and he had to force himself to look away. Staring, no matter how flattering the light, was bad form for the boss.

Andy's last cattle drive had been when he was sixteen, and he was more than aware of his current limitations—namely, his lack of recent ranching experience and his mangled reputation in Hope. Drovers were a unique lot and gaining their respect wouldn't be automatic, maybe not even possible given his current position. These were hard-riding men who were used to discomfort and had their own code, and leadership on a cattle drive would look a whole lot different than leadership in a boardroom.

Harley seemed to be keeping to himself and a couple of the other drovers were talking by the fence. Dakota buckled shut a saddlebag and glanced in his direction, her hat pushed back from her face while she worked. She was pretty in a way he didn't see very often. She wasn't Cover Girl pretty. It was something deeper; the way she stared directly at a man and he could see both the softness and sharp intelligence behind those eyes, an alluring combination. He didn't want a woman to look up to him, bat her eyes and laugh at his jokes. He wanted a woman to match him, and something told him that if she were properly invested, Dakota absolutely could.

The sun rose steadily higher in the sky, the light turning from rosy to golden. Dakota's fingers moved with the nimble deftness of experience. Her voice was low as she said something to the horse, her words lost in the few yards between them. Andy had meant to stay away, but he couldn't hold himself back any longer.

"You have enough food for the day?" Andy asked, heading in her direction. The cook would meet them at the first camp, but until they arrived they were responsible for carrying their own food. It was a question at least.

"I've done this before." She put a hand on her hip. "I'd check on the little guy, if I were you."

She nodded in Harley's direction. He and Elliot, the most experienced ranch hand the Granger's employed, were eyeing each other distrustfully from where they sat in their saddles. That didn't look promising.

"What's up with them?" Andy asked, keeping his tone low enough for privacy.

Dakota shrugged. "Don't like each other by the looks of it."

He laughed softly. "Yeah, I picked up on that."

"You sure about that horse?" she asked, nodding in Romeo's direction.

"You don't think I know what I'm doing, do you?" he asked. She wouldn't be alone in the opinion—his dad and brother had thought the same.

"I'm better at this than you are."

Her tone held challenge and she was probably right. He was no drover, he was a businessman, and while he was excellent at making a profit and driving up the value of shares, cattle and drovers weren't part of his expertise. Not anymore, at least.

"You may very well be," he said, shooting her a grin. "But I'm a quick study."

He didn't know why he felt the need to compete with her. It shouldn't matter, but he didn't want her to see him as weak or needing her help. This might be temporary, but he was still in charge until his brother got back. She'd offered to meet him halfway at civil, but he was aiming at a whole lot more than that. He wanted her respect, but that would have to be earned.

"We'll see."

Andy shot her a rueful grin and headed back to his horse. He put his boot in the stirrup and grabbed the horn, swinging himself up into his saddle. He looked around at the team he'd be riding with, and he could see that they were solid in experience, if not all entirely friendly. Harley's New Testament was still tucked into the front pocket of his jacket and he chewed on the inside of his cheek. Behind him, Elliot Sturgeon stared hard at a point just left of Andy, his reins held in a loose grip. He was good at his job and could have led this cattle drive. He wasn't Andy's biggest fan, either, which made this prickly.

"Okay," Andy said, raising his voice over another hoarse crow from the rooster sitting on the fence rail next to the henhouse. "So I think we're all pretty clear on our route. We're heading due west for about a day and a half. We've got some newbies this time, so let's not assume everyone knows everything—"

"Like you..." a low, gravelly voice said, and Andy glanced in the direction the voice had originated, only to see three drovers eyeing him with the same bland expression. It wasn't worth the confrontation right now, but he could see they didn't respect him. That could turn ugly a couple hours past civilization. He needed to address this now and a couple of different ideas flitted through his head before he settled on the words.

"I've never done this route, but I'm here because this is my family's herd," he said, keeping his voice even, and he let his gaze move over his team slowly. "You might like me and you might not. I might like you and I might not. Anyone who figures four days with me ain't worth the money, drop out now and save me the aggravation. Anyone who makes trouble on this trip can expect a pink slip when we get back. No exceptions."

No one moved, and a horse snorted. The drovers looked down, except for Harley, who looked straight at Andy, nothing against him yet, apparently. Dakota's gaze didn't drop, either, but her expression hadn't exactly softened. Romeo started to prance in place, and Andy tightened his hold on the reins.

"Good. I take that to mean you're all in. You're here because Chet wanted you here or because I hired you. You're all good at what you do, and we can make this a smooth ride. Let's review the route."

They'd ride to the first camp at Loggerhead Creek, where the cooks would be waiting. The cooks this year were Andy's uncle and aunt, and they'd drive a horse trailer over with two pack horses. The next morning Andy and the drovers would set out for the foothills where the cattle were grazing. They'd take the pack horses with them to carry the kit they needed for their next camp. They'd cross the Hell Bent River, which lived up to its name during spring runoff, and they'd round up the cattle and camp there for the second night. Then they'd drive them back. They'd stop once more at Loggerhead Creek, where they'd camp again, drop off the pack horses, and then carry enough food with them to drive the cattle home. Four days. It was a pretty smooth operation. Chet had worked out the kinks in the last three years since his marriage.

"Any questions?" Andy asked, looking over the group, the morning sun shining at their backs so that he had to squint. No one broke the silence, so Andy gave a curt nod. "Let's go."

He pulled Romeo around. The other drovers kicked their horses into motion and they all set out at a brisk canter toward the western pasture. Andy hung back and then took up the rear. His earlier bravado was starting to wane and he glanced over his shoulder, back at the ranch.

He remembered the last cattle drive he'd done with his dad and brother. Riding out with the drovers had seemed like an adventure, except that his father had always talked more seriously with Chet. He'd ask Chet's opinion; suggest different ways Chet could look at things. Chet got advice and Andy got criticism. He'd treated Chet like the heir and Andy was more like a visitor along for the fun of the drive.

Keep out of the way, Andy. Your brother has this one.

Andy, you're going to get yourself kicked in the head if you keep that up!

Andy, why don't you go start supper? We'll take care of the rest out here...

It had always been like that. Chet and Dad had a kind of bond Andy couldn't explain or share. They were alike—serious, quiet and immovable. Andy, on the other hand, had laughed louder and filled those silences his brother and father left hanging out in the stillness. And now, as a grown man, he felt the resurgence of adolescent angst. Andy had been better at ranch work than his father ever knew because, frankly, his father never stopped to notice.

Elliot dismounted and opened the gate that led into the pasture. The fence stretched out across the rolling field, shrinking and blurring into the distance until it dropped out of sight down a steep grade on one side and climbed the rolling incline on the other. A fence was a constant source of upkeep for a rancher, and Andy could appreciate the sight of a well-maintained one. The gate opened with a groan and when they'd all filed through, Elliot closed it again with the thump of metal against wooden post, fastening the latch.

The pasture opened up ahead of them, the grass rippling in a cold wind that cut across the plains with nothing to stop it. The snow might be late this year, but it would come, and overhead there was another honking V of geese moving south. Andy kicked Romeo into motion and the drovers fanned out, each taking some space as they rode.

He'd known on that last cattle drive that none of it would change. Ever. It was on horseback with the drovers that Andy had decided to make his own life and his own future away from the land he'd grown up on. Andy loved the land, too—or he had until he'd realized that it would never be his. But while his brother loved the very soil under his boots, Andy had loved the horizon—that tickle of land meeting sky, so full of possibility. He loved the disappearing line of fence as it dwindled into the distance, and the gentle touch of pink along the horizon as the sun crept slowly upward. He liked clouds that soared like battleships, leaving dark shadows beneath them, and the whistle of wind past his face as he rode at full gallop. The soil was good, but the horizon was better. He might be pushed out of the ranch, but that didn't push him out of life. Sometimes, it was best not to get attached to something never intended for you anyway.

Andy found himself watching Dakota from the corner of his eye as she slowly overtook him. She was an experienced rider and her attention appeared to be on the scenery around them. A glowing sunrise and frost melting into dew as far the sunbeams stretched. She blended into the moment seamlessly, a cowgirl cantering across the pasture, and Andy sucked in a chilled breath of morning air. He'd do well to keep his focus off the backside of Dakota Mason—she was another one never meant for the likes of him.

Watching his team riding, horse strides lengthening into a comfortable gate, riders settling into the motion, he felt that same sense of disconnect he'd felt all those years ago—he was an outsider here. But looking at Dakota ride, her ponytail bouncing on her back, her hips moving with the horse underneath her, he felt a different kind of longing. This Montana land wasn't his and it never would be, but if he could belong anywhere, he wanted it to be with a woman like Dakota. Dwight had never deserved her, and maybe Andy didn't, either, but he'd have at least treated her right.

But that had been a long time ago—too long ago to even matter now that they were all adults. He'd felt a twinge of that when he'd seen Mackenzie again four years ago. She'd reminded him of what he wanted most, too, but that had been more of a nostalgic shiver, a realization that he'd been an idiot way back then. Looking at Dakota—this rooted him to the here and now, and that was probably more dangerous.

Elliot urged his horse forward and edged their mounts closer together as he caught up. Elliot pushed his hat farther down onto his head, water-blue eyes squinted in the low-angled sunlight. The older drover gave him a curt nod of greeting.

"So you hired the kid." It was a statement not a question.

"Yep."

"You know much about him?" Elliot inquired.

"Not a whole lot. But he seems to know his stuff and he was pretty desperate for a job." It was the same question anyone around here would ask—what did they know about him? But a body was a body when you needed to round up four hundred cows.

"He's been to prison," Elliot said.

"What?" Andy looked over at Harley, who rode next to Dakota. "How do you know that?"

"Just do." Elliot made a clicking sound with his mouth and the horses eased apart again. "Keep an eye on him, is all."

As Elliot moved farther away, Andy continued to eye the kid in question. He couldn't even grow a full mustache and he had a faintly naive look about him, like dirty jokes would spoil his innocence. Harley appeared to say something to Dakota and she laughed, the sound skipping along the breeze and melting into the rippling grass.

Either Elliot was lying or the Bible-carrying kid had the best poker face Andy had ever seen. Either way, this drive was about to get a whole lot more interesting.

After a few hours of riding, the sun was shining warm and golden on Dakota's shoulders. The air was warmer now, but the wind was cold when it picked up. Autumn could be like that—bitingly cold in the morning and then unseasonably warm, all within a matter of hours. But they were in December and while it still looked like fall around these parts, the wind promised change. The land was a succession of rolling hills as they headed toward the mountains, and meandering lines of rocky creek beds spider-webbed into the cleavage of the hills. Cold mountain water babbled across stones, giving extra moisture for clusters of trees to dig down their roots and drink.

They reined in by a copse of fiery-hued trees to have something to eat and let the horses graze. When the wind picked up, the leaves swirled off the branches, circling and spinning as they sailed out over the grassland, leaving the trees just a little barer—just a little closer to naked.

It felt good to dismount and Dakota stretched her back, letting the tension in her muscles seep away. She loved riding. When she was on her own ranch, she preferred jobs like checking on the cattle or the condition of the fences because it meant she could ride all morning, face to the wind and heart soaring.

The men dismounted, as well. Dakota had been watching them as they rode. She'd spoken with a few. There was Harley, the innocent-looking kid who sparked her maternal side. She didn't know what it was about him, but she wanted to ruffle his hair. Then there was Elliot, who was silent but not altogether unfriendly. Carlos and Finn were both in their midtwenties and had flirted a bit, that is until Elliot put his horse between them and drove them off with that annoyed stare of his. Dave was goofy and joked around a lot, his humor bawdy but funny, but he knew his way around a horse.

And then there was Andy. Andy hadn't made much contact as they'd ridden. He'd kept back, surveying the land and possibly just keeping to himself. It was hard to tell. She'd expected him to talk to her somewhat, but he hadn't said a word. She wasn't disappointed about that; she was wary. Andy wasn't a man to be trusted, and she resented that he acted so honest and straight-shooting. A man who could hide his character was worse than one who wore it on his sleeve, and it looked like Andy had learned to hide a few things.

Or he'd reformed. Which was more likely?

Dakota unbuckled the saddlebag and pulled out the food she'd packed. There were two multigrain bagels filled with thick slabs of cream cheese, some dried fruit and an apple turnover.

"Are you ready for a rest?" Dakota asked softly, stroking Barney's neck. "You really are a sweetheart, you know."

The horse bent to take a mouthful of grass and she patted his shoulder. He wandered off a few paces, seeming to enjoy his temporary freedom.

Elliot, Dave, Finn and Carlos were sitting together on some rocks by a dried-up creek laughing at something—probably a joke told by Dave. He seemed to be an unending fount of raunchy humor, mostly centered on the women he'd dated, who seemed a questionable lot. Harley sat alone, a little ways off. He was opening a foil-wrapped sandwich and his gaze flickered up toward her as if he'd felt her curiosity. She gave him a cordial nod, which he returned then turned his attention to his food.

Andy sauntered in her direction and she was struck anew with those Granger good looks. He was tall, broad-shouldered, and he had the rolling gate of a man who knew how to ride.

"Hi." Andy paused a few feet from her then nodded toward a patch of shade a couple yards off. "Care to eat with me?"

No, she didn't want to eat with him, but avoiding the man wasn't going to be possible. She'd taken the job, and part of that job was dealing with the boss, so she silently followed his lead and they settled themselves on their jackets to eat. Dakota unwrapped a bagel, the scent of whole wheat making her stomach rumble.

"Nice speech earlier," Dakota said, taking a bite.

"That's a rehash of another speech I gave when I bought the dealership. That was a complicated time for worker morale."

It was strange, because she'd never really thought of Andy as a successful businessman before—more like an improperly rewarded fiend. But he did have a good sense when it came to getting people to work with him, and a team of drovers was probably the hardest group to win over. Not that he'd succeeded yet, but they'd stayed, which was more than she'd expected.

"So—" Dakota paused to swallow a bite "—you're doing well with the dealership, then."

"Yeah." He nodded. "I've built it up. When I bought it, it was barely breaking even, but after three years, it's making a steady profit. That doesn't come easily."

He'd made money, but that didn't mean he was liked—she knew that well enough. Sometimes the wealthiest men were the most hated because they'd climbed on the backs of the little guy to get where they were. She was curious what sort of boss Andy was when he was away from the town that knew him so well.

"How many employees stayed?" she asked.

"Most of them. A few were ticked off at the change of management style, and it didn't take too long to encourage them to move to something else." He took a bite of his sandwich and chewed thoughtfully then shot her a smile. "I'm good at it, you know."

Was he bragging now? It was hard to tell. Didn't he realize that he was announcing this to the woman who needed extra jobs to keep the family business afloat? In the distance a flock of birds lifted like a flapping sheet and then came back down in a fluttering billow.

"Good at what?" she asked curtly.

"Making money." He shrugged. So he was bragging. It was in bad taste and she shot him a flat look.

"What?" He frowned. "Hey, I know you all wanted me to go to Billings and fail miserably. Sorry to disappoint." He was silent for a moment. "I wanted this ranch. Well, my dad's part of it, at least."

Dakota's swallowed. "You always made it pretty clear you didn't want this life."

"I had to talk myself out of it," he replied with a shrug. "Haven't you ever wanted something you could never have? I wasn't going to get it, and I didn't feel like waiting around for the rejection. My brother was the heir and I was the spare."

"So if Chet hadn't been interested—" She wiped some crumbs from her jeans.

"Yeah, if I'd had a fighting chance at running this place, I'd have done it." He nodded. "But you've got to work with what you've got. That's life."

They were both silent for a couple of minutes as they ate. Dakota polished off the bagel and moved on to the dried apricots, sweet and tangy.

She and Andy had their desire to work the land in common, as well as their status as second-born. She'd always wanted to work her family's land, too. What would she have done if Brody had shared the same dream? Ever since they were kids, Brody had wanted to join the army. He played soldier. She played cowgirl. Knowing her brother's ambitions, her only problem was trying to open her father's eyes to reality. But what if her reality was more like Andy's and she loved the land that she'd never inherit?

But even then, she would have loved the land enough to keep it from developers. This community meant something to her, and outsiders didn't understand the heart of Hope. Maybe this was part of his talent—drawing in his employees so that they liked him against their better instincts.

"So why a car dealership?" she asked. There had to be plenty of other business opportunities around Billings. It was the largest city in Montana, after all.

"It seemed like a sound investment." He gave her a wry smile. "But no one dreams of spending fourteen hours a day on a car lot."

"So it was about the money for you?" she asked.

Andy popped the last bite of sandwich into his mouth and spoke past it. "Money? Uh-uh. I needed a life. So I built one."

So he'd settled, and in the process made a small fortune. When there were people following their hearts and just about losing their land, that seemed unfair. He might have built a life for himself, but it had come at a cost other people were forced to pay. Apparently karma had been sleeping on the job.

"What about you?" he asked. "Ever wanted to see what was out there in the big, wide world?"

"I want the ranch," she said. It was all she'd ever wanted. "And I'm not giving up on that."

"All right, then," he said, a small smile on his lips. "Do you think you'll get it?"

"You think I won't?" she shot back. "What do you know about it?"

He put up his hands. "Just asking."

She sighed. Picking fights with the man wasn't going to make this drive any easier, so she decided to answer. "I think I'll get it. Eventually."

Somehow. She was the one at home, wasn't she? She was the one working extra jobs, working the land, poring over ledgers in the evening…

"I hope you do," he said quietly. "Because if you don't, it'll be years wasted and, trust me—there will be resentment. You might think you'll be all open-minded and forgiving, but it feels different on the other side."

Andy turned back to his food and she mulled over his words. She was driven, focused on her dream for the future, but what if things didn't turn out the way she expected? What then? She couldn't see herself in any other role than this one—cowgirl, rancher. Would she have the strength to start fresh? That was a scary thought.

Angry voices cracked the stillness and Dakota's gaze shot toward the other drovers. Harley and Elliot were on their feet, glaring at each other.

"Say it again, kid..." Elliot's voice held a threat.

"You're a gutless wimp—" Harley didn't seem to be taking his opponent's size into the equation here. Elliot's expression was one of derision and he cracked his knuckles slowly, one by one, the popping sound carrying more clearly than their words. Harley quivered with raw rage, that baby face suddenly looking a whole lot meaner. The other men moved back, out of self-preservation or an instinct to let the males fight for status, Dakota had no idea, but things were about to get ugly.

"Getting tense over there," Andy said, his attention fixed on the men with a directness that belied his conversational tone.

"Are you going to step in?" It was less of a question, more of suggestion.

Andy's expression was guarded and his muscles tensed. He didn't answer her. This was where Andy was going to prove himself or fall short.

Harley was smaller than Elliot by quite a bit, thinner, shorter. He was downright suicidal to be taking on a man Elliot's size, in Dakota's humble opinion. Elliot was tougher, harder, older. Elliot didn't even see it coming when Harley threw a punch and caught Elliot in the jaw. The bigger man staggered back, shook it off, then stalked forward, a deadly look in his eye.

"That's all you've got?" Elliot challenged.

"Hey!" Andy roared, rising to his feet, and Dakota was momentarily stunned at the sheer size of him. Andy was a big man, six foot one with broad shoulders, and when he fixed that direct stare on someone it was downright intimidating.

Elliot slammed Harley in the gut, doubling him over, and Andy arrived at the scene in time to grab Harley by the collar and toss him effortlessly to the side. He rolled twice before landing on his backside. Andy stood solidly between Elliot and Harley.

"That's enough." Andy's voice was low but it carried. Dakota hurried to where Harley sat on the ground, staring at a spot between his knees. He was probably trying not to vomit after that blow to his belly. She put a hand on his arm and he jerked it away then spat. Ironically, Elliot was probably the worse for wear after that short scuffle, but given any more time, Harley would have been in very rough shape.

"That was dumb," she muttered. "He's a whole lot bigger than you, if you hadn't noticed."

Harley didn't answer.

Dakota shook her head and stood.

Andy was staring down Elliot, both men of similar height, but of the two of them, Andy was bulkier.

"Let it go!" Andy said, meeting Elliot's furious gaze. "I'm serious. Let it go."

"Or what?" Elliot growled. "You'll fire me? You can't. I work for your brother."

"Don't push me, Elliot." Andy's tone was menacing and Dakota glanced at the other men. They were looking away uncomfortably. This was going to affect their pecking order, she was sure. After a couple of beats Elliot muttered an oath and stepped back.

"What was that about?" Andy demanded, whirling

around to face Harley. "You threw the first punch—I saw that much."

"Nothing."

"Elliot?" Andy demanded, shooting an icy glare toward the other man.

"Nothing!" he barked.

Dakota could see that was as far as Andy was going to get with the two men. They obviously knew each other, had a few resentments stewing and weren't about to open up about it to the likes of Andy. Still, Andy had risen to the occasion in a way she hadn't expected. Faced with the testy tempers of a couple of drovers, he'd matched them and backed them down. That took guts and a certain amount of confidence that left her grudgingly impressed. Somehow she'd expected the city convert to have lost some of his country edge, but she'd been wrong about that.

"All right." Andy raised his voice so everyone could hear. "I'm going to say this once and only once. Anyone who gets himself beaten up on this drive is going to have to ride like that. You break it, it's gonna hurt like hell on horseback. Now clean up. We're heading out in five."

Carlos, Finn and Dave looked at Andy with new respect, and Dakota watched as Harley and Elliot headed off in opposite directions. That left Dakota standing alone, the remnants of her lunch lying in the grass a couple of yards away. She brushed off her hands and eyed the men around her.

"Idiots," Andy muttered as he came past her, his strong arm brushing her shoulder. He'd earned something this morning—something that would last for the remainder of the drive—and she was glad that he had.

Every cattle drive needed a clear leader and, for better or for worse, Andy was theirs.

She gathered up the last of her wrappers and the food she hadn't eaten, and headed out to where her horse was grazing a few yards off. Barney had completely ignored the human kerfuffle and she envied him that ability. It would be nice to be able to take his place in the open plains, melt into the wind and skim over the waving grassland, leaving her worries about the future far away.

"Dakota."

She turned to find Andy looking at her with a gentler look than she'd seen yet. He had Romeo by the reins and he adjusted his hat on his head with his free hand. "Watch yourself, okay?"

What was he worried about, exactly? She'd grown up with guys just like this; she knew how to deal with them. She'd even dated Dwight, who'd turned out to be twice as bad as these guys when he'd had a few drinks in him. Andy had said he was no lost kitten, and neither was she. She'd worked her father's land when Andy had been shirking responsibility, and she'd worked shoulder to shoulder with rougher men than these.

Andy still didn't look settled, but he gave her a nod and put a boot into the stirrup. He swung himself up into the saddle and surveyed the group with a slow, cool gaze.

She mounted once more, feeling more secure on her horse's back, and she kicked him into motion. She could feel Andy's gaze drilling into the back of her as she passed him. When she looked back over her shoulder, he gave her a nod, flicking the brim of his hat. But his granite expression didn't change. Apparently he didn't find anything to joke about in the present circumstances, and that was something she could finally respect.

This drive would be so much easier if Andy Granger could just live up to expectations and fail. It would also be a lot easier if he stopped being so blasted human.

Sympathizing with him hadn't been part of her plan, and it still wasn't. They'd never been friends, and she didn't need to be now; she was only here for the paycheck.

Chapter 4

That evening when Dakota dismounted, her legs ached from the long ride. She didn't normally ride for a full day like this unless she was doing a cattle drive. On her own land, she'd ride out to check on cattle in the nearer pastures, even escape for a morning of riding just for the pleasure, but the hard riding—the pushing forward and the not stopping, riding from sunup to sundown—happened once a year and her body had to get accustomed to the trail all over again.

They'd been riding west all day and for the last hour, the lowering sun had blinded her until it finally slipped behind the mountains in a final explosion of gold and crimson. She stretched her back, the movement feeling good on her cramped muscles. Daylight was gone and, while the sky still glowed orange at their position beside the foothills, dusk had arrived.

A fire was already roaring in a makeshift pit, some lawn chairs set around it in preparation for tired, cold cowhands. The camp was pitched beside a copse of creeping juniper and spruce trees that provided some shelter from the steady wind. The tang of sap and tree needles mingled with the mouthwatering aroma of corn bread and beefy chili that made her stomach growl, and Dakota watched as the others headed straight to the table laden with food.

"Hot cocoa?" Lydia asked with a friendly smile. She wore a knitted scarf around her neck and some fingerless gloves.

Dakota gratefully accepted a mug of frothy cocoa, two large marshmallows floating on top. She took a sip and licked her lips.

"Delicious," she said with a smile. "Thanks."

Lydia had fried sausages, canned peaches and three tubs of sour cream alongside the chili and corn bread. Within a matter of minutes, everyone was served heaping helpings of the feast.

When her own family did cattle drives, Dakota would look forward to this time of day when the work was done and they could settle around the crackling fire, talking and laughing. People said more after they'd eaten. There was something about that open sky, the pinprick of stars and the snap of a fire that made the consequences of words feel further away. Her grandfather's stories were always more interesting on the cattle drive than at any other time. He'd dug deeper out there, told the tales that were more honest and painted people as they really were. If she wanted to learn about her ancestors, the cattle drive was the place to do it.

But this was different. This was the Granger drive,

and most of the people here were hired hands. There would be no family stories told, and it only served to remind her that from here on out, they were going deeper into the wilderness, beyond the reach of roads and of rescue. The next night wouldn't be this comfortable and they'd be working hard, not just riding, very soon.

Andy stood to the side with his uncle, Bob, arms crossed over his chest. There was tension between them that she could see in the way they stood, arms crossed, a few feet apart, not looking directly at each other—they were family but Andy wasn't much more popular with his own kin than he was with the rest of Hope. Andy had made the Grangers look bad, and the Grangers cared about their collective reputation in these parts. They had a name to protect.

The other men were around the fire, dipping their corn bread into their bowls of chili and bringing it dripping to their mouths. Everyone was hungry. Her gaze moved toward Andy. He looked a lot like his brother out here with those broad shoulders and, despite the tension, his kind eyes. Funny that she'd notice Andy's eyes when she of all people shouldn't be fooled by them. Dwight had kind eyes, too, but you put a drop of whiskey into him and he got nasty right quick.

Dakota stirred the healthy dollop of sour cream into her spicy chili then took a bite. Food tasted better by firelight somehow. She glanced up as Harley sank into a lawn chair next to her, his plate balanced precariously on one hand.

"Hey," he said, taking a bite of corn bread.

She nodded to him and turned back to her own food. This was the time to fill up because after this, they'd only be able to eat what they carried and the fare went downhill quickly. The heat from the fire could reach them easily enough, and she enjoyed the way it warmed her shins first.

"So what's he like?" Harley asked past a bite of food.

"Who?" She glanced in Harley's direction again to find the kid's gaze directed toward Andy.

"Mr. Granger," he said.

"Andy?" She laughed softly. It was definitely strange to hear Andy referred to as mister, but then he probably was called "Mr." all the time back in Billings. It was only here in Hope that he'd never stop being plain old Andy. "You afraid he's going to fire you after that dustup with Elliot?"

She cast Harley an amused look.

"Will he?" Harley looked less than amused.

"I have no idea." That was the honest answer. Andy had promised anyone who caused trouble a pink slip upon returning, but then, Harley's job was over once they got back anyway, so for Harley that wouldn't make much of a difference. "I highly doubt he'll send you packing at this point. We need the bodies. You're only here for the drive, I thought."

"Yeah." Harley gulped back another bite of food. "But if there was work, I might offer to stay on."

There it was. Harley was hoping to be a little less temporary.

"What are you doing out here, anyway?" she asked, dipping the heel of her corn bread into the last of the chili in her bowl.

Harley didn't answer right away and she thought that maybe he wouldn't, but after polishing off his last sausage, he turned toward her.

"You want to know?" he asked.

"Yeah."

Dakota eyed him with new curiosity as he told his side of things—the story of what had brought him to Montana to begin with. He was old-fashioned, she realized, with a streak of wounded honor. There wasn't a lot of place for that in the modern world, but if it could fit in anywhere, it would be a place like Montana, where a man's word was still supposed to mean something without a legal contract to back it up. There could be so much drama behind the shuttered faces of these cowboys, so many stories that no one would even guess at. He sounded older than he looked with that wispy mustache and those soulful eyes, and he seemed to notice her expression because he shot her a rueful smile.

"What?" he asked.

"How old are you?"

"Twenty-two."

She chuckled. Twenty-two wasn't exactly grizzled. She was just about thirty, but she could sympathize. She remembered feeling awfully grown up at twenty-two herself. She'd already ended a relationship to an abusive alcoholic.

"You're still pretty young for those old-fashioned ideals," she retorted. She still had the urge to ruffle his hair…what could she say?

Harley didn't answer and he looked away. His jean jacket was pushed up his forearms to reveal what looked like a tattoo. It was crudely drawn, though, in the shape of a Celtic cross. Dakota tilted her head to the side to get a better look.

"What's that?" she asked.

Harley pulled his sleeve down, shielding his arm from view.

"Life experience," he replied dryly.

There was more to his story and she was willing to bet it was a whole lot more interesting than any of them had been giving him credit for. But he deserved a warning.

"Elliot's tougher than you might think," Dakota said quietly. "Don't go picking fights with him out here. We're miles from civilization and I'd hate to tempt his baser instincts."

"Noted," Harley said quietly.

Harley's gaze flickered in Elliot's direction and he nodded. At least he'd heard her warning, and she could only hope he'd take it.

Dakota glanced in Andy's direction and caught him watching her. How long had he been doing that? He had a plate in his hand now and he was chewing, his expression thoughtful. When she noticed him, he gave her a slight nod in acknowledgment and turned his attention to his food.

Andy seemed different out here, too. He looked more like the rancher, the boss, and less like the prodigal son. There was something about the expanse of grassy plains—the jagged drops and narrow crevices—and the rugged mountains that soared above them, closer now than ever. This cocktail of rugged wildness brought men and women down to their most elemental selves.

Stock markets and numbers in a bank account meant nothing out there, but a man's character meant a lot. Leadership and survival was based on an internal strength, not an external counter, and the farther they got from civilization, the clearer that difference became. There were some people she'd trust with her life out in the wilderness and others she'd never cross town lines with. And Andy…

His green eyes were fixed on her again and she met his gaze evenly. She didn't know exactly where he landed in her estimation of men and their character at this very moment, but he was standing stronger than she'd ever imagined he would.

"Come get more, everyone!" Lydia called from the table. "Eat it before it's cold!"

Dakota rose. She'd make good on that offer—this was her chance to eat before the real work started. A smart woman always took a second helping.

Later that evening Andy sat beside the low-burning fire, orange coals glowing against the dark ground. Of the four tents pitched on the far side of the fire, one glowed from the light of a flashlight. Apparently, Harley was reading. The horses munched hay, the sound peaceful and soothing. Andy was taking the first watch and Bob would take the second. He could hear his uncle's snores already from the back of the van where he and Aunt Lydia were sleeping. They were far enough out that wolves and coyotes could be an issue if they didn't have a lookout.

Andy grabbed a log and tossed it onto the fire. The coals erupted in a shower of sparks then the dry bark caught the flame with a crackle.

Andy wasn't the last one awake. Dakota stood by Barney, giving him one last brush before bed, but Andy had a feeling she'd been putting off going to bed until the men were out of the way. She could hold her own, but these ranch hands weren't her family's employees, which would change the balance of power there. She was just another drover on this drive, albeit a prettier version than the others. Her hair hung long and loose down her back, the milky white of her hands vivid in the pale moonlight.

She's beautiful.

He'd always thought she was gorgeous, but she'd been the one woman solidly out of his league. Dakota wasn't just "a girl," she was smart, opinionated and way better than any of them deserved. When she'd turned him down for Dwight, it had stung—more than stung. But then he'd met Mackenzie and Mack had actually returned his feelings. That had been the most passionate summer of his youth, but he still hadn't been content. Maybe he'd have done the same thing to Dakota back then if she'd accepted him. He hadn't exactly been mature and he'd had a mighty high opinion of his own masculinity.

Dakota finished with the horse and turned, freezing for a moment when she saw him watching her. He inwardly winced. He'd made her uncomfortable—that hadn't been the plan. He looked back at the log that had started to burn in earnest and he could hear the crunch of her boots as she came closer. She sank into the chair next to him.

"You're on watch?" she asked quietly.

"The first one," he said. "You going to bed now?"

She shook her head. "Not yet."

He found himself pleased to hear that. He'd assumed that she'd turn in and he'd be left with his thoughts, but a few minutes' worth of company wasn't unwelcome.

Harley's flashlight went out and the camp was silent and dim except for the crackle of the fire.

"You're doing better than I thought," she said, shooting him a wry smile.

"You expected me to crash and burn so soon?" Andy chuckled softly. "Sorry to disappoint."

"I didn't say I was disappointed," she replied. "You did well with Harley and Elliot. That could have gotten ugly."

Andy leaned forward, holding his hands out to the fire. "It might get ugly yet. They won't talk, so whatever caused it is still simmering."

"Harley did."

Andy shot her a look of surprise. Harley had opened up? This was information he needed but he didn't want to chance being overheard. He stood and nodded in the direction of the edge of the camp where moonlight illuminated the rough, prairie grass. Dakota rose and they made their way from the trees and tents to where the open countryside spilled out before them, bathed in the silvery wash of moonlight.

A few black clouds scudded across the star-studded sky, leaving faint shadows on the land beneath. A coyote trotted silently across the grassland, a fresh catch in its mouth.

"So what's the deal?" Andy asked quietly.

"Elliot is involved with Harley's sister," she said. "Apparently she's pregnant and wanted to get married. Elliot didn't want to. I'm not sure what happened, exactly, but Harley is under the impression that his sister could do better and he came to Montana to try and bring her back home."

Andy rolled this new information over in his head. So Elliot was about to be a father… He and Chet both. Andy found himself mildly envious. It was an intimidating amount of responsibility to have a family to support, but it was the kind of challenge that Andy had always known he wanted one day. He couldn't help feeling a small pang of envy.

"Elliot said something earlier," Andy said after a moment. "Something about Harley having been in prison."

"He didn't mention that," she said. "But he did have a tattoo on his arm that looked…amateurish."

A prison tattoo? The thought still didn't sit right with him. But then, maybe that New Testament in his pocket was more about new starts than it was about his past. His decision to take the kid on may have been a hasty one. Still, Andy was pretty good with judging character, and Harley hadn't seemed elusive.

"He doesn't seem like the type," Andy said after a moment.

A frigid wind picked up and Dakota shivered.

"Come here," Andy said.

She looked at him distrustfully.

Andy rolled his eyes and took her by the shoulders, positioning her closer to him. He angled his body so that he blocked the worst of it, but he liked having her this near to him. He dropped his hands and they stood there, barely inches apart. He was her boss—nothing more.

Dakota's hair whipped up in the wind and she pulled it back, tilting her chin up as she did to meet his gaze. She only seemed to realize then how close they stood together and she stepped back, a cautious look on her face.

"I'm not trying anything," he said, his voice low. "It's cold. That's all."

He cared what she thought of him, because while he might not be her favorite man, her dislike of him was at least honest. If she was going to resent him, it might as well be for the truth, not something false. And he wasn't making a move on her. Tempted? Yes, but controlled. If he ever did make a move, she'd be absolutely clear about his intentions.

"I know." She didn't sound as convinced as he'd have liked.

"You still think I'm a womanizer, do you?" he asked with a low laugh. "It's not true, you know."

"I knew you, Andy." She shook her head. "Dwight used to tell me stories about you."

Dwight Petersen was the reason Andy had backed off and never asked Dakota out again. Friends didn't move in on each other's girls. But Dwight had changed over the years.

He remembered one trip back home when Dakota had knocked a can of soda off the counter and it had exploded open, splattering the kitchen floor and bottom cabinets. While Andy's first instinct had been to laugh at the way she'd jumped a foot in the air, Dwight had laid into her, calling her an idiot and growling about how she'd better clean it up. A few others had grabbed towels and lent a hand while Andy had pulled his buddy aside and told him straight that he'd better get it together because Dakota wouldn't put up with that garbage for long.

He'd been right. In a matter of weeks she'd broken off their engagement, and Andy had been relieved. Dakota deserved better than a man who didn't know a good woman when he had one. Thinking about Dwight's rage still left Andy uneasy, years later, and it made him wonder what, exactly, Dwight had told her about him.

"Back then, I might've been a bit of a womanizer,

but that was then. A lot of things changed—including Dwight, might I add."

Dakota smiled wanly. "You're telling me that while Dwight turned into a drunk, you improved?"

He laughed softly. "I grew up, Dakota. We all do it eventually...except for Dwight, apparently. My last serious relationship lasted four years, and I almost married her. I've been single for the three years since. I don't think you can exactly call me a rake. Not anymore, at least. There's got to be a statute of limitations on that."

Surprise registered in those brown eyes and he felt a surge of satisfaction. At least he'd be able to blow apart one of her preconceptions.

"I'd heard you were engaged," she said.

"See?" He shot her a grin. "I'm not half as bad as you think."

Ida had been a wonderful woman. He could have been happy married to her, but there was something missing from their relationship, something he'd been looking for and never quite found. His brother had managed to find it with Mackenzie, but it was one of those intangible qualities that made all the difference in a relationship.

"You still managed to garner quite the reputation, you know," she noted.

"And you always managed to see right through me," he retorted. "You never liked me, Dakota. You didn't hide your feelings too well."

She frowned at that, cast him a sidelong look and then turned her attention to the rolling countryside.

"I didn't hate you."

"Didn't say hate," he said. "But you didn't much like me, either."

She shrugged in acceptance of that and he smiled at the irony. He'd never bonded with a woman before over her general dislike of him, but there was a first for everything.

"The thing is…you never fell for my act."

"So you admit it was an act," she shot back.

"Sure." He shrugged. "Every guy has an act." What man wanted to advertise the things that hurt?

"Is this an act now?" She looked up at him, her clear gaze meeting his, and he dropped the urge to joke or flirt. She was serious and he sensed that she needed an honest answer from him. If they were going to work together, she needed to trust him.

"I've got nothing left to fake," he said quietly. "I'm the least popular guy in town, trying to hold things together for my brother. I'm just trying to get the job done. People will think what they think. Don't worry. I know where I stand with you."

"Which is where?" she asked, a small smile on her lips.

"Halfway at civil."

Color rose in her cheeks and she looked away again. "I should get to bed, Andy. It'll be a long day tomorrow."

"You should." He'd known she wouldn't stay out with him long, but it had been nice all the same. There was something about being alone with Dakota under the big Montana sky that woke a part of him that had been dormant for too long…a part that wanted to connect, talk, share. It was a dangerous temptation and parting ways was probably the wisest choice right now. This was temporary and he had no intention of complicating matters.

She took a few steps toward the tents then turned back, those dark eyes glittering in the moonlight. "I don't want to be friends, Andy."

"I know." He shot her a grin. "We aren't. We tolerate each other at best. Like always."

She laughed softly and he felt a surge of satisfaction at having made her laugh in spite of it all. She turned away again, heading toward her tent, and he returned his gaze to the rolling countryside.

The land spread out before him in a comforting expanse of nothing. The horizon, dark and distant, still tugged at him as it always had.

Dakota might have never liked him much, but he'd always grudgingly liked her. She was strong, smart and capable, and perhaps the proof of those qualities was in her instinctual distrust of him. While the other girls thought they might be the one to hook him, she'd never been inclined to try.

And now he was the one who'd ruined her family's land. She still wouldn't be inclined and somehow that made him like her all the more. She was the one woman he could trust to be completely honest with him. And perhaps she was the only woman who wanted absolutely nothing from him.

She didn't want to be friends. And neither did he. He wasn't a lukewarm kind of guy.

Chapter 5

The next day the tents, bedding and food were loaded onto the pack horses and the team set out amid the early morning mist, climbing steadily up the foothills. The land was rockier and craggier here, the scrub that erupted from gullies and lined streams now dry and scratching. Lydia and Bob had headed in the other direction. They'd be back in two days, but with the Grangers also left their last contact with civilization for the next couple of days. Out this far, their cell phones didn't even work.

Dakota settled into the rhythm in her saddle, but her mind was sifting through more than the upcoming work of rounding up the cattle. She was thinking about her conversation with Andy in the moonlight. She'd been completely honest when she'd told him she didn't want to be friends. She had a lot of reasons to resent him, but standing out there miles away from home and the pressures awaiting her there, she'd felt something unexpected…she'd *liked* him.

Attraction was something Dakota could deal with. Attraction was nothing more than a biochemical reaction, but liking someone went deeper. And, yes, Andy was definitely attractive. He had those Granger genes, after all—the wide shoulders, smoldering eyes and perfect swagger in his boots. That wasn't extraordinary, though. There were any number of good-looking cowboys; calendar companies made a fortune off them. But *liking* him…

She'd always sworn she'd never be pulled in by empty flattery and she knew Andy from their childhood onward, so she was supposed to know better than to fall for his charms. Andy had been a teenager full of flash with no substance. Then he'd matured into a grown man who'd sold them all out to the highest bidder. So standing with him in the moonlight, listening to him tell her that he wasn't the cad she took him for…

For a moment she'd thought he was making a move on her. She would have known how to deal with that. But his respectful reserve? Before this cattle drive, she'd known exactly what to think of Andy and exactly where to file him. Now she wasn't as sure, and she had a feeling that would irritate her family to no end. For them, Andy was the villain, the scoundrel who'd ruined their livelihood. They didn't want to see any other side of him, and she didn't blame them. She didn't particularly want to see this side of him, either.

The team continued their ride westward, the rugged mountains growing ever closer as the air grew crisper. There was something about those looming peaks that made her feel smaller than ever in the countryside. Nature was bigger than the pride of human beings. Birch and aspens were more common now and the leaves were blazing in oranges and yellows. It was the kind of exuberant display that made her heart soar, if it weren't for other things weighing it back down.

A few deer watched them warily from the tree line and an elk or two could be spotted out in the middle of the plains, antlers raised in proud display. Heads would lower to the ground to graze then shoot back up at the sound of hooves echoed against stone.

They splashed across several shallow streams, the water babbling along smooth rocks, allowing the horses a chance to stop and drink. And when they did, she'd catch Andy looking at her. He never came close, but he still watched her with a guarded look on his face. Then Barney would raise his head, water dripping from his muzzle, and plod onward, hooves hitting rocks with a clatter as a cold wind whisked through her hair. She shivered. Her fingers were cold now and the tip of her nose. She rubbed her hands against her thighs to warm them.

Dakota had decided early that morning to ride as far from Andy as possible. But the closer they got to the mountains, the rockier and more narrow their path became and they were all forced into closer proximity.

"I can hear the river," Harley said, pulling his horse next to hers as they plodded along.

Dakota could hear the rush of water, too, so much deeper and intense than the trickle of creeks. It was still distant, but they'd be there soon, and on the other side would be the cattle.

"The real work starts today," she said, shooting Harley a smile. "You ready?"

"Always."

She was looking forward to this—the actual rounding up of the cattle. This was where they had less time for talk and their attention would be monopolized by keeping the cattle together and moving in the right direction. From today on out, she'd no longer be "the girl" on the drive, but another hand on a very big job.

Andy rode ahead of the team and for the next few minutes she could feel the anticipation growing with the men around her. This was what they'd signed on for.

"So what's your story with him?" Harley asked, nodding in Andy's direction.

"There isn't one," she replied.

"You sat up with him last night."

Irritation replaced her previous good humor. She wasn't about to have her reputation bandied about in the Hope gossip mill, and the fact that she'd had a conversation with Andy Granger didn't make her available for anything more than talk.

"I spoke with our boss," she said icily. "Got a problem with that?"

A leafy twig from a nearby tree slapped her in the chest and she pushed it away irritably.

"Hey, not picking a fight here," he said, easing his horse away. "It just looked like there was something more between you, that's all. Just curious."

So they'd been observed last night. The realization frustrated her. She'd thought the conversation had been private—the moment between the two of them. Realizing that it wasn't came as a rude awakening, because anything more than a professional discussion left her feeling like a sellout herself. If there was one thing Dakota believed in, it was loyalty to her family, and memories of her emotions last night left her feeling guilty.

Plus, she didn't want anyone to get the wrong idea about her and Andy. She wasn't along for the ride as the girlfriend, she was a hired hand. The difference mattered—one relied on a man's feelings for her, and the other relied on her own skill.

Her father deserved her loyalty, as did her brother fighting overseas. Andy Granger deserved nothing, and she needed to keep her position here straight in her own mind, as well as the other drovers'.

And yet she *had* liked him and definitely found him attractive in the way his direct green eyes met hers, pinning her to the spot without once touching her. If he had made contact, she would have pulled back, stomped off…but he hadn't. He'd just looked at her and shifted where he stood to keep the wind from hitting her so squarely, and somehow that act of protectiveness had kept her rooted to the spot.

Dakota kicked her horse into a faster pace, leaving Harley behind. Harley might have opened up to her about his sister, but that didn't mean she needed a confidant of her own. She had her situation well in hand.

Hell Bent River was close enough to see now as they crested a hill. It was an oxbow river meandering through the foothills. The banks farther upstream toward the mountains were lined by evergreen trees and a spattering of deciduous saplings glowing orange in the late-morning sunlight. Overhead, great, boiling clouds were moving in and, for a moment, the sunlight vanished and the trees turned from blazing orange to dull sienna. They sparked back into glory as the clouds pushed past, but the sky looked like rain wasn't too far off. That was the effect of the mountains, pushing the warm air upward until storms crashed down in a regular rhythm.

Across the river, before a stretch of forest, several acres of grassland spread out and a few cows were scattered across it, grazing lazily.

The sight of the cattle brought with it a flood of calm. Cattle had always done that for her. She wasn't sure what it was about bovine grazing that settled her in the deepest part of her soul.

"From what Chet said, the rest of the herd should be further on," Andy said.

Was he asking her input? She glanced at him and he raised his eyebrows expectantly.

"These are just a few stragglers, but we're close," she confirmed.

Andy didn't answer, but she knew he'd heard her. Whether he liked it or not, he needed her expertise out here. It wasn't bragging to note the obvious—she was better at this part of the drive than he was. The cattle would be spread out as far as they could comfortably wander over a summer, and it was the drovers' job to spread out wide and start moving them in toward the center. The river would act as a natural corral the cows wouldn't cross without some significant persuasion. It was an ideal setup.

The other drovers had reined their horses in close by and Andy raised his voice.

"Carlos and Finn, you go north. Dave and Elliot, go south. Dakota and I are circling around back to the west, and Harley, you stay with the pack horses and start setting up camp. Come west once you're done. We're bringing them all back to this spot here, and then we'll camp for the night on the far side of the river. First thing tomorrow, we'll take them across the river and start for home." He glanced around at the men who stared back, faces immobile. "Stay safe, take time to think, and let's do this!"

Andy glanced at Dakota and she pushed her hat more firmly onto her head and shot him a grin. "Let's ride!"

Without any further prompting, the six of them kicked their horses into motion, came down the other side of the hill and toward the river. The work had officially started.

Romeo stretched out beneath Andy, lengthening his stride. The horse's hooves thundered beneath him, a rumble that moved up his thighs and into his stomach. The river was wider and deeper than the other streams they'd crossed and he could feel Romeo tense the closer they came to the water. Ahead of him, Elliot was the first to plunge into the river, the water coming up to the horse's stifle as he slowed, pushing against the lazy current. Elliot urged the horse forward with a shouted, "Hya!" Behind him, Carlos surged in.

Dakota had slowed, taking up the rear, and Andy glanced back, wondering if she were keeping her distance from the other drovers for a reason. Had someone been bothering her when he wasn't looking? Because he had been looking…watching, observing. Women could ride with men and do the job equally well, but not all men saw them as equals. He wouldn't have a woman mistreated on his drive. Especially not Dakota.

The pebbles rattled under Romeo's hooves as they

approached the river, but Romeo balked and Andy could feel it in the horse's muscles.

"Let's go, Romeo," he muttered, giving him a kick to get him moving in the right direction. But the second the water hit the horse's fetlocks, he backed out again.

"Romeo, move it!" Andy ordered. "Hya!"

The other men were coming up out of the water on the other side and Elliot had already looked back, taking in the situation.

Andy grit his teeth in irritation. This wasn't the way he wanted the drovers to see him—inept in getting his horse across a river. Leadership counted, especially now.

Dakota came up beside him and Barney's big body moved right up next to Romeo.

"Let the horse do the thinking," Dakota said, her voice low.

"I would if—" Andy started, but Dakota's expression held an order. She knew horses better than he did—heck, better than anyone around these parts—so if she gave direction, he'd be wise to follow it.

"Loosen the reins," she commanded.

He did as she said, letting the reins go so that Romeo could choose his own way, and as Barney moved forward into the water, so did Romeo. They rode side by side, their knees pressed together, as the water rose up the horses' legs, splashing against their boots as they came to the middle of the river. Romeo stayed close to Barney, and Barney, being the more experienced horse, led the way. The solid muscles of the animals beneath them flexed as the horses pushed forward against the current, and soon enough, their footing grew more solid and they clambered up on the bank at the opposite side.

"Thanks," he said quietly.

"It never happened. You were waiting for me." She shot him a smile and eased Barney away.

The other drovers carried on without a backward glance, horses prancing forward as the water dripped off their sleek bodies. The grazing cows looked up in interest, trotting away as the horses approached.

She'd rescued his image back there. She could have taken the reins and led Romeo across, but she hadn't. She'd made it appear that they'd simply crossed the river together when, in reality, she'd been giving his inexperienced horse the support he needed, allowing Andy to keep face at the same time.

"That's why I recommended Patty," she said, shooting him a sidelong look.

"Point made." He grinned. "I still like Romeo."

She laughed. "You just hate taking your brother's advice."

Maybe he did. Chet had gotten it all, and there were times he wished his older brother would come to him for advice, to need something from him—anything—that would allow him to be the savior for once. But that had never happened. What did Chet need from him when he had everything already?

Except for this—Chet had needed someone to look out for the ranch when he couldn't be there. He'd needed this favor, and Andy didn't have it in him to turn his brother down. They had their own tangle of resentments, but at the end of the day, they were brothers.

"I've been away for too long," he admitted after a moment of silence. "I'm used to being the boss in my own world, not the stand-in for my brother's."

"Me, too." Her voice was almost too quiet to hear her,

and he nudged Romeo closer, closing the gap between them. "I'm the hired hand here, but at home, I'm the boss's daughter. Trust me, I know the feeling."

"And here we both are, stepping down to help out the same guy."

"No, I'm stepping down because I need the money." Those brown eyes caught his for a moment before she looked away again. "I don't have much choice."

"I had no way of knowing, Dakota."

"I know."

She seemed to blame him all the same. He heaved a sigh. She'd be rid of him soon enough, anyway.

"But even if you'd left well enough alone, I'd have done this for Chet," she said after a moment. "He'd do the same for us."

Would Chet do the same for Andy? He hadn't yet. Chet had held on to this land with a stranglehold, and he'd showed no inclination to loosen his grip—just like their father had. However, this was temporary, and it would all be over soon enough. Then Chet could take over again and Andy would go back to his own life.

"So are you saying that you helping me out back there…that was for Chet?" Andy asked with a wry smile. If it was for Chet, that was going to sting, but it might be better to know it up front.

Dakota didn't answer, but the color bloomed in her cheeks and she looked softer again. There was something about those pink cheeks that melted away his need to win this one.

"Seems to me that in spite of my mistakes—and you have to know that I'm sorry for what happened to your land—you might actually like me," he said. "You could have let me look like a fool. You could have led me across like a riding student, but you didn't."

She pushed her hat back and wiped a hand across her brow. "Don't start rumors now, Andy. I care about the integrity of our team. That's it."

But her expression had eased and there was a sparkle in her eye. She was warming up to him, he could see that much. Whether it would last was another story.

They rode due west, side by side, the sun warming their backs as they went. Harley peeled off and dismounted, and when Andy glanced back, Harley was loosening the ties on one of the pack horses.

"Give it time," Andy chuckled. "I'll grow on you."

As they cantered across the field toward the distant tree line, Andy knew for a fact that Dakota would never be a woman to lean back on. She was no quiet support, she was a mouthy challenge, and he liked that even better. Besides, she'd come back to lend a hand, and that said more to him.

If he'd made fewer left turns in life, he'd have liked to end up with Dakota Mason. But there was no undoing his past and Dakota wasn't about to step down for the likes of him.

The horses opened their strides into a gallop and Andy loosened his hold on the reins. Let him run! He looked over in time to see Dakota bending low over Barney's shoulder, and the bigger horse thundered beside him. She was inching forward, and in response, Andy flicked Romeo's flank with the end of the reins.

So she wanted to race. He couldn't help the grin that came to his face. This feeling he had as they rode across the open field, his heart racing as their horses galloped—it was best to remember it was short-term.

The land, the ranch, the cowboy life—Chet had it all. Andy's life was in the city. And what was it that their dad used to say? *Timing has a lot to do with the outcome of a rain dance.*

He could have danced until his feet were raw, the ranch had never been an option. Andy had done what he'd needed to do, and he knew that looking back wasn't productive. But when he looked to the side, there was nothing better than a woman matching your stride, ponytail bouncing behind, body surfing the rhythm of the animal beneath her…

But the timing wasn't right for Dakota, either, and keeping his eyes forward was the best thing for him.

Chapter 6

Rounding up the cattle was a release, as if a spring had been snapped and everything holding Dakota back had suddenly flung away. This was the kind of work she loved—riding at full gallop across a field as she angled around a group of cattle. Then she'd pull up, head them off and heel her horse into motion again.

Barney knew this work, too—a reason why she'd chosen him. The horse loved this part as much as she did, and she could feel his joy as they raced across the land together, mane and hair blowing back in tangled knots that would take forever to brush out. But worth it. Oh, so worth it.

Andy worked about a hundred yards off. Romeo had been a good choice for this part of the job. He was young and wound up like an explosion about to happen. He could turn on a dime, and Andy held him in easy control. He held the reins close and tight, his knees gripping expertly, and when his gaze passed over her, he shot her a grin.

Andy could ride. It was odd to only be realizing his skill level now, and she found herself feeling grudging respect. She should have had a sense of what he could do, since they'd been on horseback for two days now, but this kind of riding was different than the slow plod toward the herd. This was daring—it took guts, and it took an instinctive trust of the animal beneath you.

"Surprised?" He laughed as he cut off the last of the escaping cows and reined in next to her.

"A bit," she admitted ruefully.

"We can't all be horse whisperers like you," he said, Romeo's hooves dancing beneath him. "But I can hold my own."

She had to admit he was absolutely right about that. He was holding his own quite admirably, and for a man who hadn't been honing his skills for the last decade, he obviously had natural talent. Had his family realized this? she wondered. Or had it gone unnoticed?

"Over there!" Dakota pointed toward some cows making a dash for the golden, blazing tree line. They exchanged a look and then heeled their horses into motion. The trees were like a carpet of autumn glory rolling up the mountainside. The farther up the mountain, the sparser the deciduous trees were, heartier evergreens taking over in the shallower, rocky soil.

The cattle had a lead on them and Dakota's heart sank as several cows disappeared into the foliage. Rounding up the cattle in an open space was a much easier task than winding after them through the trees.

"Blast it!" she heard Andy mutter, and she mirrored his sentiments.

"How many went in?" Dakota asked. "I counted three."

"Me, too," he confirmed, and he let out a shout, turning around a couple steers heading toward the tree line, as well.

"Let's go in on foot," Dakota said as they approached the trees. Riding in would be more difficult, and the cows would naturally run from them. But if they went in on foot, they could get closer and encourage the cows back into the open.

They both dismounted and went in a few yards apart to try to get around the sides of the cattle and get behind them. The trees were ablaze in golds and oranges, but once they went in, it was dimmer. The fragrant leaves under their feet crunched.

"There's one," Andy said, picking up a long switch as he angled around the other side of the steer. He swatted the steer's rump and it bawled out its annoyance but headed back in the right direction. Dakota took over as the cow came closer and spread her arms to encourage it to keep moving. It erupted into the open and she turned her attention to the next cow.

It took about ten minutes to get all three cows out of the trees and back into the field. When the last one shot back out into the open sunlight, she and Andy shared a grin.

"We work well together," Andy said.

"You're actually good at this," she laughed. She could remember Andy shirking the work the few times their ranches had worked together for harvest or calving.

"Why so shocked?"

"I always thought you went to the city because you didn't have what it took." She winced. "Sorry. Is that too blunt?"

He rolled his eyes. "What made you think that?"

"That spring when you helped us with calving. My dad had that awful stomach flu, remember? We went around tagging calves. You and I were put together, and you were all aloof and disinterested in the whole process. I remember that because you didn't tag one calf. I did it all. You were just along for the ride."

"You wanted to do the work," he replied with a small smile. "You were so eager and serious."

"I was not." Had she been? She'd been responsible. That was different. "You were lazy."

"I could do the work—better than most, might I add—but I wasn't about to get in your way. You kept plowing on ahead of me every time you spotted a calf."

Dakota thought back on that summer and maybe he had a point. She'd been pretty focused then. She'd been fifteen with precisely one interest—cattle. What did that make her, a cattle nerd?

"Besides, being capable with the work wasn't what my dad was looking for," he added.

"No?" Twigs snapped under their boots as they made their way to the tree line. "What did he want?"

"He wanted a team player," he said.

They emerged into the sunlight and Dakota went over to where Barney stood waiting and scooped up the reins.

"And you aren't a team player?" she asked over her shoulder before she swung up into her saddle. The cows were grazing again a few yards off and farther away still the whoops and shouts of the other drovers filtered across the distance toward them.

Andy mounted, as well, and pulled Romeo up beside her.

"Not really," he said with a glint in his eye. "I can go rogue from time to time."

Going rogue was an understatement. He'd sold his land and left town. If that was what he called going rogue, then she could well understand his father's reluctance to groom him to take over. Accumulating that kind of land took generations and a lot of money.

"Like with Mackenzie?" she queried. He paused, shot her a sharp look. She'd crossed a line with Mack, but she wasn't sure that she cared. She wanted to know.

"What about Mackenzie?" he asked.

"You cheated on her."

"Does everyone know about that?" he asked with a shake of his head. "I was seventeen. She and I had started up fast and hot, and I didn't know how to take that forward. What was I supposed to do, get a job and marry her? I wasn't mature enough to handle that kind of intensity in a relationship. I got scared and did something stupid."

"Hmm." She was silent for a moment. "Do you wish you'd been the one to marry her?"

Andy shot her a grin. "You're meddling, Dakota."

"You never come back for the holidays." She pressed on. "Talk around Hope is that you were in love with Mack and you can't bring yourself to see them together."

"That's crap." His tone was tired but not defensive. "I don't come back for Christmas because it reminds me of when my mom died when I was thirteen. When Dad was still around, I came home for the holidays because it still felt like Mom was here…in our memories. But when Dad died, there was no point. Christmas has never been the same since."

She'd remembered that his mother had died, but she hadn't tied that to Christmastime in her own mind. Obviously, Mrs. Granger's death hadn't impacted her own Christmas one bit back then, and for that she felt a wave of guilt. The Granger boys had lost their mother that year, and it hadn't even put a hitch in her stride.

Dakota cleared her throat. "I'm sorry. I didn't realize that."

"Yeah, well…" He shrugged.

"So what do you do for Christmas?"

"I get together with some friends, we have dinner out at a restaurant, open a bottle of wine at home."

She winced. "Not much for family."

"It passes the time," he said wryly. "And I know what you're going to say. That's not what Christmas is supposed to be. It isn't supposed to be endured. But I'm not what a son is supposed to be, either—or a brother. So I do it my way. It's…easier."

They urged their horses into a trot and the cattle ahead of them started a slow move in the right direction. Dakota eased wide to keep a mother and calf moving, then edged back in toward Andy again.

"You and your mom were close?" she asked.

"Of course." He sighed. "And that was all Dad needed to solidify his view of me. Chet was his son, and I was Mom's son. My role in this family was set in stone long before I disappointed everyone."

Had he been pushed into the role of irresponsible younger brother? She'd never known Mr. Granger very well. He'd been quiet and stoic like most ranchers, but he hadn't seemed unfair or mean.

"What role?" she asked.

"I was supposed to work for my brother. I was supposed to do what Dad said, and when Chet took over, I was supposed to follow his orders."

"Ah." It was coming together for her. Andy had been expected to take his place as a support for Chet, and Andy had resented that. Perhaps that shouldn't surprise her—Andy and Chet had equally strong personalities.

"What do you mean, 'ah'?" he asked with a laugh. "Does that explain it all to you?"

"Yes."

Andy smiled wryly but didn't push the issue.

They rode in silence for a few minutes, her mind going over this new information. Andy was more broken than she'd realized. He'd covered well with his playful antics and disregard for rules, but there had been a lot more going on under the surface than she'd ever guessed.

"You were the opposite." Andy's voice broke into her thoughts. "I can analyze you, too, you know."

"You think so?"

"You weren't meant to inherit that ranch, either, but you knew Brody didn't want it, so instead of getting all disenchanted with the whole thing, you just got more persistent. You had something to prove and you wouldn't let the likes of me get in your way."

"The likes of you?"

"Am I wrong?" he countered.

No, he wasn't wrong. In fact, he'd nailed it, irritatingly enough. She'd been determined to prove herself worthy in her father's eyes, and maybe that had never stopped. She was still trying to get his approval, to show her ability. She was even taking on the financial responsibility to save up enough money for the down payment on the irrigation system. She could have left that one to her father. It was technically his ranch, after all.

"I'll take that silence for consent." Andy chuckled. "Don't worry. Your secrets are safe with me."

"What secrets?" How well exactly did he think that he knew her?

"That you're still scared you won't inherit that land," he said, his direct gaze meeting hers in a challenge. "That you're still scared you aren't quite good enough."

"Oh, I'm good enough," she retorted.

"I know it," he said. "But I'm not the one you're trying to convince, am I?"

Figuring him out was like a perplexing puzzle, but having him turn that same microscope onto her was mildly unsettling. She had more in common with him than she cared to own, but he was right. She was still trying to prove herself, and the only times she felt free of that burden was when she was out with the cattle, feeling the wind in her face. Out here, away from town, away from her father, away from all those pressures, she got to simply be.

And maybe that was something else she had in common with Andy Granger. Because out here he looked freer, too.

Dakota got quiet after that and Andy wondered if he'd said too much. He hadn't meant to shut her down. It was nice to talk to her. Of all the drovers, she was the one he felt most comfortable with—maybe even too comfortable if he was talking this much. But they had personal history. She'd been his best friend's girlfriend. Heck, he'd expected her to become his best friend's wife. They'd been together long enough.

There was something about how she reacted to the mention of Dwight, though. She shut down, froze over. It'd been several years since their split, and that kind of reaction seemed a little extreme for a couple that didn't work out. He wondered what happened there—what Dwight hadn't told him.

When Dwight and Dakota broke up, they'd been the focus of the Hope rumor mill for months. Andy had talked to Dwight a little bit when he'd come back for Thanksgiving long weekend from school, but they hadn't had much to say to each other anymore. Dwight had stayed around town and hadn't gone to college. Andy had gone to school and had a head full of business and economics.

Truth be told, Andy had thought himself better than Dwight at that point in his life. He wasn't proud of that now, but youthful arrogance had no bounds. Add a few years and a bit of life experience, and a man knew that four years of college didn't add up to anything much when it came to human value, but college freshmen weren't always clear on that, and his glossy vision of his own future had been shinier than anything else right then. So he didn't blame Dwight for not opening up too much. Now that Andy had experienced a broken engagement of his own, he knew exactly how much pain his buddy had been in. His empathy was several years too late to be much use to the friendship, though.

Regardless, Dwight had clammed up and not said much other than it hadn't worked out and Dakota had called it off. Dwight had moved back in with his mom for a bit to lick his wounds, and Andy had given him an awkward pat on the back and said something banal about there being more fish in the sea.

Again, not Andy's proudest moment.

He wished now that he'd been a better listener, because from what he could tell, Dwight had sunk into depression. The last he'd heard from him, Dwight had been talking about some sports bet he'd lost on. Andy had felt bad for him, but hadn't lent him any money to cover it. By then they'd grown apart. They had different interests, different goals, and the only things they had in common were high school memories that felt further away than ever.

One of those shared high school memories was Dakota—a memory that was in the flesh on this cattle drive—the girl who'd chosen Dwight over him.

The cattle were moving steadily toward the river now and the other drovers were closing in. This made the job harder as four hundred cows got pressed ever closer together. It was organized chaos at best. Andy was tiring—this pace was a grueling one to keep up.

Andy whooped, pushing the cattle farther in, and the thunder of hooves and echo of bawling cattle thrummed through him. Where was Dakota? She was around here somewhere—close by, surely, since they'd been riding together only a couple of minutes ago. He looked around then whooped again, heading off a cow that tried to escape.

"Hya!" he shouted. "Get on!"

The cow zagged back into the herd, and Andy scanned the mad, writhing team of cattle. It was then that he saw her—directly in the path of steer about to make a stand. Its hooves were spread, head down, nostrils flared—signs of an angry animal. Dakota's horse seemed to sense a personal assault because Barney reared up, pawing the air and, for a split second, Andy's heart stopped in his chest. But Dakota stayed seated, perfectly in control of her body, and he let out a pent-up breath of relief. Andy was impressed watching her ride out Barney's rearing, but as the horse came down, the steer thundered toward them.

Andy kicked Romeo into motion, intending to head off the steer, but before he could intercept, Barney lowered his shoulder and heaved backward, tossing Dakota clean out of the saddle as if she were a doll. She landed on the ground with a jarring thud.

Andy arrived at that moment and inserted himself between Dakota and the steer, shooting out a hand.

"Dakota!" he shouted.

She pushed herself to her feet and reached up, grabbing him by the forearm, allowing him to pull her up neatly behind him into the saddle just as the steer charged around them again.

"Thanks!" she panted as he heaved a sigh of relief.

"No problem." He looked around for Barney and saw the big black horse not far away. He headed in his direction. "Are you okay?"

"It hurt, but I'll survive." Her voice was breathy and he could tell she was in pain. It felt strangely good to have her behind him—so close that he could feel the pounding of her heart against his back. Thank goodness he'd been close enough to get to her…but still, he had a feeling she hadn't exactly been in distress. She dealt with horses and cattle on a daily basis.

When they got to Barney, she swung down and

grabbed his reins. She rubbed a hip with one hand and scowled into the horse's face.

"Not nice, Barney," she remonstrated, and Andy could have sworn he saw guilt in Barney's expression. Then she put a foot into the stirrup, grabbed the horn of the saddle and swung herself up.

"You sure you're okay?" he asked.

"You act like I've never been thrown before." Her expression was incredulous, and Andy shook his head and laughed.

"Just checking. Let's work, then."

It was quite possible she was tougher than he was, even with their difference in size. She was petite and slender, while he was tall and bulky, but she could probably take more of a beating from a horse than he could and still stand afterward.

He wouldn't be able to do this job without her, he realized. He didn't like that fact. He'd much rather know that he could do this with his hand tied behind his back, but he knew better than that. Dakota had been quietly, unobtrusively, supporting him on this drive, and if he didn't have her here, he'd likely have lost the drovers' respect by now.

She was helping him succeed…but why? Why would she do this for him when he was Enemy Number One in her family? Why put herself out for him at all? He glanced back over his shoulder. She didn't notice his scrutiny and he was struck anew by her beauty. Sitting there on the big black stallion's back, hair blowing out behind her in the brisk wind, her cheeks reddened from exertion and weather, he found himself feeling something he hadn't felt since he was a teenager.

She should have chosen me. When she'd had the

choice between him and Dwight, Dwight had been the lucky dog who'd got to spend his weekends with Dakota Mason. Andy had always cherished a little pang of jealousy because of that. He'd tried to put it to bed, especially after Dwight had asked her to marry him, but it was still there.

But this was a decade later. They'd all grown up, changed, started lives of their own… It was time to stop envying Dwight the time he'd had with her, because here Andy was with Dakota on a cattle drive, and if he really wanted to do something about it, he could.

Or could he?

Life was cruel, because while he sat here staring at Dakota Mason, realizing just how amazing she was, there were too many reasons to hold back. Her family hated him. She was as tied to the land as Chet was, and Andy was heading out just as soon as he could manage it. He was a grown man, and this was not a possibility.

He'd best keep telling himself that, so he didn't do something stupid.

Chapter 7

Rounding up the cattle kept everyone busy for the rest of the day. Whoops and shouts followed the wind across the plains as they rode, herding the cattle from the farthest reaches they'd wandered. The drovers came at the cattle from all sides, driving them steadily into a central area. Cattle could be ornery, and they bawled out their frustration at being herded, the air filled with the shouting voices of cattle and men alike.

Romeo had the energy and quick responses as Andy wheeled him around to cut off a bolting heifer—a grudging point in his favor for his choice of mount. As for Barney, he was an experienced horse and he knew what Dakota wanted from him before she even had to tug the reins. She and Andy worked well together, teaming up to cut off the running cows and herd them in the right direction.

Andy seemed to relax into the job, and if she didn't know about his life in Billings, she would have thought he was a lifelong rancher. It was in his blood—the Grangers had been in these parts for more generations than even the Masons had—and watching him work showed her a side to him she'd never seen.

Not only was he was good at this, but there was something about the look in his eye when his lips tightened to let out a sharp whistle from between his teeth that sped up her heart just a little bit. It was his instinctive ability, his intensity, and the grin of victory when he succeeded in rounding up the escaping cattle that gave her pause. Andy wasn't the spoiled city boy she'd cast him as—there was more to him than she'd given credit for.

Her father would hate this, and at the thought of her father, a wave of guilt crashed down over her. She owed her loyalty to her father, not Andy.

Four hundred head of cattle were a big job for six drovers, and they worked steadily through the day. There was no time to stop for breaks, and by the time they'd brought the cattle together into the field by Hell Bent River, the sun was setting and Harley had a fire roaring.

As Dakota rubbed down her horse, the smell of hot biscuits and stew made her stomach rumble. It looked like the kid knew how to cook over a fire, which was a welcome discovery. There was nothing worse than finishing up a day of hard work only to find that your dinner consisted of burned beans and crunchy rice. She'd been there, and it could inspire plenty of rage in the hungry drovers.

Now, with the workday over, Dakota was giving Barney a much deserved grooming. As she pulled the curry comb over his black shoulder, Barney's muscles trembled with pleasure.

"Hey..." With the word came a cloud of booze-smelling breath, and Dakota startled, memories of Dwight flooding back like a punch in the gut. How many times had Dwight approached her just like that? Her stomach curdled and she looked irritably toward Elliot, a flask in one hand and an intent, glittery look in his eye.

"I saw you working with Andy today..." Bitterness tinged his tone. "He seems to like you a lot."

The words were only slightly slurred. He was intoxicated but not diminished—a dangerous combination she was only too familiar with. She looked around. Where was Andy? She could see him across the camp, his back to them. He was talking with a couple of other drovers, gesturing about something. Her gaze whipped back to the man in front of her.

"You aren't supposed to be drinking, Elliot," she said, stepping around the front of the horse so she could move farther away.

"Just a nip." Elliot laughed quietly. "You gonna rat me out?"

She wouldn't need to, and she shot the drover an annoyed look as he came closer. "Elliot, I'm busy. Go groom your horse."

Elliot fell silent for a moment and she pretended to focus on Barney, but her heart was hammering in her chest. Dwight had been like this, and she'd always thought she could talk him out of it, but she'd been wrong. It never ended without bruises. The only thing she wanted right now was to put some distance between them, and she moved around the other side of the horse.

Only as she moved out of sight of the other drovers did she realize what she'd done, and her stomach curdled.

Stupid!

Elliot followed her, closing the distance quicker than he seemed capable of, ducking away from the snap of Barney's teeth. She wished Barney had managed to make contact, but Elliot was clear now, and coming closer.

"I think I know why Andy hired you," Elliot said, a slow smile spreading over his face.

"Because I'm qualified," she snapped. "Now, leave me alone."

"Want a drink?" He nudged the flask toward her.

"No." She took another step back, but he quickly closed the gap between them. "Elliot, leave me alone."

He reached out, presumably to touch her, but he missed, a grimy hand fumbling against the side of her face. Dakota pulled back in disgust and his hand fell to the front of her jacket. Whether his groping was intentional or not, her insides roiled.

"Elliot, get your hands off me!" she snapped. "And if you don't want—"

A heavy hand fell on Elliot's shoulder and Dakota looked up in wild relief. Elliot stumbled around to see Andy glowering down on him. Andy's normally relaxed expression had transformed to one of barely concealed rage. His hand tightened on Elliot's shoulder and he hauled him away from Dakota.

"Touch her again, and you deal with me personally," Andy growled. He snatched the flask from Elliot's fumbling grip and upended it, pouring the contents directly into the scruffy grass. "Rules say no booze. Chet will be hearing about this."

Andy shoved him toward the rest of group, now getting their servings of hot stew and biscuits. "And eat something!" he barked after the drover. "Harley, get Elliot some coffee!"

Dakota swallowed the bile rising in her throat. Elliot had scared her more than she'd wanted to admit. Sober, she could deal with him, but drunk—the booze was an impenetrable wall between the drover and his better instincts. She knew what that was like.

"Are you okay?" Andy's tone was still gruff but his eyes were gentle.

"I'm fine." She sucked in a wavering breath.

"Okay..." He clenched his jaw then slid a hand around her waist, tugging her gently toward him. She could have pulled back but she realized that she didn't want to and she followed his nudge toward him, allowing him to pull her against him. His heart beat loud and strong against her ear and she rested her face against his chest, gathering her senses once more.

"Next time, yell." His voice rumbled low in his chest.

She nodded then pulled back. "Deal."

"Come on." He let go of her and led the way toward the fire where the other drovers were already eating. Elliot sat to one side looking sullen, a bowl of stew untouched in his lap.

"Okay, men," Andy said, raising his voice louder than necessary. He glared around the fire. "I'll say it once, and after that, I'll stop being so professional and deal with you man to man. We have a lady riding with us. She's fast, strong and a heck of a drover, and I expect her to be treated like everyone else. Are we clear on that?"

The drovers stopped chewing and looked first at

Andy, then at Dakota, then around at each other. They exchanged confused looks.

"Got it, boss," Harley said with a nod. The others echoed him.

"Mind if I ask," Carlos said. "Did something happen…?"

They cared, she could see that much. Elliot was drunk, but sober he was the one chasing off the others. She didn't want to be treated like "the girl," but she had to admit Andy's help hadn't come a moment too soon.

"I'm fine!" Dakota snapped. She was irritated, and not because the drovers cared about her safety, but because she shouldn't have to worry about her safety out here. They should all be equals, doing a job they were all good at. And while Elliot had scared her, she was even more annoyed she hadn't kept her head about her. She'd slipped out of sight—retreated. She was even angrier still that she'd been in that position to begin with. If she'd been with her father's men, no one would have dared to try that, but she'd been forced down in the ranks because of Andy's idiocy when he'd sold his land. She wasn't the boss's daughter, she was a regular hired hand who needed the job for a little extra cash. She'd most certainly fallen in the world, and it was entirely Andy's fault.

She headed toward the pot of stew and pulled off the lid. Would she have been strong enough to fight off a man Elliot's size who was already numbed by alcohol? She'd have given it her best shot, but she honestly didn't know. She hadn't been able to fight off Dwight, but she'd also learned a few moves since then… Brody had made sure of it.

She glanced back at the fire. The men looked uncomfortable and Andy barked at Elliot to eat up and bed down. Elliot ducked his head and did as he was told. Andy, by all appearances, wasn't going to let go of this one easily.

Dakota scooped up a healthy portion of beef stew from the cast-iron pot, reached for a couple of biscuits from the lopsided pile and, as she did so, noticed that her hand was shaking. She pulled her fist hard against her side to still the trembling.

No man would make her shake. No man would make her tremble. If she could kick a cow into submission, she'd do the same with some drunken drover if need be, and she'd aim for his most vulnerable bits.

All the same, being the boss's daughter was a whole lot more helpful in these situations than she'd been willing to admit. She'd lost more than water rights and an ability to make a decent profit. She'd lost the status that protected her. Standing out here in the wilderness, surrounded by the soft lowing of cattle and the whistle of the cold, December wind, she'd never felt so vulnerable.

Andy tried not to watch Dakota while she dished herself some stew. The air was cold and her breath came out in a cloud. She didn't want to be molly-coddled—he could tell that much. As he turned back to his own food, he could hear the distant howl of wolves from the direction of the trees. That sound was enough to put up his hackles. They'd stay clear of the fire, and they were easy enough to chase off on horseback, but if a pack got a calf separated…or, God forbid, a drover…

"Who is first on patrol tonight?" Harley asked, wiping the inside of his bowl with a piece of biscuit.

"I am," Dakota said.

Andy glanced up as Dakota joined them, sinking to the ground by the fire to start eating.

"I could take over for her," Harley suggested, and Andy was inclined to agree, if it weren't for the baleful glare Dakota shot in Harley's direction.

"Why, exactly?" she demanded.

"If it—" Harley blushed red. "I mean, it might help—"

"You think you're a better shot than I am?" she retorted. "I can ride better and I can shoot better. I'll be fine, trust me."

Was that an indirect threat he heard between the lines there? A warning for Elliot?

"There are wolves out tonight," Andy said. "We'll have two on patrol at all times. So Dakota is first, and I'll take the first patrol with her. At midnight, Dave and Finn, then at three, Harley and Elliot, and if Elliot can't get up, I'll patrol again with Harley."

Andy didn't want to let anyone else patrol with her. It wasn't only his protective instinct where she was concerned, though. He wanted some time with her—a chance to talk—and he was looking forward to that more than he probably should.

He wouldn't get much sleep, but that was the burden of leadership. Elliot wasn't carrying his fair share of the load, and if Andy had his way, he'd be fired at the end of this, but they needed him until they got back. He hadn't liked the way Elliot had been stalking Dakota. It gave him the creeps and ticked him off at the same time. There had been more to that encounter—Andy just couldn't put his finger on it. Anyway, Andy would put in some serious effort to waking Elliot come three. It wasn't like he'd let the man sleep like a princess.

The sky was cloudy, no moon or stars to illumine their position on the plains, only firelight flickering orange and crackling with warmth. Moisture hung in the air as a promise of rain, and if the temperature dropped, snow. It would be a cold night.

The rest of the drovers turned in shortly after that. When a man had to get up in the middle of the night to patrol, every minute of shut-eye was precious. Andy saddled up and Dakota wasn't far behind. He handed her a shotgun, then slung his own across his back.

"You said you can shoot, right?" he said.

"You still doubting me at this point?" she asked with a half smile.

"I'm just making sure," he retorted. "I'd rather not get shot tonight."

Dakota rolled her eyes—the only response he'd get—and kicked her horse into motion. Andy chuckled to himself and heeled Romeo after her, heading south along the riverbank.

The cows were mostly lying down, slowly chewing their cud. They looked up as Andy and Dakota rode slowly past, the stillness of the night interrupted by the distant, bone-chilling howls. Out here, they weren't top of the food chain.

"I'm sorry about Elliot today," Andy said. "I'll deal with him."

"It was the booze," she said.

"Even so, I'll deal with him." That was a promise. Even if Dakota would rather have him leave it alone, he'd still deal with Elliot for the simple reason that he'd scared her—he'd seen the stricken look on her face—and Dakota didn't scare easily. He had no idea what Elliot had said to inspire it, but he'd make the drover pay one way or another.

They rode in silence for a few more minutes and Andy glanced in her direction a couple of times, wondering what she was thinking about. Her expression conflicted.

"You okay?" he asked.

She glanced toward him then nodded. "Fine."

"You don't look all that fine." He glanced back toward the camp. "I'll keep an eye out for you from here on out." Not that he wasn't already, but he didn't exactly want to announce that.

"I don't need babysitting."

"It isn't babysitting. It's the decent thing to do," he said. "Besides, you've helped me out of a couple scrapes already on this drive. I figure it'll make us even."

She gave him a wan smile—acceptance of the terms, he imagined. Riding with her in the moonlight reminded him of all those feelings he used to harbor for her—the longing to show her he was better than she thought, and the jealousy for the buddy who got a chance with her.

"Do you still see Dwight around?" Andy asked after a moment.

"No." She laughed suddenly, the sound low and bitter. "I keep clear of him."

There was something in her voice that gave him pause and he frowned, nudging his horse closer to hers. "I know he was kind of a jerk toward the end—"

"Did you know about that?" she interrupted.

Was there more to this than a simple breakup? Or maybe Dwight had really broken her heart—it was a cancelled wedding, after all. He'd been able to sympathize with Dwight over the ended engagement, but she'd have had an equal share of that heartbreak.

"He seemed to take you for granted a lot," Andy said. "At least, that's the way it looked to me."

"Take me for granted..." She was silent for a moment. "Yeah, I guess so, but that wasn't the biggest issue. He beat me up."

Andy felt the words hit him like ice and he whipped around and stared at her in disbelief. "He *what*?"

"He beat me up," she repeated, and it was like her words echoed in his head. "Every time he got drunk and I was dumb enough to go over to his place when he called, he'd go into some violent rage and smack me around."

The very thought of Dwight raising a hand to her was almost unbelievable, but then, how well had he actually known Dwight later on? Hot rage welled up inside him, overtaking the shock and giving him the urge to go find the man and pound on him.

"I didn't know that," he growled. "If I had—"

"You'd have what?" she countered coldly. "Told him to smarten up? Shaken your finger at him?"

Her words were sharp but her eyes misted a little as she said them. He could tell that her anger covered over a lot of pain—pain that had probably been reawakened by Elliot.

"I'd have hit him back for you," he retorted. "And I'd have made sure he didn't get up too easily, either."

An image arose in his mind of his fist connecting solidly with Dwight's grinning face. What kind of man raised his hand to a woman? Andy rifled through his mind, looking for clues he should have seen. How could his best friend have been beating on his girlfriend, and Andy didn't know?

"You should have told me," he said suddenly.

"You were away at college," she said. "I did one better and I told my brother."

Brody—yeah, that had been a good call on her part. Brody was now overseas with the army, but he'd always been about as soft as a tank. If she'd told her brother, he'd have taken care of it, although Andy would've enjoyed being part of the solution.

"How long was that going on?" Andy asked.

"He hit me on three different occasions," she replied. "I should have dumped him the first time, but what can I say? I wasn't smart enough back then. But the third time, I threw his ring back in his face and went home. Brody saw the black eye and hit the roof."

And no one had told him about this. Either no one knew and it was all hushed up, or he'd been too distanced from everything back home to even notice. Dakota had been right about one thing—he'd been pretty intent on getting out of town for good back then. If he'd been there, though—

"And that's why Elliot scared you so badly," he concluded, everything falling together in his mind. "He was drunk and wouldn't leave you alone, a whole lot like Dwight."

"A whole lot like Dwight." Her words were low.

They rode in silence for a few minutes, Andy's mind going over her words like a broken record. Dwight had been his buddy ever since junior high. They'd hung out on weekends and collaborated on science projects. Dwight had thrown Andy a birthday party just before he'd left for college, and Dakota had been there for once. She normally didn't have much to do with Dwight's friends. Everything had seemed fine—Dwight was head over heels for Dakota, and Dwight's parents treated Dakota like a daughter. They'd both been eighteen, and Andy was off to college in the city.

Then in the space of a few years, that fun-loving guy, the loyal buddy, had turned into a violent lout. If she'd just taken a chance on him instead, all those years ago when she'd had the choice between him and Dwight… But that was in the past. If wishes were horses—how did that saying go?

"Did you see any signs of it before?" Andy asked. What he was really asking was if there was anything he could have done while he was still around.

"He had a temper," she replied with a shrug. "But I'd never dreamed he'd lift a hand to me. That's why it took me three incidents to finally leave. It felt so surreal, so impossible."

Seeing Dakota flinch like that when Elliot had bothered her stuck in his head. She'd reacted in fear, and the thought of Dwight hurting her, scaring her, traumatizing her like that, stabbed him. He'd seen Dakota's body language when she'd backed away and Elliot had moved in like a predator. That was when Andy went to investigate. He'd taken care of it, but no one had been there to protect her from Dwight.

He was my friend.

He felt a pang of guilt at that little fact, although Dwight wouldn't count as a friend anymore. And Andy couldn't do too much about what had already happened. That was the most frustrating part about this—hearing about what Dwight had done and not being able to fix it himself… Because given a chance—

The howl of the wolves seemed to be moving farther away and Andy paused to listen to the lonesome sound. The cattle shifted uncomfortably—their instinct would warn them of the danger. The horses' hooves plodded evenly as they came along the edge of the herd. A few yards away, something moved—almost flopped. It was hard to see the in the darkness, and Andy pulled out a flashlight, shining it toward the spot.

A half-grown calf lay next to its mother. It struggled to stand again, but couldn't. This was a much younger calf than most of the others, and Andy reined in his horse.

"Dakota, do you see that?" Andy asked. He dismounted and gave the horse a pat before heading in the direction of the calf. A couple of cows rose and ambled a few paces off, but the mother stayed immobile, big liquid eyes regarding him.

She knew he was here to help, and he looked back to see Dakota coming the way he had, a few paces behind him. Andy squatted next to the calf and he could see the problem. It had gotten tangled up in a piece of twine that had bound its back legs together in a painful snarl.

"Poor thing," Dakota said as she arrived. "Use your knife. I'll hold its head."

She crouched next to him and took the calf's head in her hands, crooning softly to it about how everything would be just fine in a minute. Andy pulled out his pocketknife and sawed at the twine until it snapped, freeing the calf from its awkward position. It immediately bounded to its feet.

"There." Dakota released the calf and fell back as it lunged out of her grip.

Andy held out his hand and she put hers in his calloused grip. He boosted her to her feet. But once she was up, he didn't let go, and she didn't pull free, either. Maybe he was more comforting than he thought. She paused, her dark eyes glittering in the moonlight, and he flicked off the flashlight, drinking her in. What had she been going through while he'd been away? And why hadn't she given him that chance? Why hadn't he tried a little harder to get her attention? He'd been acting like his older brother, stepping back when the woman chose another guy, but Dwight had been a bad choice—worse than he'd ever realized.

They walked together around the cows and back toward the horses, and he kept her hand in his own tight grip. A cold wind whipped across the plain, the whistle mingling with the river's rush. He felt her shiver and tugged her closer against his shoulder.

She complied. When he turned to face her, she didn't pull back. The wind ruffled her hair around her face and as she looked up at him he found himself thinking all sorts of things he knew were out of bounds. But there was something about those dewy eyes and her parted lips… He took her face in his hands, running his thumbs over her wind-reddened cheeks.

"I asked you out," he said softly.

"What are you talking about?"

"Back when you started dating Dwight, I asked you out," he said. "And I'd been serious, you know. It wasn't me flirting or just trying my luck. I'd had to work up my courage to ask you."

"I'd already started dating Dwight," she said, shaking her head. "I wasn't that kind of girl."

No, she hadn't been. Dakota had been quality, the kind of woman who was loyal and principled. Right and wrong mattered to her, and she stood by her convictions. She'd most definitely not been the two-timing sort.

"I wish you'd have made an exception," he said. "Because I'd never have hurt you."

She pulled back and he released her. Had he offended her? It was true, though.

"I didn't need rescuing, Andy."

Dakota had never been the kind of girl who'd admit to needing rescuing. She'd had it all under control—at least the parts she let the rest of them see. She knew what she wanted and she went for it. But back then she'd been faced with a decision on who to let into her life, and she'd made the wrong choice, in his humble opinion. By the time she'd figured that out, he'd been long gone, building a life in the city.

"Just tell me I would've been a better choice." He caught her eye and held it. She pulled in a breath, and he stepped closer. "I'd be happy with that."

She put her hands to his chest. She only came up to his shoulder, but when she tipped her chin back to look him in the face, his lips hovered over hers. Their mingled breath was a wisp of cloud in the cold night air. She didn't answer him and, instead of questioning it further, he did what he'd been longing to do for several days now and lowered his lips onto hers. She didn't pull back. He kissed her gently, chastely, then stopped, looking into her face.

"You were the better choice," she said softly, a smile coming to her lips.

"That's what I'm talking about," he said with a low laugh, and he gathered her up into his arms. This time when his lips came down onto hers, she leaned into his kiss and her eyes fluttered shut.

She felt warm and small in his embrace, and as she strained upward toward his kiss, he felt a wave of protective longing. This was what he wanted—this impossible moment right here. He wanted wind and space, cattle and horses, and he wanted this woman in his arms. He wanted her so badly that his whole body ached with it.

When she pulled back, he reluctantly released her and his arms feeling cold and empty, the dampness of her lips still warm on his mouth.

"Wow…" she breathed.

Standing there in the cold Montana wind, the scrub grass rippling in the force of the gale, Dakota's hair whipping out to the side, her lips plump from his kiss, he had to agree that "wow" pretty much covered it. He'd never been affected by a kiss like that before, feeling it all the way down to his toes.

"We'd better get back on patrol," she said quickly, moving toward Barney.

"Dakota."

She turned, her cheeks pink with what might have been embarrassment; he wasn't sure. He just didn't want it to end like this, with embarrassment or retreat. That kiss had meant something—maybe something neither of them had a right to, but it had still meant something.

"You don't have to be nervous being alone with me."

She didn't need to be jerked around or to have her emotions go through the wringer. She certainly didn't need to be uncomfortable around him for the rest of the drive. He'd look out for her and make sure that no one gave her any trouble. Beyond that, he wasn't planning on sticking around Hope, and he knew better than to toy with a good woman. He'd kissed her, and she'd kissed him back, but she didn't owe him anything.

"Okay." She nodded.

"I won't do that again."

A long, low howl echoed across the plains, but wind whipped the sound into a tangle so that he couldn't tell the direction it was coming from. The horses danced nervously.

"We'd better get moving," she said. "There are wolves out there."

He wasn't sure if she was referring the howling beasts in the distance or the ones closer to home that betrayed her trust, but Dakota was safe with him, even if that meant restraining himself from doing the one thing he wanted most right now—kissing her all over again. As they mounted their horses once more, the first stinging pellets of rain began to fall.

Chapter 8

It rained for the most of the night and when Dakota awoke the next morning to the sound of voices, her body ached from the previous day's work. She rolled out of her warm sleeping bag, fully dressed, and pulled on her jacket, zipping it up with a shiver. As she unzipped her tent and stepped outside, she sucked in a deep breath of cold morning air.

That kiss last night had happened—something she'd questioned a couple of times before morning. She and Andy had done the rest of the patrol together and, after rubbing down their horses, Andy had paused with her in the darkness.

"What's that old rhyme? If wishes were horses…?" His voice was low and soft in her ear.

"Beggars would ride." She finished the line.

His hand brushed against hers, his fingers moving

lightly down hers, ever so close to entwining them together.

"Ever wish you had a do-over?" he asked quietly. "Ever wish you could go back and make a different choice and see how your life would have turned out?"

Dakota thought for a moment then slowly shook her head. "I wouldn't be the same woman I am today."

He nodded slowly. "That's a good thing, to live without regrets."

"What about you?" she whispered.

"I guess that leaves me a beggar who dreams of riding." He touched her cheek with the back of his finger. "Good night, Dakota."

What had he meant by that? She had a feeling he had a few unfulfilled wishes of his own. Heaven knew she did. But wishes weren't enough for ambitions or for the heart—and old nursery rhymes strove to teach the children that very truth. Wishes got you nowhere. Hard work, on the other hand, produced something.

When she'd crawled into her sleeping bag, she'd lain there for a long time, remembering the feel of his lips on hers. She'd never imagined kissing Andy Granger would feel quite so sweet. His first kiss had made her feel safe, and the second had awakened feelings inside her she'd thought were dormant. The memory warmed her in spite of the damp weather.

But the cocoon of night had evaporated and morning came as it always did. The rain had stopped, but everything was drenched and the sunrise looked more like a silver haze than the actual start of a day. Harley had managed to get a smoky fire started, but it wouldn't last long if it started raining again. Fog rolled along the scrub grass, the cows looking like shadows in the mist. Dakota's breath hung in the air and she rubbed her hands together against the chill. She looked around the camp and spotted Andy with the horses under a tarp. He hoisted the saddle up onto Romeo's back.

"Morning," Andy said. "How'd you sleep?"

"Not great," she admitted.

"My fault?" he asked, warm eyes meeting hers.

She felt the blush rise in her cheeks but before she could answer, he added, "We're starting early today, before the rain hits us."

"Okay," she said. "I'll be ready."

He turned back to buckling straps and adjusting the saddle. He hadn't known about Dwight's violent streak—hadn't even suspected—and that had been reassuring. He'd made her feel safe last night. Desired. He'd gotten right past all of her bravado and when his lips came down onto hers…that was something she hadn't allowed a man to do since Dwight. But none of those feelings changed how her family felt about Andy, and her loyalty had to be to them first. Even if Andy wasn't the jerk they all believed him to be, he was still the reason her father constantly worried about losing his land. They wouldn't understand; they'd be furious.

All she was certain of right now was that Andy had kissed her and she'd kissed him back.

Dakota took down her tent. The other drovers emerged from their own soon after and followed suit. It didn't take long to load up the pack horses and they ate a quick breakfast of leftover biscuits and hot coffee as they worked. They all stashed what they could to carry with them for later—their next proper meal wouldn't be until evening. The sooner they got the cattle across the river, the sooner they could head toward home, where they could dry out and get paid.

And getting paid was the point of this whole trip. For some reason she kept forgetting that. As she mounted her horse again that morning, Andy caught her eye with a small smile before easing his horse forward.

The kiss had meant something to him, it seemed, and she felt a wave of uncertainty. Feeling anything at all for Andy hadn't been part of the plan, and she couldn't help but remember her words to her mother that she could handle Andy Granger. She felt like a fraud. What was it about the open land that changed people?

The next hour the fog dissipated and the sky brightened, although the clouds hung low and refused to be pushed away. Dakota warmed up the best way she knew how—with work, and they herded the cattle and brought them to the river's edge. The river had swelled over night from the deluge of rain and it thundered between the banks in a brown, broiling swell. It had obviously rained up in the mountains, as well, and crossing the river again wasn't going to be as easy as the first time. Dakota looked toward Andy and saw the same expression of concern on his face. She kicked her horse into motion and cantered closer.

"Will we make it across?" she asked, raising her voice above the whistle of the wind.

A mist of light rain blew into her face and her horse pranced beneath her, anxious to get moving again.

"We'll have to try," he said and then raised his voice so the other drovers could hear him. "Okay, boys, let's get rolling!"

That was all they needed. The drovers started doing what they did best—whooping and shouting and pushing the herd from behind until the first cows were nudged forward and they plunged into the water and started the manic swim for the opposite shore. When the lead few made it to the middle, the rest tumbled into the water after them and for a long while the water was filled with mooing, bawling, thrashing, writhing life.

When they made it to the other bank, the cattle stumbled and scrambled to get a foothold in the mud before pulling themselves onto the land, being pushed forward from behind. They ran into the opposite field, dripping dirty water, their wide bodies streaked with mud.

So far the cattle were all making it across safely. There had been a few close calls when some of the large calves had struggled to keep up with their mothers, but they'd made it in the end, and Dakota breathed a sigh of relief. Losing cattle on the drive wasn't something a drover took pride in, and she felt compassion for the cattle, too. They were gentle creatures and a lost calf or comrade would be hard on them.

Dave and Finn crossed the river as the herd on their side began to thin out, leading the remaining cattle by example. Elliot, Harley, Andy and Dakota stayed behind, urging the cattle forward and into the water. It was a team effort and the hardest part of the drive by far.

An hour slid by as Dakota whooped and herded, Barney's hooves slipping in the mud as she pulled him around to cut off an escaping steer.

Overhead a peal of thunder boomed and for a moment she heard nothing but ringing in her ears. Only a few cows were left on the bank of the river—cows and the smallest of the calves. As the thunder exploded, the cows turned and stampeded away from the water, heading for the distant tree line, their calves trailing behind.

Andy wheeled his horse around and Dakota followed his example, hooves pounding as they raced after the fleeing cows. Dakota leaned low as Barney galloped ahead of the cows, then she pulled him around and cut off the leader. Andy did the same for a steer and soon they had the cows stopped and mooing in frustration. There were at least seventy or eighty adult cows and nine of the smallest calves, and as they herded them back toward the river, Andy shot her a grin.

"You're really good at this," he said.

"Told you." She laughed. "This is the fun part."

"You keep saying."

Harley was waiting for them at the river's edge, his attention focused on the swirling water. When Andy and Dakota arrived behind the protesting cattle, Dakota could see the problem. The banks had collapsed from the hooves of three-hundred-odd cows and the onslaught of water hadn't abated. The adult cows might make it across the river, but the calves didn't have a chance. On the other side, the drovers had herded the cattle into a closer unit, waiting for Andy's orders.

"Boss!" Finn shouted. "What's the plan?"

The plan. Anyone raised in the country knew that there had to be a plan. Nothing worked without one. Wishes and dreams had no place on a ranch. From a distance, grazing cattle and peaceful scenery might seem pastoral and relaxing, but a rancher never relaxed. She was always looking at the next step, preparing for the next season, the next hurdle.

If wishes were horses...

In her experience, wishes were a waste of time. If wishes held any kind of clout with local government instead of that blasted Lordship Land Developers... If wishes were dollars… If wishes could hydrate a parched field… If wishes could bring Brody home safely… If wishes could change her family's view of this complicated man in front of her… Wishes didn't count for much.

Andy looked over at Dakota, green eyes meeting hers in a silent request. He needed her advice and, right now, she was the one he trusted.

"The calves won't make it," Dakota said, keeping her tone low. "We can either wait it out here or go downstream and see if we can find a shallower spot. It's your call."

Andy nodded, was silent for a beat and then raised his voice. "We're going to take these downstream and see if we can find some shallower water for the calves. Carry on toward the camp. Lydia and Bob will be there tonight, and if we don't join you by morning, send someone."

"Sure thing!" Finn shouted back. "Good luck!"

The drovers on the opposite bank turned away and Dakota pushed her hat more firmly onto her head, pulling her chin down to protect her face from the driving drizzle.

If wishes were horses, Dwight would never have started drinking and she'd be married right now with a few kids of her own. And maybe that would have been good enough, even if Dwight had never aroused the kind of passion inside her that Andy seemed to manage last night. It would have been the life she'd always pictured, and she wouldn't be facing all these challenges and complications by herself.

She had her family, and that counted for a whole lot, except her family had no idea she'd kissed the enemy and that she was empathizing with Andy in spite of her best intentions. When it came to Andy, she was one hundred percent alone.

And, ironically, when it came to life in Hope, so was Andy.

The sky cleared the farther they rode downstream and by the time midmorning arrived, sunlight beamed down on the sodden countryside, making the drops of water shine like diamonds. Copses of leafless trees lined the banks of the river, some trees leaning heavily toward the water but still miraculously staying rooted as the rush of water ate away at the earthen banks. The cows trotted complacently ahead of them. A blue jay squawked overhead, followed by the twitter of smaller birds. These were the kinds of scenes he was afraid to let himself miss.

Back in Billings he'd sit in his office, focused on quarterly sales figures, and in some corner of his mind he'd remember some breathtaking view he'd witnessed on horseback—just sitting there in the middle of nowhere, drinking in a sun-splashed vista. This one could be filed with the others—scenes so lovely they ached when you remembered them from the confines of a city office.

Andy looked over to Dakota, but her gaze was fixed straight in front of her.

He shouldn't have kissed her.

He was letting himself feel things he shouldn't be feeling. Hope was supposed to be a pit stop while he helped out his brother and tried to somehow make up for selling the family land out from under him. Reigniting old emotional attachments wasn't part of the plan. Yet the more time he spent with Dakota, the more attached he was getting, which meant that kissing her had been a monumental mistake.

The three of them easily kept the cattle moving, and Harley rode a good distance from Andy and Dakota, leaving them in relative privacy. Andy wanted to talk to her, but he couldn't say the things that were on his mind, namely that she sparked something inside him that he'd never felt before, even with Ida. Dakota made him wish for things and hope for things, but she was as much a part of this land as his brother was, and he knew what that meant.

The Grangers put family and the land ahead of everything else, and sometimes the top priority was blurry. You couldn't separate Chet from the land without tearing off a part of him. Andy had made that separation, but it hadn't been easy.

Dakota, he knew, was the same as his brother, and feeling things for her wasn't smart. She'd put her family and that land above anything else she might be feeling. He was neither family nor sticking around, so allowing himself to feel whatever it was he was feeling for Dakota was masochistic at best. Yet he couldn't stop remembering the sight of her in the darkness. It wasn't just that she was beautiful—he'd been around beautiful women before. It was more than that—it was the way he softened around her, the way he wanted to protect her, to defend her. She was so much more than just a beautiful woman, and when he thought about the way her glittering eyes met his, how her lips parted ever so slightly—

"Do you ever talk to my brother on Facebook or anything?"

Andy's reverie popped at the sound of her voice and he dragged his mind back to present.

"Sorry?" he asked.

"Brody. You aren't connected on social media, are you? I mean, through friends of friends, or something like that."

"Uh…no." Brody had been a couple of years older and he'd hung out with a different group. Brody been in Chet's graduating class, but even so, he'd hung out with a different group of kids than Chet had.

"Okay, well…that's good."

"Why's that?" Andy asked with a short laugh.

Her gaze flickered toward him and he sensed her discomfort. Was he really such an embarrassment that she wanted to hide him from her brother, too?

"It's nothing," she said.

That was a lie—he could see it written all over her face.

"Why? Is Brody going to have a problem with you doing this cattle drive with me?" he asked.

"He can't stand you, but that's not the point." She shot him a quirky smile.

She certainly didn't sugarcoat it, did she? But no one in Hope liked him right now, so it didn't come as a surprise. Besides, it was Brody's ranch, too, that had been decimated by his sale. Regardless, Andy respected the guy—he was fighting for his country, after all—and the truth of Brody's opinion stung a little.

"I'm doing damage control," she said.

"For what?"

"He doesn't know about Nina yet."

This was one bit of gossip he *had* heard all the way in Billings. It was such a small-town-drama kind of thing to happen that Andy had been bitterly amused. But he no longer had to care—his life was in Billings. It felt different now, though, looking Dakota in the face.

"You didn't tell him?" he asked after a moment.

"No."

"Why?"

She turned away, letting out a sharp whistle that got a cow moving again, then glanced in his direction again.

"Because when he deployed, he was engaged. And then one day, a few months after Brody had left, I saw Nina making out with Brian Dickerson in the back of a movie theater. I was pretty shocked. I mean, I'd never been a huge fan of her for a sister-in-law, but..."

"Did you say anything to her?" he asked.

"I didn't have to. We looked at each other, she turned beet red, and I left." Dakota smiled but it didn't reach her eyes. "That evening Nina called me to explain. She said she didn't think she could wait for Brody to come back. My parents were the ones who came up with the plan, though."

"Which was to hide it from Brody?" Andy clarified. It looked like Brody had the same kind of family he did—the kind that pulled together so hard, they could crack a nut with the sheer force of their good intentions.

"They didn't want to spring it on him while he's dodging bullets. He'll be home in February and we'll tell him then."

"He hasn't noticed on social media or anything?" Andy asked incredulously.

"We talked to his friends and they agreed to go along with it," she said.

"And Nina?" he asked.

"She got off social media completely—the only way

to really keep this private. She answers his emails as briefly as possible, because she owes us this much. She can't crush him—not now. He'll face reality when he's home again."

"And you don't think Brody will be pissed?" he asked.

Dakota's face paled. He'd hit on it, he could tell. Brody would absolutely be angry when he got back. So that was the kind of family the Masons were: well-intentioned and so determined that they'd managed to get every single one of Brody's friends and family to portray a lie. That took a massive force of will. They took care of their own to the extreme. He had a feeling Brody was going to be boiling mad when he got home and found out what had really been going on.

"Are you judging me?" she asked. "He could get killed over there, Andy. I'd rather deal with him being angry if it means getting him home alive."

Andy shrugged. He could see the point, albeit grudgingly. "I get it. I'm not sure he will, though."

"I've been thinking the same thing," she said, her tone softening. "I'm not sure I can keep doing this."

"No?"

"I mean, the last email I sent him I told him about doing this cattle drive with you. Once I get back, I expect that you'll monopolize conversation for a bit." She winced. "He really doesn't like you. I'm just not sure how much longer you'll be a distraction."

"A distraction." He shot her an irritated look. "Is that what I am to you?"

Was that all he was, at this point? He'd thought they'd gotten to know each other over the last few days. He thought he'd been able to show her who he was underneath all the scandal associated with him. In fact, they'd gotten a whole lot closer than that.

Color rose in her cheeks. "When it comes to emailing my brother, yes."

He wasn't sure what he expected her to say, but not that. He was tired of being the bad guy, the black sheep, the prodigal son. He was sick of being glared at and ignored, worrying about the meals he ordered in local diners. He'd thought he'd been able to crack through all of that with Dakota, and the color in her cheeks suggested she was feeling more than she was saying.

"After last night, you don't think we count as friends yet?" he demanded. There was no point in dancing around it anymore. They'd shared something special, however fleeting it might be. The memory of her slender waist, the feel of her straining up toward his mouth, the way she'd melted into his embrace, the perfect fit… It was all he'd been thinking about all day.

"I don't want to talk about that."

"Why not?" He pressed on. "If you didn't want me to kiss you, you can say so. I'm not pushing myself on you."

He hadn't pushed her into that kiss. It had been very mutual, and the memory of her in his arms sped up his heart even now.

"I'm no wilting flower. If I hadn't wanted to kiss you, I wouldn't have. But—"

"But we've made it a little past friendly," he said, keeping his voice low.

Her cheeks turned pink. "I don't think we meant to do that."

She was right. He hadn't. Feeling things for her wasn't in the plan, and if he could put a brake on what he was feeling, he would. Heck, he was trying to. But that kiss had been real, and he was pretty sure they'd both felt it.

"My family hates you, Andy."

"Yep," he agreed, keeping his eyes on the cattle. He completely understood. The Masons weren't a family to trifle with. If he wanted something with her—really wanted it—then this Granger had just met his match in difficult families.

"And you're not staying." She couldn't hide the regret in those words, but she was right, he couldn't stay.

"Hope won't forgive me," he said, hearing the sadness in his own voice. "You're right. I'm headed back to Billings as soon as I can."

"So maybe what happens on the trail can stay on the trail," she said quietly.

"Don't worry, your secret is safe with me," he said.

"Which one?" she asked.

"All of it. I'm not here to make your life any harder." He looked over at her and caught her gaze for a moment. If things had been different, he wouldn't walk away so easily, but he was a practical man. He clicked his tongue and Romeo sped up at the command. "As for Brody, I say tell him. He's no idiot. I'm sure he suspects something already."

"Okay." Her voice stayed quiet. "Thanks."

For his discretion about their kiss or his advice? Maybe it didn't matter. This—the feelings sparking between them, the hopes he kept trying to slap back down—wouldn't last. Soon enough they'd return to civilization again and Dakota would slip back into her life. She was a Mason, and her family would have other hopes for her that didn't include their arch nemesis.

Whatever was growing between them right now could never survive Hope's scrutiny.

Andy eased his horse forward, breaking into a trot to head off a wandering calf. They'd gone from civil to slipping past friendship in the matter of one night. It hadn't been planned. In fact, if he'd been thinking straight, he would never have done it, but there was something about those chocolate-brown eyes and the direct way she stared at him that emptied his head of logical thought.

Do the cattle drive and get out—that had been the plan. When exactly had it gotten more complicated?

Chapter 9

The river's swell had started to decrease as evening came on and, after some debate, they decided to set up camp. Getting eighty head across a river at twilight wasn't going to be easy, and in the morning, if the river had gone down even further, they'd be in a much better situation to get across safely. Their food, what they'd been able to carry with them, had been mostly eaten, and Dakota was thinking of the rest of the group who would be arriving at their own camp at the same time—except they'd have Lydia Granger's savory cooking to welcome them.

The hoot of an owl drew Dakota's attention and she watched as the shadow swept across the field then disappeared into some trees. The evening air was cold, chilling quickly as the last of the sun vanished behind the mountains, leaving behind a dusky sky edged with red along the silhouette of the range.

This would be an uncomfortable night. No tents. No bedding. No blankets. No shelter from the elements. Fortunately, Harley proved talented at starting another bonfire, and when they all rummaged in their saddle bags, they came up with some dried fruit, a handful of nuts, two sticks of beef jerky and six granola bars.

"This will be an interesting meal," she laughed, tossing her granola bars onto the pile.

"We have to cross tomorrow morning," Andy said. "No choice. We'll have to take our chances."

Dakota had to agree. They weren't exactly set up for a lengthy stay out here, and the weather was only getting colder.

"At least the rain has stopped," Harley said from his position by the fire. He was steadily feeding the flames pine cones and old twigs, patiently building the smoking blaze.

A fallen log lay close by the fire and proved to be a convenient seat. Andy came and sat next to her, his arm an inch away from hers—close enough she found herself instinctively wanting to lean into him. What was it about Andy that made her respond like this? Normally she had her wits about her. Even with Dwight, she'd been able to pull herself together and break it off with him permanently because she could see that he was no good for her. Well, Andy wasn't much good for her, either—not if she wanted an actual future with a man—and yet she still found herself drawn to him. She glanced over and Andy smiled back, those green eyes enveloping her for a moment of warmth before he turned his attention to Harley.

"So how long are you planning on staying around Hope?" Andy asked.

Harley put another stick on the fire and leaned back on his haunches. "Don't know. As long as it takes, I guess."

"Your sister, you mean," Andy clarified.

Harley didn't look the least bit surprised that Andy knew about his personal business. Instead he reached for his pile of food, giving Dakota a nod of thanks.

"Yeah, that's right," he said. "You all might be partial to Elliot, but I'm not."

"Your sister seems to be," Dakota said with a shrug. If she'd chosen to stay with him, there must be something keeping her there. "Maybe she's happy."

Harley tore off a bite of beef jerky and chewed silent for a minute. Then he shook his head. "Do you have any siblings?"

"A brother," she said.

"And if you settled for some guy—let go of all the things that mattered to you and went off with some cowboy who had no respect for you or your family, do you think he'd have a problem with it?"

An image of Brody rose in her mind and she wondered what he'd say if he told him she was dating Andy Granger. He'd have a whole lot to say, she was sure. Just as he had when he'd found out what Dwight had been doing to her. Brothers were protective in a unique way, and if he ever found out what had blossomed between her and Andy on this drive, she wouldn't want to face him. So, would Brody have a problem with her settling for someone the family hated?

"Probably," she said with a short laugh. "But what if

I loved that cowboy? What if I didn't want to give him up? There wouldn't be a whole lot he could do."

She was feeling defiant right now, protective of this other woman's choice to choose her future because it mirrored her own situation right now…in a small way, at least. She shouldn't take it so personally. She wasn't in love with Andy and she certainly wasn't pregnant. Harley had a solid point about Elliot's bad behavior. She didn't even know why she felt this need to get involved.

"She's my twin." Harley said it as if ended the discussion.

Dakota frowned. "But she's still her own person."

"Of course!" Harley barked out a laugh. "Any man who tries to control a country woman is either stupid or has a death wish! I'm not saying that I have any right to dictate her life. I'm saying I *know* her. She's my twin sister and I know her better than anyone. She's pregnant, she feels guilty for that, and she's sticking by the man who got her into that situation."

"What happened, exactly?" Andy asked.

"She brought him home for the weekend, announced she was having a baby, and Elliot just sat there. He was the father, but he didn't make any move to reassure us that he'd take care of her. My mom suggested they get married, and Holly wanted that. She lit up at the mention of a wedding. My mom still has my great-grandmother's wedding dress, and Holly always dreamed of wearing that dress down the aisle. That wedding—it mattered to *her*. Elliot got all dark and quiet. He wasn't going to give her the wedding she wanted—I could see it in his face. And while I think that kids need both their parents, and dads matter a heck of a lot, I don't think a woman should have to stay with a man who commits only as far as a rent check. She deserves the real thing, and Elliot ain't it."

Dakota had to agree with the kid there. If Holly wanted marriage, then sharing the bills wasn't going to be commitment enough. It wouldn't be for Dakota, either. She wondered what Holly's take on all of this was.

Andy didn't say anything and he looked away, elbows on his knees and hands hanging down between. He didn't seem to be listening, his attention diverted by something inside him.

"And the family…" Harley went on quietly. "Well, we can't just forgive him. He doesn't think that Holly is worth marrying, and we happen to disagree something fierce. Holly is pretty great, and I'm not going to stand by while she puts up with less than she's worth because she's feeling guilty about an unplanned pregnancy. We were raised with church and all that, so there were expectations. But we all carry regrets in some form or other, and it's no excuse for giving up."

Dakota looked toward the cattle. A nearby cow chewed its cud in slow revolutions, big, watery eyes fixed on them as if they were interesting to her. Her half-grown calf lay next to her, curled into a ball and fast asleep. The cows always made life seem so much less complicated somehow. Everything could be solved, given enough time, enough thought.

"So what do you plan to do about it?" Andy asked after a moment.

"I'm going to talk to her."

"I thought you did already," Dakota said, pulling her attention back to the conversation.

"No, I got kicked out. That's not a conversation. That's shutting down." Harley shook his head. "I won't clear out until she and I have sat down together and talked. Until then, I'm sticking around."

Dakota felt mildly sorry for Holly. Explaining herself to her family wasn't going to be easy, and in this Dakota could empathize. She had a tight family, too, and the thing with tight families was that while you could always count on them to be there for you, they also expected something in return—transparency. You didn't get to crawl into a hole to figure out how you were feeling, because they'd dig you right out and demand an explanation. They worried. They tried to help. In Holly's situation, they'd followed her all the way to Hope. Sometimes a girl didn't want to admit that she had no idea how she felt or that she didn't have a plan yet. Sometimes a girl just wanted to hunker down and lick her wounds. Holly wasn't going to get that freedom.

There was one thing she was certain of, however, and that was that Elliot had his own sense of pride, and Harley's presence had wounded it. Ranch wisdom said you should never back something meaner than you into a corner, and frankly, Elliot was the meaner of the two.

She sighed. "You think Elliot is going to be okay with all of that?"

"Quite honestly," Harley replied, "I don't think he cares all that much about keeping her."

Maybe Harley was right and maybe he was dead wrong. Every act of betrayal—and if Harley broke up his sister's relationship, she'd most definitely see it as betrayal—seemed to start with only the best of intentions. *I was only trying to help.*

Harley had good intentions and she could understand those good intentions, because her family had the same good intentions. They took care of their own, too. They tramped over boundaries and dug people out of their holes and helped them whether they liked it or not. That's what family did—and, hopefully, you lived to appreciate it.

Dakota could only hope that Brody would understand that, because whether she came clean now or two months from now when March rolled 'round and Brody came home on leave, she was still part of that deception—at the very heart of it. And Brody would see what they'd done as a betrayal, too.

Harley took the first patrol that night. He hummed to himself as he cantered off into the darkness, his voice mingled with the soft lowing of the cattle. He had a surprisingly smooth baritone and he sang an old Christmas carol that tugged at Andy's heart. "It Came Upon a Midnight Clear"—one of his mother's favorites.

Beside him, Dakota shivered, and Andy moved closer and put his arm around her. She startled.

"Just keeping you warm," he said.

She leaned into him, fitting neatly under his arm, and they both sat in silence for a long time, listening to Harley's voice as he sang to the cattle on his rounds.

"What were you thinking about?" Dakota asked, rubbing her hands together.

"When?" he asked.

"When Harley was talking about his sister," she said. "You got this faraway look in your eye."

"Oh." Had she noticed that? He'd thought he'd managed to hide his feelings, but apparently not from her. He shrugged. "I'm not much better than Elliot."

"What?" She laughed and shook her head. "I think you might be too hard on yourself."

"I was with Ida for four years before we broke up," he said. "She wanted to get married and I—" His mind went back to the life he'd shared with Ida in Billings. She'd been a good woman—there was no denying that. He'd proposed, but he'd also had a hundred good excuses to keep putting that wedding off. "I knew she was a really great woman and, in theory, I couldn't do better, but I wasn't sure about marrying her. So instead of proposing, I asked her to move in with me. We lived together for a year before I proposed, but I wasn't in any hurry to get married. It didn't feel right."

"You broke up pretty close to the wedding, didn't you?" she asked quietly.

"Yeah." He nodded. "And the main issue was that I'd never really wanted to get married—not like she had. And Ida figured that out. She was smart enough to call it off because she didn't want to be married to someone who didn't want to be there heart and soul."

Dakota leaned forward toward the fire and he let his arm drop away from her shoulder.

"Breakups happen, Andy."

"They do, but I should have been man enough to face what I was really feeling. Instead of dodging marriage by asking her to move in with me, I should have told her the truth. Elliot's not a bad guy, but he's doing the same thing I did—dodging a marriage he doesn't want deep down. And that ends up hurting everyone."

He glanced toward her, expecting to see judgment on her face, but instead he found her watching him. Her expression was sad and gentle.

"I don't know, Andy," she said. "Marrying the wrong woman would have been a far sight worse."

He smiled. "You're quite pragmatic, aren't you?"

"A cattlewoman has to be." She shot him a grin. "You're a good guy, Andy. That's the thing—you hide it well. You manage to convince everyone that you don't care, but you do. And you're a better man than you pretend to be."

A good guy. Dakota, who never minced words and always saw through him, saw some good. It softened him and he cleared his throat, looking away.

"Coming from you, that's high praise," he said ruefully.

"Flattery is a time waster." She pushed a half-burned stick back into the fire.

Elliot might not be able to stand him, but Andy could empathize with the rugged cowboy because he'd been there. Maybe Andy had been a little more polished, but the drive was the same. When it wasn't the right fit, a man dreaded getting hitched. And now Elliot had a baby on the way to complicate things further. What if he'd gotten Ida pregnant? He'd have married her, of course, and done the right thing by her. He'd have raised his family. But that wouldn't have changed the fact that they weren't the right match. They lacked that unexplainable spark that really great couples seemed to have—couples like Chet and Mackenzie, like Ida and Calvin.

The fire popped an explosion of sparks and Andy leaned forward to put another bundle of sticks onto the blaze. The wind was getting colder and it whistled through the trees in a low moan. No one would get much sleep tonight. As he settled back next to Dakota, he slid his arm around her again, nudging her closer. She followed his encouragement and settled against his side. She felt good tucked under his arm like that, like she was made for it. There was something about having Dakota next to him that made him more alert, more aware of his surroundings. The wind whipped up again, leaves swirling and the fire nearly going out before the wind changed direction again.

Dakota shivered.

"Cold?" he murmured.

She nodded and he rubbed his hand over her jacketed arm. Andy would be surprised if there wasn't snow in the morning. She leaned her head against his shoulder and when he leaned his cheek against the top of her head he could feel the silkiness of her hair against his three-day stubble.

Back in Hope, he'd been faced with public opinion about his mistakes, and no one seemed terribly interested in understanding his side of things. *A good guy.* They could have been empty words, meant only to be polite, except Dakota had never been the type to offer empty platitudes. That was one of the things he respected about her.

"Did you mean it?" he asked quietly.

"Hmm?" She straightened and looked up at him.

"You honestly think I'm a good guy, in spite of it all?" he asked quietly. "I'm the rat who sold out, you remember."

She met his gaze evenly. "You're a good man, Andy."

She wiped a hair away from her face and she was so close that he could feel the warmth of her breath against his cheek. Neither of them moved away. He'd always trusted Dakota to see through him and he realized there was nothing quite so comforting as having a woman see right down to the heart of him. His gaze flickered from her brown eyes down to her pink lips and, before he could think better of it, he lowered his lips onto hers.

She wasn't surprised this time when he kissed her, and she leaned into him. He cupped her face with one hand and pulled her closer still with the other. The kiss quickly deepened as she moved against him, closing the cold out as his heart sped up to meet hers. He knew they shouldn't be doing this again, but for the life of him he couldn't remember why against the blood pounding in his ears.

Dakota put a hand against his chest and pushed him back. She sucked in a breath and laughed shakily.

"We've got to stop doing that."

"Yeah, we do," he agreed, closing his eyes, willing his blood to calm. "Sorry about that."

"It was me, too," she said.

Far away, they could hear Harley's voice singing "Oh, Come All Ye Faithful." His mom had liked that one, too. Every Christmas Eve she'd insisted they go to church, and those old carols had shaken that little church with the fervent voices of friends and neighbors.

"I'm feeling things I haven't felt before," he admitted after a moment. "I know it's no help, and it's not possible, but I've never felt—" He swallowed.

"Me, too." She pulled back and he dropped his hands. She felt too far away. "We should stop this before someone gets hurt, Andy."

He knew she was right. This couldn't work for a hundred different reasons. Why was it that the women who were available and appropriate didn't do this to him, but the one woman completely out of reach made his head empty of every logical thought, made him want to hold her again, no matter the consequences to his heart later on? In the moment, it always seemed worth it.

But she was right. If they didn't have a future, they

were tormenting themselves for nothing, and while he might be willing to risk his own torment, he wasn't willing to risk hers.

"My family will never accept you," she said quietly, as if reading his mind.

Was she trying to think of a way to make it work? Or was that just wishful thinking on his part? But he knew better than to ask her to cross that line. That step outside the family circle tended to be a permanent one. When he'd sold that land and gone to Billings, it had solidified something that had been in process for years. The once malleable boundaries hardened and he was officially an outsider. Was he still a Granger? In name, maybe.

"I think I understand why Holly doesn't want to go home," Andy said, trying to pull his thoughts together again. "There are points in your life, steps that you take, that change you. There isn't any going back. Harley wants her to go home, but maybe she knows better. Maybe she knows that the door is already closed and it'll never be the same again."

"Like you," she whispered.

"Yeah, like me." He gave her a sad smile. "It can be lonely out here on the outside."

She slid her hand into his and he squeezed her fingers, listening to Harley's distant singing.

"My mom used to sing that song," Andy said softly. "She was a real stickler for the real meaning of Christmas and all that."

"You're missing her," she said.

"I miss her most at Christmas." He inhaled deeply. "It's funny, though. She made sure I knew about the angels and the wise men and the baby in the stable. That mattered to her because it was what Christmas was all about in our home. Even when she was dying, when she'd ask us to sing carols with her, she believed. Oh, how she believed. She was going to a better place. But for me—" his voice broke and he swallowed hard "—the meaning of Christmas for me was listening to the angels in *her* voice. I was a boy losing his mother."

Dakota tipped her head onto his shoulder. "Don't you keep any of the traditions in her memory?"

"One," he admitted. "My mom used to hang mistletoe around the house when we were kids, and you'd have to walk around watching the ceiling, because she kept moving it. And if you stopped anywhere around the mistletoe, she'd descend on you and smother you with kisses."

"That's so sweet."

"Yeah." He smiled at the memory. "I'd put up a fight for appearances, but I liked it. Do you know what it's like to be loved by someone that fiercely? When she died, I lost seventy-five percent of the love in my life in one fell swoop. So I hang mistletoe in my apartment in Billings," he said. "For her."

He could see tears in her eyes. She wrapped her arms around herself and when he squeezed her hand, she met his gaze again.

"Keep your foot in the door," he said softly. "I can't ask you to give up your family. I wouldn't be much of a man if I did that. When the ones who love you are gone, you realize just how much you lost."

What he wanted to do was to take advantage of these last couple of hours of privacy, pull her into his arms and show her exactly how she made him feel, but that would be selfish. It would comfort him in the moment, but at her expense.

Besides, once they returned to Hope, it would be harder to then have her realize anything between them had only been a fantasy, instead of seeing it now. It would hurt more to watch the realization dawn on her, to watch the change in her eyes when she looked at him.

He didn't want to mess with her heart but, frankly, he had a heart to protect, too. And while Andy had been able to break things off with other women without too much scarring, he knew for a fact that Dakota would be a different story, and no man walked into that willingly.

Chapter 10

Half a mile downstream the river widened and slowed—the perfect place for eighty head of cattle to get across, and when the sun was still low and golden, Dakota ignored the empty gnaw in her stomach as they herded the cattle through the hip-deep water to the other side. Morning brought frost, covering the countryside in white lace that crept back as the sun warmed the ground. Their breath hung in the air and, as the morning progressed, Dakota was grateful for the warmth of the sun on her shoulders.

The night hadn't been a restful one. They'd kept the fire going and leaned against each other for support and warmth. Leaning against Andy had made her feel more of the same things she didn't want to feel. Hating him was easier. As was judging him. But understanding his perspective and realizing their attraction to each other was both mutual and powerful—that was difficult.

When Andy went on patrol, she'd lain next to the fire, and she and Harley had attempted to get some sleep. They'd need any rest so they could manage the long day coming. And when Dakota took her turn at patrol, she'd been relieved to have some solitude to try to sort out the anxiety that wormed up inside her.

They got up and saddled their horses the next morning. There was no breakfast, no coffee, and they all wanted to get moving as quickly as possible. The sooner they started out, the sooner they'd get back to the rest of the group—and food.

Things were getting complicated and she knew it. While they were out on the drive, she could push aside all the other burdens and expectations waiting for her back at the ranch, but the closer they got to home, the less she could ignore it all. She was falling for the cowboy who'd ruined her family's land.

"We'll be home tomorrow," Andy said. "Back to normal."

Normal. Did she really want everything to be normal again? Normal included a massive family secret they'd been hiding from her brother. It included her father's heavy heart as he struggled to make ends meet on a ranch that was costing more and more to run. Normal also meant being alone—no stolen kisses, no leaning into that space underneath Andy's arm that was the warmest nook she'd ever found. Normal certainly came with a price.

"We'll both be busy, I'm sure," she said. And they would be. She'd be working with their own cattle. She had a line of fencing to fix and she and her mother had plans to build a new chicken coop before winter. And then there was Brody…

She hadn't decided yet how she'd deal with him. She'd never forgive herself if she went against the family plan and he died over there. She took off her hat and pulled her hand through her hair. It would feel good to get home and shower.

The freedom to feel all these tumultuous feelings would come to an end in precisely two days, and they'd be back to obligation and responsibility. They'd be back to "normal."

"About Dwight…" Andy said. "I'm going to have a talk with him before I leave."

"Don't bother," she said with a shake of her head. "I'm fine."

"Who said it was for you?" he retorted.

When she looked over at him, she saw a teasing smile on his lips.

"That's all over now," she said, rolling her eyes. "Let it go."

"Thing is," Andy said, "he lied to me."

"What are you talking about?"

Ahead of them, Harley kicked his horse into a trot to head off a wandering cow and Dakota looked at Andy. The joking was gone from his face and his jaw was clenched. The morning sun glistened on the auburn stubble on his chin and when his gaze cut toward her, she felt warmth rising in her cheeks.

"When I asked you out and you turned me down, Dwight told me that you and he were starting things up, and I understood that. I did the honorable thing and backed off." He shot her a rueful smile. "Well, I didn't think you'd actually choose me over him, anyway. If I thought I had a chance, I probably would have been significantly less honorable. You always saw right through my attempts to be cool and collected. What can I say?"

"So when did he lie?" she asked.

"When I told him that he was a lucky guy because a girl like you—" He shook his head, started again. "You were the kind of girl who walked her own path, wasn't afraid of anything. You were special. So I told him that I'd totally back off. No hard feelings. I just wanted him to take care of you. Be good to you. You deserved that."

Dakota felt tears mist her eyes and she quickly looked away. His words had managed to slip right beneath her defenses. She hadn't realized there had been any competition going on between Andy and Dwight back then. She'd thought Dwight was the decent one and Andy was the flirt. It had all been so black and white. So simple.

"He said he would," Andy went on, his voice low. "But he didn't keep his word, now, did he? So I have a few things to settle with Dwight on my own. We were buddies. I backed off. He didn't keep his end of that bargain."

Several cows slowed to a stop and Andy pulled his horse away and went after them. She watched him go, her mind whirling. How much had she missed back then with her steel-clad certainty about how things stood? She'd always been opinionated and she wasn't easy to sway, but in that situation she'd been wrong. Dwight wasn't the man she believed him to be—he had a mean streak and fast right hook. And she'd never seen it coming.

The day wore on, hours slowly rolling past, and they pressed the cattle the limit. They could slow down tomorrow and allow for more rests, but today they needed to cover ground so they could get to the camp. They were all hungry, and Dakota was starting to feel a little light-headed. A day of riding and herding was tough with no food in your stomach, and while they were all used to pushing themselves, they also knew their limits. The camp would be a very welcome sight.

"Penny for your thoughts?"

She turned to see Harley approaching and she smiled wistfully. "Nothing."

The cattle were moving easily enough and, as they rode, the day warmed. Harley pulled off his jacket, and she caught sight of that crudely drawn tattoo on his forearm once more.

"What is that?" she asked.

"A cross."

"Yeah, I see that," she said with a short laugh. "Where did you get it?" Harley didn't look inclined to answer so she added, "Word around here is that you've spent some time in prison."

Harley cut her a cautious look then sighed. "So much for keeping a low profile. Who told you—Elliot?"

She nodded. "Sort of. He told Andy. Andy told me."

"You two are closer than you like to let on," Harley said with a wry smile.

"Me and Elliot?" she asked.

He laughed and shook his head. "Nice try. You know who I'm talking about. You and the boss. There's something there."

"We have a bit of history," she said. "But it's nothing more than that."

Or perhaps a little more than that. In fact, there seemed to be parts of their history she hadn't even known until today. Andy hid his heart well, but deep underneath it all, he cared more than she'd ever known.

"What kind of history?" he asked.

"It's personal."

"More personal that my prison time?" he quipped, and when she glanced over at him she caught Harley's boyish grin. These last four days without shaving didn't seem to make any difference for him.

"We ran in the same circles in high school," she said. "Nothing terribly interesting."

Harley let out a shrill whistle and he touched a cow's flank with a long twig. It picked up its pace. Harley had admitted to having spent time in prison, and she was still balancing that out in her head. She'd half expected him to deny it, to point out that Elliot couldn't stand him, and a part of her would have been happier with that outcome. Elliot was easier to dislike—at least for her. Couldn't something go back to being black and white?

"So what did you do to go to prison?" she asked.

Harley chewed on one side of cheek then he sighed. "I was a cattle rustler."

His words took a moment to sink in and, when they did, she stared at him, aghast. Not only did he look about fourteen years old, but he had applied for work as a drover. If he'd been imprisoned for stealing cattle, he had no business working this kind of job ever again.

"You shouldn't be working here, then," she said shortly.

"It's the only work I know," he said. "What am I supposed to do? I'm not qualified for anything else."

"Be a short-order cook," she said. "I don't really care. If you've been busted for cattle rustling, this kind of job would be a big temptation."

Harley's cheeks colored and he looked away. Was he embarrassed?

"Look, I was a kid. I got involved with the wrong guys, and I can't blame a troubled home or anything like that. I thought they were cool because they were tough and dangerous, and I was bored with the Sunday-school humdrum at home. But when my new friends needed a fall guy, guess who went to prison?"

"And the tattoo?" she asked.

"My cellmate did it for me. It has—" He looked away, out across the plains. "It has personal significance."

She nodded. Fair enough, but she still didn't think he belonged there. He was all Billy the Kid in appearances, cherubic face and Bible in his pocket. Most of the cattle losses were inside jobs these days, and Dakota took this kind of thing very personally. The Masons had lost about fifty head one year due to a shady ranch hand, and that kind of loss hit a rancher where it hurt. There wasn't a huge profit margin in this kind of work.

"I'm not the same guy," Harley said, his hand moving up toward the New Testament in his pocket. "I've learned from my mistakes. Sunday school isn't so bad, after all."

Harley was a likeable kid, but she knew better than to trust based on charisma. She might have missed the subtleties going on between Andy and Dwight, but that didn't make her blind. If a girl sat back on her haunches and kept her eyes open, she could learn a whole lot.

"There was this woman in Hope," Dakota said after a moment. "She had a reputation around town as being pretty loose. She'd slept with every available man, and a few of the unavailable ones, too. Then one day she went to church and the church members were so happy to see that she'd come looking for some answers and some faith. She got involved with all the church activities. She helped out with Sunday school and baked pies for the bake sale… Then one day, they found out that she'd been sleeping with the head elder. The *married* head elder."

Harley winced. "What happened?"

"Well, the church was rocked. I mean, this man was a community pillar. His wife left him and they got divorced. It was very messy. He and his wife had three sons together, and those boys never forgave him. The woman with the reputation ended up marrying the head elder and they moved away. Don't know where they are now, or if they even lasted. The ex-wife still attends that church, though. As do the boys."

Harley was silent for a moment. "That's too bad."

"It is," she said. "And the moral of that story is that sometimes people show an interest in religion for their own selfish reasons."

"Are you suggesting something?" Harley asked, caution entering his tone.

Dakota knew why she was angry—she'd really liked Harley. And if he betrayed them, if he was up to no good, after all, it would hurt more than the Granger profit line. Somehow she needed a bit of redemption out of this whole cattle drive—she needed it to be about something more than the feelings she and Andy could never act on.

"Are you really trying to live a better life?" she asked after a moment.

"Yes." His tone was honest and quiet. "I'm here to make a little bit of money the honest way so that I can stay long enough to talk to my sister, and then I'm going home. Simple as that."

"Okay," she said. "I've had men lie to my face before, and they've been as sweet-looking as you are. Don't be one of them."

"No, ma'am." Harley tipped his hat.

She sincerely wished him the best, but if he came around the Mason ranch looking for work, he'd be stark out of luck.

Bob Granger rode out to meet them when the sun was high. He led a packhorse behind him loaded with supplies, and they watched him approach for two hours before they finally met. He crept over the golden, rolling hills, a tiny figure with a tiny shadow, moving steadily up toward the foothills. Provisions were coming, and Andy was relieved.

Personally he could have dealt with a full day without food. It wouldn't have been comfortable or his first choice, but his relief at seeing that packhorse had less to do with his own hunger and more to do with Dakota.

She'd been getting steadily paler as the morning wore on. She was tough as leather, that woman, and she put in just as much work as he'd ever done. She'd be the last to admit to weakening, but she was hungry, and the old protective instinct kicked in. She was driving the Granger cattle, and she deserved to do that on a full stomach.

When they finally met up with Bob at noon, they all dismounted and he pulled out the food he'd brought—roast beef sandwiches, chocolate bars for energy, and dried fruit. Andy passed the first sandwich to Dakota and she didn't wait on niceties, tearing open the waxed paper and taking a big, jaw-cracking bite. Andy couldn't help the grin that came to his face.

"Last we ate was what we could scrape from the bottom of our saddlebags last night," Andy said, tossing the next sandwich to Harley and then taking one himself.

"Should have crossed with the rest," Bob said disapprovingly.

"We would have lost calves," Andy replied. Was his uncle really questioning a leadership decision in front of the drovers?

"Might have lost more than calves if I didn't come out to fetch you," Bob retorted.

"I'm fully capable of getting the cattle home," Andy said. "And coming out to bring supplies is called teamwork, Bob."

"Is that what we are?" his uncle asked wryly. "A team?"

The words were loaded. Andy had relinquished any right to call on family solidarity when he'd sold his land to the highest bidder against the family's wishes. He didn't only need to prove himself to the hired help, he needed to prove himself to his own kin. They were all waiting for him to fail—for some sort of karmic retribution to even the score.

"The river was too swollen to get the calves across," Andy said. "So we went downstream. We crossed this morning."

"Ah." Bob nodded slowly. "Lose any?"

"Not one." He'd made the right call. He knew that beyond the shadow of a doubt. And he hadn't made the decision alone—Dakota had been a big part of it. Bob would have disagreed with him no matter what he'd chosen.

"Eat up." That was as close to an atta-boy as Andy was going to get out of his uncle. Uncle Bob was Andy's late father's brother, and he saw things in a very linear way. There was family, there was land and there was cattle. And then there were the idiots who messed things up for the serious ranchers. Andy fell into the latter category.

They ate the food Bob had brought and, before half an hour had passed, they all remounted and started back toward camp.

"Elliot had a few things to say about Harley, there," Bob said, lowering his voice.

"Harley had a few things to say about Elliot, too," Andy replied with a grim smile. "Harley's leaving when the drive is done. It'll take care of itself."

"If Chet had been here, he'd—"

"Yeah, well, Chet wasn't," Andy interrupted. "And I'm here because Chet wanted me here. Let me do my job."

Andy was tired of defending himself to this blasted family. They disagreed with him. They were embarrassed of him. He was a mark on their good name. Fine. But this was emotional for them, and there came a point when Andy got good and tired of wading through everyone else's emotions. If they hated him, so be it. He'd be out of their hair in a few days and they could all settle into some nice, comfortable resentment and stew to their hearts' content.

Bob grunted but didn't say anything further. Riding was easier with a full belly, and Andy found his eyes straying toward Dakota more often than he'd care to have his uncle notice. She rode ahead of Andy, chestnut ponytail bouncing on her back, hat pushed back and one hand resting on her thigh. Her hips pivoted easily with the movement of the big horse beneath her, and when she looked out over the ever-flattening hills, he caught her face in profile.

Was she ever beautiful.

He'd always known it, but riding with her on the open countryside somehow made her more vibrant, more alive. The fact that they were now on their way back to the ranch also made this time with her all the more precious. If there was a way to make it last, he'd do pretty much anything, but there were too many things out of his control. If it were just about him and Dakota, maybe a few those barriers would have been surmountable, but it wasn't. It never was about two people. Everyone had a whole host of others attached to them, people who refused to be discounted. Family didn't just wish you well and wave goodbye. There were always strings, obligations. And sometimes the mistakes you made couldn't be atoned for, after all.

When they arrived at the camp that evening, Lydia had a meal of smoked sausages, coal-baked potatoes and creamed corn. Andy tried not to be obvious about it, but his gaze kept trailing back toward Dakota. She sat on a chunk of wood, her plate balanced on her knees, and he realized that even with greasy fingers and a little dab of ketchup in one corner of her mouth, she was still the most beautiful woman he'd ever met.

She caught him watching once or twice, and a small smile flickered at her lips. She felt it, too. He knew that she did, but they were one day away from civilization—close enough to Hope that their phones would pick up reception again once they turned them back on.

Bob and Lydia were eating now that everyone else

had been served, and Andy felt a pang of sadness looking at his aunt and uncle. They'd weathered over the years, grayed, plumped, but he still remembered the old days when he'd go apple picking at their orchard, or the year his uncle broke his leg and it was Andy's job to cut their grass on the riding lawnmower. He'd hated doing it—for free, no less—but he'd felt proud of himself all the same in that boyish emotional conflict that meant a valuable lesson was being learned.

Bob might not have a whole lot of respect left for him, but Andy hadn't forgotten where he came from. Not completely.

The low hum of voices mingled with the creak of tree limbs as the wind moved the towering evergreen boughs above their heads. The trees broke most of the cold wind, but the air was still frigid, making the fire a welcome comfort. Elliot and Harley stood away from the group, out by the edge of the trees, and what must have started as a private conversation now missed that mark by a mile.

"Everyone knows about your history." Elliot's voice carried, and Andy's attention snapped toward the lanky cowboy.

"I don't really care," Harley said. "I'm not here to make myself look better than I am. I'm here for my sister."

"I don't have her." Elliot's tone dripped sarcasm. "Have I carried her in my pocket? You're here for me. You want to make sure that everyone hates me as much as you do before you're done."

Andy and Dakota exchanged a look. Apparently the two drovers were going to sort out their business right here, right now. It might be just as well if they could manage it civilly, enough. The tension had been thrumming for days.

"I don't hate you." Harley's voice stayed controlled. "I just don't think you're good enough for my sister."

Elliot barked out a laugh. "So why come to me about that? What is this, an arrangement between men? Are we bartering her off? She's a free woman, and she can do what she likes."

"Just to be clear—" Harley's control was starting to waver "—you got her pregnant, you brought her to Montana to live with you, you intend to keep this arrangement going, but you won't give her the one thing she wants most right now?"

"How do you know what she wants most?" Elliot demanded. "You came to our door and she wouldn't even open it. Take a hint."

"Because I know *her*!" Harley's voice rose. "You sleep with her for a couple of months and you think that's knowing someone? There is a family heirloom wedding dress in my mother's closet. Do you know about that? Did you know that Holly tried that dress on just last year? When she turned eighteen, my father gave her a string of pearls and he told her that he wanted her to wear them before her wedding day so that she'd remember what she was worth. She cried when she put those pearls on, and she wore them every week to church. But when she left home to come to Montana to live with you, she left those pearls behind."

Dakota paled slightly at those words and put her plate down on the ground at her feet, turning toward Harley and Elliot, a frown creasing her forehead.

"Maybe she's changed her mind about a few things." Elliot turned away then stomped back. He seemed to have forgotten the rest of them watching. "Ever think of that? Ever think that maybe she thinks for herself now, and maybe she doesn't want the weight of all those expectations on her?"

"And maybe you convinced her that she wasn't worth those pearls anymore," Harley snapped. "Maybe you convinced her that she wasn't worth commitment, her great-grandmother's wedding dress or a man willing to promise his life to her!"

Elliot's face paled and his lips quivered with fury. "I will not—" He paused, putting obvious effort into controlling himself "I will *never* be backed into a shotgun wedding!"

"I know." Harley's face twisted into a cold smile. "And I'm glad of that. I just want her to see it for herself."

Elliot grabbed Harley by the collar and dragged him forward.

This had gone far enough. Andy crossed the camp in several strides and grabbed Elliot's finger, bending it backward painfully until he released the younger man.

"Enough!" Andy roared.

"For all your sense of honor, Harley—" Elliot spat "—your sister is embarrassed of you. If you care about her at all, you'll walk away and let her forget that her own brother is an ex-con. You think I'm disgracing her? I'm not the one who humiliated the entire family by cattle rustling! I did her a favor by keeping my mouth shut about you!"

Cattle rustling? Andy stared at Harley in shock. Was that what had sent the kid to prison?

"Enough!" Andy repeated, his voice vibrating with

repressed anger. "Leave each other alone. You can work this out on your own time—not here!"

"Speaking of family disgraces..." Elliot sneered. "You might be running this drive, but no one's forgotten what you've done, either, Granger."

Elliot jerked his arm out of Andy's grip and stalked back to the fire. The rest of the drovers sat in awkward silence, turning their attention to their food again. Harley stayed put, turned his back on all of them and stared out at the lengthening shadows across the plains as the sun sank.

Andy went back to the fire, attempting to keep his expression neutral. He wouldn't be chased off by the likes of Elliot with a few snide comments. Elliot was hired help, and Andy was there representing the family, whether the blasted family wanted him or not. There were some things he didn't like to advertise, like when a drover's snarky remarks hit too close to home.

Bob looked up and met Andy's gaze for the first time since they'd returned to camp. The firelight flickered across his features and he cradled a tin mug of coffee between his roughened hands. He didn't say a word, but Andy could read it all in that weather-beaten face.

Elliot's words had hit the mark—no one was going to forget.

Chapter 11

The next morning Dakota awoke before sunrise. The sky was still dark and when she fumbled with her watch in the cocoon of her sleeping bag, she saw it was only four. She wasn't going to go back to sleep, though. She normally woke up close to this time at home for chores, and convincing her body to do anything else would be more work than simply getting up.

The ground was cold and hard, and as she moved around pulling on clothes and running a brush through her hair, a heaviness clung to her. She'd hoped it would've disappeared during the night, but it hadn't.

She and Andy had been careful all evening—polite nods, few words, a cautious distance when they sat next to each other. They were no longer alone, and she could feel the difference that meant between them. Alone—or relatively so with only Harley for company—they were freer with each other, they'd naturally lean toward each other in the glow of the fire.

But last night they'd both been rigid, trying not to lean together lest people see them and think there was something going on between them.

Which wouldn't be wrong.

That was the thing—there *was* something between them. They could pretend otherwise, but it didn't change the truth. She'd been developing feelings for Andy, and she could see it in his eyes that he felt the same. But the people around them, the pressures, the expectations, all changed things. They weren't free to feel anything.

As Dakota came out of her tent, she could still hear the snores of the other drovers. Apparently a hard, cold ground didn't interrupt their slumber at all and she crept away from the tents, wanting some time to herself in the dimness of predawn.

Dakota did up her jacket and slipped to the edge of camp. Outside the shelter of the trees the wind was sharp with cold. Snowflakes danced in the air as the edge of the horizon glowed the deepest of mauves. A horse plodded toward her and she recognized Andy immediately. He'd been on the last patrol of the night—she should have remembered. He reined in Romeo and dismounted, all without saying a word.

"Morning," she said softly.

"First one up?" His voice was gravelly and quiet.

She nodded. She wouldn't be for long. Soon someone else would awake, make some noise, and the rest would start pulling their things together…but not yet. Right now, in these dusky moments before dawn, they were the only ones.

"Walk with me," he said, holding out his hand, and

his gesture sent a flood of relief through her. From all their careful distance last night, that outstretched hand closed the gap again. She took his hand and they walked briskly away from camp.

"We'll be home by supper," Andy said. His hand was warm, enveloping hers in comforting strength.

"It's not going to be the same," she said.

"Never is," he agreed. "Home changes everything."

Normally that would be a good thing, but not this time. Home wasn't a welcome bastion of warmth and food, it was the finish line—the goodbye. He pulled her in closer and wrapped his arms around her waist, his mouth so close she could feel his breath against her lips. Still, he didn't close the distance, his mouth hovering.

"Andy…" she whispered.

"I'm going to miss this," he murmured, and then his warm lips came down on hers, soft and tender, then growing more insistent as he pulled her closer still.

Her heart sped up and she wanted to be closer to him, away from bulky coats and prying eyes. She wanted to feel his heart against hers and rest her cheek against his neck… She wanted kisses that didn't stop.

But she pulled back—they did have to stop this. Tempting as he was, why should she torment herself with something that could never be?

"I know your parents are going to hate me for a long time," Andy said huskily. "But maybe you could point out that I'm not the devil…you know, if it ever comes up?"

He reached down and wiped a bit of moisture from her lip with the pad of his thumb. He smiled teasingly, but it didn't cover the sadness that glistened in those green eyes.

"I could try," she said with a low laugh. "I'm not sure what good it would do."

"Yeah, I know..." He stopped and pulled her around to face him. "Dakota, what if it didn't have to end just because the drive did?"

"How?" she asked, shaking her head. "We can't just ride off into the sunset, Andy. That's not real life."

"But we could ride off to Billings." He caught her gaze and dipped his head to keep the eye contact. "I'm serious, Dakota. I know this is nuts, but I'm actually pretty well off. I've got a house, a business, friends... Come back with me. We could make a life together—"

The life, the home, the promises... If anything had illuminated the fallacy of those possibilities, it was Harley's sister and Elliot. They might avoid a painful goodbye, but for what? The drawn-out pain of a relationship that didn't have what it took to last in real life, with real families?

"What about my family?" she asked.

"We could make some money in Billings—enough to buy some more land—and come back. We could figure it out," he said. "Together." And while the offer was tempting, it lacked too many things she needed in her life: the land, her family ranch, the community of Hope that she'd grown up in. It lacked *people*, the very people who had loved her, raised her, defended her when Dwight got abusive and who were a part of her deepest core. Could she just walk away from her parents? They'd be heartbroken. Brody would be furious and God help Andy if her brother got his hands on him.

"No." She pulled out of his arms. It was too hard to think with him this close. "You're offering what Elliot offered Holly, and that doesn't work. I have a family, and I can't just walk away from them. I can't be happy that way! And the truth is, they aren't going to just forgive you and or see what I see in you—"

"Which is?" he pressed.

Tears misted her eyes. "I see the guy who told Dwight to be good to me…the guy who came back to run a cattle drive knowing that everyone would hate him… You're a good man, Andy. I know that, but the rest of the town isn't so convinced."

Andy held her gaze for a moment then looked away. "I know."

"And I'm sorry." Why did this have to be so hard? They'd known it was impossible from the beginning. That was why they'd done their best not to feel this way—to nip it in the bud. "But what if…"

Dakota was almost afraid to say it. Running off to Billings couldn't answer their problems, but what if Andy didn't have to leave right away? What if they could put this goodbye off somehow and get more time to think.

"What if what?" he asked softly.

"What if you stayed?"

Andy sucked in a deep breath then released a slow sigh. "I don't belong here, Dakota. You have your family, parents who are still around, a whole community that has your best interest at heart, but I don't. They hate me here, and that's not about to change. My own uncle can barely stand to look at me. I came to do my brother a favor, and that's it. I can't stay."

And she'd known that, too. Nothing had actually changed over the last few days, except for their feelings for each other.

"Don't you see?" Anger was replacing the sadness

now—something easier to deal with, something she could wield. "We've been talking about Harley's sister this whole time, and deep down I've thought she was a little bit dumb. I mean, I'll defend a woman's right to choose her own future until I go blue in the face, but deep down I thought she was blind not to see it!"

"See what?" Andy's eyes clouded. "You think I'm no better than Elliot?"

"Yes!" She dashed a tear off of her cheek with the back of her hand. "It's the same situation, don't you see? They wanted to be together, but they didn't think it through. You're offering a life in Billings, but it's no more than Elliot offered—"

"That's not true," Andy growled, anger flashing back at her in those green eyes. "I'm not offering to share rent, Dakota. I'm offering me, all of me. I'm offering to get married!"

Dakota felt like the breath was knocked out of her and she stared at Andy in surprise. He was asking her to marry him? Did that change things? It made her heart leap, and it made her wish for things so hard that it ached inside her very core, but did it truly change anything?

"You're offering all the right things, Andy," she said, her voice choking with tears. "But you're forgetting something. A wedding isn't about just you and me—"

"It should be," he said.

She shook her head. "Those pews would be empty, and that would break my heart. I can't give up my entire family, Andy."

Andy nodded, and his eyes misted, too. "I know, gorgeous," he whispered. "I love you, and I could never ask it of you."

The horizon was pink now and the sky brightened ever so slowly, illuminating the forms of lounging cows chewing their cud. If only things could stay as simple as they were out here…

"You love me?" she asked softly.

"Would I ask you to marry me if I didn't?" He reached out to move a hair away from her eyes. "Not that it matters, I guess."

Dakota took a step back, out of his reach. If he touched her again, she'd only move back into his strong arms, and no matter how long she put this off, it wouldn't change anything.

Behind them, a pot clanked, and Dakota turned to see Lydia standing at the tree line looking at them. They'd been seen, and Lydia was making as much noise as possible to warn them.

"We have cattle to move," Dakota said quickly. She met his eyes once more, but she knew better than to take even one step toward him. His eyes held a silent request that she couldn't answer and so she did the only thing left—turned back toward camp. With every step, her heart ached more, but she wouldn't make Holly's mistake. A woman might need love, but she also needed family, and one could never make up for the other.

That day the ride was smooth. Everyone was looking forward to getting back, and the cattle perked up, remembering the warmth of home and hay. He and Dakota didn't talk much. They stayed busy keeping the cattle moving, and truthfully, it looked like she was avoiding him. Maybe that was for the best. He couldn't change her family's opinion of him so easily, and he couldn't take back the land sale that ruined the Masons' property. He couldn't give her the whole package—a loving husband who melded well with her own family. He could love her, he could be faithful and devoted, but he had no control over the rest. And she deserved to have the whole package.

When they finally got back to the ranch, the sun was sinking at their backs. They unsaddled the horses and gave them all a much deserved rubdown. And when Andy had thanked the drovers for their service and promised paychecks for the next morning, everyone went their own way.

Except Dakota. She stood there in front of the barn, her face glowing in the last of the sunset.

"I'm going to miss you," she said.

"This isn't goodbye," he said. "I still have to give you your paycheck tomorrow."

"I know." She pulled the elastic out of her hair and let it fall loose around her shoulders. It changed the look of her—softened her—and all he wanted was to push his fingers into that hair and pull her into his arms, but he wouldn't. They knew where things stood. But he had other business to take care of—business connected to her, but not entirely about her, either. Dwight had been his friend, and he wasn't about to just walk away from what he'd done to Dakota. "You said Dwight spends a lot of time in the bar," Andy said after a moment.

She nodded. "Unless he's changed overnight."

"The Honky Tonk?" he clarified.

She nodded again but looked at him dubiously. "Why do you ask?"

"I told you before," he said with a shrug. "I have a bone to pick with him."

"Andy, let it go." Her eyes flashed annoyance. "It

was a long time ago and I don't feel like dragging it up again. I've moved on. You should, too."

"Hey." Andy caught her eye and held it. "He was my best friend, okay? I'm not dragging you into anything. This is between me and Dwight."

She shook her head. "I'm not yours to protect, Andy."

"And I'm not yours to stop," he retorted.

A couple of beats of silence passed between them and color rose in her cheeks. She nodded a couple of times, swallowed, then said, "Okay. Fine. I'll leave you to it, then. But don't do anything stupid and get yourself arrested."

Was she worried about him?

"Scout's honor."

Dakota turned and walked away. She didn't turn back. She got into her truck and he watched as her tires spun up some gravel and she drove off. He had no idea what she was feeling, or if it was anywhere as aching as what he felt. Soon enough he'd be driving out of Hope for good, too, and he'd have to nurse his torn heart in Billings. Dakota would move on, of course. She'd find a good guy and settle down to have a few kids and run a ranch, and the man who ended up with her would be a lucky son of a gun.

Finding a woman who made him feel the way Dakota did wouldn't be easy. In his thirty years he'd never found one to match her.

Half an hour later Andy pulled his truck into an empty space in front of the Honky Tonk Bar. It was a seedy-looking place, squat and small with blackened windows. No one wanted to be reminded of the time of day or night when drinking their worries away.

The *T* in the neon sign flickered. When he opened

the door, he was met with stuffy, beer-scented air, the jangly, old-fashioned country music from the juke box and the jumble of laughter and voices.

He scanned the crowd—it was still pretty early, but the bar was obviously doing good business. In a far corner a few cowboys sat around a table, nursing bottles. There was another table close to them filled with women in their mid-forties, laughing and joking. A couple danced on the floor, swaying off-rhythm to the music, oblivious to anyone else around them.

At the bar sat a solitary figure, shoulders hunched. Andy hadn't seen Dwight in a few years. He'd heard that he'd gone to seed, but they hadn't actually crossed paths, so staring at the back of this fellow, Andy wasn't sure if he was looking at the right man or not. If this was Dwight, he had no idea what he was even going to say to him. He'd gone over a few different options in his head on the way over, but he still had no clue which words would come out of his mouth. He just knew that he couldn't leave this.

Dakota might not be his to protect, but that didn't just turn off his feelings. But this wasn't one hundred percent about Dakota, either. If it had been a different woman that Dwight had beaten, Andy would still be here—beating on a woman couldn't be just left alone.

As if on cue, the man turned and glanced over his shoulder. He was older, more worn, but it was Dwight Peterson, all right. He saw Andy, and didn't seem to recognize him at first, then froze.

Andy crossed the bar and dropped onto the stool next to Dwight. His blond hair was tousled and greasy. He clutched a glass of whiskey with a white-knuckled grip and shot Andy a sidelong glance.

"Look who's back," Dwight said.

"For a few days, at least," Andy said. "Long time, Dwight."

"Yup." Dwight drained the glass and put it back on the counter with a thunk. "So what do you want?"

Andy shrugged. "We used to be friends."

"Used to be." Dwight snorted. "Then you got your fancy life in Billings and didn't have time for the rest of us. So, what, you back slumming it for a few days?"

He'd gotten an education and then gotten a job. What was he supposed to do, sit around in Hope while his brother ran the ranch?

"I got a job, man," Andy retorted. "You resent me for that? How have you been?"

"Hard to get work around here," Dwight said.

"It would be when you're soused."

Dwight didn't answer that and Andy didn't expect him to. There was plenty of ranch work to be had around here if you were able-bodied and willing to work hard. Being sober would also be an asset, but from what Andy could tell, Dwight already had a bad reputation, and that was both pathetic and sad. He didn't have to turn out like this.

"Where are you living these days?" Andy asked after a moment.

"With my mom. She needs me to help out around the place…"

Andy seriously doubted he was living with his mom because the old lady needed him so badly. Likely, Mrs. Peterson would be good and glad to have her son out from under her roof, but Dwight drank away what little money he got his hands on. He had a problem—a big one. Dwight had turned out a little bit too much like his old man.

"I saw Dakota," Andy said.

Dwight nodded slowly then raised two fingers at the bartender. Andy shook his head in the negative when the bartender looked to Andy for his order. He wasn't here to drink. A filled glass slid down the counter toward them and Dwight picked it up and took a sip. Andy let his words hang in the air a little longer, but Dwight didn't open his mouth.

"You have nothing to say?" Andy asked icily.

"How's she doing?" Dwight asked at last.

How was she? She was just as amazing as she'd always been, except there was a crack in her now—a place where Dwight had broken her faith in men and she'd never quite healed.

"She told me about how you used to smack her around."

Dwight's hand trembled and he put the drink down. "That was a long time ago."

Anger coursed through Andy's veins until his entire body pulsed with it. It might have been a long time ago in Dwight's estimation, but he'd seen the way Dakota reacted with Elliot on the cattle drive, and it wasn't far enough in her past yet.

"You remember when you started dating her?" Andy asked, keeping his voice low.

Dwight shrugged. "What about it?"

"I backed off," Andy snapped. "You said you were in love with her, that you'd marry her—"

"She broke it off!" Dwight snapped. "I *would* have married her!"

This wasn't about broken engagements, this was

about broken promises. Andy stared hard at the counter, attempting to keep that simmering anger under control. “You said you’d take care of her, man. Then you started hitting her.”

“That was only—”

“When you drank.” Andy smiled icily. “I know.”

“It only happened a couple of times.”

“Three times, she said. That’s three times too many.”

“So what are you here for?” Dwight asked, looking over at Andy warily. He only met Andy’s eye for a second before he dropped his gaze like a kicked dog. He looked like he was expecting a punch, but Andy wasn’t even sure Dwight would defend himself if he did. Back in the truck, Andy had fantasized about a few different scenarios that ended in him punching Dwight square in the face, but now that he was staring at him, Andy didn’t have it in him anymore.

Dwight’s face had scars from fights, and Andy had a feeling that Dwight knew exactly what it felt like to be beaten up. Andy didn’t need to educate him in that. But under those scars, under the smell of booze that seemed to emanate from every pore of the man’s body, was the shadow of the old Dwight Peterson that Andy used to know—the buddy through thick and thin.

“I’ve gotta tell you, Dwight, I wanted to give you a taste of what you did to her,” Andy said quietly.

Dwight was silent. He shifted on the stool, looking ready to raise an arm in self-defense, but there wasn’t any pride left. Just shame and booze.

“I’ve got a better idea.” Andy pulled out a few bills and put them on the counter to cover Dwight’s bill. “Come on.”

“What?” Dwight snapped. “Where?”

"You can sit here and drink the night away," Andy said, hooking him under the arm. "Or you can come out with me."

"I thought you hated me," Dwight said.

"I still might," Andy retorted. "But you're safer with me than you are in here. Let's go."

Dwight took a moment to consider and then got shakily to his feet. "What about giving me a job at your swanky car dealership in Billings?"

"Nope." Andy led the way through the bar to the front door. "I don't hire drunks."

"So where're we going?" Dwight asked, rubbing a hand across his nose.

They stepped outside into the autumn cold and Dwight shivered.

"For a fresh start, buddy," Andy said gruffly. "There's an Alcoholics Anonymous meeting happening in the basement of the Good Shepherd church in—" he looked at his watch "—fifteen minutes." He lifted up his phone as proof, the website open on the screen.

"I don't need a support group," Dwight sneered, and he took a step back toward the bar.

"Dwight, you hit her!" Andy's voice rang out clear and sharp, and Dwight deflated once more. Andy hooked a thumb toward his truck. "I'll drive you down. I'll sit in the meeting with you."

Dwight stood in the flickering light of the neon sign, the *T* buzzing softly every time it flashed. He looked sad, worn out, empty.

"Why are you doing this?" he asked after a moment.

"Because we used to be friends," Andy said.

"Not friends now?" Dwight asked hopefully.

Was Dwight his friend? No, Andy couldn't lie and

say that he was. He couldn't be the buddy of the man who'd terrorized a woman like that, especially Dakota. But Dwight wasn't a threat to Dakota anymore. He was a broken man, and Dakota was well free of him. Dwight looked at him hopefully. He was half drunk, which might account for this sudden burst of neediness, and Andy sighed.

"You've got to pull yourself together, man," Andy said at last. "You need to go to these meetings every week. You need a sponsor. You've got to work the steps. You can be better than this."

Andy opened the passenger-side door and gestured for Dwight to get in. No, Dwight wasn't his friend anymore, but for the memory of a friendship that used to mean a lot to both of them, Andy was willing to do this. Deep down under the addiction there was a guy who used to be his buddy.

"But let me be clear," Andy said as Dwight got in. "You need to stay away from Dakota. For good."

Dwight didn't answer and Andy banged the door shut before heading around to the driver's side. If Andy ever heard that Dwight had raised his hand to Dakota again, his good will would be spent and he'd come back down here and follow his previous instinct to beat the ever-loving tar out of him.

Chapter 12

Dakota expected to drop into bed that night, exhausted from the drive, but instead she found herself lying awake. Granted, she'd gone to bed early, but it hadn't been just any cattle drive this year and coming home to her own bed didn't provide the closure it usually did. Sure, the cattle were back. Her job was done. But she'd fallen in love with the wrong man despite her best efforts not to.

Her bedroom was the same room she'd slept in since she was a child. It had changed over the years and the toys and childish knickknacks were down in the basement now. It was a sparse bedroom—white walls, a bed with several quilts on top. She had a standing wardrobe in one corner, a writing desk in the other, and a handmade rag rug that she and Grandma Mason had sewn together years ago. A bookcase held some framed black-

and-white photos of grandparents and great-grandparents, a few awards and three shelves packed tight with her favorite books.

How long should she stay in her parents' house? She'd planned on moving out a few years earlier, but then the ranch had started to dry up and the workload had increased drastically. So she'd stuck around. Besides, her parents couldn't afford to hire another worker to replace her right now, and she had as much at stake in this land as they did. So she stayed on, keeping watch over her hopeful inheritance. This land wasn't just the family ranch, it was her future, and she was willing to sacrifice certain things to see her dreams of running it become a reality.

Now she lay in bed, staring at the shadows the moonlight and tree branches made on her ceiling. Tears welled in her eyes. She'd hoped it would all feel differently once she was home again, that her feelings for Andy would fade and she'd see clearly that it was an impossibility. And while she did recognize that a relationship would never work, her feelings hadn't faded. If anything, she felt her loss all the more sharply. It stabbed deeper than she'd thought possible, deeper than even calling off her wedding had wounded her. How had this happened in such a short period of time?

"I fell in love with Andy Granger..." Whispering the words aloud wasn't as jarring as she'd hoped it'd be. Probably because it was true. She'd seen a side to Andy on that cattle drive that she'd never seen before, and when she'd looked into his eyes and felt those strong arms wrap around her, she'd known what she was giving up. In her mind's eye she could see what a life with Andy would be like—waking up in those arms each morning, starting a family, getting older… But the one thing she couldn't picture was doing all of that in Billings. And that's why it was so impossible. She couldn't just walk away from this land, and yet she couldn't tear herself completely free of Andy, either.

Downstairs the phone rang twice and then was picked up. She could hear the muffled sound of her father's voice, but couldn't make out the words. She wiped the tears from her cheeks and sat up in bed. This was no use.

She looked at her cell phone, tempted to dial Andy's number, but she didn't want to wake him up to say…what exactly? That she missed him? That her heart physically ached right now because of what she was walking away from? They'd already said it all… the only problem was that home wasn't dulling the pain for her like it was supposed to do. Coming home hadn't changed a thing.

Dakota grabbed her bathrobe and shoved her feet into her slippers. She'd go downstairs and get a bowl of ice cream or something. She ambled out of her room and started down the stairs. Her father was coming up, still dressed in jeans and a red, flannel shirt, rolled up to his elbows like he'd always worn his shirts. She stopped short when she saw his face. He was ashen.

"Dad?" Dakota put a hand out. "What happened?"

He blinked twice before he said anything and when he spoke, his voice was raspy. "I just got a call from your brother's unit commander—" He swallowed hard. "Brody's been injured…badly, they say. A land mine went off and—" Her father's voice shook. "He's in surgery right now. They don't know how long he'll be there, but he'll be sent home once he's stable enough for transport."

His words took a moment to sink in and Dakota stared at her father in shock. The worst had happened. They'd told each other that the worst couldn't happen, wouldn't happen, because of the very fact it was the worst-case scenario. They were somehow protected from it all because they'd laughed at it, refused to give it root. But Brody had been wounded—their fears had come true—and she could only pray he'd survive.

A land mine… Tears welled up in her eyes.

"Is he going to die, Dad?"

"They don't think so," her father said, sucking in a wavering breath. "But his combat days are likely over. They say his leg is in bad shape. They'll call again once he's out of surgery and give us an update."

She nodded numbly. "Okay, so that's good news, then. It could have been worse."

Her father raked a hand through his sparse hair. This was what they had been trying to protect Brody from by keeping their secret, and it had befallen him anyway. Was her father thinking the same thing?

"When he left, I was so angry," her father said. "They say not to go to bed angry with your wife, but I think it's worse to let your child leave when you're mad like that…"

"He knows you love him, Dad," Dakota said. "You two just never really saw eye to eye—"

"I just want him home safe." Her father's chin trembled. "To me, he's still my boy who wanted shoulder rides. And I want him back home in one piece…or as close to it as the surgeons can manage."

Dakota sank onto the stairs and her father sat next to

her. They were both quiet for a few moments then her father patted her knee with his gnarled hand.

"Dakota, do I put too much pressure on you?" he asked quietly.

"No."

What was too much pressure? He let her be a part of running the family land, and that came with pressure that she was gladly willing to shoulder. She was a grown woman now and didn't need to be sheltered from the hard things in life.

"Well, I'm going to tell you what I should have told your brother before he left," her father said gruffly. "I want you to be happy. That's it. You make your choices and live your life, and if you end up happy, I'll have done my job well."

Dakota leaned over and put her head on her father's shoulder. "But I am happy, Dad."

The words were hollow because she was furthest thing from happy right now. But that wasn't her father's fault. He didn't even suspect what had happened between her and Andy.

"Are you? Living here with us?" Her father smiled sadly. "Follow your heart, Dakota. I won't give you grief."

Perhaps she didn't look as happy as she claimed to be. She couldn't say that life had been easy with Dwight's abuse, a canceled wedding and the land drying up before their eyes. But happiness didn't necessarily come with an easy life, and she wasn't one to back down from the challenges. Right now, the ache inside her wasn't because of Dwight or the land, it was because of Andy. And she'd have to deal with this particular heartbreak alone.

He'd said he loved her…he'd asked her to marry him and move to Billings…

And Brody was wounded and would be on his way home as soon as they could safely transport him. Why did everything have to knot together into one unmanageable tangle?

Her father pushed himself to his feet. "I'm going to go and wake up your mother."

He walked heavily up the stairs and paused at the master bedroom door. He hung his head for a moment, as if steeling himself, then turned the knob. She heard her mother's groggy voice. "What time is it?"

Follow her heart… Did her father have any idea of where her heart led? Because right now, with every beat, it was yearning for the man who had decimated their property.

She bowed her head, meaning to say a prayer for her brother's recovery, but instead of a whispered prayer, she only met with tears. Her heart was breaking—for the man she'd fallen in love with against her better judgment, for her brother, who was wounded in the line of duty, still so far from home, and for her father, who had loved so hard but forgotten to put it into words.

Happiness might not be guaranteed in an easy life, but an easy life certainly had fewer heartbreaks. Unfortunately, she hadn't gotten a choice in the cards she'd been dealt.

The next morning they awoke to snow. It was like a mantle had been tossed over Hope while they'd slept, and when Andy crawled out of bed, he'd stared out at drifted peaks. They'd gotten the cattle home just in time.

Andy had asked the drovers to come back this morning to pick up their checks, and there was still another twenty minutes before the drovers were due. The truck bumped and slid over the back drive that led from the fields—he'd just brought some fresh hay for the feeder, the pasture being covered now—and his gaze slid over the peaceful scene. The morning sun was bright and golden, glistening off the fresh snowfall. It covered fields, topped fence posts, and drifted up the sides of buildings—winter's official arrival. The cows congregated in small groups, their breaths coming from their blunt noses in puffs of cloud.

He'd miss this. If he had to be brutally honest, he'd miss Dakota more. He could have been happy enough going back to his life in Billings if it hadn't been for her. She'd awoken him to feelings he wasn't ready for, both for her and for this land he'd thought he'd said goodbye to. But his time with Dakota made him realize exactly what he wanted—everything that was out of reach.

She would come this morning to collect her check and he'd see her again, and his heart sped up at the prospect. He knew where they stood. He knew he couldn't give her the life she deserved, and she knew it all too well. He hoped that this goodbye might make the difference. Maybe if he said goodbye to her in the light of day he'd be able to make his peace with it.

Andy pulled to a stop beside the barn and turned off the engine. His brother had called late last night to say Mackenzie had had the babies and they were doing well. The new arrivals were boys—both over five pounds—and they'd named them Jackson and Jayden. Andy had felt a strange tug of love already for the nephews he was yet to meet—there would be more Granger boys, another set of brothers. He sincerely hoped these two would have a better chance at maintaining a relationship than he and Chet had. The pressures of inheritance and future planning could be disastrous, but these kids would have an uncle who understood all that, and maybe he'd be able to give them some advice about how not to mess things up too badly.

Chet would be coming back to the ranch on his own for a few days before Mackenzie would join him with the babies. That meant Andy's time here would be up and he'd have to bow out and leave the ranch in his brother's capable hands. At the very least, he wanted his brother to come back to everything running as it should. Andy could offer that much.

Andy got out of the vehicle and headed around the side of the barn, snow melting over the leather of his cowboy boots. He stopped short when he saw a figure he recognized—Harley. Andy's hackles immediately rose, remembering Harley's past with cattle rustling. He'd expected Harley to return for his check, but he hadn't expected to see him lurking by the barn door. He appeared to be looking inside rather intently, and he didn't hear Andy as he approached.

Just before Andy spoke, he saw what had Harley's attention. Elliot stood inside the barn, his cell phone to his ear. He was shuffling a boot against the cement floor and leaning against a stall.

"I know. I know..." Elliot was saying. "I was an idiot... I understand why you kicked me out, I do... Yeah, I know. Like I said, I'm sorry about that. I want to be there for our baby and you know what? If you want to get married, I'll do that, too. Your brother said something about a wedding dress your grandmother wore and it got me to thinking…"

"Morning," Andy said quietly, and Harley whirled around.

"Scared me," Harley said with a quiet laugh. "Sorry, I was just—"

Andy raised an eyebrow and Harley shrugged. "He's talking to my sister."

Andy frowned. "He said that she kicked him out." That was news to all of them. They'd been assuming that Elliot and Holly were still together. Had all that drama been for nothing? He had to admit, he liked the idea of this unknown Holly standing up for herself and giving Elliot the boot. If Elliot wasn't going to be man enough to marry her, why should she put up with less?

Except it sounded like Elliot was changing his tune.

"Yeah." Harley scowled down at his boots. "Apparently."

Andy jutted his chin in the direction of the house. "Come with me back to the house. Leave Elliot alone. You don't want to make any more trouble for yourself."

Harley followed Andy away from the door and they headed down the worn path past the chicken coop and toward the house. A frigid wind whipped around the barn and slammed into them as they ducked their heads against the onslaught. Winter was here and they hadn't gotten back a day too soon. If it was this cold here, he was willing to bet the foothills would be freezing.

Harley hunched his shoulders against the cold but his expression was grim.

"You okay?" Andy asked after a moment. "I mean,

it's good news, isn't it? Holly didn't take his garbage. She kicked him out. Now you can rest easy. It sounded like he was proposing there, too. She'll have it her way. Mission accomplished, right?"

Harley looked over at Andy then heaved a sigh.

"Why didn't she come home? She'd kicked him out. She was on her own. There was no reason not to come back. There was no reason not to open the door when I knocked."

He felt for the kid. All Harley wanted was to bring his sister home again where she'd be safe, where he could protect her, where no one would hurt her. But, apparently, Holly didn't want that, and Andy could respect that, too.

"I don't know," Andy said. "Maybe too much changed."

"Obviously. She's pregnant," Harley retorted. "Nothing will ever be the same again."

Andy sighed. "Look, kid, I think I get it. Sometimes, when too much changes, when you've changed too much, there isn't any going home again, only going forward. Maybe that's why she hasn't come back—she's not the same girl she used to be and she's doing the only thing open to her—moving forward."

They stopped at the stairs and kicked the dirt off their boots before Andy opened the door and they went inside. The warm air of the kitchen, still scented with morning coffee and toast, felt good on Andy's wind-chilled hands. He took off his hat and tossed it onto the counter, then headed toward the table and the waiting paychecks.

"I'm her brother." Harley sounded dismal and, for his sadness, he looked younger still. "I'd be there for her."

"And you still can be," Andy said. "Maybe she needs a bit of space."

Sometimes a protective, well-meaning sibling could be the last thing someone wanted when they were trying to sort out their future. Andy could understand that all too well! He'd had a well-meaning brother of his own, a brother who'd never quite be able to appreciate the depth of his heartache. Holly might be in the same situation right now.

"See..." Andy said after a moment of silence. "We all change. Sometimes home doesn't fit anymore."

Andy picked up the envelopes and flipped through them until he came to Harley's name. He passed it over and Harley accepted it with a nod of thanks.

"I've changed, too," Harley said quietly. "I've been to prison. If that isn't change, I don't know what is. But I still came back again. So I know about home not fitting right anymore, but I also know that if you stick it out, you can find a way to fit in again. It won't be in the same way, but there's always a seat at the table for you. People might need to scoot over a bit, and they might need to fetch another plate, but there's always that seat."

Harley's words slowly sank into Andy's mind and he gave the young man a thoughtful smile. In his mind's eye, he could see those parents waiting for their daughter, still seeing their little girl in spite of it all. Holly could do worse than return to the home that loved her so much. And deep down he wished she'd give in and do just that. At least she had a home to go to. His parents were both gone, and the gap had closed behind him. He should be so lucky.

"You're wise beyond your years, Harley."

"I'm not as young as I look." Harley cast him a lopsided grin.

Andy laughed softly. "Yeah, so you keep saying."

"Thanks for giving me a chance, Mr. Granger," Harley said after a moment. "It was an honor riding with you."

"You bet," Andy said. "Good luck with everything."

"Thank you, sir." Harley turned toward the door, pushing his hat onto his head with one hand.

"Harley," Andy said suddenly, and the young man looked back.

"Yes, sir?"

"What are you going to do about your sister?"

Harley sucked in a deep breath then shrugged. "I don't rightfully know. I'll try and talk to her again, and if she won't talk to me, I'll go home."

"I'm sorry about that," Andy said. "I know it wasn't what you wanted."

Harley smiled. "That's not retreat, that's just doing the next logical thing. Home is home. It isn't going anywhere. We'll be there when she's ready."

"The seat at the table," Andy said quietly.

"You bet, sir. The seat at the table. Thanks again for everything." Harley tapped the brim of his hat then opened the door. A blast of cold air swirled past him into the kitchen and he stepped outside, pulling the door shut behind him.

A seat at the table… Harley seemed pretty optimistic about that, and Andy wondered if there was truth in those words. Was it possible to come home again after letting down your entire community? Was it possible to belong again after years away? There was only one woman he wanted to come home to, and that was Dakota Mason, but Hope had closed up after him. There might be hope for Holly yet, but he doubted there'd be a chance for him.

Unless…

Chapter 13

Dakota stood on a crate, peering under the hood of her truck. The darn thing refused to turn over and she couldn't fetch her paycheck until it did. Her father had the work truck out on the ranch, delivering hay and filling watering troughs, and the other work truck had stopped working last month. She still needed to get the parts to get that one moving, and while she had most of them, she had to make another couple of trips to junkyards to see what she could scavenge. Ordering parts at the auto shop was a last resort.

The sun was higher in the sky but the temperature had most definitely dropped since they'd gotten back from the drive. Her fingers were red with cold. She reached for her travel mug of coffee that sat on the top of the engine block and took a lingering sip of creamy warmth.

Last night they'd gotten several updates from the

hospital where Brody was undergoing surgery. All had gone well and they'd been assured that Brody would recover and keep the leg that had been so badly torn apart during the blast. He'd need nursing care when he got back, though, and her parents were already talking about the expense of hiring a full-time nurse.

Dakota had sent her brother several text messages, but she hadn't heard back from him yet. When she finally did, she'd stop worrying, but until then—

An engine rumbled into her drive and she stepped back from the truck and shaded her eyes. It was Andy's vehicle making fresh tracks over the snow-covered driveway, and her heart sped up.

What was he doing here? Didn't he have drovers to pay and a ranch to run? Seeing him again wasn't going to be easy, and she'd counted on being able to steel herself before going over. Having him show up here didn't give her that opportunity.

"Morning!" Andy called as he hopped out of his truck.

"Hi, Andy." She grabbed a rag and wiped at the grease on her hands. "What are you doing here?"

"Bringing your paycheck." He held up an envelope. "You didn't come by to get it, so I thought I'd bring it to you."

"Thanks." She accepted the envelope, trusting that the amount on the check was the amount agreed upon. She'd open it later. When she looked up, she found Andy's eyes locked on her.

"Are you okay?" he asked quietly. "You look…sad."

"It's been a rough night," she admitted. "We got a call that Brody was in an explosion and he's been in surgery. They saved his leg, but—" She swallowed hard. "So he's coming home."

"That's horrible." Andy stepped closer and slid an arm around her waist. She tipped her head against his broad chest, thankful for the brief comfort he provided. "I'm glad he survived, though."

"Me, too," she said. "And I'm glad I didn't end up telling him about Nina or I'd have blamed myself for this."

"Hey, war isn't your fault," he said seriously. "And he's coming home. That's what matters, right?"

She pulled back and nodded quickly. "That's what matters."

"When you open that envelope, you'll find two checks," Andy said. "One is from Chet for your work on the cattle drive and the other is from me."

"What?" She frowned. "Andy, you don't owe me anything—"

"Whatever," he said with a wry smile. "Of course I do. It's my fault you're struggling, and it's the least I can do to get your hydration system."

"I couldn't accept it..." she began. The words evaporated from her mouth as she caught Andy's tender gaze moving over her face and settling at last on her lips. He moved closer and bent his head, catching her lips with his. The softness of his mouth made her forget what she'd been about to say, and she felt like she could melt into his embrace. When he finally pulled back, she asked, "So is that goodbye, then?"

"No, just a kiss."

She felt the color rise in her cheeks. "When do you leave?"

"You're not getting rid of me that easily," he said with a low laugh. "I'm sticking around."

"What?" She could hardly believe her ears. "What are you talking about? I thought you couldn't stay in Hope…that they'd never accept you again, that—"

"I had a weirdly deep talk with Harley," he interrupted her. "As it turns out, Holly had dumped Elliot, after all, but she isn't ready to go home yet. It sounds like Elliot is willing to do pretty much anything to get her back."

"That's really good for them." Dakota smiled. "Harley must be relieved—even if he still isn't Elliot's biggest fan. But how does that change anything for you?"

"He was talking about how no matter how much you change, there is always a place for you at the table, so to speak. It got me to thinking. Anyway, Chet got back this morning. Mack is still in the hospital with the babies, but they should be released in a few days, and Chet asked if I'd stick around. He needs help running the ranch and Mack is going to be pretty busy with the babies, so—"

Dakota realized she'd been holding her breath and she let it out in a sudden rush. "So you're staying?"

Andy nodded. "Good news?"

She felt tears mist her eyes. "Yes…yes! Definitely."

Andy reached out and tucked a stray tendril of hair behind her ear. "I know that your family would never forgive me, but I was wondering if you'd give me a chance to just…be around you. I won't ask for more. Maybe if your family could get to know me, they'd see that I'm a good guy. I'm not the same man I used to be back then, so it won't be the same, but that doesn't mean I can't find home again here in Hope. With you.

Just give me the chance to win your father over and then if I can't—"

"Yes." She nodded.

"Yes?" Andy smiled tentatively. "I had a whole speech prepared, you know."

"My dad and I had a talk of our own," she said quietly. "Brody's injury kind of put things into a different perspective for us. Life is short—sometimes too short. We can't waste it on the things that don't matter. He said that he wants me to be happy. He and Brody butted heads for so many years, and he doesn't want to do that to me. So he gave me his blessing to follow my heart. He has no idea that my heart leads to you, but..."

Andy smothered the rest of her words with a kiss and pulled her in close. His strong arms closed around her and she twined her arms up around his neck, leaning into his strength.

"Then marry me," he said, pulling back.

"What?" she gasped.

"I'm serious, marry me! I'm not in this halfway and I'd take my time and wait for you to feel comfortable if I need to do that, but if things have changed and you're willing..." There was pleading in those green eyes. "If you're willing..."

"How would it work?" she asked. "You'd be living with your brother, right?"

"Nope." He grinned. "There are two full ranch houses on that ranch right now—one was our childhood home and the other belonged to Mack's grandmother. I'll be living in the one I grew up in. And, believe me, there's room enough for you, too...and maybe a baby or two of our own."

"Is this really possible?" she asked in disbelief.

"Which part?" he teased. "The baby or the wedding? Because I happen to know a minister who could marry us tomorrow if you wanted to get started on the babies..."

"Andy!" She blushed and shook her head.

Andy lifted her hand to his lips, looked at it for a moment, turned it over and then kissed the one clean spot on the back of her wrist.

"I'm in love with you, Dakota. I want to marry you. I'm completely serious, and I'll prove that I was the better choice for the rest of your life, if you'll let me."

"I love you, too," she whispered. "And, yes, I'll marry you."

Andy moved in for another kiss and she planted a hand on his chest, holding him back. "But one more thing," she said.

"Anything." She could see by the look in his eye that he meant it. The tenderness in his face promised so much more than words ever could.

"When we tell my dad about this," she said quietly, "you're going to have to duck. His first reaction isn't going to be pleasant."

Andy chuckled softly and pulled her back into his arms, his lips hovering over hers. "That's a deal. Hope couldn't be home without you in it." He paused, holding back just a whisper away from a kiss. "I'm a lucky guy."

Joy bubbled up inside her and Dakota grinned into Andy's warm, green eyes. "You most certainly are. Now kiss me already."

And Andy did. He kissed her long and slow, and when he finally released her, Dakota was certain that while they'd have a whole knot to untie when it came to her family, Andy Granger was most certainly worth all the trouble he was going to cause. This love would be the foundation for their very own home. And Hope, Montana, was just big enough for them all.

Epilogue

The Christmas Eve wedding was Chet's idea.

"Mom would have liked that," he said. "Besides, you need something to celebrate again, Andy. It's different for me now that I have Mack and the boys. It changes your focus, gives you someone to put a Christmas together *for*. But I'd say start now—make your Christmases your anniversary, too. Love is what Christmas is all about, isn't it?"

"Who would even come?" Andy asked. "I'm Enemy Number One around here."

"The ones who love you," Chet said. "Make it an intimate wedding. Let everyone else wonder how it went down."

It had made a lot of sense and when Andy asked Dakota what she'd thought, she'd immediately agreed. Planning a wedding in three weeks flat was a whirlwind affair, and it took both families pulling together to make it happen.

Unfortunately, Brody wasn't back in time for the wedding, which was disappointing for everyone. He got an infection in his leg and had to stay another few weeks in the VA hospital, but they set up a webcam so he could watch the entire thing from his hospital bed.

On the morning of Christmas Eve, when Andy stood in a sunlit church with his bride, the minister's words tumbling around them, he could feel all those childhood Christmases coming back again…the love, the anticipation, the bone-deep certainty that with Dakota he'd finally come home.

The actual ceremony was a blur. He'd promised himself he'd remember every second of it, but all he'd remember later was looking down in those chocolate-brown eyes of her and saying "I do" with every fiber of his being. She wore a long ivory dress with lace sleeves, her soft skin peeking through. A long veil fell back from her dark hair, cascading down over her shoulders into a frothy pool around her feet. She was promising to be his, to be Mrs. Dakota Granger until death parted them.

But it was the memories made later at the reception, in an antiques neighbor's barn renovated for social events, that would settle into Andy's heart. As they stepped into the candlelit room for the first time as husband and wife, Dakota tugged him to a stop and he looked up to find a spray of mistletoe hanging above them.

"Merry Christmas, Andy," Dakota whispered, her eyes glistening in the low light.

He dipped his head and kissed her gently, tugging

her close to him, wishing they had fewer observers for this…

Every table around the room had a sprig of mistletoe, and Andy felt his throat close off with emotion as he looked around at the glossy barn filled with the people who supported them—more than he'd imagined would be there. Chet was persuasive, and after Ken Mason's initial reaction of rage, after Dakota'd had a long talk with her dad out in a field—a talk that took an entire morning—Ken turned out to be pretty persuasive, too.

There was room at the family table—it just took a little shifting of the chairs.

And every Christmas thereafter, in Andy and Dakota's home, after the kids were born and as the years crept by, Dakota would put up mistletoe around the house, surprising Andy with a kiss when he happened underneath it. It was a tradition started by Andy's mom when she'd thought she was being playful but really was etching her love into her family's hearts. Andy's kids would grow up with the same laughter and outpouring of love, and mistletoe began to mean something a little more in Hope, Montana.

It was more than "Merry Christmas." It was the meaning of Christmas…love, family and the sound of the angels in a woman's loving voice saying, "Look up—mistletoe!"

* * * * *

Despite lying on her résumé, Amanda Lowery still manages to land a job designing Halcyon House for Blake Randall—and a place to stay over Christmas. Neither of them have had much to celebrate, but with Blake's grieving nephew staying at Halcyon, too, they're all hoping for some Christmas magic.

Read on for a sneak preview of Jo McNally's It Started at Christmas…, *a prequel in the Gallant Lake Stories miniseries.*

"Amanda, I didn't mean to upset you. I don't ever want to do anything that scares you."

She sucked in a deep, ragged breath, looking so terribly lost and sad. Her eyelids fluttered open. She stared straight ahead, talking to his chest.

"You don't understand, Blake. There are days when… when everything scares me." Her voice was barely above a whisper. His heart jumped. He thought of that first day, when she ended up unconscious in his arms.

Everything scares me.

She'd kicked her shoes off earlier, and in her bare feet the top of her head barely reached his shoulders. He put his fingers under her chin and gently tipped her head back.

He wanted to kiss this woman.

Wait. What?

No. That would be wild. He couldn't kiss her. Shouldn't.

But how could he not?

Her hair tumbled off her shoulders and down her back in golden curls. Before he knew it, his free hand was slowly twisting into those curls. She didn't pull away. Didn't look away. He lowered his head until his face was just above hers. He felt her breath on his skin. She smelled like citrus and spice and blueberries and red wine. Her lips parted and she stared at him with her enormous eyes.

"I swear I don't want to scare you, Amanda. But… may I kiss you?" His voice was a raw whisper. "Please let me kiss you."

His words came out as a plea. He'd never begged for anything before in his life. But here he was, begging this sweet woman for a kiss. Ready to drop to his knees if that was what it took. He heard his father's voice in his head, mocking his weakness. That was when he started to straighten, started to come to his senses. Then he heard her whispered answer.

"Yes."

Was there any sweeter word in the world? Adrenaline surged through his body, and his hand tightened in her hair. His eyes opened to meet those two oceans of blue. Dangerous blue. Deep enough to drown in.

She was frightened, but she was trusting him. And that realization scared him to death.

SPECIAL EXCERPT FROM

Carolyn Wiebe will do anything to protect her late sister's children from their abusive father—even give up her Amish roots and pretend to be Mennonite. But when she starts falling for Amish bachelor Michael Miller, can they conquer their pasts—and her secrets—by Christmas to build a forever family?

Read on for a sneak preview of An Amish Christmas Promise *by Jo Ann Brown, available December 2019 from Love Inspired!*

"Are the *kinder* okay?"

"Yes, they'll be fine." Uncomfortable with his small intrusion into her family, she said, "Kevin had a bad dream and woke us up."

"Because of the rain?"

She wanted to say that was silly but, glad she could be honest with Michael, she said, "It's possible."

"Rebuilding a structure is easy. Rebuilding one's sense of security isn't."

"That sounds like the voice of experience."

"My parents died when I was young, and both my twin brother and I had to learn not to expect something horrible was going to happen without warning."

"I'm sorry. I should have asked more about you and the other volunteers. I've been wrapped up in my own tragedy."

"At times like this, nobody expects you to be thinking of anything but getting a roof over your *kinder*'s heads."

He didn't reach out to touch her, but she was aware of every inch of him so close to her. His quiet strength had awed her from the beginning. As she'd come to know him better, his fundamental decency had impressed her more. He was a man she believed she could trust.

She shoved that thought aside. Trusting any man would be the worst thing she could do after seeing what Mamm had endured during her marriage and then struggling to help her sister escape her abusive husband.

"I'm glad you understand why I must focus on rebuilding a life for the children." The simple statement left no room for misinterpretation. "The flood will always be a part of us, but I want to help them learn how to live with their memories."

"I can't imagine what it was like."

"I can't forget what it was like."

Normally she would have been bothered by someone having sympathy for her, but if pitying her kept Michael from looking at her with his brown puppy-dog eyes that urged her to trust him, she'd accept it. She couldn't trust any man, because she wouldn't let the children spend their lives witnessing what she had.